Instead of replying, Morgan went up on her tiptoes and leaned forward, resting her hands on his chest, and kissed him softly, fleetingly, on the mouth.

"And you're a special man, Ryan," she said in a funny, breathless voice.

This close he could see her beautiful face perfectly in the fading light, her eyes wide and her lips parted in unconscious welcome. If she'd glanced away or turned, Ryan was sure his self-restraint would have held. If she hadn't just stood there inviting him to do something, he wouldn't have pulled her tight against him and kissed her with every shred of lust and longing he felt for her.

Acclaim for

MEET ME AT THE BEACH

"4 Stars! A sexy series starter set on an island where any-one would love to spend the summer, Sykes's latest is a winner." —*RT Book Reviews*

"As Aiden and Lily take a chance on their romance, nei-ther knows whether it will be fleeting or turn into forever. Their intense romance is sensuous and moving, with a perfect small-town setting." —*Publishers Weekly*

"V. K. Sykes has created a unique island removed from the chaos of the mainland, accessible only by ferry or private boat, and populated it with a community of strong-minded people who work hard, take pride in their heritage, and band together to celebrate the good times and get through the bad times as they protect and support each other...It's a place I want to visit with people I want to know. They've touched my heart and I'm now invested in their happiness. I can't wait to catch the ferry over for my next visit to Seashell Bay!"

—TheRomanceDish.com

"Genuine emotions plus intriguing characters make *Meet Me at the Beach* constantly enjoyable, and V. K. Sykes always keeps the reader engaged during every enter-taining scene. This author is a talented husband-and-wife writing team, and they perfectly balance duty with dreams for a very imaginative story."

—SingleTitles.com

Summer at the Shore

Summer at the Shore

V. K. SYKES

FOREVER

NEW YORK   BOSTON

Forever
Hachette Book Group
1290 Avenue of the Americas
New York, NY 10104

www.HachetteBookGroup.com

Printed in the United States of America

First Edition: June 2015
10 9 8 7 6 5 4 3 2 1

OPM

Forever is an imprint of Grand Central Publishing.
The Forever name and logo are trademarks of Hachette Book Group, Inc.

The Hachette Speakers Bureau provides a wide range of authors for speaking events. To find out more, go to www.hachettespeakersbureau.com or call (866) 376-6591.

The publisher is not responsible for websites (or their content) that are not owned by the publisher.

For Dan and Naoko

Acknowledgments

We'd like to thank our editor, Alex Logan, and the staff at Forever Romance for their kind support and help in ushering our books into the world. Many thanks also go to Debbie Mazzuca—no one could ask for a better friend. Finally, our sincere gratitude to our agent, Evan Marshall, who works tirelessly on our behalf and whose support we truly value.

Summer at the Shore

Chapter 1

$\mathcal{R}$yan Butler dumped his army-issue duffel bag onto the deck and grabbed a bench seat beside the ferry's port rail. As usual, he'd kept his gear to a minimum for a visit home. And it struck him as weird that he still thought of Seashell Bay Island as home, despite his determined escape years ago. Most summers, he'd spend only three or four days with his folks, but this vacation could last a lot longer. He had plans, of course, but his years in the army had taught him the necessity of keeping them flexible. If the island started to close in on him, he'd jump on a ferry and head somewhere else. He had some money, some time, and no responsibilities, so he could pretty much do whatever he wanted, whenever he wanted. Ryan called that freedom, and he needed a good dose of it right now.

After his latest grueling contract with Double Shield Corporation, Ryan had made it clear to his controller that he needed a serious break. For ten months, he'd been baby-sitting diplomats in Baghdad. For six more after that, his job had been protecting a Fortune 500 CEO and his team as they bounced their way across a string of countries that varied from half-assed safe to outright deadly. Those jobs paid great but left him with an even bigger dose of uncertainty about his future than when he'd left the military. A little of the hired gunslinger's life went a long way, and he sure as hell couldn't see doing it in the long term.

As for the alternatives? At this point he hadn't a clue.

A year and a half ago, simmering frustration with his army career and the lure of good money had prompted him to leave Special Operations and hook up with Double Shield, a private military contractor. But it hadn't taken long to realize that money wasn't enough. In fact, his restlessness had only increased with the corporate gig. At least in the army, Ryan had felt like he had roots that kept him grounded. Now he was drifting. His bank account was getting fatter, but that was about the only good thing he had to show for his life over the last eighteen months.

He twisted in his seat to take another look over the bay, breathing in the tangy scents of the sea air and the fishing boats. He'd taken one of these ferries between Portland and the island thousands of times, including every day of his four years at Peninsula High. The ride could be a boring pain in the ass, but it was relaxing. Forty minutes to an hour of pure peace. Put the earbuds in and zone out.

Except for the occasional mad morning rush to finish up homework before the boat docked in Portland. Okay, maybe more than occasional.

A cheerful serenity cloaked the harbor scene even though tourists and locals alike rushed to make boats to the various islands, towing children and dogs, as well as groceries in carts and battered canvas bags. Coming home had never particularly thrilled him, and yet Ryan had spent enough time eating dust and dodging bullets and

IEDs to regard the good old USA, and coastal Maine in particular, as probably the closest thing to peace he'd ever find. Yeah, it was caught in a retro time warp that certainly wasn't for an adrenaline junkie like him, but he did appreciate the laid-back beauty of the place that remained unchanged from one year to the next.

The ferry horn sounded one blast to signal the boat's imminent departure. A couple of tanned and fit young deckhands—probably students—finished securing the cargo while two others pulled the metal gangway onto the boat. Like them, Ryan had spent the summer after his high school graduation crewing on the island ferries. It had been hard, hot work, but something about that final summer, working and partying with his high school friends, had been almost idyllic.

And then he'd left for the military and soon enough to Afghanistan, Iraq, and then Afghanistan again. In the process, he'd lost too many army buddies and seen enough ugliness to last several lifetimes.

"Hold up!" a voice cried from down the pier. "Please, guys, I really need to make this boat."

Ryan recognized that feminine voice even before he saw Morgan Merrifield running full tilt boogie down the concrete platform of the ferry terminal. Her pretty face flushed and her blond hair flopping forward into her eyes, she lugged an overstuffed L.L.Bean bag in her right hand and pulled a wheeled cart with her left. Instinct made him jump up and rush down to the boat's lower deck to help her.

Though one of the deckhands was rolling his eyes at her, the other one grinned and started to push the gangway back across the gap between the platform and the boat. With the sweetest smile God ever put on a woman's face, Morgan thanked them as she set her bag down and fumbled for her ticket. Ryan waited a moment for the guys to secure the gangway and then strode across to help the girl he'd known since she'd barely started to walk.

"Yo, Morgan, it looks like you could use a hand with that. If taking my help wouldn't offend your girl-power pride, that is," he teased.

Morgan and her best friend, Lily Doyle, had always been hardheaded when it came to proving they were as capable as anybody on Seashell Bay. In Lily's case, that determination had translated into fighting the sea as captain of her own lobster boat. In Morgan's, it was all about organization. Morgan Merrifield could organize the living hell out of anything from a referendum campaign to the kids' events at the Blueberry Festival. She'd been born to be a teacher, and Ryan figured she probably ran her elementary school classroom as efficiently as an Army Ranger instructor ran his drills.

"Ryan," she gasped, her gaze widening in surprise. She stared for a few seconds, then flashed him a glorious smile that sank deep into his bones. "Oh, heck, offend away. Be warned though. That bag is heavy."

Though he easily hoisted the canvas tote, she wasn't kidding about the weight. Lugging the heavy load would have done in a lesser woman. But Morgan kept herself in shape, and today she looked as lithe and toned as ever. Incredibly feminine too, he didn't mind noting—slender but with truly nice curves in all the right places.

"What's in this sucker anyway?" he asked.

"Beer, among other necessities." She cast him a mocking glance as she maneuvered the cart across the narrow gangway onto the boat. "By the way, it's real nice to see you again too, old pal."

Ryan followed her on board, laughing at her good-natured dig. "Likewise, Morgan. But why do you need to lug beer all the way from the mainland? The stores on the island stock all kinds of it."

"I've got a regular guest who insists on having his beloved Moosehead, and damned if I didn't forget to ask the Jenkins sisters to order it in. I was shopping in town today anyway, so I thought I'd pick some up." She brushed a hand back through the silky, shoulder-length hair that kept blowing across her face, and her rosebud mouth curved into a sly smile. "We make a little money running an honor bar. It helps the bottom line a bit."

Ryan switched the bag to his other hand and helped her steer the cart around a pile of suitcases left on the deck. "Well, aren't you just the considerate hostess? Or is it host? I don't want to be politically incorrect."

"You, politically incorrect? Perish the thought. But yeah, I'll do special stuff for guests to keep them coming back. God knows we can't afford to lose any more business." For a moment, her cheery expression dimmed.

The deckhands yanked the gangway on board again and closed the gate. Morgan wheeled her cart across the cabin to the port side and found an empty bench.

Ryan plopped the bag down beside her. "Okay if I sit with you? Or would you rather be alone?"

She looked at him like he'd just lost his mind. "What, you think I'd rather be alone than sit with the hottest dude to ever walk the halls of Peninsula High School? Every female on this boat is thinking I've hit the jackpot, Soldier Boy."

Though she was clearly kidding, Ryan had a sudden flash of Morgan clinging to him like a second skin at the festival dance last summer. Neither of them had been joking then.

"Oh, come on," he said, his brain momentarily seizing up as his gaze drifted to the truly nice cleavage exposed by her blue tank top.

Lame, man. Really lame.

Ryan dropped onto the bench next to her. "Sweetheart, I'm really sorry about your dad. He was a great guy." The urge to pull her into his arms to comfort her surprised him with its intensity. He gave her hand a quick squeeze instead.

Morgan's features turned somber, her gaze drifting to the dock where the water taxis were moored as the ferry moved toward the open water of the harbor. She shifted toward him on the bench, her skirt fluttering around her tanned legs. "Thanks, Ryan. And thank you for the sympathy card. I know I should have acknowledged it, but... well..." She paused to breathe a low, heartbroken sigh that practically killed him. "I just couldn't stand to go through them all again, and then it seemed too late."

Cal Merrifield had keeled over dead of a heart attack in late April. Ryan had been stunned when Aiden Flynn e-mailed him the shocking news. Morgan had lost her mother to cancer about three years ago, and now her father was gone at just sixty years of age. Cal had owned the Lobster Pot bar and restaurant for years before selling it to buy the island's only B&B. He was truly one of the good guys, and Ryan knew that his sudden loss had devastated Morgan and her younger sister, Sabrina. According to Aiden, it had pretty much rocked the entire island of Seashell Bay.

"I heard you left your teaching job," he said, not wanting to make her dwell on the details of her dad's death.

Her face scrunched up in a grimace that would have been comical if the subject weren't so awful. "Yes, for now. I took a leave of absence."

"I assume that was for your sister's sake?" No way Sabrina Merrifield could manage the B&B. Though she'd been Cal's steadfast helper, poor Sabrina had always had enough trouble just managing her own life.

"Yes. That and my guilt."

He frowned. "Guilt?"

Morgan's gaze skittered off to the side as the ferry captain tooted his horn, drowning out the squawking seagulls. "That was a stupid slip of the tongue. Just forget I said it," she finally replied.

Because Morgan was as upfront and honest as anyone he'd ever known, her response surprised him. But then she smiled, and even though it looked to him like it might have been forced, it brought her quiet beauty blazing back to life.

Simply put, Morgan was a babe, with eyes as blue as a June sky, a smooth-as-honey complexion, and a cute nose with a slight tilt that gave her face character. She also had the most thoroughly kissable lips he'd ever seen. But though all the island guys now agreed she was a first-class hottie, it hadn't always been that way. Growing up, she'd been a bit nerdy, slightly overweight, and naturally shy. But by the middle of high school, she'd started to blossom into a very sexy girl. Morgan and Lily and their friend Holly Tyler had made one hell of a triple threat back then, and almost every teenage guy in Seashell Bay had spent considerable time and energy circling them like a pack of overeager puppies.

"Let's go up to the top deck," he said. "It's too nice a day to be stuck down here in the cabin." Morgan had probably sat on the lower deck because she didn't want to haul all her crap up the stairs, but he figured they both could use some fresh air.

"Good idea," she said, getting up.

"Want me to bring your stuff?"

She scoffed. "Boy, pal, you've been away too long. You know it's safe to leave things on the boats. Besides, there's nothing valuable in there."

"Except for the beer," he joked. Still, he decided to keep an eye on people getting off the boat at the two stops they'd make before Seashell Bay. He'd learned not to be fully trusting—not even here.

As he climbed the staircase behind Morgan, Ryan gave her rear view a thorough, if discreet, inspection. Damned if she didn't get prettier every time he saw her, with a body that just didn't quit. When she sat down on a bench at the stern, she reached into her purse and pulled out a pair of sunglasses, covering up the baby blues that he could stare into all day. It mystified him that Morgan wasn't in a permanent relationship with some mainland guy since she'd been teaching school up the coast for years. He doubted that anything would ever happen between her and any of the island guys though. Most young people in Seashell Bay regarded their island contemporaries more as annoying brothers and sisters than potential mates. Friends, yes. Soul mates and lovers, not so much.

"If you're a little cool up here," he said, "I've got a fleece in my duffel."

A refreshing breeze usually appeared around the time the ferry cleared the harbor and turned into open waters.

On a hot summer day, you could fry an egg on the sidewalk in downtown Portland and be reaching for a sweater before the boat passed the ruins of Fort Gorges in the middle of the bay.

Morgan tipped her face up to the sun for a moment. "Thanks, but I'm fine." Then she looked at him, inscrutable behind her big, movie star shades. "Ryan, I'm really surprised to see you here in June. You're usually only back for the Blueberry Festival."

He leaned back in his seat and stretched out his legs, going for casual. "Let's just say this isn't going to be my standard, quick in-and-out. I might even stay for the whole summer or most of it."

He heard the sharp inhalation of her breath. "Well, that'll be a first," she said after a pause. "Your mom and dad must be so happy. And heck, that means people might actually get a chance to know the real you, not just the mysterious tough-guy front you put on." She smiled and gave him a friendly poke on the arm. It wasn't the first time Morgan had teased him about what she called his "strong but silent" act.

"What are you talking about? I'm an open book."

"An open book with blank pages, maybe."

"Wow, that didn't tickle," he said, adopting a wounded look.

Morgan laughed, a light, melodious sound that Ryan had always found insanely sexy.

"Okay, I take that back," she said. "Maybe not blank, but written in some unbreakable code. Mr. Enigma, forever wrapped in mystery."

Yeah, and that's the way I like it.

Ryan had never much liked folks poking into his business, and poking into other people's business was pretty much a team sport in Seashell Bay. "Maybe I just don't have a very interesting story to tell."

She stared at him. "Dude, that's a big fat lie if I've ever heard one."

"Come on, Merrifield, how many times have we hung out at the Pot drinking beer and playing darts?" he said with a taunting grin. "Or danced at the festival social? Hell, it's not like I hide out in a cave when I come back to the island." Damn, he'd almost forgotten how much he enjoyed kidding around with her.

Morgan's expression went serious on him in an instant, surprising him again. "In a way, you do hide, Ryan. You hardly ever talk about yourself and never about what you actually do. All anybody knows is that you were in the military for years and then you left. Trust me, we've spent many a long hour on the island speculating about what nefarious things Ryan Butler might be up to. Some people even think you were part of the raid on Bin Laden's compound, and maybe what happened there made you decide to leave the army."

That theory was completely bogus, though Ryan had been part of operations every bit as hairy as SEAL Team Six's mission to Abbottabad. "Not even close. Besides, SEALs are navy, and I was army. Who was the wing nut that came up with that stupid idea?"

Morgan made a zipping motion across her lips. "I never reveal my sources. But if you don't like rumors, you could try to be a little more forthcoming. Inquiring minds want to know."

"You mean *nosy people* want to know. Okay, here's the deal—I was in the army, I left, and now I work for a private military contractor called Double Shield."

She rewarded him with an encouraging smile. "That's a start. Now what exactly do you do for Double Shield? Which, by the way, sounds like a condom ad."

Ryan was torn between laughter and irritation. He didn't like people pressing him for details of his life, but he knew Morgan was just kidding around. "I protect people who need protecting."

"Holy cow, you mean like movie stars and rap artists?" She batted her eyelashes in a *golly-gee* imitation of someone who was actually impressed with what he did.

"All kinds of people," Ryan said with just enough edge to signal the topic was closed for discussion.

Morgan blew out a sigh. "See what I mean? Getting information out of you is like digging for gold in Seashell Bay. Totally pointless."

"Now that's an incisive little nugget of analysis."

She groaned at his lame joke. He was really hitting them out of the ballpark today.

The boat pulled up to the Little Diamond Island dock, and a few passengers started to gather up their things.

"Call me paranoid," Ryan said, "but I'm going to head downstairs for a few minutes to make sure nobody gets ideas about your stuff." Maybe they could talk about something else besides his life when he came back.

She smiled. "If it makes you feel better, go for it. They'd be crazy to try with you playing watchdog. Dude, you look more ripped every time I see you."

Ryan flexed a bicep to make light of her comment. "Right, a regular man of steel."

Morgan told herself that her rapidly beating pulse as she watched Ryan disappear below was simply a coincidence.

Most übermasculine guys in their early thirties tended to swagger, especially around women. Ryan though...he moved with a quiet yet powerful grace that was a wonder to behold. His body was pretty damn wonderful too, with broad shoulders tapering to the classic six-pack and long, muscular legs. His Red Sox T-shirt hugged his brawny chest and showcased his cut biceps. That amazing body was the product of years of military training and his beloved kayaking, and it was all too easy to imagine how it would feel wrapped around her.

She breathed a tiny sigh and slumped against the back of the bench, turning her face up to the warm June sunshine. She'd spent hours rushing around Portland to pick up supplies. Normally she gave herself enough time before the boat's departure to use the cargo service for her goods, but too many errands today and a fender bender near the parking garage had delayed her. So it was really great that, after her mad dash, Ryan had appeared to help her. The fact that he liked to rattle her chain spoke to the easy friendship that still existed between them.

Her thoughts about Ryan had often strayed from friendship into fantasy territory over the years, and their encounter at last summer's festival dance had done nothing to change that. The two of them had ended up in a slow dance at the end of the evening, egged on by their friend Laura Vickers. A little drunk by then, Morgan had found it all too easy to melt into the dangerous shelter of Ryan's embrace.

It had been a culmination of a stressful evening, brought on by a horrible and very public confrontation between Lily Doyle's father and his longtime enemy, Sean Flynn. Morgan had been so rattled and worried for Lily that she'd responded by drinking more than she normally did, which had lowered her staunch defenses against her supersecret crush on Ryan. Her heart had pounded like a battering ram as he held her close—too close. His bristled jaw had rubbed gently over her cheek, and she'd thought he was going to kiss her right there on the crowded dance floor. Under the influence of alcohol and nerves—and yes, sheer lust—her smarts had evaporated in the heat of Ryan's mysterious gaze.

At precisely the same moment, they'd both snapped out of it. By some sort of unspoken but clear mutual agreement, she and Ryan had derailed the makings of a runaway train. Even in her instinctive relief, Morgan had been shaken to realize how good it felt to be held by him. How thrilling the moment had been in its raw sexual power.

And how insanely stupid it had been to let it go that far.

While in theory she loved the idea of having hot sex with Ryan Butler, she was not going to be a one-night stand for a hard-ass soldier who flitted in and out of the island, not even stopping long enough to make a ferry pass economical. And Ryan had clearly felt the same, because they'd quickly parted ways after the dance, never speaking a word about what had happened during those few electrifying minutes.

Dammit though, one look at him today had sent her right back in the grip of an emotional—and hormonal—tsunami. Whatever that dance at the social had stirred up, she obviously hadn't managed to bury it deep enough. Morgan knew her traitorous body would happily straddle Ryan's lap for a hot make-out session right now, in full view of a bunch of islanders who knew them both. But surely all that told her was that it had been way, way too long since she'd had sex.

Yeah, sure, that has to be it.

Ryan came back up the stairs, taking them two at a time as the boat pulled away from the dock. He sat next to her and said, "So, tell me about Golden Sunset. How are you and Sabrina making out with the place?"

She mentally winced, hating the idea of voicing her struggles with the inn. Should she be honest with Ryan or put on the brave face she maintained for all but her closest friends? Uncertain, she gave a little shrug.

"Not too good, huh?" His gaze looked both sympathetic and concerned, and she could tell he wanted an honest answer.

She capitulated. "It's been rough. An awful lot of our regular guests came back year after year mostly because they loved Dad. You know what a big personality he had, and he really knew how to make people feel welcome and wanted."

"Cal was a stand-up guy. One of the best."

Morgan took a deep breath, the grief almost choking her. "Quite a few couples cancelled their summer reservations after they heard Dad had passed. I don't know whether they didn't want to come if he wasn't there or they thought the place might be too depressing after we lost him."

Hell, despite her best efforts, the inn's atmosphere *was* depressing. It still seemed impossible that it should carry on without her dad.

"Maybe a little of both," Ryan said, frowning a bit. "It's too bad they didn't look at it as an opportunity to keep supporting the place. And you."

"Amen to that. Anyway, unless business somehow picks up, it looks like we could wind up in the red for the summer. And I think you remember how dead the rest of the year is for tourism in Seashell Bay."

The B&B's bread and butter had always been the summer vacation crowd. While most of that revenue came from tourists, a lot of island residents didn't have room in their homes and cottages for all the family and friends that descended on them in the summer, so those folks often ended up at Golden Sunset too. That kind of business would continue at various levels all year, but only at Christmas was the inn ever close to full during the off-season. If Morgan didn't manage to pull in some good summer business, her father's B&B was headed for disaster.

Ryan glanced at another ferry as it passed them to starboard on its way back to Portland. At least a dozen people waved at them, as always happened when boats passed each other. She forced a little smile and waved back.

"Have you given any thought to selling?" Ryan said. "Or will you be able to ride it out?"

Oh, I think about selling every freaking day.

"I'm not sure anybody would buy the place at this point. Everything was up in the air even before Dad died. Aiden and Lily and their partners are building that new resort...and, well, who really knows how it'll impact our little place?" Morgan was really happy that Aiden Flynn had returned to the island for good, but she had some worries about the effect of his upscale ecoresort on her small business.

"Most of your regulars should stay loyal," Ryan said. "A lot of people prefer the atmosphere of smaller inns. From what I hear, Aiden's place is going to cater to a different crowd."

Morgan gave him a wry smile. "Yes, a crowd that likes lots of comforts and the latest in modern conveniences. Our place is short on both, I'm afraid. Heck, Dad even hemmed and hawed before finally putting in Wi-Fi last year. And our rooms are pretty . . . well, basic."

She almost said run-down, but that felt disloyal. Facing an increasingly tight financial squeeze, her father had let things slide over the past couple of years, and now the place needed a lot of work, both structural and cosmetic. "Anyway, I have to try to make a go of it for my sister's sake. She'd fall apart without the B&B."

Though he'd been mostly away from the island for more than a dozen years, Ryan would know Sabrina well enough to understand. When she was a preteen, she'd been diagnosed with a learning disability. While she was a hard worker at the B&B, cooking and cleaning and doing other chores that were familiar territory for her, there was no way she could manage the operation. Most normal administrative tasks were simply beyond her, which meant they all fell on Morgan.

"So it sounds like you're putting your teaching career on hold for the foreseeable future," Ryan said.

Whenever Morgan thought about that, it felt like someone had punched her in the gut. Though she'd told her principal that she intended to be back in her classroom in September, the low number of confirmed reservations at the inn had made that an increasingly remote possibility.

"I've been hoping I could get the place operating efficiently enough this summer to let me hire a part-time manager to run it with Sabrina after I leave, but that seems more like a wish at this point than a plan. So I'm just taking it one day at a time and trying to figure things out." Morgan didn't want to surrender to pessimism but refused to bury her head in the sand either. The stakes for both sisters were too high to engage in self-delusion.

"One day at a time is never a bad idea." Ryan leaned back on the bench and stretched out his long legs. His feet reached all the way to the opposite bench. "I guess I'm going to be doing something like that myself for a while."

Morgan welcomed the shift in conversation. "So, what are you going to do with yourself on the island? Kayak all over the place and drink beer? Or will your dad need a sternman this summer?" Like a lot of people on the island, Ryan's dad was a lobster fisherman.

"Actually, I was thinking that, if I end up spending the whole season here, I'd try to kayak to every one of the Calendar Islands. Give myself a little challenge to pass the time."

The islands of Casco Bay were sometimes called the Calendar Islands, a reference to the fact that there were supposedly 365 of them. Some, however, were barely big enough to stand on.

"Well, that'll be a heck of a workout." Morgan's brain, which refused to behave itself, easily conjured up the image of Ryan's half-naked, ripped form gleaming in the sun as he paddled through the chop of the bay.

"Just a walk in the park if I stick around for a couple of months. As for helping Dad out, yeah, if he needs me to sub while his sternman takes some time off, I'll be on the boat."

"That's nice of you since you hate lobster fishing," she said, scrunching her nose in sympathy. Like Ryan, many of Seashell Bay's younger generation had no desire to follow in their fathers' footsteps when it came to the hard slog of hauling traps from sunrise to sunset.

Ryan shrugged. "I don't much like a lot of things I have to do. Doesn't mean I won't answer the call."

She smiled at the typically cryptic Ryan Butler statement. "Your parents will be happy to finally have you at home for more than a few days."

"Yeah, but I'm not going to stay with them. I want a place of my own, a place to…" He paused for a couple of moments, his gaze distracted. "Anyway, I'm going to rent a cottage or a house, hopefully one on the water."

Morgan raised an eyebrow. "Renting isn't going to be easy. Almost everything is booked by this time of the season."

"I know, but it can't be helped. I only made the decision to do this a few days ago. I figure there should be something available, even if it's a bit of a dump. I don't need anything fancy. As long as it's got indoor plumbing, I'm good to go."

Dump. On some of her worst days, Morgan had silently used that harsh word to describe the current state of the B&B. But on his lips, the word had sparked a pretty interesting, though kind of crazy, idea. She toyed with it for a few moments, testing it out in her head. Sure it might be dangerous, at least for her, but it seemed worth a try.

As the ferry cut through the deep blue water of Hussey Sound, Morgan mentally put on her big-girl panties and got ready to proposition the sexiest man to ever come out of Seashell Bay.

Chapter 2

$\mathcal{R}$yan spotted his mother on the landing when the ferry was still a quarter mile out from Seashell Bay. She wore a red-and-black plaid shirt, one of a half dozen or so she'd lovingly preserved since her college days in the seventies. They must have cost about five bucks each back then, so he had to give them credit for their staying power.

His mom had never yet failed to be waiting for him on the landing when he came home. Not once in thirteen years. And in muggy heat and bitter cold, in pelting rain and blinding snow, she wore those same plaid shirts that barely retained a fraction of their original vibrant color. Sundays and religious holidays provided the only exception to her hilariously rigid clothing routine, since she wouldn't be caught dead at Saint Anne's morning Mass in anything other than a dress. Julia Butler might be a bit eccentric, but everyone loved both her and his dad. They were hardworking, God-fearing folk who would do anything to help a neighbor or anyone else in need.

"I'll bet that red speck on the dock is your mom,"

Morgan said. She moved closer to him as she leaned against the rail and didn't flinch when he automatically laid a casual, friendly arm across her slender shoulders. The ocean breeze whipped her hair into a tangle of shimmering gold and made her dangly earrings do a little dance.

"She never misses," he said.

"It's pretty great to have someone waiting for your boat, isn't it?"

Ryan caught the wistful note in her voice, which said all there was to say about her recent loss. Had Cal met his eldest daughter every time? He knew Morgan came home a lot and always spent most of her summer on the island helping her dad and hanging out with her girlfriends.

Not wanting to make her feel uncomfortable, he reluctantly pulled his arm away. But, man, he had to resist the urge to keep touching her. "Is Sabrina picking you up?"

"No. My truck's at the landing, so it seems we're both all set."

"I'll help you load up."

"No need. I've got it covered."

There was that girl-power pride again. Ryan thought her response was more automatic than honest, and he wasn't about to take no for an answer. "Hey, you know my mom. She'll kick my ass if I stand around with my hands in my pockets while you're lugging all that stuff."

She flashed him a wry grin. "Well, since you put it that way."

Ryan narrowed his gaze over her shoulder and gestured to a lobster boat motoring just off Paradise Point. "Isn't that Lily's boat—*Miss Annie*?"

Morgan peered at the boat. "None other. She's coming

in early today." She waved, but neither Lily nor her stern-man looked in their direction.

"That's a girl on the stern." Ryan thought he should recognize the young woman but couldn't quite nail it down.

"Erica Easton. She's been working for Lily since Forrest Coolidge went down with a stroke last fall." Morgan made a little grimace. "Poor Forrest. He survived the stroke, but his days on *Summer Star* are over. It's such a shame because that's about all he ever lived for. The man fished lobster for over sixty years and pretty much loved every minute of it."

Ryan felt an odd pang in his chest. It was terrible that old Forrest had a stroke, but any man who'd been able to work at something he loved every day for more than six decades must have been a happy guy. He wished he felt the same way about his own career. He was damn good, which was why Double Shield had been only too eager to sign him up. But did he still love sol-diering? Though he'd loved it when he was fighting for something he believed in, that happened less and less, especially since his shift to private security. Even in Spec Ops, his missions had sometimes been murky, and buddies had died for no reason that made sense to him. "That's a shame about Forrest, but I'm glad Lily found a sternman."

Morgan turned and flipped up her sunglasses, fixing a serious gaze directly on him. Ryan stared back, falling into the big eyes that were framed with thick, soft lashes. Morgan's blue eyes, silky hair, and killer body were a potent and dangerous combination.

"Ryan, listen," she said earnestly, "because I'm going

to suggest something that you'll probably think is batshit crazy."

"Wouldn't be the first time," he joked, trying to get her to relax a little.

She managed a hint of a smile. "I got an idea when you were telling me about trying to rent a place for the summer."

"Yeah?"

"Well, there are plenty of empty rooms at the B&B these days. So it would be no problem for you to have one as long as we're not full up. And I wouldn't charge you anything, of course, so you'd save the cost of renting." Her gaze skittered away over the water. "But look, I certainly won't be offended if you tell me it's a nutty idea."

Ryan tried not to show his surprise. Shock, really. Morgan's offer was generous, but he wasn't a B&B kind of guy. He liked peace and quiet and even solitude, because he'd gone very long periods when there was little of that in his life. It was the main reason he didn't want to spend weeks at his parents' house with family and friends coming and going all day long.

"Uh, that's real sweet of you, Morgan. It's just that I don't—"

She looked back at him and waved a hand to cut him off. "I understand. You'd rather be on your own somewhere. I just thought it could turn out to be a good arrangement for both of us."

As he stared into her eyes, trying to read her, her expression told him nothing. Was there something going on here? He hadn't forgotten how their dance had almost flared into something a whole lot more last summer. Later, when he tried to analyze what had happened, he'd put

Morgan's amorous reaction down to stuff going on in her life, including seeing her best friend, Lily, falling in love. In the past, despite some strong physical signals Morgan had let slip, she'd always carefully maintained her distance from him.

"Well, it's obvious what would be in it for me," he said. "What about for you?"

The ferry slowed and started to make its final turn to line up with the dock. "Your mom's waving," Morgan said. She smiled at Mrs. Butler and started to wave back.

Ryan gave his mother a quick wave and turned back to Morgan. "Well?"

"To be honest, I was hoping for a little skilled labor," she admitted, looking sheepish. "Sorely needed labor, I might add."

Okay, that at least made sense. Though the proposal still didn't appeal to him, every instinct told him to help her out. "Morgan, I can do basic labor, but if you're looking for skilled work..."

He didn't finish, because Morgan flashed him a wide, sweet smile that thumped him hard. That smile, so genuine and open, had always done it for him.

"Oh, don't be so modest," she said. "Everybody on the island knows you're great with tools."

Great with an M4 or an HK416, maybe. Just okay with a hammer.

Ryan wasn't sure if her remark contained any additional meaning but swore there was a glint of mischief in her eyes. He decided not to go there right now. "What do you need help with?"

"I think the better question would be what don't I need help with." She exhaled a sigh. "Right now I've got to deal with the immediate problem of a leaky roof on top of dozens of small jobs that need to be done. I've been planning on asking Brendan Porter to do some of the work, but he's always so busy. Besides if I could get it done via a…a barter arrangement…I wouldn't have to shell out money I can't really afford."

Ryan sure hadn't planned on spending his time on the island doing handyman work. But how could he leave one of his oldest friends in the lurch? And from the anxious look on her face, he could tell it had practically killed her to ask. While she'd tried to sweeten the proposal by offering him a free room, saving money wasn't the issue for him. What mattered was that someone he cared about needed help during a rough time.

And since help was something the resolutely independent Morgan Merrifield rarely sought, that told him how rough things must be for her.

"Okay, I should be able to handle that kind of job—if I can do it in bits and pieces and still get in my kayaking and other stuff." Stuff like maintaining his intensive daily workouts so he didn't get soft and slow. "But you don't have to give me anything at all. I'll do it to help out a pal."

She twisted her mouth sideways and then shook her head. "No, I can't let you do all that work for nothing. If you don't want a room, then we'll just have to agree on an hourly rate. I won't have you working for free. I'm touched by your offer, but I just can't allow it."

Morgan's body language and the conviction in her voice told Ryan she meant what she said. So what now? She was clearly hard up for money, while he was pretty flush. So it would make no sense for her to pay him wages for his work. That wasn't a realistic option. Nor was working for free. He totally got what she was saying about that—it would eat away at her pride and maybe even end up damaging a friendship that he truly valued.

Would it kill him to stay for a couple of weeks at the B&B? The handyman chores shouldn't take longer than that. And who knew if he could even find a decent rental house anyway? Until he found a place, Golden Sunset would be preferable to living in his parents' cramped house.

Stop trying to kid yourself, you moron.

He knew the biggest reason he shouldn't take a room at the inn was Morgan. He'd been stifling his lust for her for years, and after the slip last summer, he knew he had to be extra careful. He had to keep some space between them, and that would be pretty damn hard if they were sleeping under the same roof, wouldn't it?

He should dig in his heels and say no to the room and no to accepting any money from her either. She'd have to accept help on his terms, or there would be none. That was the smart way to handle it.

Stupidly, Ryan found himself saying the opposite. "Okay, I guess I could stay at your place for a little while. Just long enough to get most of the work done."

Her head jerked a bit, as if she was surprised. Then she held out her hand. "Deal, dude. And thank you."

Morgan should be happy. She *was* happy. Then why did her stomach feel like it was doing cannonballs off a high dock?

The answer was obvious. Ryan Butler was a very dangerous man. Until last year, she'd firmly stashed him in a mental box labeled totally off-limits. It sounded silly, but to her, Ryan was almost a James Bond or Jason Bourne type of guy, a crazy-hot mystery man who did wild, top secret stuff he never talked about. He acted like a normal guy when he was home, except for the sky-high emotional walls he'd erected around himself. Ryan *never* talked about himself or his life. If that didn't spell danger, she didn't know what did.

And now she'd flat-out invited Mr. Sexy Mystery Man into her life. Into her *home*.

"For goodness' sake, Morgan, why didn't you put all that stuff in cargo?" Julia Butler asked after she finally relaxed the fierce squeeze she'd put on her son. They stood in the center of the dock as disembarking passengers parted like a wave and flowed around them.

Ryan grinned. "Because our girl had to do a forty-yard dash to make the boat, Mom. The boat crew got the gangway back in place real fast though. It looked to me like those guys knew they'd be in deep trouble if they didn't."

Morgan stuck her tongue out at him. "No, they did it because they're nice young men. Oh, and because I always slip them a good tip when they cut me a break."

Julia's eyes twinkled behind her wire-framed glasses. "You always were a very practical girl, Morgan."

"Glaring at the crew has always worked for me," Ryan said.

"Yeah, but I'm not some six-four, jacked hunk who looks like he was carved out of a granite cliff," Morgan scoffed.

Ryan's dark brows politely arched up, while his mother's eyes popped wide. Morgan mentally winced.

"Ah, I hope business is getting better at the B&B," Julia

finally said into the awkward pause. "How's it looking for the Fourth?"

The July Fourth celebrations in Seashell Bay brought boatloads of visitors. The B&B had always been fully booked during the holiday when her dad was in charge.

Not this year.

"We've still got some space, Mrs. Butler," Morgan said. "We usually get some last-minute bookings, so I'm hopeful we'll fill up."

"Let's load up your stuff," Ryan said. "You'll need to get that beer in the fridge soon."

When the three of them reached the parking lot, Julia took Ryan's duffel and headed off to her car, an ancient Jeep Cherokee even more rusted than most of the island beaters. After Morgan opened the tailgate of her dad's red Toyota pickup, Ryan helped her get everything stowed.

He opened the driver's door and handed her inside. "I'll talk to Mom about our arrangement later," he said after she rolled down the window. "I didn't want to spring it on her here."

"Sure."

"She's obviously not going to be thrilled that I won't be staying with her and Dad," he said.

"Well, take your time. Your room at the B&B will be ready for you whenever you want to move in. In fact, you can have a choice." He'd be staying in the main house while her bedroom was in the attached annex. Though that wouldn't put much distance between them, every little bit helped. "You can have the biggest one we've got. We usually reserve that room for families—"

"Morgan, all I need is a bed and a closet," Ryan interrupted, leaning on the window frame and looking impossibly tough and handsome. Her heart skipped a few beats just looking at him. "Big and fancy are wasted on me."

She laughed. "Well, none of our rooms are very big, and we definitely don't do fancy at Golden Sunset Bed-and-Breakfast."

She didn't often refer to the B&B by name because she hated "Golden Sunset." While the sunset view from the inn was often spectacular, she thought the name made it sound like a retirement home. Morgan still hoped to adopt a fresher label, but her sister was balking. Sabrina's greatest desire was for everything to stay the same. Change—almost any change—filled her with anxiety.

"I'll spend tonight with my folks," Ryan said, "and tomorrow morning we can start by going over what you want done. How's that work for you?"

Fantastic—if this plan doesn't blow up in my face. "Sounds perfect. You can't believe how much I appreciate this, Ryan."

He shook his head. "It's no big deal. Is eight o'clock too early?"

"Absolutely not. Sabrina gets breakfast started by six, and I'm usually in the kitchen helping her by six thirty. You like omelets?"

His lips curved into a sexy grin that left her short of breath. "I'll eat anything that isn't still moving."

She wrinkled her nose. "Please, spare me the detail. Eight o'clock tomorrow, then."

"Yeah, it should be . . . interesting."

After that cryptic comment, Ryan gave the roof of her truck a tap and headed off across the lot.

In her rearview mirror, Morgan watched him all the way to his mom's Jeep before she finally put her truck in gear. Ryan Butler was hands-down the hottest man she'd ever known, and starting tomorrow night, he'd be sleeping under her roof.

That evening, Morgan wheeled past the Doyle home and trap lot and up the long driveway to Lily's place. A sunset glow washed over the jumble of lobster traps, buoys, coils of rope, and the large steel shed that served as Lily's workshop for repairing equipment.

She parked in front of the two-bedroom cottage Lily had built a few years ago at the back of her father's acreage. The house was cozy as heck, with its wood-burning stove and warm, comfortable furnishings. Morgan had wonderful memories of countless meals and bottles of wine with her best bud here. In this cottage, they'd shared joy and heartbreak, and joked about island life and the trials of finding a suitable mate in Seashell Bay.

Surprisingly, Lily had finally found her true love among one of the island guys—Aiden Flynn, who had left Seashell Bay at eighteen and returned only a year ago. Soon, Lily and Aiden would be married, and the newlyweds would move into the historic Flynn family home on the other side of the island.

Lily threw open the screen door. "The beer is cold, the coffee's warm, and Mom stocked me up with fresh-baked blueberry tarts this morning."

Morgan gave her best friend a quick hug. "Oh, please. I gain a pound every time I even take a look at those darn tarts."

"After what you said on the phone, I'm guessing you'll take beer, not coffee," Lily said as she headed back to the kitchen and pulled open the fridge. Her bare feet and damp, curling hair meant she'd already showered after a hard day of hauling lobster traps.

"Yeah, like, move over coffee because this is a job for alcohol."

They settled in the living room, where Morgan took an overstuffed armchair and Lily sprawled on the sofa, putting her feet up on the battered wooden coffee table. After taking a hefty sip of her Shipyard Ale for courage, Morgan told her about meeting Ryan on the ferry.

"I can't believe he didn't tell Aiden he'd be staying so long this time," Lily said. "Not that Ryan is ever a fount of information."

"No kidding. At least he told me a bit about what he's been up to lately. He's with some private military contractor now."

"Really? Doing what? Chasing terrorists? Saving the world from an alien invasion?"

Morgan rolled her eyes. "Aiden's got you playing too many video games. No, he's been protecting diplomats and corporate bigwigs in foreign countries. I did a search for the company, Double Shield, when I got home."

"Wait, you did an Internet search on Ryan? Seriously?"

"Yeah, busted."

Lily laughed. "Oh, well, you could always make it your summer project to find out everything he's been up to, I suppose. If anybody can probe that man's defenses, it's you. Especially after what happened between you guys at—"

"I prefer not to be reminded of that particular descent into insanity," Morgan interjected. "It was a momentary aberration due to stress and alcohol."

"Uh-huh. You stick with that story if it makes you feel better, girlfriend."

Morgan tossed a throw pillow at Lily.

"Are you going to assault me or get on with it?" Lily said, after deftly catching the pillow. "There are some juicy bits, right? I bet all that wicked chemistry between you is still front and center."

Off the charts. But Morgan wasn't yet ready to admit that. "Ryan doesn't want to stay with his folks, so he's going to try to rent a house."

Lily smirked at the dodge but let it go. "That makes sense, though he must be forgetting how busy it is here in the summer."

"I told him he'd have trouble." Morgan tried to sound casual. "So I offered him one of the empty rooms at the B&B for a while. For free, of course. Just to help out a friend."

Lily set down her beer. "Uh, well, that was certainly kind of you. Probably not the smartest move you've ever made but definitely kind."

If there was one thing Morgan could always count on with Lily—though actually there were a lot of things she could count on—it was the unvarnished truth.

"It seemed to make sense in the moment," Morgan said. "You know how much work needs to be done, and I'm so strung out financially that I can't really afford to pay a carpenter or handyman to do it all."

"And what did Ryan say after he picked himself up off the deck of the boat?"

Morgan waggled a hand. "He agreed, eventually. I insisted that he either had to take the room or I had to pay him for his work. I'm not about to take advantage of the guy that way."

Though I'd like to take advantage of Ryan Butler in a bunch of other ways. Oh, yes, I would.

"So when does he move in?"

"Tomorrow."

"Mother Mary. Well, at least he'll be sleeping upstairs in one of the guest rooms, not right next to you in the annex. Temptation will still be close though."

"I'll be sure to keep my bedroom door locked in case he comes down to the kitchen for a midnight snack and gets lost," Morgan said.

Lily laughed. "Look, I totally get why you're doing this, but if the shoe were on the other foot, you'd be giving me holy hell. You were like a mama bear from the moment you got a sniff of something starting to happen between Aiden and me."

Morgan didn't buy that comparison. "Not the same, Lily. You'd been in love with Aiden since forever, so I thought you'd get really hurt when he went back to his life in baseball. But all I've ever had for Ryan was some…uh, well, let's call it hormone-related interest."

"Had? Past tense? Hey, sweetie, you can't fool me."

"Okay, so maybe I do still have a certain lust for his fine form. But it's not like I'd be courting a broken heart. It won't happen, because Ryan and I are totally different."

Lily lifted an eyebrow. "How so, exactly?"

"Well, what do we have in common? Nada, other than this island. And when it comes to Seashell Bay, Ryan steers clear of the place except for a few days a year, while I come home every chance I get. That's a pretty fundamental difference, don't you think?"

"That sounds like what I said about Aiden and me," Lily said drily. "And I still remember how you called bullshit."

"Okay then, how about the fact that he spends his life

toting a gun? You know how I feel about the gun culture, Lily. And while I support our troops, I don't think war is a good answer to anything."

"Forgive me for harping on the same theme," Lily said, "but Aiden and I don't exactly see eye to eye on a lot of issues either. And yet our differences have a funny way of seeming totally insignificant when he's got his arms around me. Or when he's making my life easier in a thousand ways."

"Did you just change your tune from a minute ago? I know you're desperate to get me married off now that you've hooked Aiden, but really..." She gave Lily a wink in case there was even a remote chance her pal would think she was serious.

Lily pointed an accusatory finger. "Hey, if a little carefree sex was all there was to it, I'd be thrilled for you. But you know it won't stop at that, and you *will* get hurt. Not because you and Ryan are so different, but because I don't see Mr. Tall, Dark, and Loner settling down anytime soon, if ever. And not around here, that's for sure."

Morgan had the urge to hunch her shoulders. "You think I should withdraw the offer?"

Lily paused and then said, "What does Sabrina think about it?"

"She was leery at first, which didn't surprise me. But once I went through all the work we needed done and how much money Ryan could save us, she was okay."

"Sabrina appreciates everything you're doing," Lily said. "She understands how hard it was for you to leave your job and come home. It was a huge act of love on your part, Morgan."

"Love *and* guilt." Morgan hated that she still struggled

to come to terms with her messed-up feelings about her dad, Sabrina, and the B&B. It was like an anchor strapped to her chest. "And my sister isn't nearly as positive about it when she's talking to me."

Lily shook her head. "Enough with the guilt trip, you. Cal had no right to expect you to give up your career and come running back after your mom died. Especially not when he had Sabrina to help him."

Morgan grimaced. "But you remember how devastated he was. Losing Mom made him think he couldn't run the place by himself. And Sabrina was an even bigger mess than he was after Mom died, so that weighed on him too. Dad pulled it together over time, but he never stopped needing my help. I let him down, Lily."

"Oh, bullshit. The B&B is still alive and kicking."

"Alive but hardly kicking. Anyway, he made me promise that, if anything ever happened to him, I'd take care of Sabrina. And he meant making sure the B&B would be there for her. If it were just up to me, I'd try to sell the place while it's still got some loyal clients. If it keeps going downhill, it isn't going to be worth much in a sale, and then we'll be in real trouble."

Still, she hated the idea of selling, because it would mean she'd failed her father and her sister again.

"You think the money you'll save from Ryan's work will be a significant help?" Lily asked.

"Define *significant*. I have very little savings left, and the bank won't extend Golden Sunset's credit. So unless I get the work done free or on the cheap, the place is going to start looking even more like an old shack." She hated that idea too. Golden Sunset didn't deserve such shabby treatment.

"It needs some updating for sure, but that place has great bones."

"Great *old* bones, Lily. And old bones break easily."

Her friend eyed her doubtfully, then reluctantly nodded. "Well, if you really do need Ryan, all I can say is please be careful, okay?"

"Don't worry, I'll be fine—as long as I give Mr. Stud Muffin a very wide berth."

Chapter 3

$\mathcal{R}$yan parked his cart next to Morgan's pickup and took a good look at Golden Sunset, the first in a long time. Man, the place did need work. For starters, the mailbox listed over, there was a missing baluster on the wraparound porch, and the weather vane atop the gabled roof looked as if the next nor'easter would rip it clean off and send the metal rooster winging across the yard. So far, three jobs had presented themselves before he'd even started a close inspection of the old Victorian house with its attached annex.

No wonder Morgan had been so vague about the extent of the problems. He had a feeling there'd be a hell of a long list of work to be done by the time they'd finished going through the place.

At least the paint job looked pretty good. The coastal Maine climate hadn't yet weathered the eggshell-white siding or the hunter-green gingerbread trim. Ryan said a silent prayer of thanks to Cal Merrifield for keeping that part up, at least, because he sure didn't want to have to paint the old barn from stem to stern. He sucked at painting, probably because he'd always found it to be fiddly, slow, and boring. Give him a nail gun or a drill and he was good to go, but a paintbrush—no thanks.

Morgan emerged from the annex as he grabbed his duffel off the cart's cargo carrier. "What time did you say you were going to be here?" she said with a teasing smile.

Ryan glanced at his watch. It was eight forty, quite a bit later than his original ETA. "I figured I should give you a bit of extra time. Didn't want to barge in while you might still be getting breakfast on the table for your guests."

He'd been awake since six. As if his brain had been hardwired at birth with a built-in wake-up call, his eyes popped open every morning at that hour, rain or shine, no matter whether he was tucked in at his dad's house in Seashell Bay or grabbing some brief shut-eye in a wadi in Helmand Province. He'd used the extra time this morning to go for an even longer run than usual and had ended up completing a full circuit of the winding road that traced the circumference of the island. Then he'd had a quick cup of coffee with his dad, who delayed his normal castoff so he could spend time with his son. Though Ryan had never wanted to be a lobster boat captain, he'd always admired his father's dedication to the challenging and sometimes dangerous life on the water. Kevin Butler was the most decent man he'd ever known, and Ryan was happy he'd be spending more time with him this summer.

"We've only got two couples, and they're early risers," Morgan said. "Everything's already cleaned up and put away."

Leaning against the doorframe, she looked so damn

beautiful that Ryan's pulse rate doubled. Her red-and-white-striped top displayed a nice amount of cleavage, and her white capris hugged her trim figure, showcasing curves that never failed to draw his eye. Her blond hair looked like sunshine. Morgan might be in a world of trouble, but you'd never know it from looking at her.

He rolled his eyes in mock aggravation. "Damn. I guess that means I'm out of luck for breakfast."

A small notebook in her hand, Morgan sashayed across the gravel drive to meet him, her sweet smile holding more than a hint of mischief. "Oh, maybe we can rustle you up something. Granola and yogurt? Herbal tea, perhaps?"

He hoped she was kidding but decided not to push it. "On second thought, maybe we should start right in on the inspection."

"I'm in your hands. Do you want to start outside or inside?"

Babe, I'd like to have you in my hands, all right. Ryan tossed his duffel up onto the porch. "Might as well start out here, I guess. I've already noticed a few things—the mailbox, the weather vane, and that missing baluster over there." He pointed to the side of the porch.

"Baluster? I just call it a post," Morgan said, "but I must bow to your obvious male wisdom." She followed her wiseass comment up with a flourishing mock bow that gave him an even nicer view of her breasts. Then she tapped her notebook. "And those three items are already on my project list, by the way. I'm afraid it grows almost daily."

Ryan liked that she seemed so upbeat this morning. When they talked on the boat yesterday, he'd found it hard to see her so weighed down by her troubles. That wasn't the girl he was used to. She always looked put together and gorgeous, but when she had that lively sparkle in her blue eyes, Morgan Merrifield was damn near irresistible.

But when she opened the notebook and he caught a glimpse of the long list she'd prepared, Ryan had to steel his features not to show his concern.

"Lead the way." He pulled a small, spiral-bound notebook out of the back pocket of his cargo shorts and a stub of a pencil from behind his ear. "I'll make some notes on the materials I'll need."

Morgan eyed the pencil, worn smooth and round at the tip. "I guess that outfit you work for doesn't pay too well. I could get you a real pencil if you like. Or maybe even a pen?" she asked. "So far, I have to say your tools aren't too impressive, Butler."

He laughed. Yeah, that was the Morgan he'd always known—smart, funny, and always ready to rub a little forty-grit sandpaper over his ass.

"Just wait till I bring out the big guns," he said as she led him along a well-tended flagstone walkway bordered by a row of flowering plants in weed-free beds. The only plants he could identify by name were the hostas. "Then you won't be laughing."

Her eyebrows lifted a bit, but then she turned and pointed at the corner of the house. "Well, Mr. Secret Agent Man, the next item on my exterior list is that loose drainpipe. Think you can handle that assignment?"

"Easy." Ryan made a note in his book. The brackets, some of them bent, had given way and created a gap between the siding and the drainpipe. "I'll replace all the brackets. Otherwise, a strong wind might rip the pipe right off."

"And that would be bad," Morgan said.

"Especially if it whacked somebody in the head as it came down."

She exhaled a sigh, and some of the fun went out of her. "That's all I'd need—a lawsuit."

Ryan gave her shoulder a sympathetic squeeze. "Look, I'll take care of that and anything else that could give you grief."

She startled slightly at his touch. "Um, thanks. Let's go around back so you can see what else we've got."

He pondered her interesting reaction as they headed under a vine-covered trellis that led to the expansive rear yard. It sloped gradually toward the rocky shoreline where the B&B's dock jutted out into a shallow cove off the Atlantic. "What does your sister think about me staying here?"

He and Sabrina barely knew each other. They'd been two years apart in school and probably hadn't exchanged more than a couple of dozen words back then. Mostly he remembered Morgan's pretty little sister as a shy, awkward girl who would sometimes lash out big-time when some jackass kid flipped her switch with too much teasing.

"She's really grateful that you're going to help us out with the work," Morgan said in a neutral voice. She stopped as they reached a big concrete patio nestled in an angle formed by the big main house and the smaller annex. Four sets of white metal tables and chairs, each with an open, green umbrella that matched the house trim, formed a loose circle.

Ryan raised his brows. "And?"

She gave a little shrug. "Almost anything new or different makes her a little nervous, Ryan. You know that. We'll just have to see how it goes, okay?"

"No problem."

He'd been doing a visual check of the roof as they talked. The asphalt shingles were a disaster. In a few areas, pieces had ripped off. On a section of the roof above the corner of the patio, a horizontal strip of plywood sheeting had become visible.

"Okay, that's a serious problem," he said, pointing up. "You need to get the entire roof reshingled as soon as you can afford it, but that section needs to be fixed fast unless you want your guests taking unscheduled baths in rainwater."

Morgan craned back to look. "That's the first item on my checklist. Those shingles blew off in a thunderstorm two days ago. And wouldn't you know it, some water leaked down through the attic onto the ceiling of one of the guest bedrooms."

"How much water?"

"Enough that the ceiling will have to be patched and repainted."

"Was there damage in the attic too?"

"Just a wet floor, and we only use the attic for storage. Anyway, I told you there was a lot to be done around here. I could keep you busy most of the summer." She dropped her gaze down at her sandal-covered feet. "Naturally, I won't ask that of you."

"Let's see what else needs to be done," he said. "Then we'll take it from there, one step at a time."

She gave him a sheepish grin. "You're more than welcome to stay here all summer whether you're still working or not." Then she shook her head, as if remembering something. "But I would need to kick you out for a week at the beginning of August because we've got a wedding party coming in. They need all the rooms. It's the only time all summer that the place is fully booked, so it's really important."

Ryan had a vision of his leisurely summer plans evaporating like morning fog on the bay. Sharing a house with Morgan, her sister, and a slew of guests was not going to cut it for long. "I'll definitely be out of your hair way before then. I should be able to find a place to rent soon enough."

"Don't count on it, pal." She took his arm and gently pulled him with her as she started across the patio. "Let's finish up out here so we can get you a real breakfast— I was just yanking your chain about granola and tea." She ran her gaze over his body. "A hardworking man of your size needs a healthy dose of protein to start his day, right?"

Ryan swore he heard a catch in her throat after she conducted her little physical check. Maybe that brief flash of fire they'd ignited at the social last summer was ready to flare up again given half a chance.

He smiled. "Morgan, you have no idea how big my appetite can be."

Ryan followed her up the porch stairs and into the center hallway. If Morgan didn't miss her guess, his gaze was probably glued to her butt. A few minutes ago, that same gaze had made a slow perusal of her entire body, which had sent the blood rushing from her head directly to points south. He was clearly appreciating her outfit. Or more likely, what he imagined was underneath it.

Then again, she'd made a little more effort today, unlike her usual and decidedly more casual early morning routine. Her top was kind of tight and showcased her cleavage without being trashy, while her capris were a snug fit. A little understated makeup had been in order too. She kept telling herself that she was simply making up for her sweaty, harassed, and rumpled appearance on the boat yesterday. After all, she didn't want Ryan to think she was on the verge of a nervous breakdown or anything.

Ha, ha. Nice try, Merrifield.

Besides, how could she object to him giving her a few once-overs when she'd been doing exactly the same thing to him? When he got out of the golf cart, it had hit her all over again that Ryan was truly a prime piece of rampant masculinity—more so every time she saw him. His soft, form-fitting Red Sox T-shirt and cargo shorts displayed a fabulous expanse of carved, tanned muscle, enough to make her start mentally fanning herself. Add in ruggedly handsome features and a dark, mysterious gaze, and everything about him screamed hot, powerful male, a guy who knew exactly what he wanted and how to take it.

And it looked like he might just want to take her.

Morgan knew her self-control was in for a very rocky time. Keep him busy all summer? Yeah, her suddenly filthy mind could pull up about a thousand ways to do that—some of them probably illegal and all of them insanely stupid, at least when it came to protecting herself from hurt.

But she knew the wild ride would be worth it.

Almost.

Passing the parlor and dining room on the left and the sitting room/library on the right, she led Ryan back to the junction between the house and the annex. Only when she reached the door to the kitchen did she realize he'd stopped and crouched, carefully inspecting an electrical outlet. He made a note, then rose and strode down the hall to join her.

"Morgan, just how old is the wiring in here?"

Her lovely Ryan fantasies crumbled under the onslaught of reality. "All I know is that everything passed inspection when Dad bought it."

"Getting through a home inspection doesn't necessarily mean that much, and that was years ago anyway," he said in a somber voice. "If the rest of the house is like this, you need to fully upgrade as soon as possible."

Morgan stifled a pathetic whimper. "That would cost a fortune."

"It would cost a lot more if the place went up in smoke."

Crap. She couldn't possibly afford new wiring now, but she'd build it into her already awful calculations of what she'd have to spend at some point to keep her increasingly bloated whale afloat.

After a quick nod of acknowledgment, she headed into the kitchen, where her sister was working at the center island, cutting up vegetables for a country-style soup. Ever deliberate, Sabrina would probably take a good half hour or more to work her way through the carrots, beans, onions, turnips, butternut squash, and celery. Though Morgan always offered to help, her sister tended to push her away more often than not. Cooking was one of the few things Sabrina felt comfortable doing, and it gave her a much-needed measure of pride.

"Sweetie, say hello to Ryan," Morgan said with an encouraging smile.

Her sister wore a white chef's apron that covered her

from her chest almost down to her knees. Underneath was a blue T-shirt, faded jeans, and black Converse running shoes with purple trim.

"Hi, Ryan," Sabrina said without looking up.

He extended his hand across the island countertop. "It's really good to see you again, Sabrina."

Sabrina wiped her right hand on her apron. Morgan had little doubt her sister's palm was damp since all through breakfast she'd been as nervous as a cat in a room full of rocking chairs. After some hesitation, during which Ryan patiently waited, Sabrina extended her hand for a tentative shake. Thank God he'd remembered Sabrina's aversion to hugging—hugging men anyway—and hadn't tried to embrace her.

"Uh, thanks for helping us out," Sabrina said.

"Those are great shoes," he said, glancing at her feet. "That purple trim is totally cool."

Sabrina looked down, then managed a shy grin. "Thanks."

Morgan started to relax a little now that the ice had been broken. She crossed the kitchen and reached down into a cupboard for an iron skillet. "Bacon, sausage, and eggs okay, Ryan? How do you like your eggs?"

Ryan moved around the island to stand next to Sabrina. "Any way is fine."

"Coming right up." Morgan grabbed her pink apron from a hook on the back of the pantry door.

"Sabrina, how about I give you a hand with those veggies?" Ryan said.

Sabrina glanced over at Morgan, looking uncertain.

"If he insists, I say we put the man to work," Morgan said.

Sabrina extracted a wide-bladed knife from a butcher

block on the counter and handed it to Ryan, who carefully ran his thumb along the edge. Then she reached down and pulled out another cutting board. "Would you mind doing the onions? They burn my eyes something fierce."

Ryan grabbed the pair of big red onions. "When you cut into an onion, it releases a gas that combines with the water in your eyes to form an acid. People have come up with a lot of ideas to avoid burning tears. I've only found a couple of things that help though."

Morgan stared at him. He was the last guy on Earth she thought would be talking about cooking tricks.

"Like what?" Sabrina asked as she sidled a little closer to him. "I've tried cutting them under water, but it felt stupid and awkward."

"Well, I start by keeping the onions good and cold." Then he started to chop with fast, precise strokes. Morgan and Sabrina exchanged startled glances.

"The key is to have a really sharp knife," he went on, still chopping, "and get it done as fast as possible. Without lopping off the ends of your fingers, of course."

Other than a few professionals she'd watched on the Food Network, Morgan had never seen anybody slice and dice as fast as Ryan. He polished off the pair of onions in what seemed like a dozen heartbeats.

"Wow," Morgan said, "maybe you should take over the cooking around here, and Sabrina and I should do the repairs."

Sabrina's eyes were practically bugging out at the sight of the neat pile of onions. "Wow, I'll say."

Ryan laughed. "Just because I'm good with a knife doesn't mean I'm a good cook. I'll leave that part up to you experts."

Morgan wasn't buying it. He was probably a damn good cook, just like he seemed to be good at everything else. And he'd handled Sabrina, skittish at the best of times, like a real pro. It reminded her again how little she knew about the grown-up Ryan Butler, mystery man par excellence.

She could only hope he stayed around long enough for her to find out who he truly was.

Chapter 4

$\mathcal{M}$organ sidled up behind Sabrina, who was stirring the soup after she tossed in another pinch of sea salt. Ryan had headed for Portland to pull together the materials he needed to start on the shingle repair. The ballpark estimate he'd given Morgan on that seemingly small job had been substantially more than the rough calculation she'd made that morning. It was because she hadn't taken into account the fact that he'd need to rent a lot of construction gear, including safety equipment. Still the cost was going to be a whole lot less than her earlier estimate of what it would cost to have a professional roofer do the repair.

Morgan rested her head on Sabrina's shoulder. "Ryan said he'll start on the roof tomorrow."

Her sister put down her spoon and moved away, leaning on the counter by the sink. "He said he really liked my shoes." She glanced down and twirled her left foot. "You think he meant it?"

"Of course he did."

"He's never said much to me before, but he was nice today."

"You've never really had a chance to get to know him," Morgan said. "High school hardly counts, and he hasn't been home that much since."

"He was just one of those big-shot athletes before he went into the army," Sabrina said, folding her arms tight across her chest. "One of those cute guys the popular girls always gushed over. Guys like that never even noticed I was alive. Not unless they decided they needed someone to bully."

Morgan had sometimes thought that, when it came to bullying, the girls at their school had been worse than the boys. But poor Sabrina had drawn fire from both, and Morgan and Lily had spent a lot of time protecting her. Sabrina had been even more painfully shy back then, almost always dressing in gray, which Morgan had figured was an unconscious attempt to camouflage herself against the slate-gray walls of Peninsula High.

"Ryan's a good guy," Morgan said. "And we've all changed a lot from high school, right?"

Sabrina's brow creased as if she was mulling that over.

"What's going on, Sabrina?" Morgan finally asked.

"I'm glad Ryan's going to save us some money," Sabrina said. "It's nice of him, and I don't want to seem ungrateful. But I still don't see why you can't borrow the money we need to get the place in shape. We both know this place needs a big makeover, not just some handyman work. We need new furniture, new everything." Her chin went up in a defiant little tilt. "Dad would have borrowed the money."

They'd been over this issue enough times that Morgan wanted to cry with frustration. "Oh, honey, we've gone through this already."

Sabrina opened a kitchen drawer, yanked out a tea towel, and slammed the drawer shut. "Don't talk to me like I'm stupid."

Patience, Morgan. She dredged up a smile. "I'm sorry. We can talk about it as much as you want."

Sabrina hugged the towel to her chest. "Dad always found a way to come up with money, so why can't you? He never had problems dealing with the bank."

Not true. He just hadn't bothered to tell his daughters about them.

Morgan remembered their father telling them that hardworking people could usually get the banks to be flexible. Maybe that was true in the old days, but not so much anymore.

"Banks are happy to lend you money as long as they're confident that you'll be able to pay it back," Morgan said. "Sadly, our bank doesn't have that kind of confidence in the B&B anymore. They say it's too risky to extend us more credit."

Sabrina shook her head. "But we've always made our loan payments. Dad told me that, and so did you."

That streak would be coming to an end next month unless a miracle happened and the remaining empty rooms suddenly got booked. "Yes, but the past doesn't count for much. I had nothing to show the manager to convince him we'd be in a position to take on more debt. We're barely half-booked for the rest of the summer, and we're wide open after Labor Day."

"But doing nothing is a guaranteed recipe for failure," her sister said stubbornly. That was one of their dad's favorite sayings, one Sabrina tended to fall back on whenever they got into this argument. "We're having a hard time getting bookings because the place is practically falling apart. But if we spend some money and make it look really nice, people will come back."

Morgan held out her hands, palms up. "Sweetie, we have *no* money."

"Well, Lily and Aiden must have plenty of money these days. He was a pro baseball player, and now they're building that fancy resort. Lily would do anything for you, Morgan." Sabrina's blue gaze had turned almost desperate.

"Their money is tied up in the resort and renovating the old Flynn house. And even if they did have some available cash, how could I ask my best friend to invest in a place that might not survive past the summer season?"

Sabrina tossed the tea towel across the room and yanked off her apron, throwing it onto the counter. "So what's the answer, then? Help from Ryan sure isn't going to be enough."

"Well, it's certainly going to help."

"Oh, stop it!" Sabrina snapped. "I'm not some child you have to shelter from reality. It's going to take real money to get this place in shape, and you won't even try to raise it."

Morgan felt her mouth gape open. "Sabrina, that's just not—"

"Don't say it's not true, Morgan. Sometimes I think you'd like nothing better than to sell this place and wash your hands of it." Sabrina stopped abruptly as her voice caught, half turning away to look out the window into the yard.

Morgan beat back the sense of frustration that threatened to choke her, refusing to rise to her sister's angry bait. That last jab had hit her in a very vulnerable spot.

"Look, you've got a great job on the mainland," Sabrina said in a lower voice, "so I get why you want to get back to it. But all I have is the B&B, Morgan. And what about Dad? Don't we owe it to him to do every last thing we can to keep his dream alive?"

Now was not the time for Morgan to talk to her sister about coming to live with her in Pickle River. That would just send the argument into the stratosphere. "Let's just take it one day at a time, okay? I'm here now, and I'm not going anywhere. I promise."

Sabrina huffed. "You don't really care about what happens to Golden Sunset. If you truly cared about Dad and me, you'd have come back and helped when he asked you to. Instead, you picked your job over your family. How do you think that made us feel?"

Man, talk about a freaking guilt trip. "Honestly, I've never seen the two as mutually exclusive," Morgan said, wishing she didn't feel so defensive. She loved teaching, and she'd worked hard to put herself through college and build the career she'd always wanted. Why was it wrong to refuse to give it up?

Still, deep in her heart, Morgan felt guilty as hell. Maybe it was the curse of the eldest child, but the guilt was beginning to take a real toll on her spirit.

Sabrina grabbed the kettle off the stove and started to fill it. "Anyway, you'd better get the idea of selling out of your head, because the only way it can happen is over my dead body."

A horrible mix of anger, sadness, and fear about where this would end up threatened to flatten Morgan. "Honey, you know I don't want to sell," she said softly.

Sabrina threw her an angry glare. "Dad left me half

the inn, thank God," she said as she plunked the kettle onto the stove. "So you can't dump this place without me, and I'm not leaving unless the sheriff comes and drags me away. I mean it, Morgan."

Morgan just shook her head. There was no point continuing the discussion, especially with her sister so wound up. She had to wonder if it was just Ryan's presence that had shaken her up, or if Sabrina was finally getting how serious things were.

Chapter 5

$\mathcal{M}$organ stepped out of the kitchen, holding a tray with one hand while she gently closed the rattletrap screen door with the other. She'd spent most of the morning tidying up in the kitchen, stewing over the latest batch of bills and fretting over last night's argument with her sister. Finally, she'd stuffed the bills in a drawer and set out making a snack for Ryan, who'd started early on the shingling job. Last evening, the poor guy had walked into the aftermath of her fight with Sabrina, and Morgan still felt badly about it. He'd quickly picked up on the tense atmosphere and made himself scarce.

She felt guilty that Ryan was giving up a perfect kayaking day. Morgan hadn't missed the long look he'd directed out at the water before he went up the ladder with a load of shingles draped over one brawny shoulder. There was little doubt he'd rather be out in his kayak instead of slaving away on a hot roof. Since he wouldn't let her do anything to help him—not that she could really envision herself crawling around the roof, lugging heavy packets of shingles—she figured the least she could do was to entice him down for some refreshment. The tray held a pitcher of freshly squeezed lemonade and two chilled glasses, along with fresh-made blueberry scones and a small container of butter.

She set it down on one of the patio tables and then, shading her eyes against the glare, looked up.

Ryan had his back to her as he hammered a shingle into place, and for the second time that morning, her breath pretty much seized in her chest. His broad, tanned shoulders and bare, muscular back glistened with sweat under the straps of his safety harness. His yummy biceps flexed with power as he swung the heavy hammer, driving in each nail with a single, smooth blow. And then there was the tool belt slung low over his cargo shorts, highlighting his truly stellar ass. Ryan Butler was the construction worker fantasy come to life.

Yep, the heat index was definitely going up around Golden Sunset, and it wasn't because of the summer sun.

Morgan cleared her throat so she wouldn't squeak when she called up to him. "Hey, you hardworking man, how about taking a break? I've got fresh lemonade and a blueberry scone with your name on it."

Ryan glanced back over his shoulder, dipping his head to peer under the safety rail. He waved and started to say something—to decline, she suspected. But then he paused and seemed to reconsider. He slung his hammer into a slot on his tool belt and stood up. "On my way down."

Morgan hurried to the ladder and gripped the aluminum rails to steady it, just as she'd done earlier that morning. It made her feel like she was doing something useful. Ryan shucked off the safety harness and smiled down at her as he swung his long legs onto the ladder. She took that smile as a silent acknowledgement of her small effort to assist.

Plus, the view from the bottom was pretty spectacular. How could she not keep her eyes glued to that glorious example of male physical perfection, especially when all he had on this morning was a pair of cargo shorts, work boots, and a tool belt? Her mouth went so dry she felt more than ready for some ice-cold lemonade.

She kept a firm grip on the ladder, as much to steady herself as to help him. As he neared the bottom, she had to resist the urge to run her tongue over his glistening back.

Get a grip, Morgan. She let the ladder go and took a quick step away from temptation.

Ryan smiled as he planted his feet on solid ground and turned to her. "There's no way I could resist fresh lemonade." He flicked his gaze over her body. "Or such beautiful company."

"You old sweet talker, you," Morgan said, trying to cover up her nerves. "I bet you say that to all the girls."

"Only the ones who serve me lemonade and homemade scones." He reached over and gently tugged on a lock of her hair.

Feeling a little breathless, Morgan led him to the table. She'd better focus on the work or she might end up dragging him into her bedroom. "I can hardly believe you're almost done already. You really know what you're doing up there."

He lifted an eyebrow. "It's not exactly rocket science."

Morgan smiled and filled one of the glasses with lemonade. "Sit for a while and relax. There's no need to rush to finish. The guests aren't going to be back for hours, so you don't need to worry about bothering them." The

Dawsons were spending the day in Portland, while the Lyles were on a boating excursion.

"No, but I'd sure like to get in some kayaking on such a perfect day."

Morgan had to repress a wince as she poured herself some lemonade. "You could always keep your kayak here, you know."

Ryan nodded. "Yeah, I guess that would make sense. It should be safe to leave it on the beach, right?"

She settled into one of the chairs, and he followed suit. Morgan couldn't help noticing that he took a long, appreciative look at her legs, all the way up to her little white shorts.

"Nobody but Daisy Whipple steals anything on the island," she said, ignoring the way her face had heated. "And I highly doubt she's into lugging your kayak home."

"She's still doing her thing, huh? My mother gave up buying garden ornaments years ago. Said she got tired of running over to Daisy's all the time to retrieve them."

"I've always thought having a town kleptomaniac added a nice dash of local color," Morgan said. "Micah always jokes that he won't charge Daisy unless she starts stealing cash or Red Sox memorabilia."

Deputy Sheriff Micah Lancaster, Seashell Bay's law officer, had been Morgan's friend since childhood. While a tough, rugged cop, he always gave islanders a break unless they proved not to deserve it. He had a particularly soft spot in his heart for poor Daisy.

Ryan laughed. "Since he's Seashell Bay's biggest collector of Red Sox junk, I can see why he'd say that."

"Junk? Deputy Lancaster better not hear you say that, my friend, or you'll be serving time behind bars."

"Hell, I've said it to him a dozen times over the years. The guy's such a nut for the Sox that he can't go to Fenway without coming home with an armload of crap."

Morgan wagged a finger at him. "I wouldn't call all those signed baseballs he's collected crap. He's got a Carl Yastrzemski, a Mo Vaughn, a Nomar Garciaparra, and a Pedro Martínez, plus a bunch of the newer stars. And he has hundreds and hundreds of Red Sox cards too, including some pretty valuable ones."

"Okay, now I'm weirded out. Have you memorized his whole collection or something?"

"No, but I did help him organize it a while back. He didn't have a good system for keeping records, which would be a problem with insurance if he ever had a loss in a fire or flood. I downloaded some free software for organizing collectibles and showed him how to use it."

A slight scowl marked his brows. "That was neighborly of you. Have you two gotten closer by any chance?"

Now there's a question I didn't expect. "Do you mean are we dating?"

"Just curious."

Morgan repressed a smile. "We're not, but we've been good friends all our lives, as you well know."

Ryan shot her a skeptical look. "Friends sometimes turn into lovers."

It was hard to tell what he was thinking from his expression, but did she detect a teeny bit of jealousy in his tone?

"Something like that would never happen between Micah and me." She paused a moment, debating whether to say anything more on the subject of the deputy and his personal life.

"But?" Ryan probed.

Morgan wanted him to be totally clear that Micah was not interested in her. Why that seemed so important was a question she wouldn't look at too closely. "No buts. It's just that, well, it's not me that Micah's interested in anyway. The deputy has developed eyes for someone else, especially since last summer."

"Like who?"

She waggled a hand. "Let's just say that it's a one-way street at this point and leave it at that."

"Oh sure, now you go under the cone of silence."

"Yes," Morgan said sternly. "And don't you breathe a word about it to Micah or I'll creep into your room in the middle of the night and smother you with a pillow."

Oh man, did I really just say that?

"Well, you're more than welcome to try." His slow, sexy grin made clear exactly what he was thinking.

Morgan was under no illusions as to what would happen if she ever did creep into Ryan's room. Her head told her it would be an epic mistake, but even the thought of it made her girl parts want to stand up and give Soldier Boy a salute.

She cleared her throat and changed the subject. "So, did you learn all your construction skills on that summer job you had after high school or did your dad teach you?"

Kevin and Julia Butler had built their house with their own hands when she and Ryan were in elementary school. Though a lot of lobstermen built additions or did renovations to their homes, few had constructed an entire house, much less one as cozy and comfortable as the Butler home.

"Both." Ryan gave a little shrug. "But shingling is pretty easy stuff, babe."

His unconscious use of the sexy endearment gave her a little jolt. *Down, girl. It didn't mean anything.*

"You're being far too modest. A lot of men these days don't know one end of a hammer from the other." She'd learned that having a reliable handyman was on virtually everybody's wish list—even in Seashell Bay, where most of the local men were as hardy and self-reliant as you'd find anywhere.

"I can't argue that." He took a long swallow of lemonade and then finally sampled the scone. "Hey, this is really good."

"Sabrina's the main baker," Morgan said, "but we both know our way around pastry. Mom was a genius with it, so I guess we got a little talent passed down in our DNA."

Morgan still couldn't roll out dough without thinking about her mother. Even now, her loss remained an open wound for both her and Sabrina. Mom had been only fifty-three when ovarian cancer took her so quickly that it had left the family stunned and overwhelmed.

"She won a lot of prizes in the Blueberry Festival contests, didn't she?" Ryan asked.

"Absolutely. Mom totally cleaned up. She and Aiden's mother always had a friendly competition going as to who was the best baker on the island."

"I still remember Mrs. Flynn's famous blueberry pies," Ryan said. "Mom would send me down first thing in the morning to get in line for them. And your mom's specialty was muffins, wasn't it?"

"Muffins and scones, like the one you're scarfing down. Somehow neither my efforts nor Sabrina's can quite measure up even though we use her recipes."

Ryan took another bite and shook his head. "Hard to believe anything could be better than this."

"Thanks. There are plenty more where it came from.

As long as you keep working, Sabrina and I will keep you well supplied." Morgan winked at him. "God knows you don't have to worry about putting on weight."   .

She tried to inject a light note into her voice, but talking about her mom always brought out the heartache, especially when she was back in Seashell Bay. Every single thing on the island seemed to evoke the memory of her parents, reminding her of how desperately she missed them. Though she'd been teaching on the mainland for years, she'd always come home at least once or twice a month and had spent all summer in Seashell Bay. In some ways, she felt like she'd never really left home.

Ryan's expression grew serious. "It must be hard. I mean, not just coping with the B&B but with losing your parents like that."

Morgan's throat went tight, but she powered through it. "I see Dad everywhere. Like, he'd sit on this patio for hours on end talking to guests. He'd tell them stories about the island—half of them made up or exaggerated—and he'd ask them questions about where they were from, what they liked, and what he could do to make their stay more enjoyable. You should take a look at the comments in the guest book, Ryan. People just loved Dad."

Some days, the old place felt so empty without him.

"When I was in Afghanistan, I thought a lot about kids who lose their parents," Ryan said.

Surprised, Morgan waited for him to elaborate.

"You couldn't walk ten feet there without seeing a homeless, orphaned kid sleeping on the street, a lot of them maimed by land mines." Ryan's fingers whitened as he gripped his glass hard. "Once you've seen it, it keeps eating away at you, even when you're no longer in country.

I give money to the Afghan Women's Mission, but that seems kind of feeble. I wish I could do more."

Though Morgan didn't really think of herself as an orphan, she was, of course. That had obviously tapped into Ryan's somber memories.

"It's not feeble at all," she said. "It's wonderful. I'll Google that charity this afternoon and make a donation too."

His appreciative smile lit up her insides.

"That would be great. You don't need to give a lot—even ten bucks makes a difference." Ryan pushed himself up out of the chair. "But now I'd better get back to work if I want to have any hope of getting in some kayaking. And thanks for taking such good care of me, Morgan. I appreciate it."

She shook her head as she rose. "Don't be silly. You're the one taking care of us. Any little thing I do for you is nothing compared to what you're doing for Sabrina and me." Instinctively, she reached out to rest a hand on his muscled bicep. But she snatched it away an instant later, blushing at the feel of his warm, naked skin under her fingers.

Or, more truthfully, how much she wanted *more* of that warm, naked skin under her fingers.

Chapter 6

$\mathscr{R}$yan unhooked the bungee cords that secured his ocean kayak and lifted the fifty-five-pound Tetra 12, propping it against the side of his truck. He reached back into the truck bed for the bag of aluminum brackets and wood screws he'd bought to repair the loose drainpipe.

From the back of the B&B's parking lot, he could see the section of the roof he'd repaired. It was a solid job that would keep the rain on the outside where it belonged, and Morgan had seemed genuinely pleased with the result. Unfortunately, when Ryan again made the point that the whole roof needed to be replaced soon, her lush mouth had flattened into a straight line and her shoulders had hiked up to her ears. Without a complete reroofing, he feared the leak he'd just fixed would be followed by many more.

He was surprised to find himself worrying about that. It had only been a few days and already he was starting to feel a sense of responsibility toward Morgan, Sabrina, and their white elephant of an inn.

He shook off that vaguely alarming sensation and focused on the options for late afternoon kayaking. The best at this hour seemed to be Cliff Island. He figured he could do that return trip in a little over two hours given the favorable weather and sea conditions. He took the brackets into the kitchen, figuring Morgan would probably be there. She'd invited him to eat with them tonight, sharing a meal of homemade spinach and cheese ravioli, and Ryan was totally down with that. By the time he got back from kayaking, he'd be ready to enjoy every scrap of food that came anywhere near him.

He knew he'd enjoy spending more time with Morgan too, and that left him feeling a bit conflicted.

The annex's screen door swung open and she stepped out, wiping her flour-dusted hands on her long apron. Ryan couldn't recall ever thinking a woman wearing an apron looked sexy, but Morgan did. Her sweet curves filled it out so well.

Her eyes, clear and blue as a summer sky over the island, latched onto him, seeming to stick on the board shorts that rode low on his hips. Then she slid her gaze past him to the kayak.

"Nice kayak. I love that deep shade of yellow." Her voice sounded a little breathy.

"Thanks. The color was definitely what did it for me too," he said, unable to stifle a little sarcasm at her girlie comments.

Morgan didn't seem to hear the dig, apparently more interested in his bare chest than his words.

"Uh, aren't you going to wear a shirt?" she said. "You know it'll be a lot cooler out on the water."

Nice try, babe. He tried not to grin. Morgan had been ogling him pretty much all day, on the roof and at ground level. "I stowed a T-shirt in the hatch just in case."

"Oh, good." She wiped her hands on her apron again, even though most of the flour was gone. "I've never done any kayaking, but I always thought it looked like fun. I should take lessons before trying it though, right?"

Her hesitant smile made Ryan wonder if she wanted him to give her a lesson but was too shy to ask. He could let her use his dad's solo kayak, and he could drill her on how to get back into it if she capsized. Ryan had to admit he'd welcome the chance to see her in a thoroughly soaked shirt, even if it was under the safety vest he'd insist she wear. "Definitely. Just getting into the thing can be tricky unless you know what you're doing."

"Then I guess I'd need a good teacher." Now her smile was teasing. "Know where I might find one?"

Before he could answer with a quip of his own, the loud, buzzing whine of a motor interrupted them. Only one golf cart on the island made a sound like that. Then again, only one golf cart on the island had the raw power of Roy Mayo's modified engine. "There goes Roy."

"No, here *comes* Roy, and Miss Annie too. They're just turning into the driveway."

He sighed. "Damn. I guess it's time for my annual lecture from Miss Annie. Too bad I didn't get onto the water five minutes ago."

Morgan poked him on the arm. "Be nice. You know Miss Annie just wants all us wayward kids to return to our island roots. I think I've had that lecture from her approximately a hundred and seven times at last count."

Ryan laughed as Roy swerved to a stop beside his truck. The cart's wheels threw up enough gravel dust that he and Morgan both took a few steps back.

"The old boy's still got it," Ryan said in a dry voice.

Roy, a ninety-plus-year-old widower, had shacked up a few years ago with the widowed Annie Letellier, Lily's grandmother. Miss Annie and Roy were the happiest clams at the shore despite their constant public bickering, and everyone adored them. Fiercely independent, proud, and loyal, Roy and Annie were as decent as two human beings could be and as quirky and unique as Seashell Bay.

Despite Miss Annie's good-natured nagging, Ryan always looked forward to seeing her and Rocket Roy.

Miss Annie eyeballed Ryan as she got out of the cart. "Well, look at what the cat just dragged in. Don't you own a shirt, Ryan Butler? We don't see you for a year, and then you show up looking like some hippie surfer who took a wrong turn on the way to California."

Despite her ball busting, Miss Annie smiled, opening her arms wide for a hug. "Come here, you rascal. Your mama and daddy must be so happy to see you. And I hear you might be staying all summer."

There were no secrets in Seashell Bay, especially not from Miss Annie. She knew everything within minutes of it happening. The feisty old gal was like a satellite dish, gathering and focusing signals from every corner of the island and beyond: When Ryan was growing up, the kids used to call her Sherlock Holmes because she could sniff out any and all of their misdeeds.

"Could be, ma'am," he said. "My plans are pretty open at the moment."

"From what I hear, Morgan is going to be keeping you plenty busy." She tilted her head to inspect Morgan. "Isn't that right, dear?"

Morgan's toothy grin gave nothing away. "Oh, there's

plenty to do around here, that's for sure. And Ryan is being very kind to help us out."

"What all are you folks doin' round here anyway?" Roy said, his thumbs hooked into his wide belt like a Wild West lawman. The old guy was tall and rangy, so he managed to pull it off. "Maybe I could give you a hand with something. God knows it's good to get out of the house for a while." He pointedly rolled his eyes at Miss Annie, even though he was smiling.

"Just a bunch of little stuff," Ryan said. "Though I've been telling Morgan that she needs to get that old roof seen to sooner rather than later." He glanced up. "The shingles are at the end of their life span."

As the four of them gazed at the B&B's roofline, a car pulled into the driveway. Ryan turned around to see a red Jeep parking next to the golf cart. It was Lily's ride, but Aiden was at the wheel.

"Hey, how come nobody told me about the party?" Aiden said as he climbed out and strode over to join them. He exchanged quick hugs with Miss Annie and Morgan and then shook hands with Roy and Ryan. "Good to have you back, Ryan, though you might have let me know you were coming."

Ryan shrugged, feeling a bit guilty. "It was kind of a last-minute decision."

Aiden made a scoffing noise that told Ryan what he thought about that lame excuse, but his friend obviously decided to let it go.

"You look good," Ryan said. "Retirement must be treating you right."

After suffering a number of injuries, Aiden had retired as a pro baseball player last fall in order to coach a local university team. He initially hadn't been happy about taking early retirement, but it seemed to have worked out just fine.

Aiden grinned. "Retirement? I've never been so busy in my life."

"The boy's become a real entrepreneur," Roy said, pronouncing the last syllable *noo-er*.

Aiden glanced at the hardware in Ryan's hands. "So, I guess Morgan didn't waste any time putting you to work."

It seemed the entire island knew what Ryan was doing. Then again, he shouldn't be surprised. If his mother hadn't blabbed about it, Miss Annie would have seen to it that just about everybody else on the island was up-to-date on his movements. That was just the way she rolled.

Ryan briefly recapped the situation with the roof, which had Morgan breathing out a weary sigh.

Aiden gave her a sympathetic grimace. "I have to admit I've been thinking the same thing, Morgan," he said. Then he turned to Ryan. "If you were up for it, man, you and I could do something about that roof. You're good at construction, and I just finished helping build my father's new house."

Roy snorted. "Yeah, and we finally got that old geezer out of our place, thank the good Lord."

Aiden's father, Sean Flynn, had been staying with Miss Annie and Roy while he worked on staying off the booze and getting his life back on track. It had been a hard slog, according to Aiden, but the entire island had come together to help Sean deal with the fallout of a lifetime of alcohol abuse and depression. They'd been there for Bram, Aiden's recovering alcoholic brother, too.

Miss Annie poked Roy in the ribs. "Stop your nonsense, Roy. You and Sean got along together like biscuits and gravy. Lily called it a bromance, didn't she, Morgan?"

Morgan laughed, but then her expression turned serious. "Aiden, that's really sweet of you, but you're so busy. And you're still working on your family home."

"I've got some free time now. I have to wait for Brendan to do some finishing work before we can install the rest of the flooring." He glanced at Ryan. "Look, you and I could strip and reshingle that roof pretty fast. And if we need another hand, I'm sure we could recruit Brett or Josh or Micah."

"Hell, what about me?" Roy protested. "I can help too. It wouldn't be my first time on the dance floor when it comes to swapping out a roof, let me tell you."

Miss Annie looked horrified. "You old coot, have you completely lost your marbles? You're ninety-one years old, for goodness' sake, and you are *not* going to be fooling around on that steep roof. Not if you want to still be puttin' your boots under my bed. You can kiss that good-bye, Charlie Brown."

Ryan mentally winced. No way he wanted to envision Roy and Miss Annie doing the nasty, and the slightly appalled look on Aiden's face suggested the same reaction. Morgan, however, was obviously trying not to laugh.

Roy shot Miss Annie a lethal glare. "Shee-it, woman. Didn't I do some work on the roof at Sean's new place with this guy?" He jerked a gnarly thumb at Aiden. "Did I break my neck then? Well, did I?"

"No, praise be to God," Miss Annie said. "But that was a one-story cottage, not this...this skyscraper. You're too old for such foolishness, Roy Mayo. I've been widowed once, and I don't mean to go through it a second time. And certainly not for the likes of you."

Roy's weathered face wrinkled up even more. "Widowed a second time? Was I in a coma or something when we got hitched? I seem to have missed it."

Morgan jumped in before Miss Annie could sock him. "That's incredibly kind of you to offer, Aiden, and you too, Roy. I'm touched, but I'm not sure I could afford the materials right now even if you guys did all the work yourselves." Her expression told Ryan how much it cost her pride to admit that.

Aiden crossed his arms, looking stubborn. "Morgan, Ryan's absolutely right. As for the money, I'll loan you what you need. You really do have to deal with that roof before your business floats away in a flood."

Morgan's shoulders started to hike back up around her ears. Though Ryan didn't like that they'd put her in an obviously uncomfortable spot, he agreed it was too important to back off. Aiden had come up with a workable solution to the problem, and Ryan had no intention of letting it slip away.

"Same goes for me, Morgan," he said. "Aiden and I will cover the cost of the materials, and we'll do the work ourselves. And if Roy wants to help, I'm sure we can find plenty of work for him to do down here at sea level."

"Oh, sure. Treat me like I'm some crapped-out old invalid," Roy groused.

Ryan ignored him, zeroing in on Morgan because she seemed to be wavering, her eyes flicking between him and Aiden. "Let us help you, okay?" he said gently. "Isn't that what neighbors always do for each other around here?"

That little nugget might sound presumptuous coming

from a guy who hardly ever set foot on the island, but that truly was how things worked in Seashell Bay. He sometimes tended to forget that.

"Besides," he added, going for a lighter note, "if you say no, all your nosy neighbors like Miss Annie and Lily will get on your case until you do say yes. They'd drive you nuts."

Miss Annie shot him the obligatory scowl before grasping Morgan's hands. "I would never do that, dear, but these boys won't give you a moment's peace. I guarantee it." She flicked a warning glance around their little circle. "Really, have you ever met three more stubborn men in your life?"

Aiden's eyes were glinting with laughter. "It's true, Morgan. We'll just keep bugging you until you give in."

Morgan managed a small laugh as she threw up her hands. "Well, stubborn, maybe, but I don't think I've ever met three nicer men either. All right, gentlemen, I humbly accept your gracious offer."

Ryan slipped an arm around her waist and gave her a quick squeeze. Helping her out was definitely the right thing to do.

It surprised the hell out of him how good that made him feel—almost as good as her sweet body tucked under his arm.

Morgan almost passed out when Ryan slipped his arm around her waist, especially since he did it in front of other people. It almost felt as if he was staking a claim, and that made her face heat with a no doubt bright red, totally embarrassing blush that could probably light up half of Seashell Bay in a blackout.

When he let her go, she forced herself to shrug off her crazy emotional reaction and focus on the plan to fix Golden Sunset's roof. When it came down to it, how could she afford to say no? Still, accepting the generous offer went against the grain. Ryan had nailed it when he said that neighbors helped neighbors in Seashell Bay, but she loathed the idea that people might think of her as a charity case.

Morgan had always fought for financial independence. She'd been self-sufficient since she was old enough to hold down a summer job, so flirting with financial calamity scared the hell out of her. So did being in debt to people who wanted to help her, even people who were friends.

But given the situation and her responsibilities to Sabrina, she simply couldn't say no, at least not right now. All she could do was make a solemn, silent vow to pay back every cent, even if Golden Sunset didn't survive. It would take a while, especially if she had to drag her sister back to Pickle River and support her there, but she'd do it.

When Ryan waved a hand in front of her face, she realized she'd missed the last several moments of the conversation.

"Well, how about it, Morgan?" he asked. "Come on, it'll be fun."

She mentally regrouped. "I'm sorry, guys. I kind of zoned out for a moment while I was trying to figure out how I could repay you." She smiled as brightly as she could manage. "Now, what were you saying?"

Roy gave an amused little snort that drew an elbow in the ribs from Miss Annie.

"Aiden and Lily want us to go to the Sea Dogs game

with them tomorrow night," Ryan said with a hint of a smile. "Aiden's got free tickets, and Lily will take us all into town in her boat."

"That's what I came over to ask," Aiden added. "We'd love it if you and Ryan could make it."

Was this idea supposed to be a double date? "Um, well…" Morgan scrambled to come up with an answer. She wasn't a sports fan, and minor-league baseball didn't exactly turn her crank. And then there were all the potential complications of spending social time with Soldier Boy.

"Come on, don't make me be the third wheel," Ryan said.

"Jesus, Mary, and Joseph," Roy butted in. "If she's going to pass up a free ticket, I'll go."

"You're not the fourth Aiden had in mind, Roy," Miss Annie said. "Anyway, buy your own damn ticket if you want to go."

They all laughed, including Morgan. And, heck, she actually did want to have a fun night out with her friends. Take in the game, have a drink afterward, and then head straight home to bed. It should be no big deal.

Except, of course, when your date happened to be Ryan Butler.

Chapter 7

"That was one hell of a play," Aiden mumbled.

Since his friend was currently stuffing his mouth with a Sea Dog Biscuit, a calorie-laden concoction of vanilla ice cream and two big chocolate chip cookies, Ryan could hardly understand a word he said. He, however, had steered clear of the junk food and headed directly past go to the beer. "Yeah, the kid's got game," he said.

They'd just watched Portland's young left fielder make a leaping grab of a ball that would have been a home run. The Sea Dogs were already down by three to the Trenton Thunder, and a three-run homer might have put the game out of reach.

"I don't recall ever seeing you make a catch like that," Ryan added, ribbing his friend.

Aiden snorted. "Yeah, well, how about we talk about the fact that you set the record at Peninsula High for most errors in a season by an outfielder?"

"Long since broken, as you well know. But okay, since we're taking a walk down memory lane, how about the home run record I broke in my senior year? *Your* record, as it happens. And my mark still stands, last I heard."

Aiden polished off the ice cream sandwich in one massive bite. "Too bad your batting average never made it past two-sixty, and you ran like a wounded water buffalo."

Sadly, Aiden wasn't far wrong. Ryan had been a good high school player with fearsome home run power, but he'd lacked the kind of all-around skills that would have taken him to the big leagues. He'd swallowed that bitter pill early on and had rejected a couple of baseball scholarships at small colleges, preferring a future in the military to a slog in the minors.

Still, he felt the occasional twinge of envy that Aiden had carved out a solid pro ball career and then a retirement that enabled him to continue working in the sport he loved.

"Anyway, the girls are sure missing some great action." Morgan and Lily had hiked off some time ago to check out the stadium's souvenir store. When they were still gone two innings later, Ryan suspected they were probably nursing microbrewery beer in the concourse and talking about subjects that had nothing to do with sports or souvenirs. "I'm not holding my breath waiting for them to come back, are you?"

Aiden shook his head, intently watching the pitcher as he struck out the next batter. Then he flicked that intensity in Ryan's direction. "Can I ask you a question?"

Ryan mentally sighed at the familiar sensation he got whenever somebody was about to pry into his life. It almost always started with asking if it was okay to ask him a question. What was he supposed to say—no, mind your own damn business?

Not when it was Aiden, that was for sure. Though they didn't see much of each other and didn't keep in really close touch, Ryan regarded Aiden as a very good friend. "Shoot," he said.

"Look, man, I don't want to get all up in your grill, but something's been bugging me about why you left the service. Like there's more to it than what you've been telling people."

Ryan had given Aiden the same story he'd given everybody other than his parents. He couldn't lie to his mom and dad, but as far as he was concerned, it was nobody else's business. Still, Aiden's instincts were right. The last thing Ryan wanted to do was keep bullshitting his best friend.

"Like I said, I needed a new challenge. And the money was part of it too." He paused a moment, still thinking about how much he should say.

"And?" Aiden prompted.

Ryan gave a little shrug. "Okay, let's just say my last command sergeant major wasn't the president of my fan club. The guy made it just about impossible for me to stay in the unit and still keep my sanity. I figured, if I didn't leave, I'd end up in a court martial after I slugged him."

There had been moments when Ryan thought he'd happily face military justice so he could give that prick Strohmayer what he deserved. But that had just been his testosterone talking, and he'd managed to avoid a physical showdown.

Aiden's brow furrowed. "What the hell was his problem?"

"I was...uh, well, a special case for him." Ryan said. "We were just two people who weren't meant to coexist in life, much less in a tight fighting unit."

Ryan didn't want to get into any of the stupid details

with Aiden—details like the fact that the reason for Strohmayer painting a target on his back had nothing to do with Ryan's service and everything to do with the lies that Strohmayer's niece, Callie, had spun to her family. Ryan had been with Callie for more than two years. He'd thought he loved her, and she loved him. But near the end of his final tour in Afghanistan, Callie had sent him an e-mail—a fucking e-mail—with a six-line message that said she'd fallen in love with one of his best friends, a civilian who worked on the base. Her final sentence had asked him to respect her decision to want a different kind of future. He'd respected her decision, all right, but he hadn't respected her lies.

After he'd gotten over the shock and the hurt, he'd tried his best to move on. But Callie wasn't done with fucking up his life. She came from a steadfast military family who'd all liked Ryan and approved of him. Lacking the guts to come clean with her parents that she'd been screwing around on him while he was deployed, Callie had told them Ryan had been unfaithful to her.

He hadn't. Never.

"I had some asshole managers in my career, so I can relate," Aiden said. "But couldn't you have transferred into another unit?"

"That's where timing came in. I had a couple of Spec Ops buddies who'd gone to work for Double Shield. When they told me DS was on the hunt for new operators, it just felt right to make the move. I was ready."

"You went with your gut."

"Best way to go, right?"

"I went through something like that last fall," Aiden said. "I had to decide between heading out to California to play or to retire here and coach at USM. I'd been pretty desperate to land a spot with some other team after the Phillies dumped me so, when I got an offer from Oakland, it should have been a no-brainer. But I went with my gut and stayed here, and I've sure got no regrets. You don't find this way of life in very many places."

Unlike Aiden, who'd hated Seashell Bay because of his abusive father, Ryan had grown up happy. He'd just never seen a future for himself on the island as a lobster fisherman. "You decided to stay because of Lily, didn't you?"

"Actually, she was ready to come with me to California."

"Are you serious? Lily without her boat and lobster fishing?" Ryan shook his head. "Man, she really must love your CFA ass."

"I sure as hell hope so, since we're getting married. But I think I can safely say that the good people of Seashell Bay no longer see me as a Come-From-Away. Believe it or not, it feels like home now."

"I guess people just needed to know that you weren't a stuck-up asshole with your big-city celebrity ways. Even though you are, of course," Ryan joked.

"Some celebrity," Aiden scoffed. "That's why I still have to work for a living." Then he elbowed Ryan in the ribs. "Let's go grab another beer and track down the girls."

"Something tells me they might not appreciate us horning in on their conversation. Especially since I'm thinking I might be the subject at hand."

"Yeah? Are your ears burning?"

Ryan grinned. "Hell, they're on freaking fire." And as far as he was concerned, that was a damn good sign.

* * *

The Commercial Street bar was jammed, the rock music from a local band was frenetic, and Morgan was well on her way to getting more than tipsy. She'd downed two beers at the ball game and was finishing her second in less than an hour at the bar. Ryan and Aiden were way ahead of her and yet didn't show any visible effects, which figured since they were such big, brawny guys.

And it also didn't take a rocket scientist to figure out why she was tempting fate with alcohol. She was feeling sorry for herself, and she really, really hated it.

Lily, of course, was understandably and boringly sober, allowing herself only one ball game beer. She was the designated boater, and Lily Doyle never screwed around when she was at the wheel of *Miss Annie*. The safety of her passengers meant she'd stuck to mineral water at the bar even though it would probably be a while before they'd make the return journey to Seashell Bay.

"Not to be an old lady," Lily said as she and Morgan headed to the restroom, "but I'm not sure it's smart for you to be blitzed when you and Ryan get back to the B&B tonight."

Morgan pushed the door open and glanced around the restroom to make sure they were alone. "Come on, Lily, can't I have some fun for once? I've earned a night off."

At the stadium, Lily had gently grilled her again about her feelings for Ryan as they sat near the concessions. She knew Lily was concerned about her, but the only thing their little chat had done was ratchet up her anxiety about all the ways her friendship with Ryan could go off the rails.

Her pal frowned. "You sure don't look like you're

having fun. You might fool the guys, but you know you can't fool me."

"Not having fun? Am I not laughing hard enough when one of the guys tells a joke?" She winced, knowing that sounded bitchy. She reached into her bag and rummaged around for lip gloss.

Lily lifted skeptical eyebrows.

Morgan heaved a sigh. "Okay, this little outing is a wee bit harder than I thought it would be. It's like the four of us are on some goofy double date."

Lily gave her an encouraging smile. "Keep talking."

Morgan could read between the lines—*Before you get truly drunk and do something stupid, like screw your brains out with Soldier Boy.*

"I'm just feeling a little overwhelmed, is all." Morgan faced the mirror, trying not to notice the slightly manic look in her gaze. Grimly, she swiped a little more gloss onto her lips. "My life is so up in the air right now, what with the mess at the B&B."

"It's not just the B&B, honey."

True, but how could Morgan tell her best friend that it made her totally jealous to see Aiden and Lily all over each other while she had to keep a safe distance from Ryan? How high school was that? Never had she felt more aware of her single status, especially since the bar they'd chosen was basically a hookup hangout.

"Look, I'm being an idiot," she finally said. "You should just ignore me."

Lily rolled her eyes. "I get it, honey. I know it's hard to be with Ryan without jumping his bones. But you can't let that keep you from having fun. God knows you deserve it. And Ryan looks like he's enjoying himself.

You two should just kick back and have a few laughs, like old pals."

"Old pals?" Morgan huffed out a laugh. "From what I've been seeing over the past couple of days, I'm guessing he'd totally be up for a booty call." She could get so down with that, but what an epic mistake it would be.

"We talked about that, didn't we? You two have enough sexual energy to light up the town, and now you're staying in the same house. You just have to find a way to deal with it." Lily frowned. "He's not pushing you, is he?"

Morgan leaned against the wall, next to the hand dryer. The tile felt cool on her overheated skin. "No. But I could have sex with Ryan in a New York minute. He's making me crazy. But I know exactly what it would be for him— a fun little fling and then good-bye." She frowned. "And then I look at you and Aiden, and all I can think about is *that's* what I want—a real relationship with a good guy who loves me. Not just some dumb summer fling with a man who's going to basically forget about me as soon as he steps onto the damn ferry."

Lily just patted her shoulder. After all, what could her friend say? Facts were facts, and whining about them wouldn't change a thing.

The beam from Portland Head Light stood out strong and bright against the inky darkness of the water and sky. It was a warm, still night, the stars were out, and the bay waters were gentle. Feeling no pain, Ryan relaxed as he hung out with Aiden on the port rail of Lily's boat.

Morgan, on the other hand, huddled close to Lily at the wheel and still looked wound up. Less than an hour ago, the women had returned from the bar's restroom looking pretty grim, and within minutes, Lily had started talking about how she needed to call it a night. That made sense, given that she had to be up and out on the water at dawn, but Ryan had the feeling something else was going on.

Something with Morgan.

His cute little innkeeper had been sending him mixed signals all night. She'd been fairly flirty early on, but then she'd pulled back, focusing on Lily or Aiden. And he got where she was coming from. Like him, she was feeling the heat that was building between them. But unlike him, she was trying like hell to deny it.

On that score, nothing had changed since last year. She wasn't the kind of woman to want a one-night stand, or even a summer fling. He respected that.

But man, he wished she would go for it. He'd have to be dead from the neck down not to want to get gorgeous Morgan Merrifield between the sheets. And he figured he could handle a summer fling without getting bent out of shape about it, especially since sporadic sex with no involvement had been all he'd known over the past few years.

But Morgan obviously wasn't there, and he'd begun to think she never would be.

So he'd adjusted his attitude, trying to just be friends. He'd given her lots of space—a hell of a lot more space than Aiden had given Lily tonight for damn sure. Those two couldn't get enough of each other. Ryan had felt a few twinges of envy as he watched them. That, unfortunately, had led to a few semidrunk lapses on his part, where he'd slipped his arm around Morgan and pulled her close. The second time it happened, she couldn't shimmy away from him fast enough.

Man, she looked so damn hot in a little white tank top that revealed plenty of soft, creamy white cleavage. The sexy top with her skintight jeans and her high-heeled sandals had done a real number on him all night, and he hadn't been the only guy at the ballpark and the bar giving Morgan a lust-filled eye.

Still, it felt like more than just lust. She'd been his friend since she could walk, and what was now happening between them felt pretty earthshaking. Sure, good friends sometimes turned into lovers. He had personal experience with that. In fact, it had bitten him in the ass seven years ago when Callie, the girlfriend he'd cared a lot about, had gotten it on with one of his buddies during one of Ryan's deployments.

But this was totally different. He and Morgan were both free agents. No one else would get hurt if they gave in to all the explosive chemistry that had been building between them.

Aiden glanced at him, giving him a wry, understanding smile. Then he got up and went to stand behind Lily, wrapping his arms around her waist and nuzzling her neck as she steered the boat. Morgan stepped away, taking the chair next to the captain's seat. But Ryan didn't think he was imagining the melancholy on her face as she stared straight ahead into the night.

What was she thinking? Did she envy her friends? Because Ryan had to admit he was feeling that way. Lily and Aiden were so obviously in love and so physically hot for each other that it was like they had some kind of weird aura surrounding them. They were about to start married life in the place they wanted to be, doing what they wanted to do.

Still, it wasn't the life *he* wanted, and he was damn sure about that.

As he studied Morgan's expressive features, he also felt pretty damn sure that she *did* want that life—white picket fence and all.

Too bad he wasn't the guy to give it to her.

Chapter 8

$\mathcal{M}$organ pushed her way through the swinging door between the kitchen and the dining room, a pot of Earl Grey tea balanced on a small tray. Though Ryan had been helping to serve guests this morning while she made breakfast, he hadn't come back to the kitchen after dropping off the tea order. She spotted him now sitting with the Stringers, deep in conversation with gray-haired Charley while Lydia, Charley's wife, fiddled with her cell phone.

Despite Ryan's reluctance to share personal details, he clearly had no trouble chatting up the guests.

Normally, Morgan handled breakfast by herself on Wednesday mornings because Sabrina had her weekly appointment with a psychologist in Portland. Sabrina had been seeing the counselor once or twice a month for several years. But after their dad died, the psychologist had told Morgan that Sabrina needed more frequent support. The cost was a killer, but Morgan didn't begrudge one cent of it. Other things could be sacrificed. Her sister's well-being was not going to be one of them.

She set the white Belleek teapot, cheerful with its pale green shamrocks, in the middle of the table. "Charley, Lydia, can I get you anything else? It's last call for the kitchen."

"We're good, sweetheart," Charley said with a smile. "I was just telling Ryan about my time in Korea. The Battle of Chosin Reservoir."

"Charley was with the Fifth Marines," Ryan said, his tone admiring. "They were outnumbered and fought their way out of a Chinese trap in brutally heavy fighting. Charley's company was called the Chosin Few."

Morgan raised her eyebrows. "So you two fellas have a lot in common, I'm guessing."

"Damn right," Charley said. "Although Ryan served longer than I did. Sometimes I wonder about young folks these days, Morgan. And then I meet a guy like Ryan and get my faith back."

Ryan looked slightly sheepish at the praise. "I'd have been proud to serve alongside you, sir. But I'm falling down on the job, and I don't want the boss to get mad at me. It was great talking to you, Charley." He smiled at Lydia. "You too, ma'am."

"Hope you folks have a great day," Morgan said to her guests before following Ryan into the kitchen.

"Sorry, I didn't mean to get into a big discussion out there." Ryan started to load the dishwasher.

She was happy he'd been able to share stories with a fellow vet. "You were entertaining our guests, which is a big part of an innkeeper's job. Dad wanted people to feel like this place was a second home. Heck, I just might offer you a job in the kitchen and dining room once you get finished with the repairs."

"*If* I get finished with the repairs, you mean," Ryan said wryly.

It had rained for three days straight since their night at the ballpark, making it impossible for him to work on the roof. All the materials were now on-site, including the ladder lift, nail gun, and compressor that Ryan had rented from a Portland supplier. He'd told her that Aiden would join him on Saturday, and in the meantime, he'd work on repairing the water damage in one of the guest rooms and replacing insulation in the attic.

Though the poor weather had frustrated Ryan's kayaking plans too, he'd been easy and good-natured.

But distant. When he wasn't working or visiting with his parents, he was usually tucked up in his room in the main building. Only once had he shared dinner with her and Sabrina. The other nights, he'd headed to the Pot and come back to Golden Sunset late.

And not once since that night at the ballpark had he touched her.

Morgan didn't think Ryan was angry with her for being so cool that night. He'd been friendly enough whenever their paths crossed. She just figured he'd probably absorbed the unspoken message that she wasn't up for some no-strings-attached sex.

Though she should have felt relieved, his cool approach had only made her feel worse and made her want him even more. By the second night, she practically had to handcuff herself to her bed to make sure she didn't creep up the stairs and slip into his bedroom. Poor Charley and Lydia were in the room next door to his, and the walls were pretty thin. The thought of that dignified old couple hearing her and Ryan go at it like sex-starved bunnies was horrifying to contemplate.

"I want to get at that roof tomorrow," Ryan said. "The delay is really bugging me now."

"I warned the guests about noise," Morgan said. "They're fine as long as you don't start banging around too early."

"You'd better define early, then."

"Ten, I guess. You can't really blame them for not wanting any hammering until they've cleared out for the day. When you did that little repair a few days ago, you can't believe how loud it sounded all through the house."

"Sorry, but you can't drive nails with a foam rubber hammer."

"Ha, ha, funny guy. I get it, but I can't afford to shut down for a week either. These guests are helping to pay the mortgage and put food on the table. And we want first-timers like the Stringers to come back."

"Got it." Ryan leaned a hip against the island counter and studied her. "So what are you going to be up to for the rest of the day, boss?"

Morgan sighed. "Bookkeeping, shopping, laundry, cleaning silverware. Making dinner with Sabrina. Same old, same old. No rest for the wicked."

His gaze dropped to her chest for a leisurely moment before flicking back up. "Wicked? I haven't noticed you being wicked. Not yet, I mean."

Oh, boy. The heat in his eyes that had been missing for a few days sparked to life.

She swallowed, flustered by his sudden sexual innuendo. "It was just a figure of speech, Ryan. People say that all the time around here. Irony, get it?"

His gaze narrowed as if he was irritated that she wasn't going to play along. "All joking aside, you do work too hard. You need to have some fun too."

Like having crazy-hot sex with you?

She practically clutched her head in frustration. Of course jumping into bed with Ryan would be the first thing that popped into her head when she thought about fun.

"Well, you did say you'd give me some kayak lessons. That sounds like it would be fun," she said in an insanely cheerful voice, trying to compensate for the lewd images playing through her mind.

Though she wasn't crazy about the idea of being wedged into a precarious plastic shell, a nice paddle along the eastern shoreline of Seashell Bay might be relaxing. She sure needed to relax.

Sex would be relaxing, Morgan.

She wished she could tell her damn brain to shut the hell up.

"I'll be all over that if it ever stops raining." Ryan moved a little closer, close enough that Morgan had to repress her instinct to take a step back. "But I had another idea. How about I take you and Sabrina out for drinks and dinner tonight at Diamond Cove? You guys have been great to me, so I'd like to do something nice for you."

Now *that* she hadn't expected. It was certainly a sweet and generous gesture on Ryan's part. Including Sabrina was not only kind, it also told her that he didn't see the dinner as some kind of date. He couldn't have known that Sabrina would certainly decline the offer.

She struggled for a moment to find a lighthearted response but gave up when all she could come up with sounded stupidly flippant. "That's sweet of you. I'll talk to Sabrina as soon as she gets back."

I'll sort out my feelings about being alone with you later.

Morgan couldn't help noticing that she'd already made up her mind to accept the offer, even though Sabrina wouldn't be there as a buffer between them.

Her sister hated going out, other than an occasional night at the Pot with Morgan and her closest friends. Whenever Sabrina had to be in a public place off the island for more than a few minutes, she often started to act jittery. She said it made her anxious, and that she couldn't enjoy the food or the company. Sabrina's idea of fun had always been to curl up on the cozy love seat in her room with her nose in one of the library's murder mysteries. She devoured them like chocolate.

"Great," Ryan said, smiling. He had the best smile. It practically melted the panties right off her body. "I'll check the ferry connections and make a reservation for seven thirty."

"Sounds good."

He took off his server's apron and hung it up. "And now I've got a heavy date with some insulation."

"Well, you wouldn't want to disappoint her," Morgan said. "I hear she can be a real taskmaster."

Ryan's smiled turned thoughtful. "Nothing I can't handle."

As she watched him leave the kitchen, Morgan thought that there was very little in life that Ryan Butler couldn't handle.

Including her.

Ryan attacked his sixteen-ounce New York strip with enthusiasm. "Great steak. How's your tuna?"

Morgan took a small bite, her eyelids fluttering half shut with pleasure. "Mmm, divine," she purred. When she let out a happy sigh and licked her lips, Ryan felt it all the way down to his groin.

And she was just eating, for God's sake. Just imagine if she were really trying to turn him on.

Everything about her was so delicate, including how she ate. He'd always punched food down fast, no matter how fancy or fussily prepared. And he'd take a good steak over seafood most of the time, even in Maine. He had little enthusiasm for lobster, no doubt because he'd grown up eating it almost every day. When he was in school, he'd sometimes trade his mom's lobster rolls for PB&Js or, better yet, sandwiches made out of ham from those little round tins. He'd never had a shortage of mainland kids happy to swap.

"I have to say it again, Morgan—you look amazing tonight."

She wore the proverbial little black dress—nicely short, he was happy to say. It lovingly hugged her slim form and exposed her tanned arms and shoulders. On the ferry, she'd covered up with a black lace shawl, leaving it on in the cool restaurant. A gold pendant with its single pearl nestled in her sweet cleavage, and her gleaming blond hair looked like silk and begged to be touched—preferably while he was buried deep inside her.

It had practically killed him not to draw her tight against him as they sat thigh to thigh on the short crossing from Seashell Bay to Diamond Cove. Though it was a thank-you dinner, not a date, people on the boat had sure looked at them like they were a couple. And no wonder, because the sexual energy between them was almost palpable.

"Tell me as often as you want," she said with a smile. "By the way, you clean up pretty nicely too."

Ryan had worn his navy blazer—the one he kept at his parents' place—along with gray dress slacks, a white shirt, and his Iraq vet tie. "Thanks. I only wear this jacket about once a year, so I don't even know if it's in style."

She rolled her eyes, as if the idea of him caring about style was ridiculous. Which, of course, it was.

He glanced around at the casually upscale restaurant. It was great other than the fact that they had to dine inside instead of on the lawn or expansive deck. Everything outside was still soaked, but the drizzle had finally tapered off and a few muted purple rays from the setting sun colored the picturesque Diamond Cove marina.

"Sabrina doesn't know what she's missing," he said. "It's too bad she didn't want to come."

Morgan scrunched up her nose. "She didn't mean to seem ungrateful. You know she's just built a little different from most people."

"I like her. Always have, even though the feeling wasn't exactly mutual."

"She was touched that you wanted her to come."

"Yeah, she told me that this afternoon."

Morgan blinked. "She did?"

"She yelled up at me while I was in the attic." He couldn't help grinning as he remembered looking down through the access door to see Sabrina at the bottom of the ladder with her hands on her hips, her face all serious and intent. "Before she ran off, she also said she knew I'd have a good time with her sister."

Morgan's eyebrows hiked up. "Really? She didn't mention any of that to me."

"I thought it was kind of sweet. But maybe you'd better not tell her I mentioned it."

She made that cute zipping motion across her lips she'd used before.

"Sabrina had it right," he said. "I am having a good time with her sister. I always have a good time with you."

Except for that weird night in Portland when you looked like you wished I'd fall into the bay on the way home.

She blushed and gave him a hesitant smile. "I'm having a good time too." Then she laughed. Man, he loved her laugh. "It's hard not to when you're eating sushi-grade tuna and drinking fine wine. So I must thank you again, Ryan. This is special."

Then she put her glass down and gave him a mock scowl. "But hey, all we've talked about is the B&B and Sabrina and me. Don't we get to talk about you for a while? Fair is fair after all."

He mentally flinched. Morgan probably thought this was exactly the sort of setting for sharing secrets. A nice dinner, a couple of glasses of wine, and before you know it, you're blabbing out your life story. Well, that was never going to happen with him.

Then again, he was happy she was feeling relaxed enough both to ask and to think he would answer. He could afford to share a bit with her.

A bit.

"Just don't waterboard me for info, okay?" he said drily.

"You are just so funny," she mocked. "How about you start by being a little more forthcoming about your military career? All anybody seems to know is that you fought in both Afghanistan and Iraq. It seems to me that you must have liked army life to have stayed in the service so long."

Ryan hesitated, weighing his response. He'd have preferred Morgan to pose a specific question or two instead of probing for some kind of bullshit self-analysis of his military career.

"I did two tours in Afghanistan and one in Iraq," he said. *Next question, please.*

Morgan smiled when he didn't elaborate. "That's the way you want to play it, huh?"

Ryan shrugged. "Why don't you ask another question, and we'll see how far we get."

Morgan propped both elbows on the table and rested her chin in her palms. "Some people think you were Special Forces, and that a lot of stuff you did would be classified. Is that why you don't talk about it?"

"Not to get too technical, but they're actually called Special Operations, not Special Forces—unless you're referring to what people sometimes call the Green Berets."

"Okay, professor."

"Anyway, I trained for Spec Ops after Iraq. And you're right that some of what we did is classified. But most of our time was spent training and making sure we were ready to go on a moment's notice."

She gave him a sheepish grin. "I will admit to spending some time on the Internet researching U.S. Special Forces—I mean Special Operations. I'm thinking you might have been Delta Force since they're army." She paused. "That is, if Delta Force even exists. Apparently there's some doubt about that."

"Ah, the good old Internet." As far as Ryan was concerned, the Internet was often a cesspool, especially when it came to things military. He never talked about Delta or what he'd gone through to get chosen for that elite unit, nor could he ever reveal anything about the counter-terrorism missions he'd been part of in half a dozen countries.

"You're not going to talk about Delta Force, are you?" Morgan said with a smile. "Mr. Enigma."

"I can't talk about any Spec Ops units I might or might not have been in. I *can* tell you I was a sniper in a Ranger regiment for a while."

Her eyes popped comically wide. "A sniper? Really?"

If that revelation had bowled her over, it would be interesting to see how she reacted to some of his hairier missions.

"What was it like to be a sniper in Iraq? It must have been terrible over there." She sounded torn between admiration and horror.

"It wasn't as bad as you might think," he said, shading the truth. He wouldn't talk about all the overwatch missions he'd been on, covering army and marine units as they fought to clear out al-Qaeda-infested neighborhoods. "We patrolled at night and slept a lot during the day because it was so damn hot outside. Spent a lot of time playing volleyball and cards and working out."

Morgan looked uncertain. "But...you killed people, right? That was your job as a sniper, wasn't it?"

"Sure. Terrorists who were killing our soldiers and kidnapping and murdering journalists and any Iraqis or Afghanis that stood up to them. Real sweet dudes who loved to behead people."

Ryan had no regrets about enlisting after 9/11 and heading to Afghanistan eight months later. Nor had he ever second-guessed his decision to join the Rangers and then Delta. But more than a decade on the front lines had been enough. His units had completed their missions with effectiveness and honor, never leaving a man behind.

She went silent for a few seconds, a common reaction. "I tried to find as much information as I could about Double Shield Corporation too," she finally admitted.

"You really should think about getting a PI license if you ever get tired of teaching. You're a regular Philip Marlowe."

She wagged a finger at him. "Sarcasm is not your forte, Butler, especially dated sarcasm."

He shrugged.

"From what I read, it sounds like Double Shield's main business is supplying mercenaries to dictators and big corporations around the world," she said.

That unexpected shot hit him like a bullet to a ballistic vest. Her tone, while light, held a note of disapproval. He cautioned himself not to overreact. "Some people put that slant on it. Actually, we're all about keeping people safe in dangerous environments and situations. I've helped a lot of good folks who would be in big trouble unless they had us to stand between them and the bastards who want to kidnap or kill them."

Becoming aware that he'd tensed up and was leaning forward in what Morgan might interpret as an aggressive posture, he took a couple of deep breaths and relaxed back into his chair. But hell, his fun night was starting to go south fast.

She nodded, looking ultraserious. "I totally get that, Ryan, but how long can you keep doing something so dangerous? Don't you worry that your number will come up sooner or later?"

Jesus, what was he supposed to say to that?

When he didn't answer, she let out a sad little sigh and toyed with the base of her wineglass. "I was always worried that something might happen to you in Iraq or Afghanistan. Now it looks like I'm never going to be able to stop worrying about you."

Ryan froze. His mother had said the same thing in almost exactly the same words. But from Morgan? Unless he was reading her all wrong, the kind of emotion he saw in her sky-blue eyes was a whole lot more than concern for a longtime friend.

And he wasn't quite sure how that made him feel.

"I'm sorry, Ryan. I made it all about me when it's about you. Just ignore me."

He reached across the table and gave her hand a gentle squeeze. "Morgan, you don't need to worry about me. I just do my job, and if I do it right, everybody should end up safe."

Ryan hoped that would reassure her. In truth though, there was only so much he could control in any given situation. And he wasn't going to say it to her, but hell yeah, of course he thought about getting his ass shot for the sake of protecting people who could be either very good, or unethical jerkoffs.

"I hope so," she said softly, clearly not convinced.

He closed his eyes for a couple of seconds as he tried to think of some way to end this conversation without worrying her even more. For some reason, that now seemed very important. When he opened them again, he gazed across the table into a haunted, beautiful gaze that made something tighten up in his chest. "I don't see doing this job forever, but right now it's not a bad place to be. I make great money and work with good guys. Besides, there isn't much else I can do to make a living other than play bodyguard."

Actually, someday he'd have other options with Double Shield—ones that didn't involve being on the business end of a gun. Those would take considerable time to pan out though. He didn't have enough years in yet with the company to earn a transfer to a different role.

Her expression lightened when she scrunched her nose at him. "Don't underestimate yourself, Ryan. You could do just about anything you set your mind to. Look at how you're handling the repairs at the B&B."

Ryan forced a smile. While she was trying to be supportive, Morgan's comment only brought his situation into sharper focus. He had a high school diploma and no training in anything other than combat and security. His options were limited. Not that money was particularly important, but he could never make the kind of salary that he was earning at Double Shield anywhere else. Not even close.

And especially not in Seashell Bay.

When he didn't respond, she said, "Do you ever think about putting down roots somewhere, someday?"

"Sure. Somewhere, someday."

"But not here, I presume."

"There's not a lot of call for bodyguards on the island, Morgan. There's nothing for me in Seashell Bay."

When she flinched, Ryan mentally cursed. "That didn't come out right," he added quickly. "I just meant that there's no work for me here unless I want to haul lobster traps."

Her jaw went up in a stubborn tilt. "That's exactly what Aiden thought until last year. Now he's coaching college baseball and constructing a fancy ecoresort, not to mention building his father a new house, renovating the old family Victorian, and—most importantly—getting married to my best friend. If that doesn't show how a person's life can turn around on a dime, I don't know what does."

Then she blinked, and her expression went flat. Ryan suspected she was thinking about her own life, and how it had so quickly turned for the worse after her father died. He had to switch the conversation to something less intense or the evening would end up a disaster.

He refilled her glass and smiled. "On a lighter note, let's talk about kayaking for a minute."

She frowned a bit at the abrupt switch, but then gave him a tentative smile. "Okay."

"I suggest we start by going out in my dad's tandem," he said. "That way I can give you some of the basics before we put you in a single."

"Sort of like flying with an instructor before you solo?"

"Exactly. And if you feel comfortable after a while and the sea is calm, maybe we could even paddle across to Peaks Island."

She narrowed her eyes. "Does your kayak have room to carry snacks and beverages? I refuse to go anywhere without snacks. Preferably ones with chocolate."

He laughed, his spirits lifting with hers. "There's plenty of space in the hatches. You can take just about anything you like."

"Awesome. I'm going to kick some kayaking ass." Morgan reached out to give him a fist bump. "I can't wait."

Ryan decided he felt exactly the same way.

Chapter 9

$\mathcal{M}$organ was dumping laundry into the washing machine when she heard a vehicle pull up in the driveway. She quickly got the wash going and hurried back into the kitchen, raising the blinds on the window above the sink. It was Ryan. He'd borrowed her truck to pick up his dad's sleek, bright yellow kayak.

Ryan had just started to untie the craft when Christian Buckle pelted across the yard to greet him. The ten-year-old had arrived yesterday with his parents, Tim and Kristi, for a short visit with his grandparents. That extended family was among Golden Sunset's best clients. Chester and Dottie Buckle had five sons and daughters, all with kids, and none of them wanted to stay at their parents' two-bedroom house near Wreckhouse Point. Christian had glommed on to Ryan almost right away, which Morgan had to admit was pretty cute. The shy boy and the hard-ass warrior made an unlikely combination.

She headed out to the truck.

"Please, Ryan?" Christian said. Rail thin with black glasses, the boy reminded Morgan a little of Harry Potter.

Ryan, unloading the kayak, gave Morgan a comical look that said *help me*.

She bit back a smile. "Please what, Christian?"

"I was asking Ryan if he could take me for a ride in his kayak," the boy said shyly. "He told me he was going back to his dad's house to get the two-seater."

Even though Christian was shy, he was an adventurous kid who loved exploring Seashell Bay. A couple of summers ago, he'd wandered off along the coastline and picked his way down the bluffs through dense underbrush so he could explore the big rocks on the remote beach. When he hadn't returned after two hours, his parents had frantically mounted a search along with Morgan, Sabrina, and their father. Morgan had found him sitting contentedly atop a tall boulder, contemplating the waves. Since then, his parents had banned Christian from going anywhere near the bluffs.

Considering that island kids had all done that sort of stuff at one point, Morgan thought it was overkill.

"Ryan's pretty busy, I'm afraid," she said. Ryan was starting the big roofing job today, and she knew he wanted to get on with it.

"Just a little ride," Christian said as he turned back to Ryan with pleading eyes behind those big glasses. "Please?"

"Maybe if both the big bad boss here and your mom say it's all right. What do you think, Morgan?" Ryan gave her an irresistible wink.

She laughed. "Okay, Christian. Go inside and ask your mom."

"Yes!" Christian pumped his fist and ran around to the front door.

Ryan went back to untying the kayak. "I'm not going to start on the roof until people clear out anyway," he said over his shoulder as he started to slide the big kayak out of the truck bed. "Or did I screw up and get his mother pissed off at us?"

Morgan scoffed. "Pissed off at me, maybe. Kristi's never been a big fan of mine, but she had a considerable and very annoying crush on you back in high school."

"And here I thought you never cared," Ryan teased.

Morgan wasn't going to touch that one. "Speaking of going for a ride, when do you plan on giving me my turn? Or do you want to spend the whole day crawling around on my roof?"

He checked his watch. "Late this afternoon? We can bring some dinner along and make an evening of it if you're up for it. Dusk doesn't set in until nearly nine o'clock."

Now that definitely sounded interesting. "Perfect, but we'll take a trial run to see if I'm comfortable before setting out across Hussey Sound, won't we?" Morgan didn't worry too much about the crossing—not with Ryan behind her in the tandem kayak. Making a trip like that in the smaller single would be a different story.

He gave her a reassuring smile. "Absolutely."

The front door banged open, and Christian ran across the gravel with Kristi trailing behind. "Mom says it's okay!"

"Yes, it's fine for you to take him in your kayak." Kristi slid an arm around her son's shoulders after she caught up. "It's so hard to keep Christian occupied on the island, and I totally trust you, Ryan." A slim, pretty woman with short, blond hair in a pixie cut, she let her gaze drift appreciatively across Ryan's body.

Yikes. Morgan wasn't thrilled that Kristi had been making her interest in Ryan clear since she arrived. Fortunately, her son was too young and too excited about the kayak ride to notice.

Morgan wasn't quite sure about Kristi's husband though.

"You have a safety vest that will fit him, I presume," Kristi added.

Ryan mussed Christian's lank brown hair. "No problem. We can go now, Christian."

The boy bounced up and down on his toes. "Yay!"

Still ignoring Morgan, Kristi clamped a hand on Ryan's forearm, looking like she'd never let go. "You know, I was just thinking that if he likes the ride today, maybe you could give him some lessons? Kayaking might give Christian something healthy to look forward to when we come back every summer. I'd pay you, of course."

Ryan glanced at Morgan. She thought he was silently asking for her opinion, if not her approval.

She gave a little *whatever* shrug, not wanting to push him one way or the other. But anything that would help keep the Buckle family returning to Golden Sunset was just fine with her, even if Kristi was irritating as hell.

"I guess I can spare a little time to teach Christian some basics. But I won't take your money, Kristi. Just call it a favor from one islander to another."

Kristi gave him such a sugar-sweet smile that Morgan's teeth started to ache.

"I guess we'll always be islanders, Ryan, even though we've both been gone a long time," she cooed. Then she turned her brilliant smile on Morgan. "You're *so* lucky to have this guy, Morgan, you sly thing."

Huh? There was definitely some sexual innuendo in

that comment, which clearly suggested that her luck must involve getting more than handyman work out of Ryan.

Well, Morgan could play catty with the best of them. "Oh, don't I know it, Kristi," she cooed back.

Looking vaguely alarmed, Ryan tapped the kid's shoulder. "Uh, Christian, could you hold up one end of this thing all the way to the beach? Because the sooner we can get the gear down there, the sooner we can get out on the water."

"I'll do my best," Christian said resolutely as he looked at the big tandem.

Ryan could easily hoist the kayak and carry it down himself, but it was sweet how he was trying to include Christian. He showed the boy where to place his hands and then held on to one end of the kayak while Christian lifted the other. "Got it?" he asked.

"Got it," Christian echoed, lifting his end. He grinned with pride.

Ryan started walking backward with careful steps, keeping close watch on Christian all the way.

Kristi sighed. "I sure wish Tim was as patient with Christian as Ryan is."

"It's easy to be patient when you're not actually the parent," Morgan said. "I bet Tim is a really good dad."

Kristi didn't really appear to be listening, her focus instead fastened on Ryan and her son. "I'll tell you one thing," she said. "I bet *that* guy will make a hell of a husband and father if some lucky girl ever manages to get him to the altar."

Then her gaze flicked back to Morgan. "Not that anyone in Seashell Bay is likely to ever find out. After all, why would a guy like Ryan stick around a place as boring as this?"

*   *   *

Christian sat in front of Ryan in the tandem kayak, gripping his big, black paddle for dear life. As they hugged the shoreline near the southern tip of the island, Ryan had to swallow a chuckle as the boy flailed at the water.

What Christian lacked in technique he more than made up for in enthusiasm. Ryan had suggested he sit back and enjoy the ride instead of paddling his ass off, especially since the adult-sized paddle was too big for him. Not happening. The kid had insisted on doing what he called "his share of the work." Impressed, Ryan had decided to leave him alone for now instead of hammering away at him about technique. Technique would come later with lessons. Today, he just wanted Christian to have fun. To think of kayaking as something that made him feel good, something he might want to do all his life.

That was how Ryan felt. How could you beat skimming across the water under the open sky, totally in control, going anywhere you wanted at whatever pace you wanted? Ryan had done some of his best thinking in his kayak, while at other times he'd spent hours not thinking at all. He never felt happier or more at peace than when he was out on the water.

Which, he supposed, meant he had at least some part of the island imprinted on his DNA. After all, he had come from a long line of men and women who'd built their lives around the sea.

He steered them through the narrow passage between Seashell Bay and the tiny, treeless chunk of volcanic rock known as Coogan's Island. "Hey, Christian. Think it's time to turn around and head back?"

The boy stopped his furious paddling long enough to

look back over his shoulder. "Can we keep going a little bit longer? This is really fun."

Yeah, but I'm not getting any work done on that roof.

Ryan was having fun too. It was kind of unexpected because he wasn't a guy who'd ever spent much time with kids. "Okay, five more minutes and then we have to go back. Your mom might start to worry if we're gone too long."

Christian let his paddle dangle over the side for a moment. "She's always been overprotective. My dad too."

"Maybe," Ryan said. "But your mom's letting you take kayak lessons, isn't she? Nothing overprotective about that."

"I guess not."

He wasn't sure why he was defending Kristi, except to make Christian feel better. Because the looks she'd given him earlier had struck him as wildly inappropriate, and they clearly hadn't sat well with Morgan either. Aside from the fact that her kid was standing there, Kristi was a married woman. In Ryan's world, once you made a serious commitment to someone, you didn't go around ogling other people who caught your eye.

And you sure as hell didn't go around sleeping with them either.

Ryan figured he'd better make sure to keep his distance from Kristi, even though it was unlikely she'd really come on to him with her husband and son in the same house. She probably thought it was just harmless flirting, but something that seemed harmless could lead to things that weren't. Things that left wounds that could take a very long time to heal.

Even now, years after the betrayal that had fucked up his life, Ryan's wounds could still throb when poked.

Chapter 10

$\mathcal{M}$organ couldn't believe that Kristi Buckle's mean-spirited words were still rolling around inside her head as she and Ryan neared the other side of Hussey Sound. The woman had really pissed her off. If her family hadn't been such loyal clients, she might not have been able to hold her tongue.

Dammit girl, focus on the great view.

She caught sight of the massive, rust-colored rock formation on Peaks Island known as The Whalebone. Even the short passage from the B&B dock to Peaks, not much more than a mile in length, had seemed daunting at first. Still, the combination of a tranquil sea and the supercompetent man in the rear seat of the tandem kayak had made her say yes when Ryan proposed they paddle to Casco Bay's most heavily populated island. She didn't regret it either, because it was one thing to explore the bay on a ferry or even a little lobster boat but quite another to be slicing low through the waves in a fourteen-foot plastic shell, your butt mere inches above the water.

Exhilarating was the best word to describe the feeling.

Tiring was the second best. Although she exercised regularly, did yoga, and thought of herself as in good shape, Morgan knew she'd be sore tomorrow.

"You're awfully quiet up there, buddy," Ryan said as they paralleled Peaks Island's rocky northern shore. They were heading for a beach where they'd stop, rest, and have some of the food she'd stowed in the hatch beneath her thighs.

"I was just trying to keep it together back there in the deep water, Captain. I didn't want you to keelhaul me for capsizing us," Morgan joked.

Actually, it had been hard to concentrate on her stroke while fuming over Kristi's nasty comments. Morgan had always dreamed of walking up the aisle of the old village church of Saint Anne's, surrounded by her family and friends, about to be married by a beaming Father Michael Malone. And she couldn't deny that more than once Ryan had been the stand-in for the nebulous groom of her dreams.

"You didn't really think I'd let us capsize, did you?" Ryan asked.

Morgan took a quick glance over her shoulder. Man, he looked mysterious—and hot—in his wraparound sunglasses. "The thought did cross my mind when we caught those big swells from that lobster boat."

Ryan laughed. "Come on. The guy slowed practically to a crawl when he saw us."

Casco Bay lobster fishermen were always considerate of other craft on the water, something Morgan couldn't say about the joyriders that liked to rip up and down the bay, dodging buoys and traplines. Fortunately, she wore a lightweight safety vest, and Ryan had already taught her how to get back into the shell if the kayak went over. She was a good swimmer and, with the vest on, she was in no danger unless she somehow got hit in the head and knocked out. Even then, Ryan would make sure she survived. The guy's strength and skills were downright amazing.

"Getting tired?" he asked, after they passed through the narrow passage between Pumpkin Knob and Peaks.

"Who, me? On second thought, just drop me off at the ferry dock, and I'll meet you back in Seashell Bay." She was kidding. Though her shoulders and arms had started to burn, a rest should give her enough gas in her tank for the return crossing.

"Then we'd better rest up now. Over there." He pointed to a stretch of sandy, seaweed-strewn beach where a line of trees partially concealed the houses perched above. "If you're still tired after the break, no worries. You can just take it easy on the way back and let me do all the work."

Though that sounded pretty awesome, the last thing she wanted was for Ryan to think of her as soft or wimpy. "Forget it, pal. I'm up for the challenge."

"Tough girl, huh? I'm impressed. Good for you." The admiration in his voice gave her a funny but nice feeling in her stomach.

Ryan rolled out of the kayak as they neared the beach. He shoved it up onto the sand with Morgan still in it, clutching her paddle. A little wobbly, she got out and popped open the hatch beneath her, pulling out a soft-sided cooler with tuna salad sandwiches, chips, and a Hefty bag with carrots, broccoli, and celery. Ryan retrieved four cans of iced Moosehead beer from a hatch behind her. A minute later, they were sitting side by side on the warm sand, drinking cold beer and munching the food while they enjoyed the cooling breeze off the bay.

They sat together in silence, just enough distance between their bare legs to remain respectable and safe. Morgan gazed out across the picturesque straight between the islands. Two Casco Bay boats passed each other, horns blowing, the passengers waving at each other and at people onshore. Her whole life, watching those trusty little ferries had always given her a sense of peace. The boats seemed somehow symbolic of life on the bay, reliably plying the same routes as they hopped from island to island, rain or shine or snow, season after season, year after year. Those colorful boats had carried her to school, shopping, dancing lessons, proms, vacations, and so many other events in her life. Some of her happiest moments had come when she stepped onto a ferry that would take her home to Seashell Bay and her family and friends.

All that had changed the day she'd boarded a homeward-bound boat in April, grief stricken as she rushed back to deal with the aftermath of her father's sudden death. Some of the magic had gone out of life on the bay ever since, and Morgan had started to wonder if it would ever fully come back.

Ryan gently bumped her with his shoulder. "Hey, girl, you've been in another world most of the afternoon. I'm starting to think I must be boring company."

She gave a guilty little start. Nothing could be further from the truth, though Morgan had to admit that her mind kept wandering. So often these days she just naturally gravitated toward melancholy. While she was fighting as hard as she could for the inn and to take care of her sister, she couldn't brush off a persistent hollowed-out feeling—like control of her life was slipping away a little more with each passing day.

She pulled her knees up and twisted to look at Ryan. He was so awesomely masculine that he took her breath away. His long body—tanned, lean, and hard—was bare except for his blue-and-white board shorts. His chest was worthy of endless admiration, and his strong legs stretched out a mile in front of him.

Morgan dug down deep for something mildly amusing. "Uh-oh, I didn't realize you were such a delicate flower. If there's one thing you'll never be, it's boring, Butler. So quit fishing for compliments."

He gave her a mock salute with his beer can. "Then why so quiet?"

She shrugged. "The usual. My mind keeps wandering back to all the problems I've got to deal with. I'm sorry about that, because I am having a good time. Really."

He draped an arm around her shoulders. "I get how hard it is for you right now with Sabrina and the B&B and everything. But don't forget all the things you've got going for you too."

His arm felt so darn comforting that Morgan gave in to a natural instinct to lean into him. What she would *not* give in to was the instinct to snuggle close. "And what exactly would those things be?"

He tightened his grip a bit. "How about we start with the fact that you're smart, accomplished, beautiful, and incredibly nice."

Morgan's girlie heart gave a little flutter. "Wow, that's only the start? Then by all means keep going, sir."

"Well, let's just say not every sister would be as devoted to Sabrina as you are."

Oops. Wrong thing to say, although that wasn't his fault. Morgan always felt like she wasn't good enough when it came to her sister. Wasn't doing enough.

She pulled back a bit. He loosened his embrace but didn't let go.

"Kristi said something interesting while you and Christian were lugging the kayak down to the beach," she said. "Something about you."

"Please tell me it wasn't X-rated. That woman is terrifying, by the way."

"She managed to keep it PG."

"That's a relief. So what did she say?"

"Oh, that you'd make a great father if some lucky girl ever got you to the altar. That's pretty much a direct quote." She watched carefully for his reaction.

Frowning, Ryan took his arm from around her. "She thinks I'd make a good father just because I was nice to her son?"

"You've always had a natural way with kids, Ryan. You might have forgotten that."

"I don't know. Christian's just a really nice kid who wants to be good at whatever he does. So he gives it maximum effort every time out. I really like kids like that."

"So do I," Morgan said. "The poor little guy just wants to please his parents, and I don't think he finds that easy."

"Well, with his attitude, I'd put my money on him over a more gifted kid who thinks everything should be handed to him on a silver platter."

Morgan agreed. "So you're really going to take Kristi up on the lessons?"

"Why not? I figure it should be a nice break from work."

"Christian will be thrilled, and so will his mother," Morgan said drily. She thought for a few seconds before deciding to take the plunge. "And speaking of his mother, it was obviously none of Kristi's business—or anyone else's—as to when some girl gets you to the altar."

Okay, not the most skillful probing, but his reaction would be instructive.

Ryan's jaw tightened, and he stared grimly across the channel. "You got that right."

As a matter of fact, she did get it. "Well, people get curious. Folks here are always sliding questions at me about my so-called love life—when I'm going to get married and start popping out babies. All that stuff. It's worse now because I'm getting older and don't have a mother around to field the questions. People sometimes just come right out and ask me point-blank, or tell me I should be married, like saying it will make it so."

Ryan drew his legs up and propped his arms on his knees. "Mom gets her fair share of that sort of thing when it comes to me."

"What does she say?"

"I think the gist is that I'm too busy running around the world to settle down."

Morgan suppressed a sigh. "Sounds about right, huh?"

"Pretty much."

She didn't want to press him. He was obviously closed up pretty tight on the subject.

A moment later, Ryan turned to look at her. "What do *you* say when people ask stuff like that?"

Her heart skipped a beat. Was he really prodding her to talk about her love life? Ryan Butler? The more important question was, why?

She faced him. "You really want to know?"

"I wouldn't ask if I didn't," he said.

"Okay, mostly I try to blow it off. But if people persist, I'll go so far as to admit that I do want to get married and have children someday. Only with the right man though. I don't think I have it in me to be a single parent. It would be too hard." She let out a dramatic sigh. "Boring, huh?"

Ryan pushed his sunglasses up on his forehead, his dark eyes studying her so intently she began to feel nervous.

"Not boring," he finally said. "Nice. You deserve the right man, Morgan. And he'll be a damn lucky guy when he finds you."

And maybe I'm already right under his nose.

She strongly doubted that he was thinking along any such lines, which meant she shouldn't either. "It'd probably be easier for him to discover the cure for the common cold than unearth the love of his life in Pickle River, Maine, population ten and falling."

Ryan choked out a laugh. "That bad, huh?"

She wrinkled her nose. "Trust me, I'm barely exaggerating. So what about you, mystery man? Are you waiting for the right woman? Because you certainly deserve to find her," she finished with a teasing smile. She didn't want him to go squirrely on her now by getting too serious.

Ryan turned away again, gluing his gaze on the water. Her heart sinking, Morgan wondered if he was simply ignoring the question.

She shimmied back around, picked up a pebble from the beach, and tossed it as far as she could into the channel. It made a barely perceptible splash. Ryan looked at her again, and she got a jolt at the grim set to his gorgeous mouth and something that looked like pain in his eyes.

"I don't think of it in those terms," he said. "In fact, I try not to think about it much at all."

Annoyed by his cryptic response—and annoyed that she was annoyed—Morgan scrambled for a light response.

"More fun to keep playing the field, huh? I can see why. You must have to fight off scads of women who'd like nothing better than a little attention from big, strong you. You're such a badass." She batted her eyelashes.

Weirdly, his gaze narrowed with even greater intensity. It surprised her that he didn't take the easy out.

"I've learned the hard way that it's not a great idea to get involved," he said. "Even if somebody could put up with the danger and with only seeing me once in a blue moon, I'm not into that kind of a relationship. They hardly ever work."

The obvious conviction behind his words took her aback. "You know there are successful military marriages, Ryan, despite long deployments."

His smile was grim. "You know what the divorce rate is in Spec Ops units?"

Morgan wasn't about to guess.

"I've heard it's around 80 percent," Ryan said. "So your chances of success are one in five. And believe me, it's no better for guys who work for private military contractors."

She stared at him. "That's awful. But you won't be doing that kind of work forever. You told me that at Diamond Cove."

"No, but it's where I am now. Would it be fair to a woman to pretend we could have a relationship that would actually last?" He picked up a pebble and launched it out into the channel, far beyond where hers had sunk.

Boy, how could she even respond to that kind of cynicism?

"You've told me that teaching means more to you than anything else," Ryan went on, as if challenging her. "Would you sacrifice your career even if you thought you'd found the right guy?"

His attitude was starting to piss her off. "I don't know about that, but I've certainly given it up now, at least for the time being. Maybe for a long time." She stared at him, feeling defiant. "And I did it because my sister needs me. That's more important than my career."

He grimaced. "Jesus, Morgan, I didn't mean—"

She held up a hand. "It's fine, Ryan. Really." She flashed him a smile. "We shouldn't be getting this heavy anyway. We're supposed to be enjoying ourselves."

His smile didn't reach his eyes. "We can blame it on Kristi."

"Yes, let's. And speaking of Mrs. Buckle, mark my words, that woman is hot for you, husband or no husband. You're only sleeping about twenty feet apart, so I'd advise you to keep your door locked at night if you want to avoid a midnight visit."

This time, the smile did reach his eyes. He slid an arm around her waist. "If I wanted company, Kristi's not the woman at Golden Sunset I'd want in my room." His arm tightened around her waist, gently pulling her against his naked torso.

Morgan froze, staring at him. The slowly building heat in his gaze sure didn't look like a joke, nor did the arm around her waist feel like just a friendly gesture—not when she was plastered against all that warm, brawny muscle. And honest to God, she hadn't a clue how to react.

Liar.

His eyebrows ticked up, then he sighed and withdrew his arm. "Sorry. I made you uncomfortable."

"You just kind of surprised me." Morgan swallowed past a lump in her throat. God, she didn't want him to let her go. "But we seem to be making a habit of this, don't we?"

He smiled wryly. "If twice constitutes a habit."

She sucked in a deep breath and decided it was time for some frank talk. "You know I'd be lying if I said I wasn't feeling the same, Ryan. Like practically every minute since I saw you on the ferry."

"I hear a 'but' coming."

How could she explain how terribly vulnerable she felt? Between her father's death, her worries for Sabrina, and her insecurity about her own future, she was close to being an emotional basket case. How could she possibly risk a summer hookup with Ryan? That would lead to a world of hurt down the road—especially since he'd just made it blazingly clear that he avoided long-term commitments.

"But I'm...I'm not there emotionally, Ryan. I don't think I could handle it, no matter how much I might want to. I'm kind of a wreck right now." She briefly nestled her face against his shoulder. "I'm really sorry."

"Don't be. I get where you're coming from." Ryan gave his head a shake. "I'm just finding it damn near impossible to ignore all this crazy chemistry between us. Hell, sometimes it feels like I've got a grenade inside me."

Boy, that was exactly how she felt. If Ryan grabbed her and kissed her now, she'd probably be lost. They'd end up naked on this pebbly beach, getting busy in plain view of every boater sailing down the channel.

It was appalling how much she wanted that.

"The chemistry exists all right," she said. "Like a hurricane exists. I just don't think I want to find out what happens when we get sucked into the vortex."

Ryan studied her, but Morgan couldn't read his expression. Then his gaze shifted away. A moment later, when he slid his arm around her shoulder, his light touch felt like that of a buddy offering comfort. "I understand. I just hope I haven't screwed up our friendship."

Moved by his consideration, Morgan slid her arm around his waist. For a moment longer, they quietly leaned into each other like the old friends they'd always been.

Chapter 11

$\mathcal{M}$organ's head had started to droop minutes after Ryan pushed the kayak away from the beach. Before they reached Pumpkin Knob, she'd slumped all the way forward, giving in to exhaustion. He'd nudged her awake once, but she'd blearily muttered something unintelligible and nodded off again. Since she was strapped into the kayak with her paddle stowed and wasn't in an uncomfortable position, Ryan decided to let her doze. The combination of the alcohol, the heat, and the gentle rolling motion of the kayak had clearly been too much for her.

He'd insisted she relax on the journey back to Seashell Bay and let him do all the work. She'd protested, of course, but he could see the relief in her eyes. Even with freeloading a ride home, she would no doubt feel the effect of all the paddling by tomorrow morning.

The image of Morgan stretching in a long, hot shower, trying to work out the kinks in her muscles, was pretty much driving him nuts. In his mind, he was right behind her in that shower, doing his level best to relax that oh-so-sweet body of hers. It was a picture he couldn't shake loose, no matter what he tried to think about.

At least Morgan had finally admitted in words what her body language had been telling him since the day he arrived. She wanted him as much as he wanted her but just couldn't bring herself to let down her self-imposed barriers. She was clearly afraid of wanting more from him than he could give, and then having to watch him head off from Seashell Bay yet again.

But the way he looked at it, he and Morgan had this insane attraction that just wouldn't quit. Fighting every day to ignore it was just going to make it worse for both of them, so why bother? They could scratch the itch and still be careful enough of each other's feelings to make it work. After all, they were both clear on the limitations of each other's lives, so why not have some fun? Morgan damn well needed and deserved that, and Ryan figured he was the guy to give it to her. With all the pressures on her now, a risk-free fling was exactly what the doctor ordered—not some intense, emotional affair that would only confuse things and make her life more complicated.

Besides, flipping back the pages to some we're-just-friends mode would be like trying to stuff toothpaste back in the tube.

The return crossing of Hussey Sound had passed quickly with Ryan paddling hard all the way, his rhythm falling into the smooth and automatic stroke that placed him in the zone. As he passed the B&B's small floating dock, he slowed to a crawl and got ready to jump out and push the kayak up onto the beach. The sun had dipped low behind them.

Morgan must have sensed the speed change, because

she jerked upright. She reached her arms up, twisted, and stretched, giving him a sweet view of her breasts. Then she looked back at him with a sheepish smile. "Wow, I missed almost the whole ride. Sorry about that."

Ryan climbed out. "Beer makes you sleepy. That and physical exhaustion." He gently guided the craft toward the shore until it grounded.

Morgan followed him out and lifted the bow, helping him carry the kayak a few yards past the high tide mark. Just to be on the safe side, Ryan had driven a metal stake deep into the sand and now used it to tie down the tandem. In the heavy dusk, he could barely make out the path that led down the gentle slope from the house to the dock. Proper lighting away from the main house was probably another thing Cal Merrifield hadn't been able to afford.

Morgan peered up toward the brightly lit B&B. "It's a good thing I called Sabrina to let her know we'd be late, otherwise she'd be worried that I might be lobster food by now."

Ryan put a hand on the small of her back and guided her over the pebbled beach. "She knows you're a good swimmer. Not to mention that you're in extremely capable hands."

Morgan grinned over her shoulder. "So I've heard, Mr. Modest."

He nudged her on. "I do know my way around these waters, babe."

When they reached the path, an overgrown line of flat stones that meandered up to the house, Morgan stopped and turned around. It was dark enough that he could barely make out her expression.

"Ryan, before we go back inside, I just want to say

thank you. Thank you for all the work you're doing, for being so great with Christian, for dinner last night, and for giving me a wonderful day. I actually felt relaxed for once."

"Relaxed? Try comatose."

She gave a husky little laugh. "Well, yes, that too. Anyway, it was a very special day."

Ryan clenched his fists so he wouldn't give in to the temptation to pull her into his arms and kiss her stupid. "A special woman deserves a special day."

Instead of replying, she went up on her tiptoes and leaned forward, resting her hands on his chest, and kissed him softly, fleetingly, on the mouth.

"And you're a special man, Ryan," she said in a funny, breathless voice.

For some reason, she stayed in that position, staring up at him.

This close he could see her beautiful face perfectly in the fading light, her eyes wide and her lips parted in unconscious welcome. If she'd glanced away or turned, Ryan was sure his self-restraint would have held. If she hadn't just stood there inviting him to do something, he wouldn't have pulled her tight against him and kissed her with every shred of lust and longing he felt for her.

Morgan froze as he claimed her lush mouth. Her hands were wedged between their bodies, primed and ready to push him away. Even in the midst of a kiss that blasted through him like lightning, Ryan expected to get shoved or maybe even slapped.

But it didn't happen. Morgan's rigid hands slowly relaxed until they slid down his torso and around his back. At the very same time, she moaned and let him fully in.

He went hard in an instant, almost staggering under the passion arcing between them.

Sweet Mother of God.

The kiss was everything Ryan had thought it would be. Every bit as perfect as he'd fantasized since that night last year—the night he realized how badly he wanted to taste her lips, sample all the glories her body had to offer. It had been a long time coming and was all the more thrilling for the delay.

Ryan doubled down on the kiss, tipping her jaw up and adjusting the angle for a deeper taste. He slipped his other hand under her tank top, loving the feel of her baby-soft skin under the roughness of his palms. And Morgan was into it too. Man, was she ever. Instead of breaking away, she pressed herself against his thigh, breathing out a whimper. Now he was so damn hard he could have driven shingle nails with his dick.

He clamped his other hand on her gorgeously rounded ass and pulled her tight against him. Morgan moaned with the sweetest sound of hunger he'd ever heard, and his own burn of desire raced through his blood. The kiss was wet and silky and so hot that he wanted to ease her up against the closest tree and do her right there. Ryan felt like he'd waited forever for this moment, and every cell in his body urged him to take her.

Take what rightfully belonged to him.

The crazy intensity of that thought almost jolted him out of the moment. But Morgan pulled him back in when she hooked a leg around the back of his thigh and snuggled in close. Her sharp nails pressed into his back, and he could feel her hands shaking. When she nuzzled his mouth, then bit down gently on his lower lip, Ryan was lost. He didn't think he could pull back from her if a fucking military parade marched down the beach behind them.

Instinctively, he lifted her off the ground, cradling her against him. Morgan broke free from the kiss, clutching at him to keep her balance.

"What...what are you doing?" she stuttered.

He swooped in to nuzzle a brief kiss across her parted lips, walking her a few steps over to the small stand of trees just off the path.

"I just want you to be comfortable." He stopped under the shadow of a tall birch, putting her down and gently pressing her back against the smooth bark of its trunk.

Morgan huffed out a breathless little laugh. "Comfortable for what? Ryan, we shouldn't be—"

"Shhh, babe," he said.

She stared up at him, her gaze heavy-lidded, her mouth trembling just a little bit. Even in the deep shadows under the trees, he could read her uncertainty. Sense how vulnerable she was. His brain told him to pull back, but the rest of him wanted to soothe away her worries and the months of sorrow, making her forget everything but the fire burning between them. Stepping away from her now seemed impossible.

Ryan didn't even try. "Just relax, Morgan," he murmured. "Let me take care of you."

He could tell she was wavering on the knife-edge of retreat. Every muscle in his body went tight, urging him to charge ahead. But he forced himself to go slow and give her time to come along with him.

He moved a hand to stroke up her slender neck and then curled his fingers around her delicate, stubborn jaw.

Ryan loved her jaw. Loved the way it defiantly tilted up when she had the bit between her teeth, ready to battle any obstacle that stood in her path. When he tipped her jaw up and traced his thumb along her full lower lip, she let out a tiny sigh. The hot whisper of her breath drifted over his fingers, and then her eyelids fluttered shut. She opened her lips in silent invitation.

Ryan took it—took her mouth in a demanding, forceful kiss. He went deep, craving her taste, wishing he were deep inside her body at this very moment. Soon he would be, and his need for her had his body vibrating with tension.

She was right there with him. Morgan snaked her hands up between them and wrapped them around his neck. She went up on her toes, pressing into his chest, all the while devouring him with a hunger that matched his own. His erection throbbed, already aching for release, and he couldn't help nudging against her, letting her know just how much he wanted her.

Through the thin fabric of her tank top, he could feel her nipples go hard. And as much as he wanted to keep kissing her, to drink his fill of her after so many long months—years—of waiting, Ryan couldn't wait to explore. Morgan had a gorgeous body, slim and strong, with killer curves in all the right places. He couldn't wait to show her what he could do once he got her stripped naked.

He eased back. Her whimper of protest changed to a moan of satisfaction when he feathered kisses across her cheek to her ear, then down the long line of her neck. Her skin was warm and smooth, tasting faintly of coconut suntan lotion and salt, and the heat of the long summer day. He licked down to the hollow at the base of her throat, her rapid pulse fluttering under his tongue. When he kissed down to the swell of her breasts, she clutched at his shoulders. For a heart-attack-inducing moment, he thought she would push him away. But instead she arched up and angled her head back, lifting herself to meet his caresses.

When his hands slid down to the hem of her top, she shivered. "Ryan, please," she groaned, her voice so soft and full of hunger he thought he might explode on the spot.

He rubbed his cheek across the rigid tip of her nipple, poking against the fabric of her top. "What do you want, babe?" he murmured.

"I want...you."

The broken whisper pushed him over the edge. He dropped to his knees on the soft grass and pushed her shirt up around her neck. Even in the near darkness, her skin gleamed pale and smooth, her breasts perfectly framed by a bra that barely contained her generous curves.

"Damn, you're gorgeous." He leaned in and rasped his tongue across one of her nipples through the barely there material of her bra, loving the feel of the stiff point under his tongue. Morgan jerked a bit, her fingers digging into his shoulders. When he sucked on her, she let out a moan and seemed to collapse against the tree at her back. Ryan slid his hands to her waist and followed, keeping his mouth on her breast. But he wanted more, he wanted it all, so he reached up and hooked his fingers into the bra cups and pulled them down.

Her beautiful breasts popped free and, for a moment, all Ryan could do was stare as they quivered right in front of him. She was gorgeous, and nothing could have prepared him for the mind-blowing intensity of how much he wanted her.

He cupped both breasts in his palms and leaned in, taking her in his mouth.

"Ryan!" Morgan choked out, biting back what sounded pretty close to a startled shriek. Her fingernails dug in again, this time no doubt leaving marks on his skin.

For several deliriously fantastic moments, she let him play with her. Ryan's hands joined the game, stroking as his mouth went from one breast to the other. Morgan's hands cradled his head as she held him against her chest, her breath coming in fractured sobs.

And still it wasn't enough. Not even close. He needed to be inside her—right now—as deep as he could go, with her long legs wrapped tight around his hips as he pounded into her.

So hungry to get her naked that he could barely think straight, he broke free and pulled her bra back up. He quickly came to his feet, pulling her shirt down at the same time. Morgan staggered, and he had to grip her upper arms to keep her from tumbling.

"Let's get out of here," he rasped. "Go someplace we can be alone."

The B&B was too small for them to have sex in either his guest room or Morgan's bedroom, which was right beside Sabrina's. Maybe they could head down the beach, find some soft sand, and do it under the stars?

Hell, yeah.

It sounded perfect—Morgan, naked and writhing beneath him on the beach under the darkening night sky. It was every guy's summer fantasy coming to life. He'd been having it about her for years.

But then she froze under his hands. He felt the change in her, the stiff set to her muscles, the sensual fog obviously clearing from her brain as she realized what they were about to do. What they'd almost done.

He had to repress the urge to curse long and loud.

She slipped her hands between their bodies and pushed, stepping away from the tree trunk. "Oh, God, I can't believe this is happening again." She took another step away, straightening her clothes with hands that visibly shook. "Ryan, this is insane. We *cannot* do this."

"Morgan, you were doing exactly what you wanted to do." He almost growled with frustration. "And the same goes for me. You can only hold back a raging tide for so long."

Okay, it was a dumb cliché, but he was a guy and he didn't do feelings. Still, he hoped it conveyed what was going on inside him. Sure, maybe it was a simple lack of self-control. Or maybe it was just acknowledging reality.

Finally.

Morgan fussed with her clothes for a moment longer. "Yeah, well, tides come and go whether you want them to or not," she said, her voice a little shaky. "And they can drag you under and kill you too. So, extending your very apt metaphor, giving in doesn't sound like such a great idea."

And now it's time for a very cold shower. "So what was that all about, then? What just happened out here?"

She folded her arms across her middle. "Chalk it up to some kind of hormonal hysteria. I guess that's what can happen if you have sex like, about, never."

Yeah, that was a bullshit answer if he ever heard one. "That's it? It was just some crazy hormonal thing?"

She looked away. "You're the one who keeps talking about chemistry," she said defensively.

Definitely cold shower time. "And you're really sure you don't want this?"

Morgan flapped an agitated hand. "It's not a matter of what I want or don't want, Ryan. Lord knows I wish it was as simple as that."

That answer didn't tell him much.

Ryan waited her out, hoping for more. But when the silence stretched out, Morgan refusing to look at him, he finally nodded. "Okay, I'm not going to push. Nothing's going to happen between us until you're ready. So what happens from now on is up to you, Morgan."

Morgan's shaky legs barely kept her moving ahead, and it wasn't just from physical exhaustion. Ryan had just completely rocked her world, skewing it right off its axis.

It had been incredibly stupid to offer up that little peck of friendly thanks, even though at the time it seemed natural and right. What she hadn't counted on was her inability to move away from him and his almost instantaneous, passionate response. He'd seized the moment, that was for damn sure, and her resolve had gone totally AWOL.

As for her body? That had gone boneless when he gripped her in his brawny, protective embrace.

Lost in that moment—okay, several long minutes—of stunning pleasure, Morgan had forgotten where she was or maybe even who she was. Because she wasn't that girl who threw caution and modesty to the winds, ready to do it up against a tree, only a few dozen yards from a house full of people. Thank goodness she'd been able to snap out of it and make her clumsy exit.

Morgan stopped for a moment when she reached the back porch. She let out a shaky sigh as she fluffed her hair, smoothed her top again, and prayed she looked relatively normal instead of like a sex-starved maniac. How were she and Ryan going to keep working together, living together, when it seemed like every look or fleeting touch set off an explosion?

At least Ryan had told her that everything would be up to her from now on, which gave her some degree of control over the situation, no matter how laughably small. Sex might just be sex for him, but Morgan knew it couldn't be that way for her. She already cared about Ryan far too much to have a casual fling, content to let the emotional chips fall where they may. There was simply no way she could check her heart at the door before she crawled into Ryan's bed—the episode under the trees had made that unmistakably clear.

Through the screen door, she could see Sabrina leaning against the island counter, her thin arms crossed tightly over her faded blue Seashell Bay T-shirt. She shot Morgan an angry glare. "Well, it's about time."

Morgan opened the door and crossed to the refrigerator, yanked out a carton of orange juice, and poured herself a small glass to keep her blood sugar from crashing. She was in no shape for this discussion.

"Dammit, Morgan, I was really worried," her sister said. "You shouldn't be out on the water when it's nearly dark. It's too dangerous."

Morgan drained the juice in one long swallow and turned around as she heard Ryan come in the front door. She put a finger to her lips so Sabrina wouldn't start an argument while he was in listening range.

"I called you just so you wouldn't worry," Morgan said after he was upstairs. "Not that you needed to fret. I wasn't exactly making a transatlantic crossing."

Her sister swallowed hard. "I saw what you and Ryan were doing out there, Morgan. It...it upset me."

Crap, crap, crap.

Morgan had thought it was too dark outside for anyone to make anything out at such a distance. Apparently there had been enough twilight for her eagle-eyed sister.

She managed to feign a casual shrug. "Sweetie, it was just a kiss to say thank you for taking me on a fun little outing in his kayak."

Sabrina took two steps forward and put her hands on her hips, riveting Morgan with her eyes. "Morgan, I didn't see everything, but I know what a little thank-you kiss looks like. That sure as hell wasn't it."

Morgan's cheeks burned with heat. Part of her wanted to tell her sister to mind her own damn business. She wouldn't though. Ryan's arrival had been a huge upheaval for Sabrina, one she'd barely started to get used to. Now she was probably thinking his presence posed an even greater threat.

"Really, it isn't something you need to think about," Morgan said in what she hoped was a normal voice.

"Are you going to have sex with him?" Sabrina snapped. "Because that's exactly what it looked like to me. Am I going to hear Ryan slipping into your room in a few hours? Because I'll be lying awake all night thinking about that."

Sabrina could be brutally blunt. Fortunately, Morgan was used to it. Her sex life was none of Sabrina's business, but her sister's poor impulse control sometimes led to thoughts spilling out unfiltered and hurtful. She always regretted it soon afterward.

"Do you seriously think I'd have sex with my sister listening through the wall?" Morgan said with a teasing grin she hoped would break the tension. "That would hardly be fun for anyone."

A flush crept up Sabrina's neck. She pursed her lips and remained silent.

Morgan thought her sister might be too embarrassed to admit she'd gone too far. "Sweetie, please don't read anything into what you just saw. And please try not to stay awake worrying about it, because I am not going to have sex with Ryan tonight."

When Morgan closed the gap, holding her arms open for a hug, Sabrina angrily shook her head and took a step backward.

"Not *tonight*," Sabrina said. "Does that mean you will another night?"

Morgan felt her patience slide away. God, she was so tired of handling everything. Tired of trying to keep her emotions in constant check. "Sabrina, if you want to keep talking about this, fine, we'll talk. In the meantime, please stop making false assumptions, and stop throwing accusations at me. It's very unfair."

Her voice had risen in pitch to the point where Sabrina's eyes widened. Morgan almost never spoke to her sister in a harsh tone.

Tears started streaming down Sabrina's pale cheeks. "I'm sorry, Morgan. It's just that I'm…scared. Really scared."

Disgusted for losing her temper, Morgan pulled her sister into her embrace. This time Sabrina didn't resist.

Her sister sniffled and dug in close. "I'm scared about...about everything."

Including losing Morgan, so much so that a kayak ride was cause for worry. Throw a hot guy into the mix and disaster loomed.

"I know, darling. I'm a little scared too. We're both still trying to find ways to cope without Dad. But we'll get through this together. I promise we will." She pulled back a bit, making Sabrina look at her. Her sister's teary, scared face just about tore Morgan's heart in half.

"Listen to me," Morgan said. "I will never, ever leave you. And I will do everything I can to save this place."

"Promise?" Sabrina asked with a big sniff.

"I promise."

While the future was ridiculously uncertain, Morgan knew that she would never abandon Sabrina. She'd be at her sister's side for as long as she needed her.

There was nothing else that mattered more, not even Ryan.

Chapter 12

$\mathcal{W}$hile not quite as big a deal as the Blueberry Festival, July Fourth was the second biggest event of the summer season. Relatives and visitors jammed the island for the holiday, filling up the B&B.

At least when Morgan's father had been alive, that is.

This year, only the Buckles, the Stringers, and the Boylans—the family of longtime local schoolteacher Rosemary Boylan—were staying at Golden Sunset. Three rooms out of six were filled, not counting the one occupied by her hardworking soldier and, for the past few days, studly roofer.

Morgan couldn't stop thinking about the B&B's bottom line as she tossed her sports bag onto the passenger seat of her truck. It wasn't surprising since she'd spent much of the morning going over the books again, racking her brain for some way to conjure up more business. Ryan and Aiden had lifted a huge weight from her chest by providing a new roof at little immediate cost, but a half-empty inn during a prime summer event was another warning sign of calamity on the horizon. She'd pared expenses at the inn to the bone, so there were no more savings to be found. The obvious solution—the only solution—was to bring in more revenue, and that meant attracting more guests. How to do that remained a mystery.

Her only comfort was the big wedding party coming in a month's time. Without that, her calculations showed her running out of cash before the end of August, and with no help from the bank in sight, Golden Sunset's doors would have to close after Labor Day. Morgan and Sabrina would then have to unload the place for whatever pittance they might get. Potential buyers were going to choke when they reviewed the inn's cratered financial statements.

Ryan had left much earlier to head down front to take part in the traditional July Fourth morning flotilla of lobster boats and pleasure craft that cruised down the channel from Wreckhouse Point to the south end of the island. It was always a colorful, fun parade with flags and banners flying from masts, and boats jammed with people waving at onlookers that lined the town landing and beaches up and down the coast.

Aiden had invited Ryan to ride in *Miss Annie* with Lily, his brother, and a few friends. Morgan had been invited too, as always. In fact, she couldn't recall missing a flotilla since Lily bought the boat. But yesterday she'd called Lily and begged off, making a lame excuse about working on a presentation she was going to make to another bank. While it was a bald lie, she hadn't been able to think of a better excuse. Lily had been skeptical but hadn't pressed. Morgan felt certain that her old pal would cross-examine her when they met up later today though.

The truth, of course, was that she didn't want to spend the morning in the tight confines of Lily's lobster boat with Ryan. Not only might that have reinforced everyone's impression that something was going on between them, it would have felt awkward and weird after what happened the night they came back from the kayak trip. In fact, every moment of the intervening few days had felt horribly awkward, which wasn't surprising, given how far things had gotten. She and Ryan had been circling each other warily, trying to act normally around the guests and Sabrina. Suddenly the jokes and quips didn't come easily, and Morgan found she was acutely conscious of every move she made and every word she spoke to the man she'd known for years. As far as she could tell, he was doing the same thing.

What had been an easy friendship had turned into a tense and uncertain standoff, one fraught with a crazy amount of sexual heat. Every day, Morgan had to convince herself that it made no sense to give in to her ever-present desire to jump into bed with him. It was a battle she knew would go on until the moment he took the boat back to the mainland and to his life as a hired gun.

A life that could never include you.

As if she needed a reminder.

At the landing, she parked in front of the Rec Center and headed toward the tents and gazebos. A red-and-yellow bounce castle and a portable dunk tank had been set up behind the Rec Center to keep the kids happy. A pair of propane barbecues occupied their usual spot beside the drinks table, and the tantalizing scent of sizzling burgers wafted her way.

She was wearing a yellow tank top and navy shorts, both of which had seen better days. They were only for her scheduled duty time in the dunk tank anyway. Every summer, both on July Fourth and during the Blueberry

Festival, she volunteered to be soaked as part of a fund-raiser for the town's small but thriving library. Once her shift was finished, she'd change into jeans and a T-shirt for the tug-of-war competition she'd organized with Brett Clayton.

"Hey, Morgan! Over here!"

She glanced to her left and saw Aiden waving to her. With him were Bram and Ryan, the three guys towering above the rest of the crowd. Though she could barely make him out through the throng, it looked like Sean Flynn was the fourth member of their little circle. The last thing she wanted was a cozy little chat with a group that included Ryan, but she couldn't be rude.

Aiden slung an arm around her shoulder and gave her a friendly squeeze. "How's my second favorite island girl today?"

Morgan gave him a little dig in the ribs. "If you value your man parts, you'd better not let Miss Annie hear that, my friend."

He grinned. "Nah, Miss Annie's in a class by herself, right? I wouldn't dare compare her to anybody else."

"Class by herself? Jesus, you got that right," Aiden's father said in a raspy voice that reflected years of sucking back cigarette smoke and alcohol. "They broke the mold when they made that old bat, thank the good Lord. She rags my ass something fierce."

Despite his crusty attitude, Sean's smile conveyed the affection that had grown between him and Miss Annie now that their decades-old feud had finally been laid to rest. It made life on the island better for everyone.

Ryan lifted an inquiring eyebrow.

"She took Dad in last fall after he got out of rehab,"

Aiden explained, "and made sure the grumpy old coot didn't stray off course."

"I'm standing right next to you, son," Sean said drily.

Ryan smiled. "Yeah, I heard you two got real close, Mr. Flynn. It's great to hear."

"Annie's all right," Sean said gruffly. "She can be a real ballbuster when she wants to be though." He tilted a can of Coke to his lips and slurped a mouthful.

While most of the partygoers had bottles or cans of beer in their hands, all four of the men were drinking Coke. Morgan knew Aiden rarely drank alcohol around his father or brother, and Ryan had apparently followed suit. He and Aiden were such good guys that it made her heart hurt.

"Where's Lily?" she asked.

"She was a little concerned about how her diesel was running during the flotilla, so she wanted to stay back and take a look at it," Aiden said. "She should be along soon."

"Why didn't *you* stay and help your bride-to-be, Aiden Flynn?"

Aiden's eyes bugged out. "Are you kidding? You know Lily won't let me within a country mile of that engine."

"Especially after he wrecked Dad's last summer," Bram piped up.

"Don't remind me," Sean groaned. "I'm still not over it."

"That was Roy's fault and everybody knows it," Aiden protested.

Bram shook his head. "Roy wasn't driving the boat, man. You were."

"And don't forget how hot you were for Roy to juice my diesel," Sean said. "So you could beat that little Doyle of yours."

"I just hope you dudes are as pumped up about the tug-of-war. I'm not about to lose to the firefighters again this year." Morgan gave Ryan a fake scowl. "And I'm looking at you when I say that, Butler."

"You're coming to the social tonight, aren't you?" Aiden asked as he and Ryan headed toward the tug-of-war pit.

It had been years since Ryan had gone to the St. Anne's July Fourth social. His visits home were always later in the summer.

"Don't think so," Ryan said.

"Why the hell not?" Aiden asked. "What else is there to do on this rock? The Pot's going to be dead."

Though Morgan hadn't said anything about going, Ryan figured she'd be there. She liked dancing and hanging out with her pals. "It's been a little weird between Morgan and me for the past few days. It's probably better for me to give it a miss."

Aiden gave him a questioning look. "She made herself scarce most of the time we worked on the roof. What was up with that anyway?"

Ryan didn't want to talk about it.

"Come on, man," Aiden said, elbowing him. "Lily said something cryptic about a kayak trip you guys took to Peaks."

Suddenly, he found himself wanting to talk to Aiden about it instead of keeping it bottled up. "I kind of made a move on her when we got back from Peaks."

Aiden's dark brows lifted. "Oh-kay, then. What kind of move are we talking about here?"

"A kiss." He wasn't about to elaborate on the details.

"Just a kiss?"

"Okay, a fucking hot kiss," Ryan admitted. *Like five-alarm-blaze hot, along with pretty spectacular groping.*

"So you two played suck-face for a while and then it all went to shit? Have I got that about right?"

"More or less. She froze up when I, uh...suggested that we might continue what we were doing in a more private place."

"Like somebody's bedroom."

Ryan shrugged.

Aiden slung an arm around Ryan's shoulders and spoke in tones so low there was no chance of anyone else hearing. "Look, I can't say I'm surprised. From what I know of her and from what Lily's told me, Morgan's not going to get involved with a guy unless she's convinced it'll go somewhere. Yeah, she's hot for you—hell, everybody on the island knows that by now. But you're just passing through, man. You can't blame her if she wants to protect herself."

Ryan figured his friend had it right—Morgan Merrifield was that kind of woman. And he admired her for it. Unfortunately, that didn't stop him from wanting to get her in bed. He now felt like Morgan had a grip on him in a way no other woman ever had—not even Callie Strohmayer, the girl he'd once figured was *the one*.

But unless he and Morgan could take the next step and see where the fire between them might lead, neither of them would ever know what might or might not have been possible. Morgan just didn't trust him alone with her. And based on what happened behind the B&B, she probably shouldn't.

"I don't blame her at all," he said. "I told her the other night that it was up to her if anything was going to happen between us." He gave a little snort. "I guess I'll just keep taking cold showers."

But in truth, Ryan wasn't sure that he could keep his distance from Morgan, pretending that he didn't want her like crazy.

Aiden pulled his arm away and studied him. "Dude, it's not like Morgan's the only single woman on the island," he said. "Or you could check out some of the bars in Portland if you're looking for that kind of action. The city's crawling with tourists looking for a good time."

"I'll pass," Ryan said. "I didn't come here to trawl bars. I came to think and relax."

"How's that going anyway?" Aiden said. "You're not exactly hot to go back to Double Shield, are you? That's the vibe I've been getting while we worked."

That was the million-dollar question. Ryan kept telling himself he had a great life, traveling all over the world and raking in a hell of a lot more money than he'd ever earned before. And yet in the middle of the night, or out on the ocean in his kayak, doubts always returned. "I'm kind of lukewarm about it, to be honest. But it's not like I've got a lot of options."

"Sometimes the options aren't obvious. Hell, I never thought I'd end up coaching a university baseball team. And if you'd told me a year ago that I'd be in the middle of developing a frigging ecoresort, I'd have laughed my ass off."

Ryan shrugged. "That's what Morgan said. Look, I'm glad for you, man, but the kind of thing that happened to you isn't going to happen to me."

Aiden gave him a mocking smile. "What, now you can predict the future too?"

"Shut up, asshole."

"Just come to the damn social, dude, and stop being an idiot," his friend said, punching him in the shoulder.

Morgan peered down at the muddy pit. Every year, the tug-of-war challenge was held on a patch of scrubby grass behind the Rec Center. The "moat," as the locals called the pit in tug-of-war lingo, was really just a small rectangle of dirt that had been thoroughly watered with a garden hose and was now a gooey mess.

Though she was trying to focus on the challenge match that she organized every year, she could barely think of anything other than Ryan.

A big crowd had gathered eight or ten deep behind the Rec Center, forming an oval around the pit. Most of the spectators had pledged money to sponsor one or the other team, and the proceeds from the competition would go, as always, to a small women's shelter in Portland. Morgan had started up the challenge years ago with Lily's help and had been honored with a plaque from the shelter last year for her efforts. It was one of her favorite events of the year, both for the great cause and because it was fun.

She glanced up when Micah tapped her on the shoulder. "Any replacements from the lists you two exchanged yesterday?" he asked her and Brett Clayton. Micah was serving as this year's ref.

Every year, Brett's posse of firefighters and EMTs defeated any team the other islanders threw at them. Morgan had a hunch things could be different this year. She'd organized the "town team" for the past four events and had never won, but now she figured her team had a decent chance to go over the top. Why wouldn't they, now that they'd added studly Ryan Butler to their ranks? She'd asked Aiden to be the team's anchor, but he'd tagged Ryan as the better, stronger choice, without a handicap like Aiden's bum knee.

Brett shook his head at Micah's question. "Everybody's here. Jessie Jameson, Laura Vickers, Connie Taylor, and Chrissie Laughlin are the women. Josh Bryson, Brendan Porter, Frank Laughlin, and myself are the men. Boone Cleary's our coach, same as always."

The women were all volunteer firefighters, EMTs, or the wives or girlfriends of firefighters. Each team had to comprise an equal number of men and women.

"We're all here too," Morgan said. "Erica Easton, Tessa Nevin, Jen Cassidy, and me." Erica and Jen were strapping lobster fishermen, while slightly built Tessa was replacing Lily, who'd pulled out a couple of days ago with a sore wrist. "Our guys are Bram and Aiden Flynn, and Kevin and Ryan Butler. Miss Annie's our coach, of course."

"Keeping it in the family, huh?" Brett said with a confident-looking grin. "The Flynns and the Butlers. Nice."

Because Fire Chief Laughlin always insisted on joining the firefighter team, Morgan felt duty bound to have someone on hers from the older generation. Ryan's dad always volunteered for the job. A big, rugged lobster fisherman, he always held his own against the fire chief's pulling strength.

"Well, each team's combined weight is within thirty pounds of the other," Micah said. "Are we good to go?"

Brett nodded.

"Yep," Morgan said, glancing toward Ryan and Aiden. Ryan caught her eye and grinned. Her heart pounding harder with nerves and excitement, Morgan shook hands with Brett before she headed over to her team.

Aiden handed her a piece of paper. "Here's the order."

She'd picked the team, but Morgan had let Aiden determine the lineup since he had a better handle on tactics. She hoped Aiden had put her in the middle of the pack to compensate for her relative weakness. Of all the islanders in the event, only Tessa was a less powerful puller.

Morgan repressed a sigh. Aiden had put her in the number seven spot, right between him and Ryan. As usual, her old pal was getting up to mischief by pairing her with Ryan. The rest of the line consisted of Jen, Kevin, Tessa, Erica, and Bram, in that order. Morgan got them all organized and then went to her spot near the end of the rope. Ryan was there talking to his parents.

"You look lovely today, Morgan," Julia Butler said with a warm smile. "Your skin is always so beautiful."

With her hair still wet from the dunk tank and with zero makeup, Morgan knew that wasn't true. But Julia was the nicest person on the planet.

"Thanks, Mrs. Butler. We're sure happy to have Ryan on the team this year."

"If only he could be here all the time instead of gallivanting all over the world," Julia said with a wistful sigh.

"Julia Butler, that is so much malarkey," her husband said. "Our boy is fighting the good fight like he always does. And that's a damn sight more important than catching people's dinner."

Ryan gave his dad a fist bump.

Julia wrinkled her nose at her husband, then smiled. "Don't get me wrong, Morgan. I'm so proud of Ryan I could burst. But I just miss him so. Watching him get on that ferry and leave again is always the worst day of the year for me."

Ryan wrapped his mother in a tight hug. "But I always come back, Mom. And I always will."

Morgan was thrilled he had such a close, loving family, but the sweet exchange hit her like a punch in the stomach. God, she missed her parents. She would miss Ryan too, more than she cared to think about.

Fortunately, Micah blew his whistle before she could get too maudlin.

"Come on, guys, let's go," Aiden ordered, holding the rope in his big hands.

"Yes, time to get the lead out, people," Miss Annie said as she bustled down the line, giving her team friendly pats on the butt. "Let's wipe the grins off those smoke eaters' faces."

"Duty calls," Ryan said. After he kissed his mom and got in position as anchor, his dad moved forward to take up his place near the head of the line.

When Ryan wrapped the end of the thick rope around his waist and let the remaining few feet trail behind him, Morgan shook her head. "You can't wrap the rope around your waist. That's not quite in keeping with the rules for the anchorman, dude."

Ryan lifted an eyebrow. "Really? Well, you're the pro." He unwrapped the rope and handed it to her. "Show me," he said in a deep, low voice that made it sound like he might want to do something far sexier with the rope than just play tug-of-war.

Oh, boy. Rope and Ryan Butler was not a combo she should be thinking about.

"Okay, it goes underneath your arm, like this." Morgan

threaded the rope under his arm and circled behind him. "And up over your other shoulder, like so." She couldn't help running her palm down his bicep before she looped the rope back under his arm again so the loose end trailed behind him. "That's what the rules require," she finished, a tad breathless.

When she touched him, Morgan swore she could feel sparks—and a whole lot of glorious hard muscle.

"If you say so, boss lady," he murmured. "But I figure there are plenty of other rules we can break."

Morgan moved into position, hyperaware of his presence behind her. "Get your mind out of the gutter, anchorman," she flung over her shoulder.

"Get your mind *into* the game, Ryan Butler," Miss Annie scolded as she came down the line to them. "You too, Morgan Merrifield. Don't think I don't know what's going on between you two."

Morgan had to bite back a groan, but Ryan just chuckled at the reprimand.

Roy took a couple of steps forward as if to talk to Miss Annie but instead leaned in toward Aiden. "I got twenty-five bucks riding on you guys, so don't let me down. That's a lot of money to a senior citizen, sonny."

Morgan knew Rocket Roy wouldn't be the only islander who'd placed a bet on the outcome.

As Aiden reassured the old man, Morgan clutched the rope tightly and dug her feet as hard as she could into the short grass. She kept her eyes glued on Micah, standing off to the side and clearly about to whistle the start of the match.

"Your ass is seriously distracting me, Merrifield," Ryan murmured in her ear. "If you had a dime in the back pocket of those jeans, I bet I could tell if it was heads or tails."

Lord, help me. Morgan tried to ignore the little flutters in her stomach. "That excuse isn't going to cut it if we lose, Soldier Boy," she hissed, glancing back.

She didn't know whether his amused grin infuriated or excited her. Both, she guessed.

When Micah blew the whistle, whoops and cheers erupted all around the field. "Pull!" yelled Miss Annie at the exact moment that Boone Cleary boomed out the same command to his team.

Morgan pulled on the rope with all her strength, but it felt like cement under her hands. Nothing moved either way as both teams strained for advantage. "Pull!" Miss Annie yelped again, trying to get their rhythm going.

Morgan kept her eyes fastened on Aiden's back and strained at the rope.

"Come on you no-good Flynn boys, pull!" Miss Annie bellowed. For a little old lady, she had quite the set of pipes.

The crowd's cheering seemed pretty evenly split, though Morgan was so focused on trying to maintain a solid grip on the rope that she was barely aware of more than a jumbled roar. When she looked down the line at the firefighters on the other side of the moat, she saw something that made her blink. She swore she could see genuine surprise on their faces, especially Brett's. Those guys always figured they had the tug-of-war contest in the bag, but maybe not this time.

After a few tense moments, her team fell into a good rhythm, with Ryan and Aiden leading the way with huge pulls. At Miss Annie's barked commands, each pull was followed by a barely perceptible moment of relaxation before another hard yank on the rope. While it felt to Morgan like she wasn't doing much of the work, she knew it wasn't true. A team couldn't win the match without all eight pullers doing their jobs. She'd be damned if she would be the weakest link—not when they had a real shot at winning.

And *especially* not in front of Ryan.

"Harder!" Miss Annie shouted. "We're gaining ground!"

As Morgan strained, she glanced down the line. Miss Annie was right. It hadn't felt like she'd moved, and yet the center marker looked like it was now at the edge of the moat on her team's side. Across the gap, the fire chief's face was as red as his engine as he strained at the rope.

Behind her, Ryan's breath came in harsh, rhythmic pants. He was like a tractor behind her—a huge, powerful machine set in slow reverse. With each pull, Morgan now had to take a half step back to keep her balance. She got a renewed burst of energy and doubled down as hard as she could.

They had the firefighters on the run, and the crowd was going crazy. Morgan had never heard anything like it—probably because her team had never had as much of a chance of winning before.

"Put your back into it, Bram Flynn!" Miss Annie was jumping up and down like a terrier on steroids, screaming into Bram's ear.

"I am, Miss Annie!" Bram shouted back. "We're kicking their asses."

"You bet we are!" Miss Annie crowed.

"We? I don't see you yanking that rope," Roy said

loudly from right behind the old gal. "Stop distracting the boy."

Miss Annie shot her soul mate a glare that promised future retribution, but then swung her attention back to the line, calling out encouragement.

As hard as she was trying, Morgan felt like she was mostly just hanging on. With each mighty pull from Ryan, she had to scramble back. His strength was freaking amazing.

"One or two more and they're done," Ryan growled. "Put everything you've got into it, Merrifield."

"What do you think I've been doing so far, you lunkhead?" Morgan panted back.

"Pull!" Miss Annie shouted.

Morgan leaned hard onto her right foot, gave a mighty heave, and felt her balance give way. She was falling. Instinctively, she let go of the rope and flailed her arms in a last-ditch attempt to stay on her feet. But it was no use. She was headed down.

Suddenly, a pair of strong arms circled her chest, pinning her against the rock-solid body beneath her, shielding her from a hard tumble.

Unfortunately, the rest of her teammates weren't so lucky. They tumbled like a row of bowling pins. Aiden and Bram went down in a tangle of long arms and legs, Bram ending up facedown in the dirt and grass.

"Jesus Christ," Bram yelped as he lifted his head and glared at Aiden, who was laughing his ass off. Poor Bram spit out a mouthful of grass. "What the fuck are you doing, bro? Trying to break my neck?"

Miss Annie smacked him on the back of the head. "Stow that nasty language, Bram Flynn."

"Don't be such an old biddy, Annie," Sean said as he helped his son up. But he was laughing almost as hard as Aiden.

"Are you okay?" Ryan asked, his breath warm on Morgan's ear. His big hands were clasped tight under her breasts, and she was pretty sure a very solid erection was nudging into her butt.

"I think so," she managed. "If you let me up, I'll find out."

The crowd was cheering like the Red Sox had just won the World Series. Julia Butler appeared through the crowd to stand over Morgan and her son. "Morgan, sweetie, are you all right?"

She scrambled to right herself as Ryan finally loosened his grip. Apparently her team had won, since her teammates were going crazy. Miss Annie was hugging Bram, while Roy slapped Aiden on the back. Kevin Butler and Erica Easton were cheering, while Tessa and Jen were jumping around like maniacs.

Morgan dusted herself off. "I'm fine, Mrs. Butler."

Ryan bounced to his feet and came up behind Morgan. "The ground was a little soft there—it made me go down when I gave that final pull."

"And took the rest of the team down with you," Morgan said wryly.

"Hey, we won, didn't we?" Ryan protested.

"Yes, and you were—"

"Way to go, son," Kevin boomed out as he clapped Ryan on the back. "Lord, I felt like I had a locomotive pulling me with you and the Flynns at my back."

"And what about the girls?" Julia said indignantly. "It wasn't like they were standing there filing their nails, Kevin."

"Oh, jeez, my big mouth's getting me in trouble again," Kevin said, one arm around Ryan's shoulders and the other around Morgan's. "But I'm proud of both these young people. They're the best of Seashell Bay, and that's no lie."

Now that was a nice bit of irony. Both Morgan and Ryan had fled the island right after high school, while folks like Kevin and Julia Butler had been pillars of the Seashell Bay community all their lives—and were clearly happy with the choices they'd made.

"Hey, Morgan, are you sure you're okay?" Ryan asked, frowning down at her.

Morgan faked the biggest grin she could. "After that monster win? Heck, Butler, I couldn't be happier."

Chapter 13

$\mathcal{L}$ily and Aiden were definitely having a good time, drinking and dancing at the Saint Anne's social. Even Sabrina was having fun. Yet to Morgan, absolutely nothing felt right. She'd have split an hour ago if she didn't have to worry about upsetting her sister.

"Come on, Morgan, it's about time I got you dancing," Aiden shouted across the big, round table as the band's lead guitar player hit the first few thundering chords of "I Love Rock 'n' Roll." "You're the best dancer in the place."

"Yeah, go for it, Morgan," Brett Clayton said. "Don't just sit there moping all night." Brett, there with Laura Vickers, could always be counted to throw fuel on any fire.

Lily shot Brett a glare before grasping Aiden's hand as he got up. "Let her be, Aiden. She's tired."

Aiden grinned down at his bride-to-be. "Okay, then, I guess you'll have to do." He tried to pull Lily to her feet, but she wasn't budging.

"Punch him, Lily," Sabrina piped up with a giggle. The three beers she'd drunk had clearly anaesthetized most of her shyness and jittery nerves.

Lily finally got up. "Sabrina, I assure you I have much better punishments in mind for my betrothed later tonight."

"Promises, promises," Aiden muttered as he swept an arm around his fiancée's trim waist and led her into the throng of dancers.

"They're so sweet together, aren't they?" Sabrina said with a wistful smile. "Aiden just loves her to death."

"Nothing could be sweeter." Morgan belted down a swallow of beer from her Solo cup. She loved her friends with all her heart and liked to have a good time as much as anybody, but tonight she felt like a millstone around their necks. She just couldn't shake her gloom. What had been a dreadful financial outlook for the B&B was now bordering on the catastrophic, and all it had taken was one lousy phone call.

Until then, it had been a pretty good day. She'd made it through her dunk tank duty, her team had won the tug-of-war challenge, and then she'd enjoyed a late barbecue lunch with Lily before watching the afternoon parade with Sabrina and the rest of the crowd that had lined Island Road. Led by the pair of big red trucks from the volunteer fire department, the parade had been a Seashell Bay tradition since before Morgan was born.

But not long after she and Sabrina got back from the parade, any joy she'd taken from the day had evaporated like morning fog under a hot sun. Without divulging any of the details, Kerwin Longstreet had called to inform her that his daughter's fiancé had called off the wedding. That meant he'd have to release all the rooms he'd booked at Golden Sunset for family and guests.

Morgan had almost dropped the phone to the floor.

She'd felt an immediate stab of sympathy for the bride, of course, but then she'd shuddered as the implications for Golden Sunset sank in. Only when Kerwin baldly asked if she could see fit to refund his deposit had her mind snapped back into sharp focus. In better days, she might have entertained giving him a partial refund. Not now though. Not even if it meant losing Longstreet's future business. While the deposit wasn't huge compared to what she would have made from all those occupied rooms, she needed every penny of it.

What future business would there be to lose anyway? Her hopes of meeting the mortgage and paying the bills until the end of August were dashed. Closure had gone from a frightening possibility to a devastating probability.

Morgan hadn't thought about much else since the call. She hadn't told Sabrina yet because she was still searching for some way to reassure her that this setback wasn't going to constitute a fatal blow. But Sabrina was the furthest thing from stupid, and Morgan knew that dog wasn't going to hunt. Still, she'd decided to let her sister have some fun tonight and delay sharing the bad news until tomorrow.

She let out a small sigh and watched her friends rock out on the dance floor. Aiden had been right about one thing—Morgan liked to dance. And she was pretty good at it too. When they were teens, she and Sabrina had spent endless hours listening to rock music on their boombox and dancing all over their house. And in college, Morgan had signed up for every dance class she could take. In fact, as a teacher, she always included a dance component in her classwork, no matter how young her students. She supposed that was one thing she could look forward to if

Golden Sunset went down the tubes—at least she could teach again.

"Jeez, look who just walked in the door," Sabrina whispered in Morgan's ear. "I guess he can't stay away from a party. Or, to be more accurate, from you."

Morgan whipped her head around toward the double doors that separated the church hall from the foyer. Ryan was leaning against the doorframe, scanning the crowded room. He wore a black silk shirt that showcased his broad shoulders, and tan chinos that made his legs look a mile long. His hair looked wet, as if he'd just showered. He looked so damn crazy hot that Morgan practically had to start fanning herself.

Had Ryan really decided to show up to be with her? Maybe he just wanted to dance and flirt with the other women there, which was a truly horrifying thought. She told herself she shouldn't care, but hell yeah, she cared. Heaven help her if he made a beeline for a hottie like Jessie Jameson or Tessa Nevin.

Get a grip, Morgan. Maybe he just wants to hang out with his friends.

She watched as Aiden caught Ryan's eye and pointed him toward their table near the center of the dimly lit room. While Morgan had no trouble seeing Ryan since he was standing in the light of the doorway, she doubted that he could make her out yet. Part of her wanted to crawl under the beer-stained tablecloth and hide before he did. And yet another part of her couldn't help feeling a thrill that he might have come to search her out. It sent her mind racing back to the Blueberry Festival social last year when they'd clung to each other dancing as if they'd made the most astonishing and wonderful discovery in the history of the entire world. She'd never felt such a powerful and surprising connection, and deep down she wanted it again.

Wanted it to be with Ryan.

Her heart pounding like a trip-hammer, Morgan tracked him as he wove his way through the tables, stopping to chat with his parents who were sitting with Lily's folks, Father Michael, and some other friends. Was he really going to hang out with the old folks for the evening?

About a minute later, though it seemed like an hour, Ryan gave his mother a peck on the cheek and headed straight toward Morgan.

"Hey, bro." Brett jumped up and pumped Ryan's hand before ushering him into some space he'd made between him and Josh. "I'll grab a chair for you."

As Brett borrowed a chair from a neighboring table, Ryan shook hands with Josh, then nodded to Laura, Sabrina, and Morgan. His eyes lingered for a moment on Morgan, but if there was any kind of message there, she couldn't decipher it.

"I guess you didn't want to ignore us after all," Sabrina said in the blunt manner she tended to adopt once she got hammered. "I'll switch seats with you for a price," she said with a snort.

When Morgan jammed her elbow into her sister's side, Sabrina responded with a phony wounded look.

Ryan just gave Sabrina a smile.

"Sit down, man," Brett said, shoving the chair at him. "I'll get you a beer. Anybody else ready for another?"

Morgan, Sabrina, and Laura all held up their hands. "Jeez, the women on this island are all lushes," Brett said before heading off.

"He's right, Ryan," Sabrina said. "You'd better stay

sober, because the way we're going, Morgan and I are going to need you to drive us home. Otherwise, Micah will confiscate our keys."

"Speak for yourself," Morgan countered. "One more beer and I'm out of here. Ryan can take *you* home if you want to get loaded. *More* loaded, I mean."

Sabrina grinned and flipped her the bird.

Ryan's gaze locked onto Morgan. "Hey, whatever you need."

The sudden flare of heat in his eyes told Morgan there was more than one meaning behind those words. Any doubts she'd had about who he'd come to see evaporated, leaving a flush of warmth in its place.

"You'd better accommodate me too, Ryan Butler," Laura piped up. "I'm claiming this slow dance with you right now."

"I thought you'd reserve that honor for Brett," Ryan said.

Laura flashed him a flirty grin. "I've always been more partial to soldiers than lobstermen."

Though Morgan knew that Laura and Ryan were old friends, it didn't stop her from feeling insanely jealous at the thought of tall, gorgeous Laura swaying across the floor in Ryan's arms, clinging to him the way Morgan had last summer.

"You're on, then, gorgeous," Ryan drawled, getting up and holding out his hand to Laura.

Morgan couldn't look at them on the dance floor. She knew she was being a total asshat and a big baby, but she turned to Sabrina and started talking earnestly about trivial details at Golden Sunset. Fortunately, her sister seemed too tipsy to tune in to how she was feeling.

When the song ended and the band's female singer announced that they'd be taking an extended break, it was time for karaoke, another island tradition for the past couple of decades. Morgan had belted out her share of songs over the years, always rock tunes unless Lily talked her into a duet, in which case she inevitably deferred to Lily's preference for country. Ryan brought Laura back to the table and then headed off, meeting up with Aiden at the bar.

So much for wanting to spend time with Morgan.

Jessie Jameson, looking cute as a button, fiddled with the karaoke machine while her boss, boatyard owner Mike O'Hanlon, took the microphone as emcee. He started with a mildly off-color joke, earning a reprimand from Father Michael and a laugh from everyone else. "Sorry, Father," he said with a sheepish grin. "Anyway, everybody knows Roy likes to open the festivities every year with his, ahem, unique version of that Stevie Wonder classic, 'You Are the Sunshine of My Life.' "

Half the room broke into applause while the other half groaned. Roy cranked himself up out of his chair and gave a low bow. Miss Annie, seated next to him, rolled her eyes at her boyfriend's dramatic gesture.

"Unfortunately, we're going to have to forgo that wonderful treat tonight," Mike went on, "because Roy's throat is acting up on him again. He said he's got a little head cold, though Miss Annie tells me he got hoarse yelling at the TV last night when the Red Sox were blowing that big lead."

More laughter from the peanut gallery.

"Hell, no," Roy groused in a scratchy voice after the din subsided.

"Hell, *yes*," Miss Annie countered. "Boys will be boys."

Despite her glum mood, Morgan couldn't help smiling. It wasn't a party on Seashell Bay unless Miss Annie and Roy were bickering.

She glanced over at the bar, where Aiden and Ryan seemed to be having a small argument. Whatever Aiden was saying, it made Ryan emphatically shake his head. Aiden kept at him though.

"So who's ready to kick things off tonight in Roy's stead?" Mike asked.

Aiden waved a hand. "Ryan and I are going to lead off with a duet, if that's okay with everybody. Since neither of us has been able to make it back here on July Fourth for years, it'd be a real privilege to give it our best shot. It's about time, right?"

People in the room started applauding, cheering, and whistling. Ryan seemed pained at first, looking straight at Morgan. The only times she'd ever heard him sing was in the church choir, but his voice had grown deep and rich when they were in high school, bypassing the crackly stage most young guys went through.

Morgan gave him a thumbs-up sign. Ryan rolled his eyes but smiled.

After a quick huddle with Jessie, Aiden looked relaxed in the corner of the dance floor as he held the karaoke mic while Ryan—with the other mic—shuffled his feet, looking embarrassed. It was incredibly endearing as far as Morgan was concerned.

Jessie slid a CD into the machine. The men switched their attention to the small screen in front of them.

"Folks, please don't take any message from this song

choice," Aiden said. "It just happens to be one Ryan and I both know."

Morgan recognized the song from the opening guitar notes—Garth Brooks's "Friends in Low Places." She couldn't help a chuckle, hoping none of her sometimes-prickly fellow islanders would take offense.

Aiden led off with the first verse, and then Ryan joined in on the chorus, adding his smooth bass to Aiden's baritone in a harmony that sounded pretty good to Morgan's ears. By the time the men reached the second rollicking chorus, more than half the people in the room were singing along. That clearly surprised Ryan and Aiden, who grinned at each other and started singing even louder. By the time they finished, just about everybody was standing and clapping. Morgan found herself applauding as hard as anybody, while Sabrina stuck two fingers in her mouth and blew an earsplitting series of whistles.

It was a stellar performance, and by the end of it, Ryan had clearly been enjoying himself.

The two guys returned to the table, shaking hands and getting high fives and fist bumps as they passed through the crowd. "Wow, *Ryan* can really sing," Lily said pointedly to her fiancé.

"Har, har, funny girl." Aiden said, thumping down onto his chair. "Anyway, I told him I hoped he wasn't going to let me embarrass myself up there."

Ryan smiled. "I've heard that tune in places so low it would make your hair curl. So I figured I might as well give it a shot when I'm in a room with the people I care about the most."

He looked straight at Morgan, his expression conveying so much sincerity that she was taken aback. Ryan rarely gave any glimpses into how he felt about Seashell Bay. Most of the time she thought he'd left the island so far behind that he barely even thought about it anymore.

Suddenly, she felt overwhelmed—by everything. A wave of anxiety swept through her.

"Whew, is it hot in here or is it just me?" she said, struggling to sound normal. "I'm going to have to grab a few breaths of fresh air."

Lily leaned over to whisper. "Want me to come?"

"Thanks, I'm fine. I really do just need a bit of air." *And a few moments to get my head back on straight.*

She hurried out through the foyer and down the rear steps of the hall onto the path that connected the church and the cemetery. The air outside was still warm and some humidity had set in, so there wasn't much relief. She raked both hands back though her hair, getting it off her face and behind her ears as best she could. She felt flushed, and a little sweat had already dampened her once-crisp, pink cotton blouse.

Even worse, she felt furious with herself for wanting Ryan as much as she did. A big part of her longed to head straight for her truck and take off back to the safety of her bedroom at the inn.

But she wasn't that much of a coward. She wouldn't run away from either Sabrina or her friends, no matter how uncomfortable she might feel under Soldier Boy's penetrating gaze.

Ryan quickly drained his beer and excused himself, claiming he needed a restroom break. He didn't want the others at the table to think he was chasing after Morgan, though that was exactly what he was doing.

He'd fought the temptation to show up at the social tonight. He'd gone back to the inn after the parade was over and done some more work because he thought it might distract him. But it hadn't. Morgan had never left his thoughts for more than a moment. He'd then headed to the Pot for dinner before going back to Golden Sunset after Morgan and Sabrina left. An evening holed up in his room with a book had seemed a safer option than having to face the lure of being with Morgan in a setting all too reminiscent of last summer's encounter between them at the VFW.

That plan had gone up in smoke when his mother called from the church hall and asked sarcastically if he was sick. She wouldn't have believed a lie anyway, so Ryan told her the truth about not wanting Morgan to feel uncomfortable. He knew he didn't have to elaborate since his mom and apparently everybody else on the island knew that he and Morgan were having trouble sorting out exactly how they felt about each other.

Mom, of course, had laid on guilt about how he was giving islanders a slap in the face by not showing up when it was the only time in recent memory that he'd been on the island for July Fourth. She'd then told him Morgan had been looking all evening like her dog just died, and he'd darn well better come down and try to cheer her up.

After ten minutes of straight-on mom lecturing, he'd given in, deciding to show up for a while and see what happened. And maybe it was time that he and Morgan finally got things out on the table, because it was pointless and frustrating for them to pussyfoot around each other for the rest of the summer.

Ryan slipped out the side door of the hall. About thirty feet away, Morgan stared up at the starlit sky above the stand of pines bordering the historic little cemetery. His adrenaline went immediately into overdrive at the sight of her. She looked sweet enough to eat in a sleeveless pink blouse and slim-fitting black capris.

Her body language sucked though, with her shoulders hunched and her arms wrapped around herself.

There was a low, steady hum from inside the church, but otherwise the warm summer night was silent except for the sound of crickets and the breeze sighing through the tall pines. That quiet was one of the things Ryan had always loved best about coming home to Seashell Bay.

War zones were rarely quiet.

"Communing with our sainted ancestors?" Ryan said in a soft voice as he walked over the grass toward her. Actually, she was pretty near her parents' graves, so communing probably wasn't far off the mark.

Morgan pivoted, and her lips opened in a little gasp. "What are you doing out here?"

Ryan quickly closed the gap between them. "I was worried about you."

She stared for a moment before giving him a tight smile. "No need. I was just getting a little overheated in there."

"I suppose my arrival didn't help matters, did it?" There was obviously more to her down mood than she was letting on.

She gave a casual shrug but looked about as uncomfortable as he'd ever seen her. Frustration rippled through him.

"Talk to me, Morgan. What can I do to make things right with you?"

She turned half away from him, her shoulders practically crawling up around her ears. He had to repress the instinct to pull her into his arms. He so wanted to make things better for her, but he was afraid he didn't know how.

"I'm sorry, Ryan," she said in a flat voice. "It's not really you. Well, it is, but that's not the big thing right now."

"Okay, then tell me what is."

"Remember the Longstreet wedding I told you about? The one that had booked all our rooms for a week?"

"Sure. You said I'd have to move out by then because you'd be full up."

"Well, no worries about that anymore. They called off the wedding. Cancelled the whole damn booking."

Shit. Again, he had to fight the instinct to yank her into his arms. "I'm really sorry, Morgan. I know what that booking meant to you."

"The difference between life and death?" Then she flapped a hand. "Cripes, that was stupidly dramatic, especially since you've actually lived through that sort of situation."

Ryan didn't know if she was being too dramatic or not, and he wasn't about to guess. "Hey, no worries, babe."

Morgan sighed and rubbed her forehead. "I'm racking my brains to come up with something, but our hole is getting so deep I'm not sure we'll be able to climb out. I really don't want to believe that this cancellation is fate's way of telling me it's time to face facts and walk away."

"Well, I don't believe in fate. Not that kind of fate anyway. If anybody can get the inn back on its feet, it's you. You'll find a way."

She flashed him a look halfway between a smile and

a grimace. "Okay, then maybe *you* can give Sabrina the bad news, Soldier Boy. She already thinks I'm a complete failure."

His heart twisted at her attempt to make light of the situation. Morgan had more guts than some of the guys he'd fought with, and he hated to see her up against the wall. "You're no kind of failure at all. As for Sabrina, the girl idolizes you. She always has."

Morgan made a soft scoffing noise.

"Hey, none of that crap, Merrifield," he said. "It's obvious to everyone how Sabrina feels about you. But you can't spend your whole life trying to insulate her from every bad thing that could possibly happen. She'll never be able to handle anything if you keep coddling her."

She plopped her hands on her hips. "Excuse me?"

"Okay, maybe that was out of line. But I was just trying to say that you shouldn't forget you've got your own life to live too. Stop being Sabrina's doormat."

The last person on Earth who should feel guilty about anything was Morgan, and he wanted her to hear that loud and clear.

"Ryan, would you do me a big favor and make sure Sabrina gets home in one piece?" Morgan finally said after a few tense moments of silence. "I think I need to get out of here."

He took her by the arm and gently reeled her in. "Not yet, honey, because I've got a thought about how we might attack the problem."

She resisted a bit but came reluctantly back. Then she let out a short laugh. "Okay, I guess a cemetery is the right place to hold this discussion anyway, given the state of my finances."

"Good, but just so you know, it would have to involve spending—no, investing—more money," he said.

"Oh, wow. I guess I could always fetch my old piggy bank from Pickle River," she said sarcastically.

"Very funny. Can I just lay out my idea?"

"Actually, I do have a few ideas of my own, but you go first."

"We run full out with an advertising blitz," he said, throwing it at her in one go. "As all out as we can afford, because we've got to reach more people. We've got to get to folks who've never heard of the B&B or the island or even Casco Bay. And we offer them discounts for last-minute bookings right through to the end of the summer."

Morgan slowly nodded. "Right, but that kind of advertising would be mad expensive. We need to find a way around that."

"Maybe we could concentrate on travel web sites, plus ads in a few selected newspapers."

"Nope. Still too expensive."

Screw that. He refused to let her lack of cash stand in their way. "Why don't you let me pick up the cost? I can afford it. What I can't afford is to let the inn go down, taking you and your sister with it."

More head shaking, now emphatic. "You know I can't let you do that."

"Sure you can. Because what's the alternative?"

She narrowed her eyes, and Ryan had the notion that she was doing a series of quick mental calculations rather than actually looking at him.

"All right, I agree, except for the part about you paying the costs," she finally said. "We definitely should advertise last-minute bookings, though not spend a lot of money on ads. But I'm thinking for that to work, the discounts would have to be huge. Forty percent, maybe even fifty. We need to go big, or go home."

"Now you're talking, babe. I'm happy to go big, as you well know."

"Seriously lame, Butler," she said, shaking her head.

He just grinned and carried on. "A full house at even half the normal rate is a hell of a lot better than empty rooms producing zero cash. Since you and Sabrina do all the work yourselves, your overhead is almost as much when the place is empty as when it's full. Most of what you'd take in through the discounted rates would go straight to the bottom line."

Morgan perked up, starting to look genuinely enthusiastic about the plan. "We should focus hard on the online options. A lot of sites don't charge that much for ads, and some are even free. Maybe that will leave me with some money to do one or two print ads."

"Great, but what about the cost?"

"I'll handle it somehow," she said. "The piggy bank might have enough left in it since we're talking pretty small potatoes, especially with the websites. I've already done a little research on them."

Okay, he'd let her play it like that—for now.

"Let's do it, then." He was surprised to feel his energy surging, excited that he was able to help her find a way out.

She wagged a playful finger at him. "Now, don't get too cocky. We can't keep up that kind of discounting for long—not with the mortgage and all our other fixed costs."

"No," he acknowledged, "but you might not even make it through the summer otherwise. Let's try it and see where things stand when Labor Day rolls around."

Morgan slapped a hand to her chest and widened her eyes. "Am I hearing you right, Ryan Butler? Because that sounded to me like you're going to be in this thing with Sabrina and me until at least Labor Day."

She looked so damn cute that he wanted to sweep her into his arms and kiss her senseless. But instinct told him that making a move on her now would be stupid. Ryan had spent the past couple of days thinking Morgan was ready to kick him out of Golden Sunset. At times, that prospect had even looked good. But he couldn't walk away from either the B&B or Morgan yet. And sure as hell not when she was making it clear that she wanted him to stay.

"You're hearing me exactly right," he said.

The smile that lit up her face made his heart go wonky. "Okay, let's do this thing. Let's chop the hell out of our rates and see what happens."

"Seal the deal with a hug?" Ryan said with a grin.

She rolled her eyes. "You are so bad, but why not?"

He enfolded her in his arms, enjoying the warm softness of her body against his for a couple of moments before forcing himself to let her go.

"We'd better go back inside before they send out a search party," he said. He could hear the gravel in his voice. "And I promise not to ask you to dance if you sing at least one karaoke number for me."

Morgan swiped a hand across her brow in mock relief, but her sweet smile told him he'd said exactly the right thing.

Chapter 14

$\mathcal{M}$organ felt like skipping from her office to the kitchen. "Chalk up another booking!"

"Yes!" Sabrina, up to her elbows in flour, dropped her wooden roller and pumped her fist. "For how long?"

"Two rooms for a full week in late August. Two couples are coming in by boat to explore the islands. They'll use Golden Sunset as their base."

"At 50 percent discount?" Sabrina asked, going back to rolling out dough.

"Forty, because this one's not last minute. Like Ryan said, it sure beats having empty rooms."

The day after her ads went up on a slew of social media and advertising websites, bookings had started to roll in and had continued at a decent pace for the past three weeks. For the Blueberry Festival, the inn was now booked solid, and every day in August had at least four rooms reserved already. People were hungry for cheap vacation deals.

The inn's projected bottom line now even looked better than before the horrifying wedding cancellation. Morgan had to wonder why she'd never thought of discounting rooms before and could only chalk it up to a bad combo of grief, false hope, and tunnel vision.

Then again, she was a teacher, not an innkeeper or marketing expert.

Though Ryan's room wasn't producing revenue, his work around the B&B was worth more than any rate she might have charged. And despite the ongoing temptation of having him close by, it was wonderful to have him around. He made her feel, well, grounded for lack of a better term, and Sabrina had told her that Ryan made her feel safe.

Unfortunately, that was going to change sooner than she'd hoped.

"Ryan's still sticking around at least through Labor Day, isn't he?" Sabrina asked.

Morgan poured a cup of coffee and stirred in some cream. "Yes, but he'll be moving out of here soon."

His mother had just let him know that a friend of hers was spending the month of August on the West Coast and that Ryan was welcome to use her house. Morgan could hardly blame him for wanting a place where he'd have more space and privacy.

Sabrina grimaced. "Can't you get him to change his mind? I'm getting used to having him around. Who knew such a hotshot could cook so well?"

The way Sabrina had finally warmed up to Ryan had been a revelation. She never made it easy for anyone—least of all men—to get close to her. But Ryan had managed to slowly breach her defenses. He'd made a point of working with her in the kitchen almost every day, most often deferring to her skills and saying he was eager to learn from her. The true turning point might have been the July Fourth social, when he'd danced with Sabrina more than anyone else. While most island men steered clear of Morgan's prickly sister, Ryan had made her feel like the belle of the ball.

Watching his kindness to her baby sister, Morgan had fallen for him even harder than before.

"Maybe *you* should tell him you want him to stay," she said to Sabrina, leaning her elbows onto the island counter, "since you two are getting so tight. I've already made it clear that he's more than welcome to keep his room as long as he wants."

Sabrina nodded, looking determined. "I will, then. He makes me feel like..." She stopped, searching for words.

"Like what?" Morgan prompted gently.

"Well, I guess he makes me feel like everything might turn out all right here after all."

Morgan's throat went a little tight. "I know what you mean, sweetie."

He'd done so much for them, not only reroofing the entire house but also with a dozen other repairs to the house and annex. Even though she kept asking him to give her the bills for the materials, Morgan strongly suspected he was tossing them in the trash.

That, of course, made her feel loads of guilt, exacerbated by the lack of time he spent kayaking. He squeezed in short trips on most days, but it was clearly not what he'd expected. The guy had come home to relax and explore the islands, not bust his ass fixing the never-ending stream of little problems that kept cropping up at Golden Sunset.

So she'd been pleased today when Ryan told her he intended to paddle all the way to Bailey Island and back. He'd be bone-tired by the time he finished such a long trip, so she and Sabrina had decided to surprise him with his favorite dish, spaghetti and meatballs.

When Morgan's cell phone rang, she glanced down at the call display. *Holly's home number.* Surprised that her friend wasn't at her Boston marketing firm at this hour on a workday, she snatched up the phone. "What's wrong?"

Holly's gentle laugh reassured her. "Calm down, sweetie. Boy, I thought I was the one needing a tranquilizer."

Morgan slumped against the counter. Man, her nerves *were* totally strung. "Seriously, are you all right? You never call from home at this hour. Hell, you're hardly ever at home, what with that crazy-ass job of yours."

Holly breathed a little sigh. "I'm okay. Well, sort of anyway."

"Tell me."

"Well, I was out for a run along the Charles yesterday when my left foot went out from under me. I can't even describe the pain, Morgan. It felt like something inside there was ripping in half."

"Oh crap," Morgan groaned.

"To make a long story short, an MRI showed I'd ruptured my *peroneus brevis* tendon. It's the one that allows you to flex your foot. Not a smart thing to snap, huh?"

"I'm so sorry. They can fix that surgically, can't they?" Morgan recalled that Roy Mayo had undergone an operation for a ruptured tendon in his foot a few years back. He'd suffered through a miserable convalescence but was as good as new now.

"Yes, it's a relatively simple procedure. You're supposedly in and out of the hospital in a few hours. I go under the knife the day after tomorrow."

"Wow, that's pretty fast."

"I'm very lucky that the orthopedic surgeon was able to schedule it so quickly."

Though her good friend sounded remarkably calm, Morgan couldn't help wondering how Holly would manage on her own during a long recuperation. It made Morgan wish she had the whole summer off as she had in the past. She'd have moved in with Holly until her friend was healed and fully mobile.

"You'll need someone to help you out for a few days," she said, her mind jumping ahead to the practicalities. "I'll drive down tomorrow." Sabrina could handle the inn for a little while, especially since Ryan would be around to share the load.

"No, no. Thank you, darling, we've got it covered. Aunt Florence is coming tomorrow night, and the next day she'll drive me up to Seashell Bay to convalesce. The surgeon tells me I absolutely have to keep my weight off my foot for four weeks, so I'll be with you guys for most of the summer. That's at least one good thing to come out of this stupid accident."

Ordinarily, Morgan would have been over the moon to have her lifelong friend come home for that length of time. But she simply couldn't imagine how Holly's elderly aunts, who'd raised her after their niece had been orphaned, would manage the amount of assistance Holly would need. "Are you sure Florence and Beatrice are going to be physically up to that? Aren't you going to need more, uh, robust help?"

Holly hesitated for a moment. "I do worry about that a little, especially for the first week or two while I'm getting used to crutches." She gave a mirthless little laugh. "I was wondering how I'd manage the stairs up to my bedroom, but Aunt Florence said they'd get somebody to clear out the dining room and set up a bed for me down there."

She'd be sleeping in the dining room? That was a crappy solution. "Look, Holly, you should let me help you instead. I'll take you to and from the hospital, and then we'll drive up to Portland when you're ready. You can have my room at the B&B, and I'll take one of the guest rooms upstairs. Remember, we've got a wheelchair ramp too."

When Holly started to protest, Morgan talked right over her. "You'll be in a wheelchair sometimes, right? Because crutches are awkward and exhausting. And by the way, I'm not taking no for an answer, so get that out of your stubborn head right now."

"Oh, all right," Holly said with a sigh. "You're truly the best, Morgan, but please don't think the reason I called was to ask you to do this."

"Of course not. It'll just make it easier on everybody, especially your dear aunts."

"Everybody except you," Holly said. "You don't exactly need another burden. Not with what you've already got on your plate."

"Holly Tyler, I'm more likely to sprout a pair of wings and fly across the Atlantic than I am to ever think of you as a burden," Morgan said firmly.

"What if you need that guest room? And I *will* pay you, by the way."

While the inn was indeed fully booked for one week— around the Blueberry Festival—Ryan would be gone by then. "No, you won't, and it's not a problem. I'll even try to add a few touches to my bedroom to make it as girlie as yours," she said.

Holly laughed. "That's impossible unless you paint the whole thing pink. Now, just out of curiosity, is Ryan still there?"

"For the moment, but he's going to spend August at a house that one of his mother's friends is letting him use."

"And how's it been going with him lately anyway? Or should I be minding my own business?"

The last time they'd talked, Morgan had filled Holly in on the gist of what had happened the day she and Ryan paddled to Peaks Island. "It's fine, but let's just say that being around him remains a challenge. Like every hour of every day."

"Details, girlfriend. I need details. I'm totally bored with being an invalid already."

"Relax, you'll have plenty of time to interrogate me after tomorrow."

"True enough," Holly said. "I can't wait to see you and Lily again. Being able to spend a month with the people I love most in the world is almost worth rupturing a tendon."

"I'm glad you said *almost* or I'd have to drive you straight to the psychiatric hospital after surgery." Holly was pretty much a workaholic.

Her friend laughed. "I guess I'd better call Aunt Florence now and let her know she's off the hook. I hope Sabrina doesn't mind me crashing at your place. You'll tell me if she has any problem with it, right?"

"She'll be fine. Sabrina loves you like a sister."

"I love her too, and I can't wait to see both of you. And Ryan too."

"I'll call you tomorrow when I'm leaving town," Morgan said.

"Okay. Love you lots," Holly said and disconnected.

Sabrina's eyes were wide when Morgan turned around. Clearly, her sister had heard everything. "You're okay with all that, right?" Morgan said.

Sabrina shrugged. "It's no big deal for you to go to Boston. Not as long as Ryan's here with me."

At Mackerel Cove, Ryan beached his kayak. He popped open the forward hatch and pulled out a clean Red Sox T-shirt so he could look half-assed presentable at the restaurant. By stopping here, he could walk the length of the small island to Cook's Lobster House for lunch.

He started off at a quick pace along the narrow road. There wasn't a lot to see—just a smattering of modest houses and the little motel with the miniature lighthouse out front that had survived since his last trip here. He had so much energy he could easily have run all the way to the restaurant and back. Since starting work at the B&B, he'd felt better physically every day—and mentally too. Helping Morgan and Sabrina had given him a different kind of purpose this summer. Kayaking, working out, and lazing around like he'd planned would've had a certain purpose too, but taking care of business at Golden Sunset made him feel like he was doing something important.

The work had been hard at times, and reroofing the B&B in blazing heat had been a bitch in particular. Yet it brought its own set of rewards, like the camaraderie he'd shared with Aiden and Roy as they worked and joked around on breaks. Like the joy in little Christian's eyes every time Ryan took the awkward, enthusiastic kid out for a kayak lesson.

But hands down the biggest reward came from Morgan. She'd thanked him about a million times, even for the most minor things, and had flatly credited him with saving the inn with his idea about last-minute bookings. Sabrina had grown closer to him too, which really surprised him. She'd even told him a few days ago that she sometimes wished he could stay forever.

Which was, of course, a completely crazy idea.

Still, moving out of the B&B wasn't going to be easy, because part of him wanted to stay with Morgan for the rest of the summer or maybe even longer. He loved coming downstairs every morning and seeing her in the kitchen or puttering around outside, usually in a tight little tee and cute pair of shorts that showcased her long, gorgeous legs. She always greeted him with a sweet smile and a quip that seemed to start the day off on the right foot.

The truth was he loved seeing her at any time of day, though it was murder to have to be so careful with her. Ryan wanted her as much as ever, but he'd meant it when he said the ball was in her court. Unfortunately, it looked like she intended to keep that ball carefully tucked away, at least for now.

So it was probably a good thing that his mom's friend was letting him use her house for a month. And maybe it was time to focus a lot harder on what he was going to do with his life instead of getting so comfortable in Morgan Merrifield's cozy little world. At this point, it was probably better for both of them if he moved out of Golden Sunset and generally moved along.

After all, he would be leaving the island once the summer ended. Then life would get back to normal—which meant he'd see Morgan, his family, and his friends only once a year.

He shrugged off the discomfort that came with that

thought, picking up his pace. As he neared Cook's Lobster House, he gazed across to the picturesque little harbor and bridge. The blue of the Atlantic, gently rolling in the distance, made him stop and suck in some deep breaths of fresh sea breeze. Lobster boats were everywhere in sight, both moored in the harbor and sailing on the open sea past the granite slabs of the Cribstone Bridge. It was living art that he'd seen a hundred times, serene and beautiful. And for some reason today, it stopped him dead in his tracks.

Man, I'm really going to miss this.

The realization hit him like a thunderbolt, mentally rocking him back on his heels. He'd always enjoyed coming home to Maine a few days every year and, yes, he loved the place. But he'd never really missed it when he was away. It was great knowing that places like Seashell Bay could still exist in the world, but he'd never had any desire to live in them. Sleepy little towns just weren't for him.

Now, though, the prospect of coming back for only a handful of days a year no longer seemed nearly enough.

A gray-bearded lobster fisherman in Grundéns waved at him from the stern of his moored boat. Ryan grinned and gave the old guy a wave and a thumbs-up. Everybody waved or said hello when you passed on the road or at sea, no matter if you were an islander or a CFA. It couldn't help but make you feel pretty good, even if a lot else might be wrong.

In the past, every time Ryan had boarded the ferry to the mainland after a visit home, he couldn't help feeling a sense that he was making his escape from a life that he feared would bore the hell out of him. He'd always needed his world to be bigger than a little island in Casco Bay or even a city like Portland. But now, this part of the world was starting to feel more like a refuge than a prison, someplace he really might want to be someday.

And Ryan's instinct told him that the unexpected feeling started and ended with Morgan.

Chapter 15

 $\mathcal{H}$ er face flushed with the effort, Morgan maneuvered Holly's wheelchair across the gangway and up the concrete ramp from the ferry to the dock. Ryan's body tensed as he suppressed his urge to elbow his way through the teeming crowd to help her. People were coming off the jammed boat in a solid wave, many of them towing suitcases or carts, so he had to shift out of the heavy stream and wait.

Though Morgan had been gone less than forty-eight hours, Ryan had missed her. The B&B had felt weird without her. And over a beer on the patio late last evening, Sabrina had confessed tearfully that she couldn't even imagine her sister going back to Pickle River after all this time, and that just the thought made her sick. That hadn't squared with what Morgan had said about her sister feeling more hopeful, but Ryan had taken Sabrina's words to heart. He couldn't blame her, because a lot of things felt up in the air to him too.

"Hey there, soldier," Holly called out as Morgan wheeled her through the throng. "It's awesome to see you again, though these wouldn't have been my preferred circumstances."

Ryan leaned down and gave Holly a warm hug. She looked as gorgeous and put together as always, but her gaze revealed both pain and fatigue from yesterday's operation.

He glanced down at the blue cast covering her left leg from below her knee to her toes. "Some people will do just about anything to get a few weeks off work."

"Jerkwad," Holly shot back with a grin. "Just because I'm in Seashell Bay doesn't mean I can't work. Ever heard of the Internet?"

"Yeah, word about it reached the island yesterday. Us rubes here in Seashell Bay hear it's really something." He leaned past Holly and gave Morgan a quick hug. It was one-sided and perfunctory since she didn't let go of the wheelchair. "You put the bags in cargo?"

"Of course. Holly doesn't travel light," Morgan said. "Ever."

Holly glanced back over her shoulder, smiling at Morgan. "Well, certainly not when I'll be staying this long." Then she looked at Ryan. "How wonderful is this woman anyway? I ask you, how many other people would turn over their bedroom to a friend for weeks?"

· "She's special all right," Ryan said, smiling at Morgan. He hadn't been surprised that she was bringing Holly back here to recuperate. Morgan had always been like that, generous almost to a fault.

Morgan laughed. "Oh, stop it, you two. I'm not doing anything special. Islanders always take care of each other, or don't you fancy-pants mainlanders remember?"

"Mainlanders?" Holly said with a smile. "Isn't that the pot calling the kettle black, dear heart?"

When Morgan's gaze went flat, Ryan figured she was thinking about her teaching career up on the mainland.

She seemed to shrug it off. "There's the luggage now," she said brightly as deckhands wheeled several polyethylene-wrapped carts off the boat. "I'll grab it."

"Hold on," Ryan said. "Just show me which ones are Holly's."

"Take your time," Holly said. "I'm perfectly happy just sitting here and enjoying the sun and the lovely sea air. In Boston, I sometimes forget what it's like."

"Yeah, nothing beats the combination of stinky bait and diesel fuel down here by the dock." Ryan grinned at Holly before following Morgan to the cargo carts.

"You can grab those two." Morgan pointed to a matched set of hard-shell suitcases in some plaid pattern. "I'll get the other one." She reached into the cart and pulled up a stuffed garment bag. "Oh, and we can't forget the crutches."

Morgan put down the bag and started to reach for them.

Ryan grasped her hand. "Let me get them."

Her flushed face went even rosier before he let her hand go.

Ryan lifted the metal crutches and both suitcases out of the cart and set them down. The suitcases had straps to tie them together for wheeling, so he started working on that. "Didn't you tell her there's a washer and dryer at the B&B?" he joked.

She rolled her eyes. "You think this is a lot of clothes? You should see the walk-in closet in her apartment. It's like a whole freaking floor of Neiman Marcus. I wanted to move in."

"She must be doing great at that marketing firm then."

"I get the impression she's something of a star," Morgan said, slinging the garment bag over her shoulder.

"Couldn't happen to a nicer person."

Morgan nodded, going kind of solemn again. "She's worked hard for her success. And you know how much she's already had to overcome in life."

Holly had lost both her parents and her husband, Drew Tyler, an army helicopter pilot. Drew had been killed along with a group of SEALs and Rangers when a Taliban RPG took out his chopper's tail rotor late in the Afghanistan war. That tragedy had hit Ryan hard too. He'd grieved both for Holly and for the family of a Ranger buddy he'd fought alongside.

"Yeah, I know," he said quietly. He realized again how lucky he was to have survived the war, coming home to his family and friends.

To Morgan.

"Let's load up and get home," she said as she placed the garment bag on Holly's lap and grasped the handles of the wheelchair. "I think we could probably all use a drink."

"A drink will do a better job than crummy pain pills," Holly said. "Damn the doctor's orders."

"Roger that, ladies." Ryan tucked the crutches under one arm and hauled the heavy suitcases with the other, leading the pack down the dock to Morgan's truck.

An hour and a half later, Morgan was happy to be finally alone with Holly. After wolfing down two of Sabrina's blueberry-cranberry muffins, Ryan had headed off to paddle over to Long Island to have a beer with a fellow kayak enthusiast. Sabrina had stayed longer to chat before going off to her room for a power nap. Holly was still nursing the last of her double Glenlivet as Morgan put on a pot of coffee.

"Ryan looks so amazing," Holly said, parked by the kitchen table. "He's been ripped and gorgeous forever, but honestly I've never seen him look so..." She shook her head, as if words failed her. "Happy," she finally settled on.

Morgan pulled a pair of mugs out of the cupboard. "It's because this time he feels like he's actually a part of this place, not just a visitor to the island. I think it's made a big difference."

Holly slapped a hand to her chest. "Don't tell me that our international man of mystery actually told you that. He who never speaks a word of emotion?"

Well, that part hadn't changed all that much, although he'd allowed Morgan a few peeks into how he felt about life.

"It's more just a feeling I get," she said vaguely. "And he's been so great around here. So committed. Not just with the repairs either. Like I said, it was Ryan's idea to offer deep-discount deals for the rest of the summer." She scrunched up her nose at her friend. "Which I'm sure you would have told me if I'd thought to ask, you being a marketing guru and all."

"Maybe I could have come up with something like that. I just wish I'd known more about how rough things were here at the B&B before yesterday," Holly said.

"I know I should have been more forthcoming," Morgan admitted.

Holly tilted her head, her auburn hair falling in perfect waves around her shoulders. "But you're obviously getting more optimistic now."

"What choice do I have?" Morgan said in a light tone. "The damn thing refuses to die and let me get back to my real life."

"You'll figure it out," Holly said, smiling. "You always do. Nothing ever stops you."

"Yeah, well, better keep your fingers and toes crossed. Sabrina's counting on me, and I'm feeling the weight a little more every day." Morgan poured the coffee and brought the mugs over to the table before going back to fetch cream and spoons.

"Returning for a moment to the subject of your hottie handyman," Holly said, "I'll tell you something else that hasn't changed—the way the dude has looked at you ever since the festival social last summer. And from what I saw in his eyes from the moment he caught a glimpse of you pushing me off the boat, he still wants to do you, girlfriend. Like, big-time."

"I guess you're feeling better, since the interrogation is now commencing," Morgan said drily.

Holly laughed. "You bet. Am I to assume that nothing's happened yet on that score? You're not keeping secrets, are you?"

"Oh, he's made a couple of moves," she said, trying to sound casual. "But I made it clear that I wasn't summer-fling material. You know that's not me."

"It must have been tempting though. He's so freaking sexy. Hard not to get a little hormonal when he's around."

No kidding. "Ryan's always been a great guy." Morgan exhaled a sigh. "But he's a soldier, Holly. You and I feel the same way about getting involved with a guy like that."

Holly had made it crystal clear on more than one

occasion that, if she ever married again, it couldn't be to a man who carried a gun for a living.

Her friend's smile faded, and she looked thoughtful. "Are you sure Ryan's committed to that kind of life? He did leave the army after all. Maybe the next step will be to get completely out of dangerous jobs."

"He told me it's all he knows how to do. I can't just hold my breath waiting for the possibility that he might give it up. Anyway, all that's academic. If Ryan wants anything from me other than our friendship, it's some sex for the summer. That's it."

"Well, a lot of women would be more than happy to take Ryan on any terms," Holly said. "But if sleeping with him isn't right for you, I'm sure he fully respects that."

"He does. But it doesn't mean it isn't crazy hard being around him every day, looking but not touching. I tell myself at least twice a day that I'm certifiably insane not to take advantage of what's clearly there." Morgan paused a moment, thinking. "And it's not just a physical thing for me. I'm finally feeling like I know Ryan, and I like what I'm learning. A lot."

"Except for the soldier slash mercenary part, huh?"

Before Morgan could say yes, a loud knock sounded on the front door. She got up and hurried down the hallway to see Micah waiting on the other side of the screen door.

She opened it, smiling up at the six-foot-four deputy sheriff. "What brings you to my humble establishment, Deputy? Am I flouting some municipal bylaw? Or are you looking for Ryan? He's over on Long Island, meeting a buddy."

As if I didn't know exactly what brought you here today, my friend.

Micah pushed his sunglasses up onto the top of his head. "Actually, I just heard that Holly was going to be here for a while to recuperate. I wanted to drop over and let her know that I'll be happy to help with anything she needs."

"That's nice," Morgan said, backing out of the way so he could get his brawny self inside. "She's very tired though."

"I only planned to stay a minute anyway. Got a ton of paperwork to take care of back at the station," he said with a sardonic smile.

"One can only imagine," Morgan said, playing along. "Criminals are proliferating on this island at an appalling rate."

"I'll say. Can you believe Boone Cleary's oldest boy tagged the side of the fire hall last night?"

"Oh, no," Morgan said, clapping a hand to her cheek. "Graffiti in Seashell Bay? You'd better stomp on that before everything goes to hell in a handbasket around here."

Actually, the only crime on the island was an occasional drunk and disorderly charge, usually involving some visitor from the mainland. Once in a blue moon, one of the locals teetered on the edge of more serious trouble, but Morgan knew Micah always did his best to pull whoever was screwing up back from the brink.

Micah laughed. "Don't worry. I had him down there all day scrubbing it off. And after the lecture Boone gave him, I almost felt sorry for the kid."

"Is that Deputy Lancaster I hear giving you a hard time?" Holly shouted from the kitchen. "Tell him to get his sorry ass over here and say hi to me."

Something seemed to spark in Micah's dark gaze when he heard Holly's voice. Morgan had to smother a grin.

"None other." Morgan led him to the kitchen, where Micah got down on one knee beside Holly's wheelchair, wrapping his muscular, tanned arms around her for a squeeze. Her willowy figure was practically swallowed up in his embrace.

"I'm sorry about your foot, Holly. What rotten luck." He got back on his feet and gazed down at her. "But you look fantastic, as always. And happy. Those pain meds must be something good."

Holly gave him the beautiful, sweet smile that was the envy of every girl on the island, especially since it attracted men like flies to honey.

"You are such a smart-ass, Deputy Lancaster," Holly said.

He snorted. "Yeah, that's me. Always kidding around."

If there was anyone on the island who wasn't a kidder, it was Micah, and everyone knew it too. He was a total good guy, but he took life very seriously.

"Coffee, Micah?" Morgan asked.

"I'd better not, thanks. I'm sure you two have a lot to talk about and didn't need me barging in here." He focused his dark, intent gaze on Holly. "Holly, I just wanted to let you know that if there's anything you need—anything at all that I can do to help out—you just have to call."

Morgan had an idea of something practical Micah might do to help but wasn't sure she should be dredging up ways for him to spend more time with Holly. Still, when she looked at the obvious sincerity in his eyes, she couldn't hold back. "I can think of one way you could help, Micah."

"Name it."

"She won't be able to get around on crutches very well,

so I intend to take her for some walks in her wheelchair. I could use a hand with that if you have some time."

"Hold on," Holly said, shaking her head at Morgan. "I don't want you struggling to push me up the hills around here. You could lose your grip." Her chocolate-brown eyes took on a mischievous glint. "And I'd go barreling out of control down the hill and fly right into the bay."

"Oh, like I'd ever let that happen," Morgan said indignantly.

Micah waved a hand to cut them off. "Say no more. It'll be my pleasure to take you for some walks, Holly."

Holly smiled. "That's settled, then."

"How about tomorrow afternoon?" Micah said.

Holly blinked, looking a little startled. "Um, okay, if you're off duty then."

"I'm not, but I'm not chained to my cruiser." He tapped the small radio unit attached to his shoulder.

"So, Ryan's over on Long?" he asked.

"Kayaked over. Dude must be aiming for the Olympic team," Morgan said.

Micah shook his head. "Man, he really loves that little thing, doesn't he? I can't see the attraction myself. I'll take my big powerboat any day."

"Ryan says paddling keeps him in shape both physically and mentally," Morgan said. "I get what he means too. He's been giving me a few lessons, and I love it."

And looking at his gorgeous, half-naked self isn't too hard to take either.

Unfortunately, she wouldn't be enjoying that particular benefit for much longer.

Chapter 16

$\mathcal{R}$yan stared at the ceiling, cursing the fact that he couldn't sleep despite the long paddle this afternoon. After dinner with the ladies, he'd also gone for a walk along the beach to stretch his muscles before heading upstairs to his room to read until he dozed off.

That had been more than three hours ago, and his mind continued to twist and roll like a giant roller coaster. It was almost August, and Labor Day wouldn't be long in coming. Decisions would have to be made soon enough—decisions keeping him awake tonight.

Like, what the hell was he going to do with the rest of his life?

At nearly two in the morning, the big old house rested silently about him. The only sound Ryan heard was the faint, rhythmic hiss of the ocean waves as they broke on the beach below the inn and slapped against the pilings of the dock. The noise should have propelled him toward sleep, but so far it hadn't. Frustrated, Ryan threw off the light quilt and slid out of bed. He'd slip downstairs, grab a glass of ice water, then come back and read some more in the cushioned rocking chair. Maybe that would finally do the trick.

He didn't bother to put anything on over his T-shirt and boxers. No one was up now because he'd have heard—the walls of the old house could barely stop a whisper. As he opened his door, he looked at Morgan's directly across the hall. She'd moved into that room so Holly could have her bedroom in the annex.

And yeah, he'd already fantasized about softly opening Morgan's door and slipping into bed with her.

He suspected that was one of the things keeping him up tonight—pretty much literally—as thoughts of her took over his imagination. What would she be wearing? Flannel pajamas? A camisole and little lace panties, or an oversized T-shirt? Even in PJs, she'd be sexy as hell. He'd love to strip her naked before kissing every inch of her soft, golden skin and taking it from there. The fact that they'd have to do it all in silence would make it even more interesting.

He turned down the hallway toward the stairs, moving carefully to avoid making any more noise than necessary on the creaky pine floorboards. When he grabbed the newel post to swing down onto the staircase, it hit him, stopping him dead.

Smoke.

Was it coming from outside? There were occasional tree fires on undeveloped parts of Seashell Bay. Not that a blaze in one of the island's forested areas was welcome, but they rarely caused damage to homes or property. He hoped to God that was the origin of the odor.

He glanced toward the window at the end of the hallway. The casement was open a couple of inches. Maybe he could smell it from there.

He swung around, all his senses on full alert. He didn't get far down the hallway before it became sickeningly clear that the smell was not outside. It was above him and was growing stronger. Stopping under the attic hatch, Ryan stretched up with his right arm to see if the wood was warm to the touch. Before his hand reached the surface, he saw smoke starting to squeeze through the gaps around the door.

Fuck. Fire in the attic.

His gut twisted at the thought of all the old wiring in the house, wiring he'd known needed to be replaced.

The hallway smoke detector should be going off in seconds. Wisps of smoke were already filtering toward it along the ceiling. His instinct was to yank down the hatch and climb up the ladder to take a look, thinking the fire might still be containable.

When he gingerly touched the hatch door, it was already hot. And now smoke had started to seep out in a steady stream. He was pretty sure there was no time to run down to the kitchen and race back up with the fire extinguisher. By the time he got up into the attic, smoke could be thick enough to kill people, and he couldn't take that risk—and sure as hell not one in a wood-frame building where ten people were sleeping. The fact that there was a young woman on crutches and an elderly guest who wobbled with practically every step made any risk taking out of the question.

The alarm started to beep.

Get moving!

"Fire! Fire! Everybody up and out!" Ryan yelled as he started to pound on the doors of the rooms that were occupied by guests. He gave each door a couple of sharp knocks before he reached Morgan's at the end of the hallway. He hammered once and threw it open. "There's a fire in the attic and a lot of smoke already up here. We've got to get everybody out right now."

Morgan, looking disoriented, was feeling around for her robe on the bed. "A fire? In the attic?"

"Let's go!" he barked.

She rolled out of bed and shoved her feet into a pair of Crocs, in the process answering Ryan's earlier question. She'd been sleeping in a pink sleeveless T-shirt and lacy white panties that were not much more than a scrap of fabric.

Ryan tore his eyes away. "Can you take care of the guests? I'm going down to get Holly and Sabrina. I'll come back up as soon as Holly's safe."

"I've got it, Ryan. Go!" she ordered as she flung her robe on. He could tell she was scared as hell, but he didn't have time to reassure her.

In the hallway, the smoke was already heavy near the ceiling and sinking fast.

Morgan rushed out and called after him. "Don't worry about Sabrina—she can take care of herself." She was punching numbers into her phone. "I'll call 911, and I'll make sure everybody up here gets outside."

Ryan was relieved to see she'd pulled herself together so fast. He turned and raced for the stairs. A couple of guests had now poked their heads out their doors. "Please get downstairs and outside now," he shouted at them. "Don't dress or try to gather up belongings. There's no time."

"Don't you have a damn fire extinguisher?" Frank Bairstow growled from the door of the room next to Ryan's.

"Get me one, and I'll go up there and douse the damn thing!"

"Frank, the fire department is on the way," Morgan yelled. "Please, everyone, head downstairs as fast as you can, and stay well away from the building."

Ryan hesitated at the top of the stairs. He wanted to get down to Holly fast, but would Morgan be able to handle the belligerent old guy who apparently figured he could take care of the fire single-handedly?

"Ryan, go get Holly," Morgan said, giving him a little push. "I've got this."

The steel in her voice told Ryan she did. He flew down the staircase, barely touching the steps, and raced through the kitchen into the annex to Morgan's bedroom. The door was open, and Holly was sitting on the edge of the four-poster bed, looking slender and frail in her thin night-gown. Sabrina was trying to maneuver the wheelchair into a position where Holly could slide off the bed into it.

"I've got her, Sabrina," Ryan said, reaching for Holly. "Just bring the wheelchair, okay?"

He had to give Morgan's sister props. Instead of coming upstairs to see what the commotion was all about, she'd wisely decided to get Holly safely out of the house.

"What's happening up there?" Sabrina's eyes darted back and forth between him and Holly. She was wearing a navy T-shirt and white sleep shorts plastered with little red hearts, and she looked scared to death.

Ryan scooped Holly up in his arms. Though she was tall, her slender frame carried no more than a hundred twenty-five pounds, and Ryan barely felt her weight. "There's a fire in the attic and a lot of smoke upstairs. Morgan's called the fire department."

Holly gasped. "How did it start?"

"Maybe the wiring. It's old." Ryan angled her through the narrow door, across the kitchen, and out into the graveled parking area. Sabrina followed close behind, squeezing the wheelchair out the screen door.

As Ryan gently lowered Holly into the chair, Sabrina groaned. "Oh my God. Look at the smoke coming out that upstairs window."

Ryan glanced up. Smoke was billowing out the second-floor window at the end of the hallway. His insides torqued as he thought of Morgan up there trying to wrangle the guests all by herself. "Sabrina, I'm going back inside. Stay with Holly, okay?"

"Hurry!" Sabrina said tearfully. "Please don't let anything happen to Morgan."

Ryan told himself that Morgan was strong and smart and brave, so she'd be fine. Maudie and Morry Granger, however, were a different story. They were in their late seventies, and Morry was seriously overweight and arthritic while Maudie suffered from balance problems that had been giving her on-and-off trouble walking, even with her cane.

"The Bairstows are out!" Sabrina said, pointing a finger toward the front of the house. Pugnacious Frank and his wife Maureen had emerged and were hurrying around the side of the house toward them.

"Two guests down, four to go," Ryan growled. He rushed back in through the same door.

Only a couple of minutes had passed since Ryan barged into Morgan's room and scared her half to death, but she needed to get the Grangers outside before they collapsed from smoke inhalation. The Bairstows had already gone down to safety, and the gay married couple from Toronto—Owen and Nolan—had emerged from their room a second time, now dressed in T-shirts and sweat pants and clutching computers under their arms. Morgan knew those two fit thirtysomethings could take care of themselves, so she focused her full attention on the older couple.

Outside the Grangers' room, the closest one to the attic hatch, the smoke was so heavy and acrid that Maudie was choking as Morgan slipped her arm around the elderly woman's waist. Morry struggled to support his wife on the opposite side. Morgan wished she were strong enough to lift Maudie in a fireman's carry and lug her to safety, but the woman weighed at least fifty pounds more than she did. Morry was in no shape to help much either, though he was trying mightily to do as Morgan directed.

Even in the chaos of the smoke, the heat, and Maudie's gasping behind her husband's handkerchief, Morgan couldn't stop thinking about how this disaster could have happened. Maybe it was the ancient wiring Ryan had warned her about. In any case, the fire was on her. Her obsession with getting things done on the cheap had probably caused this catastrophe.

She gave herself a mental slap. There would be time for self-recrimination later. The fire chief would be able to tell her what caused the blaze, and in the end, it didn't much matter what started it anyway. All that truly mattered was getting people out alive.

But she wanted to burst into tears that her father's beloved inn was probably entering its death throes.

"Morry, get my purse," Maudie cried as Morgan and

her husband shuffled her toward the stairs. "It's on the dresser."

"No way," Morry grunted. His bald head was streaming sweat. "The damn roof could fall down on us any second. To hell with the purse, Maudie. You're all that counts. Everything else can be replaced."

Maudie managed a smile at her husband. "Thank you, dear heart."

Morgan felt like she was in a walking nightmare, with her heart racing and her airways already burning from smoke. But her sick feeling was eased by the moment of tenderness between the Grangers. Morry might be an out-of-shape, grumpy old guy, but he was a hero in Morgan's book.

By the time they reached the second step down, Ryan was already bounding up the stairs, three at a time. The smoke was thick enough that Morgan thought he might barrel into her before he grabbed the banister and jerked to a stop.

"Ma'am, can I carry you down?" Ryan had obviously assessed the situation instantly. "It'll be a lot faster that way and safer too."

"Yes, yes. Take her, Ryan," Morry said, coughing. "Get her out of here."

Ryan carefully eased Maudie over his shoulder, clutching her thighs after making sure her flannel nightgown was pulled down past her knees. All Morgan could feel at that moment was overwhelming relief that Ryan was here. Holly and Sabrina must be safe, and now he was making sure the Grangers would get out too. The inn might wind up burning to the ground, but Ryan had saved them all.

What am I going to do without him?

She shoved that desperate thought aside, summoning up all her energy as she put her arm back around Morry's waist.

He surprised her by pushing away. "I'm fine, Morgan. I can do this."

Morgan wasn't so sure. She stuck close to him, her hand gripping his arm as they descended together. By the time they made it three more steps down, Ryan and Maudie had already disappeared out the wide-open front door. Morgan could barely see with her stinging, watery eyes, and Morry coughed and hacked every step of the way until they were finally outside. With Ryan's help, he slowly folded himself down onto the grass right next to Maudie, where he put his fleshy arm around her shoulders and hugged her close.

Blinking her eyes clear, Morgan rushed over to Holly, who was clutching the arms of her wheelchair with white fingers. Sabrina was rigid beside her as she stared up at the house with a look of abject horror on her ashen face. When Morgan followed her sister's gaze, her stomach dived at the sight of huge billows of black smoke pouring out the gable vents on either end of the house. Though the fire hadn't yet burned through the attic floor when she was inside, Morgan knew it might not be long before flames penetrated down and set the entire old structure ablaze.

Tears streamed down Sabrina's cheeks. "This can't be happening, Morgan. Not after Daddy. Not after everything we've gone through."

Morgan hugged her sister. "We're going to be okay, sweetie. We're together, and that's all that really matters."

On the other side, Holly grabbed Morgan's hand and squeezed. "At least everyone's safe," she said. "And Sabrina was a real hero, helping Ryan get me out."

Morgan smiled at her friend, blinking back tears as she held on to her sister.

While Sabrina would have been able to help Holly to safety, and she and Morry might have been able to get Maudie out in time, Morgan knew it would have been a very close thing. That was brutally, sickeningly clear to her, especially now as she looked again at the volume of black smoke pouring out of the house. "I'm just thankful Ryan was here. I don't know what we would have done without him."

She clamped down hard on semi-hysterical tears. She would *not* lose it in front of Holly or her guests, or her poor sister. People would be counting on her to cope, to take care of them, to find them somewhere to go. She had to turn her mind to that and fast, even as she struggled to comprehend the enormity of what was happening to the inn. The Grangers would be all right. Morry's cousin, Andrew, could take them in temporarily at his house near Paradise Point. But vacationers like Owen and Nolan and the Bairstows had nowhere to go at this hour. Morgan would have to ensure they had somewhere to sleep, at least for tonight.

Ryan came up and pulled both Morgan and Sabrina into a sheltering embrace. "You guys did great."

"Thanks. You too," Sabrina said. She moved away to stare again at the inn.

Morgan let herself melt into the warmth of Ryan's body, resting her head against his muscular shoulder for a brief moment before she realized that Holly had started to shiver. Maudie also had her arms wrapped tightly around herself, obviously cold too. "I'm going back into the annex for some blankets," she said. "People are cold."

"Like hell you are," Ryan said in a low rumble. "I'll go. Where are they?"

Hearing the steel in his voice, Morgan knew it was pointless to argue. "In the linen closet across from Sabrina's room. Bring everything you can."

"You got it." Ryan sprinted across the lot and into the annex through the kitchen door.

The fire trucks arrived a minute later, lights flashing. The ladder truck was first, followed by the engine, and at the rear of the parade came Fire Chief Frank Laughlin in his department's SUV. Josh Bryson was the first man out of the ladder truck, and Morgan raced over to him. "Everyone's out, Josh, so don't worry about that. It looks like the fire started in the attic."

"You're a hundred percent sure everyone's out?" Josh said. "And you're okay?"

"A hundred and ten percent sure," Morgan answered. "We have six paying guests, plus Holly and Ryan. Sabrina's out too. All fine, I think, though Jessie should check those two over." She pointed to Maudie and Morry. "They're not very healthy to begin with."

Josh made a gesture to Jessie, one of the EMTs, as Laughlin strode over, his radio microphone in his hand.

"Morgan says it's clear, Chief," Josh said.

"Good. Do you know if the fire is still confined to the attic?" he said to Morgan.

"It was when I got out a few minutes ago. That's all I can tell you."

Laughlin nodded. "We're going to try attacking the fire

through the gable ends. That looks like the best chance to minimize the damage to the interior."

Minimize the damage.

The words slashed through Morgan like a dozen spinning blades. She wasn't dumb enough to think the damage would be anything less than horrific, not when the firefighters were going to flood the attic with water from their high-pressure hoses. Much of the house and furniture would be a sodden shambles, even if everything wasn't destroyed by fire and smoke. The only question in her mind was whether or not the structure itself could be saved.

She watched a pair of firefighters power through the front door. Others maneuvered the ladder truck into place at the chief's direction, raising the ladder toward the gable end at the front of the house. Though the Seashell Bay firefighters were volunteers, except for the chief, Morgan had total confidence in their skill and dedication. She'd grown up with most of them and knew they were all really good guys who would do their utmost to save Golden Sunset.

She could only pray for their success because the inn's insurance coverage was pretty bad. Though it would cover some of the costs, she'd have to absorb a big loss thanks to her poor dad's misguided attempt to save money with the crappy policy he'd signed shortly before his death.

But at the end of the day, who was she to criticize? Dad had done his best, and it wasn't on his watch that a houseful of guests had almost been killed in a fire that probably could have been prevented.

That was all on her.

Chapter 17

$\mathcal{R}$yan stared up at the ceiling fan that rotated lazily above him. It had been daylight for hours already, and he'd heard his father leave for his mooring before six. He'd risen and quietly made himself a cup of coffee while his mom remained in bed, then he'd showered, dressed, and lain back down again on his bed. He couldn't think of a damn thing except Morgan and the B&B.

But there wasn't much he could do until nine o'clock. That was when he and Morgan had agreed to meet back at Golden Sunset. He didn't even feel like taking his usual morning run. All he wanted to do now was to focus on what the hell he could do to help her deal with this catastrophe.

Growing up in this house, Ryan hadn't experienced many sleepless nights, conking out like most kids for nine or ten hours. Only when he joined the army and was shipped overseas did he find out what sleepless nights truly meant—senses tuned to every noise, every smell, every movement around him, even a slight breeze or a faint rustle.

Last night had been a little like that, lying awake in his creaky old bed and endlessly going over the horrifying events of the night. He'd felt so freaking helpless as he'd watched the fire crew working to keep the house from being reduced to a smoldering heap of ash. Watching a tight-lipped Morgan comfort her sobbing sister and the distraught guests, he'd wanted to comfort her, but she'd flung up some pretty impressive emotional barriers as she dealt with the aftermath. She needed to stay in control, and he sensed that she'd break down if he came on too strong.

But he was incredibly proud of her. In the midst of the chaotic scene, she'd pulled out her cell phone and arranged for the Bairstows to stay with Miss Annie and Roy, and the two guys from Canada to go to Mike O'Hanlon's. She'd called Morry Granger's cousin, and he'd arrived in his robe within ten minutes to scoop up Morry and Maudie. Finally, she'd talked to Lily, who immediately offered her guest room for Morgan and Sabrina to share. Holly had called her aunts, and Florence had soon picked her up too.

A lot of islanders had been woken last night, and every one of them had come through.

Ryan was lucky not to have to worry about where he would go. In Seashell Bay, he always had a room waiting and parents who would do anything for him. He only wished Morgan and Sabrina were as fortunate. But they no longer had any family on the island, and Morgan wouldn't want to keep imposing on Lily. She wouldn't have much choice though, unless she gave up on Golden Sunset and headed back to Pickle River with Sabrina in tow.

He just hoped the fire wasn't the thing that finally forced her hand, because that would emotionally trash her.

And he sure hoped that the insurance would cover most of the damage. If she got a big enough settlement, then the islanders would do what they could to help Morgan and Sabrina get back on their feet.

There was going to be a hell of a lot of work to do, but Ryan was certain of one thing—whatever help was needed, he was going to be here to make sure Morgan got it.

Morgan could hardly breathe much less speak. She stared up the oak staircase toward the second floor, still cordoned off by fire department tape. The choking smell of smoke, combined with her sense of horror, threatened to knock her to the ground. Only the fact that Ryan stood quietly behind her, one hand resting solidly against the base of her spine, kept her on her feet.

Fire Chief Laughlin had given her the good news/bad news report this morning. The fire had definitely resulted from an electrical malfunction in the attic, a fairly common problem in attics where old wiring was involved. The firefighters had managed to keep most of the fire contained at the top of the structure, so even though the roof was compromised and the attic storeroom gutted, the damage to the living areas was largely due to smoke and water, not fire. Still, out of caution that sections of the attic floor could collapse, Laughlin had barred anyone other than firefighters from going upstairs until a full assessment could be made.

"We need to get a restoration company in here right away," Ryan said. "The quicker they deal with the smoke and especially the water, the less likely we are to have long-term problems like mold."

We.

Just that one word gave her heart a tiny lift.

She turned around to face him. "You're thinking Servpro?"

"Yeah. Or we could try a smaller outfit my dad said we might want to check out."

"Smaller as is in cheaper?"

Ryan nodded. "I'd think so. I'll make the calls if you want and get some cost estimates. And I'll be happy to deal with getting the restoration work going."

Morgan stared into his calm, handsome face, her heart twisting with a killer combination of gratitude and love. The man exuded competence and unflinching support, something she desperately needed right now, especially given Sabrina's current state.

Her sister was a wreck. She'd been pretty solid last night until the firefighters dumped God-only-knew how many gallons of water on the house and it became clear that the damage was going to be devastating. By the time Morgan got her over to Lily's house, Sabrina was going into a full-scale emotional meltdown. It had taken Morgan and Lily over an hour to calm her down and get her into bed. Fortunately, she was still sleeping when Morgan had left to come over to Golden Sunset this morning.

Though Morgan felt like her world was coming apart too, having Ryan beside her gave her both comfort and hope. Despite getting as little sleep as the rest of them, he looked ready to tackle any problem in his black T-shirt, faded jeans, and scuffed work boots.

Still…

"Ryan, I can't ask you to do that," she said. "It's not your responsibility."

His gaze went narrow and intense. Combined with his

beard stubble—he obviously hadn't shaved this morning—it made him look a little dangerous and a whole lot sexy.

"We're not gonna get in a tussle over this, babe," he said. "I'm doing it."

Morgan pressed her hands together over her stomach. She so needed his help, so wanted to give in. But it truly wasn't his problem, and she shouldn't make the mistake of getting too dependent on him.

His gaze softened, and he reached up a hand, cradling her cheek. "Morgan, just say yes."

The affectionate gesture, combined with his wry comment, did her in. "Okay, tough guy," she sighed. "I'd be very grateful if you could do that."

"No problem. What time is the insurance adjuster coming?"

"In about an hour. The rep I talked to on the phone was really helpful. They have a twenty-four-hour hotline to report emergency situations."

"Good. The adjuster should approve hiring a restoration service right away. It's the only way to prevent more damage and an even bigger claim."

"That sounds good," Morgan said cautiously.

She'd lain awake for hours trying to recall the details of the inn's insurance. Her father had opted for cheap insurance because Golden Sunset was skating on thinner and thinner ice, a very bad move in light of last night's disaster. But she'd screwed up too. She should have been quicker to upgrade the policy. Again, it had been cost that stopped her. Morgan had told herself she'd do it as soon as the inn had the cash flow to handle that and all its other expenses.

Ryan's gaze narrowed again. "Morgan, there isn't a problem with the insurance, is there?"

"Um, let's just see what the adjuster has to say." She brushed past him into the hallway. "I want to take a good look at the annex now. The damage to the ground floor doesn't seem as bad as I thought it might."

"It's hard to tell how all that water is going to affect the walls and floors," Ryan said, following her. "We need the restoration company to tell us whether it can all be dried out or whether we're going to have to rip the place down to the studs."

Down to the studs? Might as well give up, if that was the case. "At least the furniture looks salvageable," she said, trying to be positive.

"Down here maybe. It'll be a total loss upstairs." He paused. "Hopefully you have full replacement coverage."

She didn't answer.

As they stepped into the annex, Ryan grasped her forearm and held her back. "Morgan, what aren't you telling me? Obviously the insurance hasn't lapsed, since an adjuster is on his way."

"The policy is current," she hedged.

He studied her for a moment, then sighed. "But inadequate, right?"

She waggled a hand, not wanting to come right out and say it.

He grasped her firmly by the shoulders. "Okay, we'll deal, whatever it is. What you need to know right now is that you don't have to go through this alone. I've got pretty broad shoulders, and I've had to deal with my share of disasters."

The kind of disasters where friends and brothers-in-arms wound up getting maimed or killed, she knew. And it was a reminder that, in this disaster, no one had been hurt, or had died. While she and Sabrina were in trouble, things could have been much worse. She needed to remember that and try to be grateful for large mercies.

She gave him an impulsive hug. "Thank you, Ryan. I'm so incredibly grateful that you're here. I'm not sure we could get through this without you." She pressed her cheek into the hard warmth of his chest, letting herself give in just for a moment. "And don't think that doesn't piss me off to admit it," she added only half-jokingly.

He huffed out a soft chuckle as he stroked her hair. It felt so good and so right, like somehow his embrace could restore balance to her messed-up little world.

"I know, tough girl," he said. "But that's what we do here in Seashell Bay, right? We help. And we'll do it together, Morgan, whatever it takes. You, Sabrina, and me."

Ryan tilted her head back a bit and gently kissed her forehead as his fingers snaked through her hair. Every part of her body urged her to stretch up and give him a real kiss. Wasn't that what he wanted? The bulge in his jeans left no doubt about that. And she wanted it too. Wanted it as much as she wanted air to breathe.

But she also knew she'd never been more vulnerable in her life. Now was not the time to slide into another huge emotional situation with the potential to wreck her.

She reluctantly pulled out of his arms. "Thanks, Ryan. You can't know how much that means to me." Then she turned and started down the hall again. "The chief said there's only water damage in here."

Ryan stayed silent, following her. Was he angry with her for breaking away?

She kept on talking. Babbling, more like it.

"I was hoping all night that Sabrina and I could some-how move back in down here soon. Maybe we could at least clean it up enough so that our bedrooms and the kitchen are usable." She forced herself to step into the kitchen and then breathed a sigh of relief. "Oh, thank God. It really isn't too bad in here."

Except for some pools of water on the plank floor and huge wet spots on the ceiling where water had dripped through, the kitchen seemed relatively unscathed. Sunlight streamed in through the south-side windows and bounced off the cheery yellow walls. She crossed through to the hall and stepped quickly over to her bedroom and glanced inside. It looked almost normal too, and she exhaled another relieved sigh. "Yep, that looks doable. I want us to get out of Lily's hair as soon as we can."

When she turned around, Ryan was almost on top of her. His eyes were locked onto the four-poster with its gauzy, flowered canopy. She adored that bed and was so grateful it had been spared damage. And by the way Ryan was letting his gaze drift over it, he seemed to like it too. But for different reasons, she suspected.

He met her gaze. "The problem is you won't have power right away."

Right, she'd forgotten that part. "Do you think the fire department will coordinate with the power company, or should I be calling them myself?"

"We should talk to the chief about that. I'm sure Central Maine Power won't come near the site until they get an all clear from him. It might take a while."

The whisper of hope in her heart faded. "Some of the wiring must have been destroyed by the fire."

Ryan nodded. "I'm sure we're going to need a full

repair and upgrade through the entire structure before power can be brought back in from the road."

"The annex seems okay though," Morgan said. "Could power be restored to just this part of the house?" She was starting to sound desperate, but she couldn't help it.

"Only the power company or an electrician can tell us for sure. Since it's got its own panel, I don't see why the feed couldn't bypass the main house and go straight to the annex."

"I'd really like to get back in here as soon as I can, Ryan. It would be really good for Sabrina." And for her sake too.

He gave her shoulder a comforting squeeze. "Let me talk to Frank for starters. And I'll get some estimates and time frames from electricians for a wiring retrofit. But it'll take time, Morgan. No instant results."

She could tell he was trying to give her the most optimistic assessment possible, which was really depressing because it was still a pretty bleak take on things.

"Message received," she said, forcing a smile.

Ryan blew out an impatient breath as Dermot Delaney laboriously made some notes on his clipboard, using the hood of Ryan's truck as a writing table. The baby-faced insurance adjuster looked about seventeen, despite his buttoned-up look and his serious attitude. Hard to believe he held the future of Golden Sunset B&B in his hands.

A moment later, the adjuster looked up at Morgan with a smile. It obviously didn't reassure her, since her shoulders stayed hunched up high and she kept her arms wrapped tightly across her chest.

"Ms. Merrifield, as you know, your policy provides for replacement cost on the structural elements and finishing, less the fifteen-thousand-dollar deductible. So that will certainly stand you in good stead. You do realize though that the contents are insured for only their current value?"

When Morgan gave a grim nod, Ryan blinked in shock. He wasn't surprised about the stipulation on the contents of the house, but he'd never expected the B&B's policy to have such a whopping deductible. It meant Morgan would be out-of-pocket for fifteen thousand bucks, plus whatever the replacement furniture cost over and above the insurance company's coverage. And then there was the cost of upgrading the wiring that wasn't damaged. The whole thing could total forty grand, maybe even more. Unfortunately, after the cost of the advertising, the balance in Morgan's bank account had to be a lot closer to forty bucks than forty thousand.

Morgan didn't look surprised though. She'd known exactly what was coming, which he should have picked up on by the way she'd been hedging on his earlier questions about the insurance.

At least the adjuster had authorized a restoration service. Ryan had already lined up the company his dad had recommended. They were set to begin work that afternoon once he gave them the go-ahead.

"I have the list of contents your father submitted to us last year," Delaney continued. "If you could take a look at it right away and update it with any additions or deletions, it would speed the process along."

"My sister and I will work on it this afternoon," Morgan said.

"Good, because I need you to sign off on a final version before I can finish calculating the depreciated values and approve the claim."

Morgan nodded, her blue eyes shadowed with exhaustion. "I understand."

"If you're ready, we could meet at my office tomorrow and go over the list. I'll do some preliminary calculations this afternoon so, if there aren't too many changes, I expect we could finalize that part of the claim and issue you a check as soon as you confirm the damage with photos."

"That sounds good," she said, forcing a smile. It practically broke Ryan's heart to see her struggling to hold it together.

Delaney checked his cell phone calendar. "Ten o'clock, then. I'll look forward to seeing you." He gave her a big smile and a nod and started to walk away.

"Don't you want me to drive you back to the ferry?" Morgan said.

"No, thanks. It's a beautiful day. I love coming to Seashell Bay. It's a little corner of paradise if you ask me."

Morgan's blank look suggested that Seashell Bay was the opposite of paradise for her, right about now.

After the adjuster disappeared down Island Road, Ryan wrapped his arms around Morgan and gave her a quick hug. "Now I get why you didn't want to talk about the insurance policy."

She pulled away and sighed as she leaned against the truck. She wore jeans and a wrinkled cotton shirt, having changed earlier in her room. Her clothes were fine other than suffering from a little smoke smell. Ryan's stuff, on the other hand, was still quarantined in his room upstairs.

"I thought the deductible might be a disaster waiting to happen as soon as I found out about it," she said. "But reducing it was going to cost an awful lot, so I hoped I could get away with it until the inn was making money again. I guess it's just a case of Murphy's Frigging Law."

He wasn't about to pile on more misery. "Babe, it's not like you didn't have a million other things to deal with. Not to mention coping with your father's death and taking care of Sabrina."

"I appreciate that, Ryan. But this is going to cost fifteen thousand right off the top, then a lot more to replace all the ruined furniture. The stuff upstairs was on its last legs to begin with. We'll get next to nothing for it from the insurance."

Ryan couldn't argue the point. The furniture in his room had all been old and in need of replacement. From what he'd seen of the other guest rooms, the same thing applied. "Maybe we can find stuff at secondhand stores and auctions that'll do the job. I don't see why not."

"Probably, but it'll still cost tens of thousands of dollars to get the place back on its feet, and in the meantime, I've got a mortgage to pay and no income. I can't borrow any more from the bank. The only option I can see is to somehow keep the repair costs down to what we get from the insurance." She threw up her hands, finally starting to look pissed off. "How am I supposed to manage that? It's not like I can afford to close down any of the rooms. We need all of them to be booked to keep open."

He leaned against the truck and gazed out at the spectacular view of the ocean. "Okay, let's not worry about that for now. We should stick to the immediate issues, like getting the restoration company going and cancelling all the guest bookings for—"

"Forever," Morgan interrupted.

Ryan shook his head. "I'd say a month. Maybe even a little less."

She turned to face him, slapping her hands on her hips. "Are you kidding? The place is half-burned and mostly waterlogged. What planet are you living on, Ryan Butler?"

Boy, she was really rattled to be snapping at him like that. She was a woman who rarely lost her temper or her cool.

"Morgan, honey, you have to start believing that you can figure this out. You're smart and creative and you've got a whole island full of friends ready to help you out." He slung an arm around her shoulders. "And you've got me. I'll be here with you every step of the way until the place is back up and running."

Morgan squeezed her eyes shut for a moment and then shook her head. "You are many things, Ryan, many wonderful things. But I don't think you're a magician. And that's what this place needs."

He squeezed her a little tighter. "You might be surprised."

She opened her eyes and looked up at him. The vulnerability and grief he saw in her gaze practically killed him.

"Please don't give up, Morgan," he said. "We can do this. We can do anything if we want it bad enough."

As long as Morgan was willing to keep fighting, he'd be right at her side. He'd never once let a buddy down in the field, and he sure as hell wasn't going to let down the woman he'd come to care about more than he'd ever thought possible.

Chapter 18

$\mathcal{R}$yan could tell Aiden was giving him the hairy eye-ball from behind his Oakley shades.

"We should have taken my truck," Aiden said. "It's a long way down to Miss Annie's at the speed of this piece-of-crap golf cart."

"The whole point of coming home was to slow down, you moron. Take it easy and contemplate life." Ryan threw his friend a taunting grin as they passed the trash transfer station on their way to the south end of the island.

Aiden laughed. "And how's that working out for you? You've been busting your ass ever since you got here, and now you're about to take on a Mount Rushmore–sized project."

Ryan had filled Aiden in on his plans earlier, after Lily had left for her lobster boat and Morgan had caught an early ferry to Portland to meet the insurance adjuster. Not that Lily wouldn't be involved up to her neck in what he had in mind—he just didn't want her talking to Morgan before he had some of the key pieces in place. Later, he'd made calls to three guys he wanted to rope into helping do some of the repair work at the inn. All had responded with generous enthusiasm.

"Seriously?" he scoffed. "This coming from the guy who's building a big-ass resort and coaching college baseball at the same time?"

"I'm not exactly *building* the place. I'm just coordinating some stuff."

That was a hell of an understatement from what Ryan had heard. "Well, I'm thinking in the same terms about Golden Sunset."

Aiden snorted. "You do realize that, if you get Field Marshal Annie Letellier involved, there's no chance you'll be in charge of the army, right? Miss Annie doesn't play second in command to anybody."

"Sounds good to me."

A few minutes later, Ryan eased the cart to a stop on the grass beside Miss Annie's two-story clapboard house. The eighty-year-old place sat on a piece of coastland that had belonged to the Letellier family for over a century and a half.

Roy Mayo opened the door and sauntered out onto the small porch, barefoot and in jeans and a sleeveless T-shirt that showed off his still-fit build. The old guy was a walking example of the island's hearty stock.

"Well, if it isn't Seashell Bay's very own baseball heroes." Roy had been a vocal spectator at most of the Peninsula High ball games back in the day, always supporting the local kids. "You boys want a beer?"

"Jesus, Roy, it's not even ten o'clock," Aiden said, stepping out of the cart.

"So? Did the government pass a law that stops a man from enjoying a beer at home in the morning?" Roy held the door open. "But hell, if you're going to be pussies, there's coffee too." His resigned shrug seemed to suggest that the world had come to a sad state.

Miss Annie bustled out of the kitchen as Roy pointed them toward a comfy sofa covered by a red, white, and blue afghan. "So nice of you boys to drop in on a couple of old coots."

When she held her arms open, both Aiden and Ryan gave her warm hugs. "Well, Miss Annie, it's always a pleasure to see you and Roy. Actually, not Roy," Aiden said with a grin.

"Miss Annie, we wanted to talk to you about Morgan and Sabrina," Ryan said.

She nodded. "I'd been hoping you boys would come see me about that." She sat down primly in her favorite plush blue armchair. Roy remained standing, rocking back and forth on his heels. "Roy, why don't you get these boys some coffee?" Miss Annie suggested patiently.

The old guy rolled his eyes but trundled off to the kitchen.

"I'm just heartbroken for the girls, and I feel bad for the guests too," Miss Annie said. "The people who stayed here for the night said almost everything they had was ruined."

The fire department had retrieved the guests' belongings from the upstairs rooms late yesterday afternoon before clearing Morgan and Ryan to go upstairs. Ryan had chucked his sodden, smoke-damaged clothes straight into the trash. The contents of his wallet had been mostly okay after they dried out.

"A restoration company has been on site since yesterday," Ryan said. "They say the lower floor and the annex are going to be fine, but we're looking at repairing a section of the roof and replacing just about everything upstairs except the studs, floorboards, and plumbing. Almost all the furniture is shot, and all the wiring is going to have to be replaced."

Miss Annie exhaled a weary sigh. "Poor Morgan. She's been trying so hard, and all she gets is one setback after another. Still, if I know that girl, she'll find a way to bounce back. I always told her father that she was the most resourceful young lady I'd ever met. She and my sweet granddaughter Lily. Like peas in a pod, those two."

"That's what we're here about, Miss Annie," Ryan said. "We're worried about Morgan. The fire has really kicked the, uh . . ."

"Stuffing out of her," Aiden interjected.

Miss Annie scoffed. "You don't need to protect my delicate ears, Aiden Flynn. And I'm sure Morgan knows that, whatever she needs, we'll be there to help. I don't know a soul on the island who doesn't love that girl."

That sounded good, but he needed something more concrete. "Here's the thing, Miss Annie. The insurance that Cal had on the place isn't going to cover the costs—not even close."

"Especially not if Morgan has to hire contractors to do the work," Aiden said.

"And that's where we come in," Ryan said. "Aiden and me. Josh, Brett, and Micah too. We're ready to do as much of the work as we can ourselves, so that'll cut the costs down a lot. But even with all that, the bill is still going to be huge. It's going to take a lot of new material and a lot of hours of skilled workmanship for the stuff our guys can't do. And then there's all the replacement furniture on top of that."

"Morgan has no resources beyond what she'll get from insurance, Miss Annie, and the deductible is a killer," Aiden added as Roy arrived with huge mugs of black coffee.

"I've offered to lend her money," Ryan said. "Aiden too. She won't take it because she's not sure she'll be able to pay it back."

"That sounds like Morgan all right." Miss Annie slapped her thin, blue-veined hands on her khaki-clad legs. "That means we'll just have to raise the funds she needs, won't we? I presume that's what you boys came here to talk about?"

"Yes, ma'am," Ryan said. Miss Annie was probably already a step ahead of him. Relief flooded through his veins, and the hammering that had been going on in his head all morning started to recede.

"That's all well and good, Annie," Roy piped up, "but maybe the fool girl will be too proud to take that kind of help either."

Roy was just being Roy. He loved Morgan and hadn't intended to disparage her. Besides, there might be truth to his words.

Still, Miss Annie shot her boyfriend a steely glare. "The only fool around here is you, you old codger." Then her attention switched back to Ryan. "While Seashell Bay folks are nothing if not proud, we take care of each other. I'll make sure the girl accepts our help."

Ryan smiled at her. As a kid, he'd wanted nothing more than to escape the stifling confines of the island and see what the world had to offer. Now he'd seen more than his share, and too much of it had left a bad taste in his mouth. Whatever the drawbacks of life in a small town like Seashell Bay, folks did take care of their own. If you needed help, you got it. In his book, that unquestioning generosity was starting to count for a hell of a lot.

"Could we ask you to take over that part of the operation, Miss Annie?" he asked. "There's nobody better to head up a fund-raising campaign than you." He took a swallow of Roy's superstrong, sludgy coffee and nearly gagged. "Just don't let Roy make the coffee for any of the events."

"Hell, boy, you are a pussy," Roy said with a smirk. "That coffee will put hair on your scrawny chest."

"You did a hell of a job organizing the battle against the car ferry," Aiden said, ignoring Roy's barb. "That's the kind of effort we'd need."

She waved her hand. "Lily can take most of the credit for that. But it did turn out rather well, didn't it?"

"It did at that," Aiden said with a smile. "For everyone on the island."

"Well, we're not about to let that sweet old inn close its doors for good," Miss Annie said with conviction. "It might not be the Ritz, but it's an institution around here, and we're darn well not going to let it die if we can help it. It would be like letting a piece of our history die."

Ryan hadn't thought of it that way, but Miss Annie was right. The inn had changed hands a number of times, but it had been in operation for decades—first as an old-fashioned boardinghouse and then as a small family hotel.

"I took a run down there after dinner yesterday," Roy said. "Looks to me like you got a big demolition job, for starters." He poked a bony finger against his chest. "So listen up, because this is the guy you want for that kind of work. I did that stuff for a living back when the T. rex was kicking the shit out of everything else."

Ryan remembered how adamant Miss Annie had been that Roy not be involved in anything dangerous when they were repairing the B&B's roof.

But she simply eyed Roy and then nodded. "If these boys are foolish enough to want you there, then fine. But if you fall through the ceiling or something, it's straight into the nursing home for you, Roy Mayo. I'm not taking care of some codger who tries to act like he's still thirty years old."

"Yeah, well, in some ways, it's like I still am thirty, isn't that right, Annie?" He gave Ryan a wink.

Miss Annie shot him a look that should have slayed him dead. Ryan figured he and Aiden better get out of there fast before all hell broke loose.

"I'll talk to Lily as soon as she gets home tonight," Aiden said, backing toward the door. He probably felt as alarmed as Ryan did at the prospect of hearing details of Roy and Miss Annie's sex life. "You know she'll want to be on your fund-raising committee."

Miss Annie popped to her feet. "The girl's busy. She's getting married soon, or have you somehow forgotten that?"

Aiden's grin made it clear to Ryan that he was used to his future grandmother-in-law yanking his chain. "Yeah, but don't forget that Morgan's her maid of honor."

"Then we'd darn well better make sure that the maid of honor is happy so they can have a good time at the wedding," Miss Annie added. "I'm looking at you when I say that, Ryan Butler," she said, turning her eagle eye on him.

The old gal was nothing if not perceptive and direct.

"Got it, ma'am," Ryan said. "Loud and clear."

*   *   *

Morgan eased her pickup through the gap between the hedge and the two Kingsley Restoration trucks that clogged the driveway. She parked beside the annex and headed in through the kitchen door, automatically glancing around to see if Ryan was there. Boy, she missed him. Though they'd seen a lot of each other since the fire, no longer sleeping under the same roof had brought home how quickly she'd become used to his reassuring presence.

She'd followed his advice to treat herself to lunch and a stroll through the shopping district after meeting with the insurance adjuster. After a painful discussion with Delaney, she'd needed it. First she'd tried to relax at Starbucks with a decaf latte and a copy of *USA Today* that someone had left on the table. That had been an utter failure, so she'd pulled out some paper and a pencil and jotted down rough estimates of what she figured it was going to cost to replace each item of lost furniture. When she totaled up the figures and compared it to what Delaney had said the insurance was going to pay, she'd come up with a horrifying deficit.

New furniture was simply out of the question.

Hopefully Ryan had been right when he said they should be able to find replacements by trolling consignment and secondhand shops and maybe even auctions. In fact, she'd even felt a little frisson of pleasure when she thought about the two of them poking their way around Portland or even farther afield. It was such a thoroughly domesticated and couple-like thing to do, and something she'd certainly never have imagined doing with her Soldier Boy.

She dropped her keys and bag on the kitchen counter. "Ryan? Are you still here?" she called out.

"Upstairs." His voice barely carried over the low, steady whine of the industrial dehumidifiers Kingsley had placed on both floors.

She went out to the hall and headed upstairs. Ryan emerged from the guest room she'd been using before the fire, his big work boots clomping on the pine floor. As always, seeing his gorgeous, masculine self had her stomach going kind of funny.

"Huh." She dropped her gaze to her cute summer sandals. "Maybe I should be wearing work boots up here too."

Ryan's mouth quirked into a grin. "You'd look darn cute in them. Especially if that was *all* you were wearing. Now that's a fantasy I could get down with."

Her mouth dropped open, but she regrouped. "I see your dirty mind has already returned. I don't know whether to call that progress or regression."

"I was just trying to see if a day in the city had lightened you up a bit," he said, moving closer. "Tell me you managed to have at least a little fun."

Not so much. Most of the time when I wasn't agonizing over the B&B, I was tying myself up in knots about how much I was going to miss you when you go.

Even with everything else she had to worry about, Morgan couldn't shake the image of Ryan waving goodbye to her from the ferry. Yes, he'd said he'd stay until the inn was back on its feet—or closed—but the day would come all too soon when he'd go back to his life.

His real life.

"It was a good idea," she said brightly. "I'm glad you pushed me to do it."

"And how was your friend Delaney? I think he has a big-time crush on you."

Morgan answered with a little snort. "He's being helpful, at least for an insurance adjuster."

Ryan made a fake grimace. "Okay, now I am jealous."

Morgan couldn't believe how upbeat he seemed. He'd been solid and supportive every minute since the fire, and now he was practically bouncing on his toes. "Why do I get the feeling something's going on here?"

He grasped her elbow in a gentle grip and steered her back to the stairs. "Let's go outside and talk. I'm done up here for now."

Despite her pleasure at the feeling of his hand on her arm, anxiety stirred. What did he want to talk about now?

"Let's go down to the beach," he said. "I'd like to say hello to my kayak. She must be thinking I've abandoned her again."

His joking words had her wincing with guilt. "Oh, dear. Well, if you're talking about a plastic boat like it's a woman, I'd say she must hate my guts since I'm the one keeping you two lovers apart."

He interlaced his fingers with hers as they strolled down the path to the dock. It felt so comforting, so *right*. Why couldn't he see what she did? That what was happening between them was more than just simple friendship spiced with a healthy dose of hormones.

"I'll make it up to her eventually," he said. "Once we start to get this place in some semblance of shape, I'll have a paddle in my hands every day until I leave."

And there it was—the answer to her unspoken question. Ryan was always going to leave.

"I hope so," she said, forcing a smile. "Otherwise, I won't survive the self-imposed guilt trip from hell."

He squeezed her hand. "There's nothing to feel guilty about. Whatever I'm doing, it's because I want to."

She squeezed back, too touched to say anything without bursting into stupid tears.

He guided her off the path, and they walked hand in hand across a strip of grass to the narrow beach, where the seaweed-strewn sand was exposed at low tide. "I've been thinking hard about the money we need for repairs."

"Me too." She pulled on his arm, forcing him to stop. "I've decided to call my bank in Pickle River and see if there's any way I can get a second mortgage on my house. Maybe I'll be able to get enough to cover the shortfall from the insurance."

Unfortunately, she didn't have all that much equity yet, but it was worth a shot.

Ryan stared at her as if she'd told him she was going to rob the bank, not ask for a loan. "A second mortgage? Seriously? After you told me you were going to have a hard time making your current payments until you go back to teaching?"

"Ryan, what other options do I have? We obviously have to get the damage repaired and get back in business. After that, if the debt load is just too high to manage, Sabrina and I will have to put Golden Sunset up for sale."

Morgan dreaded the conversation she was going to have with her sister about that. But Morgan was the one who would have to absorb the loans and the debt, and she couldn't afford to ruin her credit rating—especially since she would probably be supporting Sabrina for the rest of her life.

"That's not going to happen," Ryan said. "We don't need to let it happen. That's what I wanted to tell you," he added in a patient voice.

She scrunched her nose at him. "I'm sorry. I should shut up and listen."

He dropped a kiss on her nose, pulling back before she could react. "Yeah, Miss Bossy, you should."

She smiled back. "Bossy? Me? You must be talking about some other hard-up innkeeper. I'm the mildest-mannered person you'd ever want to meet."

He snorted, pulling her down with him onto the sand. She sat close to him, letting her shoulder touch his, and hugged her knees.

"Look, I get it," he said. "Maybe because we've both spent so much time away from the island, we think we have to do everything on our own."

"Maybe," she said tentatively.

"And that's nuts, because if there's one place in the whole damn world where you can count on folks, it's Sea-shell Bay. Nobody here wants to see Golden Sunset close down, and everybody loves you and Sabrina." He bumped his shoulder against hers. "Everybody."

Her heart practically leapt into her throat.

Ryan carried on like he hadn't just brought her to her emotional knees. "People want to help, Morgan. All you have to do is reach out and let them in on how much trouble you're in. Until you do, people are going to think you'll be okay because of the insurance."

She fastened her gaze on the beach, poking around a bit as if searching for sea glass hidden amongst the pebbles and sand. "I've never been too good on that score," she finally admitted.

"No, all you do is help other people," he said gently. "Now it's time to let them help you."

That sounded good, but what did it entail? She couldn't

bear the thought of being indebted to the people she'd grown up with.

Ryan shifted to look directly at her. The tenderness and open warmth in his dark gaze seized her breath. All she could do was stare back at him as her insides went soft with love and her brain went stupid with longing.

"Morgan, there's a good chance we can get the B&B back up and running without it costing you anything more than what you'll get from the insurance," he said. "And you won't have to owe anybody a dime."

That jolted her out of her goofy, romantic haze. "How, by selling lottery tickets?" She widened her eyes at him.

He laughed. "We can manage better odds than that. For starters, I've put together a crew to help me do a lot of the basic construction work. Aiden's on board and so are Micah, Josh, and Brett. Even Roy's offered to help with demolition."

Any moment now she *was* going to burst into tears, so she resorted to lame humor. "Jesus, no," she said, pretending to clutch her chest. "I can't be responsible for Roy's untimely demise. But seriously, I can't tell you how much that means to me—and what it will mean to Sabrina too."

"We're all happy to do it. The only work you'll have to pay for is the electrical repairs and a little plumbing. Aiden's pretty sure that Brendan will donate his time to do the finishing carpentry we need." He gave her a look that said she didn't have a choice in the matter. "We're not going to stand around and let the B&B shut down or see you buried under a mountain of debt."

She sucked in a deep breath, forcing herself to calm down and think. As awesome as this all was, it wasn't nearly enough. "But the cost of the materials, the electricians, the plumbers, the upstairs furniture..." The figures she'd added up a few hours ago remained fresh in her mind. "I'll still have to get a second mortgage—if somebody will give me one."

"No you won't. Free labor is only half the answer," Ryan said, shaking his head. "Fund-raising is the other half."

Uh-oh. She knew it was too good to be true.

"A lot of folks on this island are going to be happy to open their wallets to support you and make sure Golden Sunset stays alive. Miss Annie's already agreed to head up a fund-raising drive, and you know how persuasive that lady can be."

"Um, okay," she said cautiously.

Morgan didn't know what to think. She'd taken part in dozens of fund-raising drives over the years in Seashell Bay but had never for a moment thought she might one day be the subject of one. She instinctively rebelled at the idea of being reduced to a charity case. But it wasn't just about her. There was Sabrina to think about, along with the trust her father had placed in Morgan to make things right. If there was ever a time to swallow her pride, it was now.

Ryan patiently waited her out.

"You were the one who came up with all this, weren't you? With everything." It was almost too much to comprehend all that he'd done for her. How could she ever repay him?

And how could she ever find the strength to keep it together when he finally walked away?

He waved a dismissive hand, now starting to look a bit uncomfortable. "Aiden was all over it too."

She sensed his discomfort with all the emotion and did a pullback. "So, while I was screwing around in the city, eating sushi and, yes, having a beer, you were putting together a plan and enlisting an army. Nice morning's work, Butler."

He gave her a crooked smile. "Don't give me any medals just yet. If I hadn't done it, I'm sure Lily and Aiden and Miss Annie would have been right there anyway."

"Well, you do deserve a medal," she said. "I'm so grateful. I don't even know how to begin to repay you, but I'll find a way. I promise."

When his gaze turned dark and smoldering and one big hand came up to cradle her cheek, Morgan blinked up at him in surprise. It looked like she'd been wrong after all. Ryan didn't look the least bit interested in pulling back—or pulling away.

In fact, he leaned in even closer. "As a matter of fact, I have an idea about that."

Chapter 19

$\mathcal{G}$ood Lord, they were finally going to do it. And she was more than ready. She'd spent weeks resisting her endless, impossible desire for Ryan, and suddenly that seemed like it had been the dumbest thing in the world. If there were any lessons to be gleaned from that awful fire, it was that life was both precious and random all at once. That being cautious and careful couldn't always protect you from the bad things, which she should have learned in the wake of her father's death. That being too cautious and careful could cut you off from the things you wanted, the things you loved.

That she loved Ryan was beyond doubt. Morgan knew with absolute conviction that saying no to him now would be a missed opportunity she would regret forever, whether he stayed in her life or got on the ferry at the end of the summer and sailed away.

He took his time, gently resting his forehead against hers, inhaling deep breaths as if drawing in her scent. She thought he was giving her one final chance to say no.

"Yes," she breathed. "Yes, Ryan."

She wouldn't have been able to say anything more, even if she'd had the words, because he dipped his head and claimed her mouth with a searing kiss that stole every ounce of strength from her body. His hand spread wide over her back and drifted down to settle at the base of her spine. He loomed over her—big, brawny, and muscular—his very presence making her feel protected and cherished.

And turning her on like crazy.

She reached up and sank her fingers into his hair as he deepened the kiss. Boldly, she pushed her tongue between his lips, sweeping inside and claiming him the way he'd claimed her only a few weeks ago. She let her hunger drive her, pulling back to trace the edges of his firm mouth with her tongue before stealing back inside for a deeper taste of him.

Finally, Ryan eased his grip and broke the kiss. She felt a slight tremor in the big hands that wrapped around her upper arms. "Jesus, Morgan, if you don't want to go any further, say so right now. If you're not ready . . ."

"Does it feel like I'm not ready?" she said in disbelief. "I've been ready since we were in high school. Probably since junior high, although it's probably really tacky to admit that."

"You're sure? Because I don't want this if it's just a gratitude thing," Ryan said, frowning. "That's not why I've been trying to help you. You know that, don't you?"

She let out an exaggerated sigh. "You are such a dope, although I guess I can't totally blame you. I've been Mr. Dithers for weeks about this."

A smile eased his lips up. "You're way cuter than

Mr. Dithers. But I get it, and I just want to make sure that you're sure."

She rested a hand on his chest, then slid it down to his waist, letting her fingers drift along the top of his cargo shorts. "Oh, I'm sure, big guy."

Ryan's dark eyes lit up. He dipped to nuzzle her neck, trailing soft, hot kisses as she arched into him. It felt like heaven to finally give in to what she'd been fighting for so long. Relief had her wanting to jump up and spin around in crazy circles, like a kid high on sugar.

Or rip his clothes off and do him right on the beach.

Classy, Morgan. Real classy.

Honestly, at this point she almost didn't care. She felt liberated from something that had been wearing her soul down for the longest time.

"Kevin told me just before you got back that they were finishing up for the day." He slid his lips onto hers for a short, hot kiss. "They'll be gone any minute now, and if not, we'll tell them to get lost."

"Well, that might get some tongues wagging around town," Morgan said.

"Do you care?" he murmured as he moved to her neck. His breath was hot against her sensitive skin, making her shiver deliciously.

"Let them wag," she managed.

"I like the sound of that." He nibbled gently at her ear. "It looked pretty dry to me in the downstairs bedrooms. Especially that big bed of yours."

"I don't mind getting wet if you don't." She winced when he laughed at the unconscious double entendre.

"Actually, it sounds like a great way to kick off the new and improved Golden Sunset, don't you think?" he said.

"Yes, and I'd challenge you to race me back except for the fact that my legs are feeling a little weak right now," she said, smiling up at him. "Thanks to you."

"I have a solution for that." He pulled her to her feet and scooped her up in his arms, then started for the path.

"I'm too heavy for you to carry me all the way back," she protested with a giggle.

A giggle. Morgan couldn't remember the last time she'd giggled.

"Babe, my army gear and pack weigh more than you do."

He must have been telling the truth, because he was practically jogging back to the inn, carrying her as if she didn't weigh anything at all.

And like he couldn't wait to get her into bed.

She wrapped her arms around his neck and clung to him, nibbling at his ear. A few lingering doubts tugged at her, demanding she pay attention. But that was just habit, her tendency to always worry about the future instead of living in the moment. Right now, she wanted only today. She would leave tomorrow to bring what it would bring.

Carrying Morgan, Ryan practically jogged up the path to the B&B. Fortunately the workers' truck was gone, because he probably looked like a teenage boy about to get laid for the first time. He'd never wanted a woman like he wanted Morgan. It was crazy how much he wanted her—almost scary. But it also felt better than anything had in a long time. It felt right—deep down in his bones right, and that was a feeling he never took lightly.

"Hey, Soldier Boy, don't drop me," Morgan said. "I guarantee there will be no nookie if I end up on my ass."

He stepped onto the back porch of the annex, pausing for a moment to kiss her cute nose. "A very fine ass it is, and I'm not about to let any harm come to it."

She grinned back at him, so clearly happy that his heart soared. The look on her face when he'd told her about his plan to fix the inn had made him feel like a freaking hero, as ridiculous as that sounded. He didn't want hero worship from Morgan; he just wanted to make her life easier. In fact, that was now a mission, as important as any he'd ever undertaken.

"I'm glad to hear it," she said. "Because I'm quite attached to my ass."

He groaned. "Merrifield, that was bad, even for you."

She wrinkled her nose. "Yeah, kind of lame. I guess I'm a little nervous."

Ryan paused outside the screen door, shifting her so he could reach for the door handle. "You've got nothing to be nervous about, babe. I promise."

She rested a hand on his cheek, forcing him to look at her. A smile tilted up the edges of her mouth, but her eyes held his in a serious, steady gaze. Her vulnerability came through, and it was like she'd just wrapped her hand around his heart and squeezed.

"Aren't *you* nervous?" she asked.

He turned the question over in his mind. "Not really, but then I have such a raging hard-on that I can barely see straight."

She dropped her head and laughed. "Butler, you can be such a guy sometimes. It's kind of appalling."

He finally got the damn door open and strode into the

kitchen with her. "I bet you're pretty happy about that right now though."

She brushed a stray lock of silky, blond hair out of her eyes and smiled at him. "You have no idea."

"Well, there you go. I'd say this is turning out to be a very good day."

He carried her down the short hall to her bedroom.

"And I hope it's about to get even better," she said, her voice dropping to a husky purr.

Man, didn't that just make his dick want to stand up and salute?

He set her down and shoved the door shut. Sabrina was staying at Lily's, but he didn't want any surprises. Not when he finally had Morgan exactly where he wanted her. If he had anything to say about it, they wouldn't be leaving this room for several hours.

Morgan crossed to the window and opened it wide. There was a hint of smoke in the room, but it wasn't a problem. The white lace curtains framing the window fluttered in a breeze coming off the water, bringing with it the tangy hint of ocean air. She braced a hand on the post at the head of her bed as she balanced to kick off her sandals.

Ryan studied the old four-poster bed. It was obviously an antique, beautiful and in great shape. It was clear that Morgan loved it. She'd draped a gauzy, almost transparent swath of white fabric over the top to create a canopy that cast soft shadows. The duvet was gold colored and looked thick and soft, piled high with lots of satiny white and pink pillows. It was a total girlie bed, perfect for her and perfect for making love.

He strolled to the foot of the bed and leaned a shoulder

against one of the posts. "I've fantasized about doing you in this bed since the moment I saw it."

She choked out a laugh. "Isn't that just the most romantic thing I've ever heard?"

He shrugged. "Like you said, I'm a guy." He eyed the posts, then glanced down to look at the frame. "This is strong enough to support us, right? I do not want to break your bed."

She nodded. "Trust me, it's very solid. I know."

When he raised an eyebrow, she flapped a hand at him. "Not because of *that*. Ryan Butler, you have the dirtiest mind."

He moved a few steps to rest his hands on her shoulders. "Oh yeah, and I bet you know what I'm thinking this very moment."

She smiled, her cheeks flushing a faint pink under her tan. She looked a little shy and incredibly cute.

"I bet I do. And speaking of which, what's next on the agenda?"

"The first thing is to get you out of those clothes," he said, starting on the buttons of her blouse.

"What about you? Don't we have to get you out of your clothes?" She reached for his zipper.

He brushed her hands away. "You first. Besides, it'll only take me a few seconds since I'm only wearing shorts and boots."

"Commando, eh?"

"Are you complaining?"

"Heck, no."

Ryan slipped her blouse off and pretty much lost his breath. She was gorgeous, a spectacular combination of toned and curvy, with smooth skin kissed golden by the sun. And she had great breasts. As far as he was concerned, all breasts were great, but hers were in a league by themselves—full and pale, with rosy nipples barely concealed by the lace of her simple white bra.

"Babe," he said, "you're gonna kill me."

"I hope not," she said with a self-conscious laugh.

Then she surprised him by reaching back and unhooking her bra, dropping it to the floor. Her nipples were already tight—gorgeous, hard little points he couldn't wait to sample.

Fully recognizing what a lucky bastard he was, he cupped both full, perfect weights in his hands and thumbed her peaks. Morgan sucked in a breath, her blue eyes going soft and heavy-lidded.

"Let's get you undressed all the way," he murmured, reaching for the snap on her short denim skirt.

A moment later, she stood before him, clad, God help him, in a lacy white thong. Ryan contemplated leaving it on, but decided to leave the games for later. He hooked his thumbs into the elastic waistband and skimmed it down over her slender legs. Morgan rested a hand on his shoulder and stepped out of the thong.

His heart almost stopped. She was unbelievable, glowing golden in the sunlight pouring through the frilly lace curtains and washing lovingly over her body. Morgan was the most beautiful thing he'd ever seen, from her flaxen blond head to the sweet golden curls at the notch of her thighs to her neat painted toes, glittering with a nail polish that seemed to match the rest of her.

She lit up the room, and she sure as hell lit up his heart.

He must have looked like a moron standing there gaping at her, because she propped her hands on her hips.

Ryan was almost tempted to laugh at her schoolmarm expression. She was without doubt the hottest schoolmarm on the planet.

"Well, Soldier Boy," she said. "What the heck are you staring at? Get those clothes off and get to work."

He did laugh at that. "Yes, ma'am. I'll get right on it."

As Ryan hopped around on one leg, hauling off a boot, Morgan swallowed a giggle. It was mostly from nerves, which were making her a bit light-headed. And no wonder—she was standing here stark naked while the guy she'd been crushing on for years had practically eaten her up with his eyes. It was heady, empowering, and truly scary to think that she and Ryan Butler were finally going to do it after all these years.

And in broad daylight too, which somehow seemed to make it even more official. No sneaking off for a furtive coupling on the beach late at night. Clearly, Ryan had no problem with what they were doing, which meant she shouldn't either. Not even if that tiny voice in her head still whispered a warning that she was risking a world of hurt.

When Ryan unzipped his cargo shorts and skimmed them down, every remaining thought in Morgan's head fled.

Oh. My. God.

He was amazing, every muscle cut, his body bronzed by the summer sun. Totally jacked. She knew that already, of course, but to see him stark naked just made everything seem...more muscular. And even bigger.

And boy, when it came to his equipment, *big* was exactly the right word.

Ryan gave her a salacious grin. "Now that you've had a good look, would you like to touch?"

"Uh, you first," she answered inanely.

Honestly though, she didn't even know where to start. Morgan wasn't a nun by any means, but no guy she'd ever dated came close to Ryan's physical presence. Her soldier boy was definitely in a class by himself.

"That would be my pleasure," he said.

He prowled over to the bed and pulled her close, sliding his hands over her butt. Morgan quivered at the feel of all that hot, hard flesh pressed against her. His erection lay thick and heavy between them, and she couldn't help squirming a bit, rubbing it against her belly. Ryan made a noise low in his throat, halfway between a hiss and a growl. Then he dipped down and took her mouth in an openmouthed, deliciously wet kiss. He clamped his hands on her, massaging her butt as he slowly rubbed against her.

Morgan sighed, slipping her arms around his neck. The coarse hair on his chest tickled her nipples, and sensation streaked down to her core, spiking arousal and heat. As she'd done on that night when they'd first kissed, she pulled up her leg, bringing her sex into direct contact with his hard thigh. Already she throbbed with a sweet ache and instinctively searched for relief.

But it was so much more than last time. Now they were naked—all hot skin and nothing between them, their bodies doing exactly what they wanted.

He broke the kiss when she pressed even closer, hooking her ankle behind his knee.

"Fuck, babe," he growled. "That is so hot I could take you standing up, right against the wall."

Her stomach gave a little flip at the image of her jammed against the wall, Ryan pounding into her.

"In fact," he said, "I'd have you facing the wall, your hands up high and your legs spread wide. Then I'd take you from behind, so I could touch all of you while I was inside."

Wow. Morgan had to admit that he made it sound damn tempting. She clutched at his shoulders, staring up into his face. His features were taut, and his gaze glittered with dark intensity. She had to swallow before she could answer.

"I . . . uh, that sounds awesome, actually," she stuttered.

He let out a low laugh. "Yeah, it does, but not for our first time. I want to be looking into your gorgeous eyes when I'm inside you."

Morgan went up on tiptoe—and, oh, did the slide of her breasts across his hard chest feel fantastic—and kissed his mouth.

"I want that too," she whispered.

He touched his forehead to hers. "I thought you'd never ask."

He picked her up and plopped her on the bed, high up on the pillows. He started to follow and then froze. "Shit," he muttered.

She raised herself up on her elbows. "What?"

He stood up straight. Morgan couldn't help focusing on his impressive erection, now pretty much at her eye level.

"I can't believe it," he said in a disgusted voice. "I don't have a condom on me."

"Don't you carry one in your wallet? I thought all guys did that."

"I left my wallet back at my parents' house. Didn't think I'd need it today." He gave his head a rueful shake. "I'm sorry, babe. We can do other stuff, but—"

"It's not a problem," she interrupted. "I'm kind of embarrassed about this, but I bought some condoms the other day. They're in the top drawer of the dresser."

He grinned. "Planning a little action, were we? You little devil, you."

Morgan guessed she was probably blushing from head to toe. It had been an impulse buy at the drugstore the other day, and she'd silently ragged herself all the way home. Now, she was glad she'd done it.

"Hardly, but it's always a good idea to be prepared for any situation."

"That's my motto too, babe," he said as he stepped over to her dresser. "No wonder we're so good together."

Joking or not, his last comment caught her right in the heart. She wanted so much for them to be good together, on every level, even though it probably wouldn't last beyond the fading of the summer season.

He found the condoms and came back, his gaze focusing on her face. "You still okay there, Merrifield?"

She gave him a smile, pushing aside her silly second thoughts. She'd been waiting for this for a long time and firmly intended to enjoy every minute.

"I'm just wondering what's taking you so long," she said. "You don't want me to get bored, do you?"

His gaze glittered with amusement and something much hotter. "No chance of that happening, babe. Scoot over."

He joined her, sliding an arm under her shoulders and cradling her. He leaned down and sealed his lips over hers in a kiss so delicious that Morgan had no choice but to collapse into his powerful embrace. And boy, did he take his time kissing her. He savored her, seducing her with hot glides of his tongue even as his hand started exploring her body. When it drifted down to caress her breast, Morgan moaned against his lips.

Ryan moved back and gently pulled the stiff bead of a nipple, making her gasp. Sensation streaked from her breast right down to her womb. "Does that feel good?"

"Um, better than good," she managed as he continued to stroke and play.

He flashed her what could only be described as a lascivious grin. "Let's see if we can get to awesome, shall we?"

Then he bent down and took the same nipple into his mouth, sucking it in. Morgan cried out as her back instinctively pulled into an arch. Awesome didn't even begin to describe the pleasure pouring through her body as he lavished attention on her breasts. He went from one to the other, kneading and massaging with a pressure that both soothed and drove her wild. His mouth and tongue played over her, teasing and tormenting.

The fact that it was Ryan—*Ryan*—driving her into a sexual frenzy made it all that much hotter. She grabbed his shoulders, hanging on for dear life as she went under in a storm of sensation.

Finally, when she was all but sobbing with need, he pulled back. He gently cupped one breast, his thumb stroking softly back and forth across her nipple.

"So, how was that?" he asked, his voice so deep it rumbled. "Good or awesome?"

Morgan practically had to unroll her eyes from the

back of her head to look at him. His gaze was smoky with desire, but his mouth was curled up in a self-satisfied, all-male smile.

"Not bad, but I'd like to see what else you've got." Of course the fact that she could barely talk made that lie plain as day.

He huffed out a laugh as he let his hand drift down over her stomach, lightly brushing over her curls, and then gently pushing her thighs wide. When he cupped her sex, Morgan lost her breath again.

"Babe, everything about you is just perfect." His tone was low, serious, and surprisingly emotional.

That was hardly true, but the words brought tears to her eyes anyway.

When he stroked his fingers across her slick folds, it sent an erotic jolt through her body. "Ryan," she cried, grabbing his arm.

"You're so ready for me," he murmured. He was teasing her, driving her crazy.

Driving himself crazy too, from his almost ferocious expression. Morgan clamped her fingers around his wrist. "Ryan, please. I want you now."

"I'm so down with that," he rasped out. He shifted, moving between her legs and coming up on his knees. He reached for the box of condoms.

Morgan watched him roll one on, loving the sight of the man looming over her. He was so big and so damn beautiful, and he was Ryan, the man she'd been dreaming about for so long. Feeling a little light-headed, she wondered if she would pass out.

Don't you dare.

Ryan came down, bracing himself on his forearms and

brushing an incredibly tender kiss across her lips. "Ready, babe?"

She took his face between her hands, smiling up at him. "So freaking ready."

"Me too." He flexed his hips and slowly pushed into her. Morgan felt her eyes go wide, while Ryan's fluttered shut as he let out a groan.

It felt incredible—tight, but good. Really good. She pulled her legs up around his hips as he went deep inside, filling her all the way.

Her body and her heart.

Ryan breathed out a shuddering sigh when he was fully inside her. "You feel fucking amazing, babe. So incredible."

It was a total guy thing to say, but it made her throat go tight. It was the tone of his voice that did it—hushed, almost reverent.

His eyes opened, and he stared down at her. His gaze was open, honest, and blazing with raw emotion. He'd finally dropped his barriers, and that simple, earth-shattering fact brought tears to her eyes. She'd held everything in for so many long months since she'd come home—grief, anger, frustration, and fear—and it felt like it had all been washed away in this moment with Ryan.

He brushed another tender kiss across her lips. "Don't cry, beautiful. Let me make you feel good."

She smiled through her tears and wrapped her arms around his neck. "Promise?"

"Oh, yeah," he said. "Right now."

And then he started to move, and her body came alive in his arms. It took only a few minutes before he sent her flying—over the edge and farther than she'd ever been.

If only they could stay there, forever.

* * *

Morgan raised her glass in a toast. "Here's to you, Ryan. Honestly, I'll never be able to thank you enough for what you've done for Sabrina and me."

Ryan touched his glass to hers and took a drink, then reached for the champagne bottle in the wine bucket next to their table in a quiet corner of the restaurant. He topped up their glasses. "Thanks, but you know that folks would have rallied around you anyway, don't you?"

"But you were the one to take charge." She cast him what was no doubt a totally sappy look. "Just like you took charge this afternoon. At the beach and...after."

"Well, you weren't exactly Miss Shrinking Violet, as I recall. Some of those audibles you called, man..." He gave her a comic leer.

She pretended to toss her half-eaten roll at him. "I told you I was sex starved."

"Not anymore?"

"Let's say not for the moment. If you think I'm through with you, mister..."

He gave her what could only be described as a shit-eating grin. "It went pretty well, didn't it?"

"You know exactly how well it went, dude. I'm surprised my eyes didn't roll permanently back into my head."

"In the immortal words of Karen Carpenter, we've only just begun, babe."

She laughed. "Really? Karen Carpenter? That was the song my parents danced to the first time they went out. Which seriously dates you, my friend, at least in terms of your taste in music."

According to her mother, it had only taken one date

and one dance. Her parents had never gone out with anyone else after that. They'd had a great love and a happy marriage but never got the chance to grow old together, to see their children settled and happy. Possibly to one day see their grandchildren.

The knowledge that she would never share that future with her parents totally sucked.

Ryan reached across and took her hand. "Why don't I flag down the waiter so we can order?"

"I'm sorry," she said, wrinkling her nose at him. "It just hits me sometimes all over again, that they're both gone."

He nodded. "I get it, and you never have to apologize. Grief has a way of sneaking up on you at weird moments."

He would know that of course, having lost friends while overseas.

Morgan squeezed his hand back. "I'm okay. Really. And very glad to be here with you."

At Ryan's suggestion, they'd crawled out of her thoroughly mussed bed not long before dusk and hurried to catch the ferry into Portland so they could have dinner at a bistro on Exchange Street—to celebrate the B&B's new beginning, he'd said. She'd agreed, but not before extracting a promise that they'd return to the inn and her bed for another bout of lovemaking before going their separate ways—to Lily's and his folks' house.

He'd been more than down with that plan.

"I'm glad too," he said. "But I can tell you're still stewing about everything. This is supposed to be a treat for you, remember?"

Morgan nodded. "I know." Then she let out a soulful sigh. "And I'm truly worried that I might lapse into a terrible funk if you don't keep me...fully occupied. I know it's a lot of pressure, but I expect you not to let me down."

His lips were curved in a smile, but his dark eyes sparked with heat. "Man, how am I going to get all that work done if you keep dragging me off to your bed and making me your sex slave?"

"Prioritize, Butler. Beside, you'll rise to the occasion, I'm sure."

Ryan rolled his eyes. "That was really bad, Merrifield, even for you. So bad I might just have to spank you when we get back to the island."

Morgan ran her tongue across her glossy lips. "Oh, good. More treats in store."

He looked torn between laughter and genuine interest in her mocking comment. "Let's put a pin in that, shall we? I want to talk about something else first."

She pouted. "Must we?"

"Nice try, but you won't distract me with your sultry ways, woman. I have an idea that's been kicking around in the back of my mind for the past few days."

"Okay, Soldier Boy, fire away."

"I've been wondering about repositioning Golden Sunset in the tourist market. Reconstruction might be an opportunity to do something like that. To rebuild and reopen with some added focus."

"Added focus?" Morgan echoed. "Translate to English, please."

"My guess is that Aiden's new resort is going to be a game changer for the island. It's obviously got its area of specialization with the emphasis on environmental tourism. So it makes sense that Golden Sunset should have a specialty too. I have a hunch you might need to be more than small and homey to attract new clients once the new resort opens."

Morgan had always worried about that, in spite of her conviction that the kind of people who patronized the B&B were unlikely to prefer an upscale ecoresort. As long as the inn was living on a knife-edge though, that worry would remain. At the very least, Aiden and Lily's resort would add a whole new element of uncertainty to Golden Sunset's prospects.

"I don't disagree," she said.

He plucked the champagne bottle from its ice bucket and topped up both Morgan's glass and his own.

"You're killing me with all this suspense," Morgan said.

"Sorry. Anyway, I've been doing a lot of thinking as I've been paddling all over the islands these past few days. And giving Christian those lessons gave me the idea too. This part of the world is beautiful, and it's really cool to be able to kayak so easily from one island to the other. Morgan, I really think you could position Golden Sunset as a center for people who want to explore the islands in a kayak or canoe."

Morgan stared across the table at him, dumbfounded.

He took her hand and started playing with her fingers. "Look, you've seen for yourself how fantastic it is to explore the bay in a kayak. I've never been anywhere more peaceful, and I've been just about everywhere in the world."

She couldn't disagree with any of that, so she nodded.

"I figure you could offer all sorts of services out of the B&B," he continued, obviously getting into it. "Like lessons, rentals, tandem rides, tours. It could become a destination both for kayakers who want a base and for folks looking for a relaxing introduction to the sport."

He stopped, waiting for some kind of response from her.

"Yeah, I hear you," she said. "It feels a little out there right now, with everything that's going on. I think you'll have to give me a minute to catch my breath."

Ryan picked up his glass. "Sure. Just let it roll around in your mind for a while."

Unlike her father, Morgan didn't know that much about the hospitality industry. Still, she was pretty sure that any kind of hotel, resort, or B&B that offered a specialized set of services had an advantage over one that didn't. That was the whole idea behind Aiden's resort. While that kind of specialization could obviously be risky, it could bring big rewards too.

But a kayaking destination? Not only would that take some investment in facilities and equipment at the outset, it would require expertise to operate it on an ongoing basis.

Morgan took a couple of sips of champagne to give her more time to think. Since Ryan was the kayak expert, was it possible that he was trying to tell her something about his own plans and how she fit into them?

Get a grip, Merrifield.

"In theory, it makes a lot of sense," she finally said. "I see some problems though. One big one, in particular."

His gaze narrowed. "Which is?"

"I'd obviously need to hire someone to run that part of the operation since I barely have a clue about kayaking. You know I still can hardly keep from capsizing." She managed a little chuckle. "And even if I could find someone with expertise who was willing to take it on, how could I afford his salary? Or hers?"

Ryan shook his head. "There are lots of college students around the area who have enough experience to do it. I think a student would gladly take it on as a summer job, and probably work part-time during the school year too. Especially if you were able to offer free accommodations."

She nodded, even though it felt like he'd just given her a jab to the throat. Ryan's grand plan clearly didn't include him sticking around.

Which only made sense, as she should have known. Why would he be interested in working as a part-time kayaking instructor at her little B&B? Really, wasn't that a laughable notion for a man like him? Ryan wasn't even interested in staying in Seashell Bay, much less carving out that sort of small-time career. Apparently, her sex-addled brain had decided to leap over that little fact.

"I could ask around in Portland," Ryan said when she didn't respond to his reassurance. "Check out some people who might be available for the last few weeks of the season after we reopen."

Morgan reached for her glass again. "That would be good," she said.

Ryan gave her a questioning look. "I know it's a lot to take in, but I really think we could make this work, Morgan."

There's the problem. There is no "we."

Which, she reminded herself for the umpteenth time, she'd known going into this. She refused to start acting like a baby about that now.

Ryan was right—his idea was well worth exploring.

And how lucky was she to have him around to do some of the groundwork? She should be darn grateful that he cared enough to come up with yet another idea to help her and Sabrina save the B&B.

"I'm sorry," she said. "I am excited about the idea, really I am. I guess I've just been so mugged by life lately that my optimism has taken a bit of a dive."

Ryan's lips curved into a smile. "Nah, you're just keeping your powder dry until you can get better organized. You're killer smart and determined, Morgan. I know that." He paused to exhale a long breath. "Not to mention so damn beautiful and sexy that I'm thinking I should get a hotel room here instead of killing myself to keep my hands off you until we get back to the island. I'm already so hard I probably won't be able to walk."

She choked back a laugh. From the heated look in his eyes, he was definitely ready for action. And the more she thought about it, the more she liked the idea. A lot.

"You're serious?" she asked. Her girl parts were starting to feel enthusiastic about his suggestion, so she hoped he said yes.

"Hell, yeah, I am."

"I'll have to call Sabrina or she'll worry."

"She'll be able to guess what happened," Ryan said. "You told her we were going to dinner in the city tonight. I doubt she'd think you've been accosted or something."

Not with a former Special Ops guy at my side, that's for sure.

Ryan was right—Morgan didn't need to have that conversation tonight. There would be time enough for Sabrina to weigh in on the dangers of sleeping with Ryan Butler. Still, she'd text her later. Her sister worried about everything, and Morgan wouldn't put her through any more than she had to.

"How about we order some appetizers to go and then get out of here?" she said.

Ryan's gaze devoured her. "You got it, babe. Because what I'm hungry for right now, they sure don't have on this menu."

Chapter 20

$\mathcal{M}$organ poked her head inside her sister's bedroom. "I'm home," she said, not quite sure what to expect. She'd spent the night in Portland with Ryan, which would certainly make it clear to Sabrina what was going on.

Her sister, who was stuffing her backpack with clothes, glanced up. "Hi. I was just getting a few more things to take to Lily's."

Morgan gave her a quick hug and then sat on her bed. "I've got some really good news. The power guys just told me that we should have electricity in the annex later this morning, so we can move back here right away."

Ryan was still outside talking to the crew from Central Maine Power, getting all the details. But when Morgan found out they could move back in, she felt like jumping into his arms and celebrating all over again. In bed, preferably, and she was hoping there would be plenty of time for that later.

Sabrina blew out a relieved sigh. "Oh, thank heavens. I really love Lily, but I felt kind of edgy without all my own stuff." She glanced around her room, smiling at her neatly arranged desk with its computer, widescreen monitor, and Xbox game console. Luckily, none of it had been ruined in the fire. "This is the only place I ever feel comfortable."

And safe, Morgan said to herself.

"I know. It will be good to be back home." She paused, but decided to face it head-on. "Honey, are you okay about last night, my staying in Portland? You really don't have to worry about anything, I promise."

Sabrina shook her head. "Morgan, I've got bigger things to worry about than your sex life." Her face scrunched up, and she looked like she was about to cry. "Golden Sunset was on its last legs before the fire, and by the time it's fixed up and ready to reopen, the season will be over and we won't be able to make the mortgage payments. I might not know that much about our finances, but I know what'll happen then."

Morgan opened her mouth to answer, but Sabrina cut her off. "You'll tell me that our only choice is to sell, and I suppose you'll be right."

When Morgan got up and went over to hug her again, Sabrina stiffened and took a step back. That hurt, but she tried not to take it personally since her sister was clearly upset.

"Let's not get discouraged, okay? After yesterday, I feel a lot more hopeful than I did before."

Sabrina stared at her and then shook her head. "Wow, if that's what getting laid does for you, then I really should work harder at getting some of that for myself."

Under other circumstances, Morgan might have laughed at her sister's comment. "Actually, I need to talk to you about some ideas Ryan's been working on. He told me about them yesterday, and I think they've got real possibilities."

Sabrina nodded cautiously. "Good, because we could use something positive right now."

Morgan briefly explained about the fund-raising initiative and about Ryan's idea for turning Golden Sunset into a destination center for kayaking in the islands. Sabrina was clearly excited about the fund-raising drive and the volunteer labor for repairing the building, but looked less thrilled about the proposed kayaking project. Fortunately, she perked up at Ryan's offer to set the wheels in motion.

"Do you think that means he might stay?" Sabrina said hopefully. "I mean, after what happened with you guys last night, and now with him coming up with this idea, it makes me hope..." She trailed off.

How times had changed. A few weeks ago, Sabrina had tearfully blurted out her fear that Morgan would end up abandoning her for Ryan. Now, though, she was clearly hoping Ryan would stick around and be part of their lives.

But even in the hazy glow of yesterday's amazing encounters, Morgan wouldn't let herself hope that Ryan would stick around past Labor Day. Still, it was better not to completely shatter Sabrina's hopes. Better to have her feeling optimistic about things.

"Honey, I just don't know," Morgan said. "We really can't count on him being here for much longer, so we have to make sure you and I are able to do everything that has to be done. But let's just take things one day at a time, okay? I know we can't control a lot right now, but I'm definitely feeling better about the future."

Sabrina dropped her gaze, obviously disappointed. "Yeah, well, at least you've got a future, Morgan. You'll always have teaching. I've got nothing without this place."

"Not true. If you didn't have one single other thing in

this world, my beautiful little sister, you'd always have me. That's going to be true no matter what else happens."

Sabrina grimaced, obviously edging closer to tears. "You've said that to me my whole life, and I've always believed you. But I'm not a kid anymore, Morgan, so please don't say it again unless you mean it."

Morgan reeled her sister in for a hug. "I mean it more than ever. Remember when we were little and you used to come running into my room in the middle of the night during big thunderstorms? You always came to me, not Mom and Dad."

"You'd make a tent by draping a sheet over the bed-posts, and I'd bring that little electric lantern. We'd stay up talking and making up stories until the storm passed," Sabrina said, hugging Morgan back.

"Yes, and I'll always be there to make us a little tent whenever we need one. Always, I promise."

"Okay, then." Sabrina sniffled, loosening her grip.

"Okay, then," Morgan echoed. "How about we get our rooms squared away and then get to work on the kitchen? We've got a huge job ahead if we're going to get this old pile back in shape anytime soon. Ryan and the rest of the guys are going to do amazing things for us, but in the end it's up to you and me, right? It's our inn and our home, and we're going to make it work, come hell or high water."

Ryan made one last note on his clipboard. "That should do it for now. We've got all the measurements we need so I'll order the lumber, the truss clips, and all the other stuff later this afternoon. I really appreciate your help, Micah."

The deputy leaned his big frame against the twelve-foot stepladder he'd been using for taking measurements in the attic. Both his T-shirt and his hands were grimy from handling blackened lumber and drywall, and his tanned face gleamed with sweat. "No problem. But I've got to head out. I promised Holly a long walk this afternoon." He looked down at his soiled shirt and rumpled cargo shorts. "Gotta shower and change before I show up at her aunts' store or they'll think I've turned into a derelict."

Ryan could barely suppress a smile. Micah had been doing his level best to make everyone think his attention to Holly was just that of a helpful cop assisting a local pal. Ryan wasn't buying it, nor was anyone else close to him. In truth, the badass deputy was a total marshmallow when it came to Holly—although Micah would beat the crap out of Ryan if he dared to say anything close to that.

Unfortunately, the real problem with that gooey-sweet scenario was that Holly had a New York boyfriend, some rich Wall Street type. Ryan feared that Micah was in for a world of emotional pain.

"I'm going to do the same thing myself," Ryan said. "Shower and change, I mean. Not show up at Holly's."

"Maybe you should. She's bored, and she loves having people hang out with her. I'm doing my best, but I can't take her for a walk every single day."

You're not fooling anybody, pal.

Micah always tried to act nonchalant about her when he was with the guys. They let him, mostly because it was the smart thing to do.

"I'd like to," Ryan said, "but this is going to keep me busy."

Micah nodded. "You're doing Morgan and Sabrina a hell of a solid. This sure isn't the way you figured you'd be spending your summer at home."

At home. There it is again.

Ryan couldn't count the number of times one or another islander had casually assumed that Seashell Bay was still home for him. "It's no big deal. If we don't do it, this place is going to close or be sold. I think that would destroy the girls, to tell you the truth. Can't let that happen, right?"

Micah held out his fist for Ryan to bump. "Damn straight. But are you going to be able to stick around long enough to see it all through? Aiden told me yesterday that Double Shield is pushing you to sign a new contract."

Ryan hadn't even mentioned that problem to Morgan and didn't plan to. It would just upset her. He'd only told Aiden because his friend had overheard part of his phone conversation with his Double Shield controller. He should have told Aiden to keep that news under his hat.

"I'm planning on seeing Golden Sunset reopen," he said. "Double Shield can wait awhile."

In truth though, Ryan wasn't sure how long the corporation would continue to let him stall. His controller in North Carolina was cutting him some slack, but the higher-ups at HQ wanted answers sooner rather than later. Ryan wasn't sure exactly how he was going to handle that problem. But given what was happening with him and Morgan, he was more committed than ever to staying until he'd done all he could to get the B&B back up and running.

In fact, he was beginning to hate the idea of walking away from her, although he knew damn well he'd have to do it eventually.

"Well, if you ever get tired of being a hired gun, I figure you could make a good living doing repairs and renovations around the islands." Micah wiped his grimy hands on some paper towels. "There aren't many handymen around. Brendan's so busy that people often have to bring in guys from the city. That really ratchets up the cost."

"Kind of surprises me," Ryan said. "I guess because Dad does almost all his own work, I always figured that must be true for most lobster fishermen. They're a self-sufficient lot."

"Not every guy is handy like your dad, and most are so wiped at the end of a long day fishing that they just want to rest up. Besides, look at how many summer residents we've got these days. They're only here for a few weeks or months, but they need work done too. Most of them can afford to keep their homes in top condition or even build additions."

"Maybe, but it's not really how I see things working out for me."

His friend gave a little shrug. "I guess it's crazy to think you'd want to come back here when you get to travel all over the world like that. Seashell Bay must seem pretty boring after Paris and Berlin and Singapore and... what were some of the other places you said you spent time in last year?"

"Johannesburg? Lagos? Port-au-Prince?" Some of the most dangerous places in the world, in fact. People rarely needed bodyguards in Paris or Singapore.

"Right," Micah said. "Those don't sound all that great, come to think about it."

Every city had presented its particular dangers to the people Ryan had been tasked with protecting. Those three, though, had been the worst of his globetrotting odyssey. Nobody in his party was allowed to go anywhere with-out at least two heavily armed operators from the Double

Shield team at their side. Kidnapping was an ever-present danger, and there was often a good chance of being struck down by intentional or stray bullets.

"That's an understatement, my friend," Ryan said.

"No wonder you needed a break," he said, giving Ryan a little grin. "So maybe you should think about making it a permanent one and just stay here."

Ryan shook his head, wondering if there was some kind of coordinated campaign going on to bring him back to the island. Morgan, Sabrina, Aiden, Lily, and now Micah had been banging away on that subject since he got here. It gave him a weird feeling in the pit of his stomach every time somebody brought it up.

"Oh, come on, I see how Morgan looks at you," Micah protested. "I've known that girl for a long time, and I've never seen her look like that at anybody else, dude. Yeah, she won't want to admit it, but the woman's obviously got it bad for you. Of course, I'm not sure why somebody so fine as Morgan would want to hook up with you, but there it is."

"Since when did you turn into a fucking matchmaker?" Ryan asked.

"Hey, I get to give you some free advice, asshole. After all, I am the law of the land around here." Micah gave Ryan a friendly punch to the shoulder. "Now I've really gotta run."

Ryan watched him climb down from the attic, annoyed that his friend was so spot-on when it came to him and Morgan. With every day he stuck around Seashell Bay, he could feel himself getting pulled in, both head and heart. Yeah, he'd been pretty surprised by how much he was enjoying his time on the island, but it was Morgan who was the real draw. She had burrowed her way into his heart like no one had in a long time. Or ever.

Which pretty much sucked. While he couldn't leave yet and didn't want to anytime soon, he knew the day would come soon enough that he would go. That day might just bring some pain that would be a long time healing.

For both of them.

When Ryan slid his callused hand across the pickup's console and rested it on Morgan's bare thigh, the sudden rough warmth almost took her breath away.

"Happy to be moving back into your room?" he asked.

He'd offered to drive her when she went to Lily's to pick up her things. With Sabrina and Micah and a raft of utility crew guys working around the inn, they hadn't had a chance to talk about, well, things. Things like what was going to happen between them after last night, for however long Ryan remained in Seashell Bay. Morgan had spent the day cleaning and organizing the kitchen and generally tidying up, her mind coming back every minute or so to Ryan and what had happened between them. It felt like the Earth's axis had shifted, throwing her completely off-kilter. Mostly it was wonderful and exciting, but an undertow of anxiety had her mentally going sideways.

"Yes and no," she said. "The way Lily fussed over us, it was like a minivacation. But don't get me wrong—I'm glad to be going home. Anything that moves us closer to getting Golden Sunset back to normal is a step forward."

Normal? Morgan had probably chosen the wrong word. The B&B hadn't been in any state of normality for months and certainly not since her father died.

Ryan's long fingers went down her leg in a sexy glide that produced a sweet little ache between her thighs. "I don't suppose we're going to be doing it in your bed again anytime soon," he said. "Not with your sister on the other side of a thin wall."

Morgan could barely stop herself from grabbing his hand and pulling it right up to where she wanted it to be. But sex in a pickup truck wasn't going to happen no matter how much she wanted him at that moment, especially with the very likely chance that a neighbor or friend or—God forbid—Ryan's parents could drive by in the opposite direction.

But, oh, she did want him.

"She does go into Portland once a week for therapy," she said helpfully.

"Once a week? Man, I can't wait to get into my own place."

Morgan almost laughed at the frustration coloring his voice.

"I hear you, dude," she said with a grin. Every minute she was with him, she wanted to crawl on top of him and get busy.

He gave her thigh another little squeeze. "How about we head back into Portland tonight? Same time, same place?"

She tipped her sunglasses down, looking at him over the top of the frames. "Are you a sex fiend or something? How many times did we do it yesterday?"

"Why? You have a weekly limit on orgasms or something?"

She laughed. "Hardly, but hotels cost a lot of money."

He glanced over and waggled his eyebrows. "Money

well spent, in my book. And it's no problem. Double Shield paid me a ton to babysit those corporate guys."

Morgan had a clear impression that money didn't mean a lot to Ryan. Though he still hadn't told her much about how he lived his life, she knew he rented a one-bedroom apartment in a Raleigh high-rise and drove an older SUV. But he'd also said that one reason he'd been attracted to the high-paying life of the private soldier was because having a solid nest egg would buy him the freedom to walk away after a few years and not worry about what he did for a living. As skilled as Ryan was at many things, he seemed to think he didn't have many options given his lack of formal education.

"Sabrina and I had a talk this morning," Morgan said a bit abruptly. "It turns out she wasn't mad at me for...for you know."

"No? That sounds like progress."

"I think it's got something to do with the fact that she's come to think that Ryan Butler walks on water."

Ryan blinked as he pulled his hand back. "You're joking, right?"

She wished he'd left his hand right where it was. "Well, as one example, she said she wished you could stick around permanently and help us run the place. She likes everything we talked about yesterday—the fund-raising, the focus on kayaking, the whole package. But I had to deflate her hopes about you staying."

That wasn't strictly true, but she didn't want him to worry. "I get where she's coming from," she went on, stifling a sigh. "Because sometimes I can barely imagine you not being here anymore."

There. Let's see what you do with that.

Ryan didn't say anything for a few moments, turning his head as if to check out the homes that bordered on Island Road. "I'm trying not to think too much about that," he finally said.

Oh, boy. Don't let me in on your feelings or anything.

"Right. Take it one day at a time," she said. That was probably what he wanted to hear. "Like Buddhists say, yesterday is a memory, tomorrow is the unknown. The present is all there is."

"Um, yeah," Ryan said, clearly uncomfortable.

She had to stifle another sigh, this time of frustration. She'd never met a more generous or kindhearted man—or one who had such a hard time expressing his feelings.

"So," he finally said just before they reached the turn to Lily's cottage, "we've talked about me and what I'm going to do, but what about you, Morgan? Can you see yourself staying on the island even if the B&B started turning a profit? Because I didn't think that was ever in your plans."

It isn't. Not without you anyway.

But that was just her gut reaction. In truth, Morgan didn't know what she was going to do. She couldn't imagine not teaching, yet that meant going back to Pickle River or somewhere else on the mainland. The chances of a job opening up anytime in the near future at the Seashell Bay elementary school were minimal, given the ages and plans of the current teachers. That left the enormous problem of what to do about her sister.

"I don't know anymore," she said. "That's the honest answer, Ryan. I dread the idea of not ever teaching again, but…this isn't just about me. You know I have to take care of Sabrina. I want to do everything I can to help her find a happy life. If it turned out that the only way I could do right by my sister was to stay here and keep the B&B afloat, then, yeah, that's what I'd have to do."

He gave her one of his trademark enigmatic looks, then nodded. Whatever his opinion was, he was obviously keeping it to himself.

Chapter 21

$\mathcal{M}$organ's heart felt lodged in her throat. This was finally it. In just a few minutes her best friend would finally be married.

She stood at the front of Saint Anne's church with Aiden and his best man, Bram. Lily hadn't wanted some big march up the aisle, so the small wedding party had simply gathered up front, waiting for the bride to appear. But at the last minute, Father Michael had inexplicably bustled over to the sacristy, apparently looking for something. It was a departure from what they'd rehearsed last night, and it had Morgan tapping her toe with irritation.

Today, everything *had* to be perfect. Lily deserved perfection, especially since she and Aiden had been forced to fight so hard for their life together. That Aiden had returned to Seashell Bay and that he'd finally decided to make a life on the island because of his love for Lily still seemed nothing short of a miracle.

"You do realize you're the luckiest dude alive," she said out of the side of her mouth to Aiden.

"Morgan, don't ever doubt that for a second," Aiden said warmly. "I'll love Lily till the day I die."

"You'd better if you know what's good for you," she said, curling her lips back in a mock snarl.

Aiden glanced around and then leaned in close. "I bet Lily will be saying exactly the same thing to Ryan when she's standing up here waiting for you."

Morgan almost dropped her bouquet of pale pink roses. What the hell was she supposed to say to that? She frantically tried to gather her wits. "Uh, you know something I don't?"

"Only if somehow you haven't figured out that the guy's in love with you." Aiden winked at her.

"You've suddenly developed ESP or something?" Morgan hissed, totally flustered. Boy, this was *so* not an appropriate conversation to be having right at this moment. She flicked a nervous glance around the church, praying that no one sitting close by could hear them.

Aiden rolled his eyes. "Look, I spent a lot of years around tough guys who killed themselves *not* to look like they were head over heels. Ryan's been giving off that vibe ever since the fire, if not before."

She stared at him, just barely keeping her jaw from dropping to the floor. Her heart was racing a mile a minute, but she forced herself to clamp down on the insane combination of hope and excitement, countering it with cold, hard facts. Aiden had to be reading it all wrong. She could agree that Ryan was totally hot for her and was certainly into their summer fling, but nothing had changed when it came to the big picture.

After one quick glance, Morgan had studiously avoided looking at Ryan since taking her position at the altar. The last thing she wanted was for people to see her mooning at him in public. He was sitting next to Laura on the groom's side of the aisle, and when she'd caught his eye, he'd given her a wry smile and a wink. He looked so damn handsome in his dark blue suit that her knees had gone a little wobbly, but she'd simply given him a quick nod and turned her focus to the groom. Yes, she and Ryan had been dating, for lack of a better term, for the last two weeks and everyone on the island knew it. But that was hardly a reason to act like a love-struck idiot in front of all their friends. Ryan would no doubt hate that.

She forced a smile when Father Michael finally emerged from the sacristy. A moment later, the pianist began playing an old seafarer's hymn—so sweet and perfect for Lily—and the congregants stood in a Sunday-best wave. She and Aiden and Bram all turned to the red-carpeted center aisle, where Lily and a beaming Tommy Doyle were beginning their walk.

Morgan had to suppress an instinctive laugh at the look on Aiden and then Bram's face. Like everyone else on the island, they were used to seeing Lily in T-shirts, jeans, and sneakers, often covered in fish guts.

Not today. Not by a long shot.

Lily's off-the-shoulder gown in duchess satin positively glowed in the late afternoon sunlight that streamed through the church's stained glass windows. A wreath of wildflowers, picked from her mother's garden, circled her head to anchor a lovely wisp of a veil. With a four-foot train draped behind her, Lily stepped slowly but gracefully. Her gaze was locked on her groom, her face lit with transcendent joy.

Morgan blinked back her tears as best she could. Now

was not the time for the maid of honor to fall apart. She'd already cried enough over the past twenty-four hours—much of which she'd spent with Lily and her mom and Holly—and there would be opportunity for her to indulge in maudlin sentiments later. Right now, she needed to keep it together and not let her own emotions, too close to the surface these days, draw focus away from the ceremony.

"Get a grip on the tears, Merrifield," Bram said sotto voce behind Aiden's back. But he punctuated the comment with a sly grin. "By the way, have I told you how smokin' hot you look in that dress?"

"Shut up, Bram," she whispered.

When Father Michael let out a little *tsk*, frowning at her and Bram, Morgan gave the priest a sheepish smile. It was the second time today that Bram had called her "hot." Morgan had already received more compliments than she could count about her royal-blue bridesmaid's dress with its scoop neckline and sheath silhouette. Still, she had very nearly stuck her tongue out at Aiden's not-so-little brother, and wouldn't that have made a pretty picture for the wedding album?

Lily arrived at the altar with her dad. Tommy gave his daughter a fierce hug—he'd been blubbering the entire way up the aisle—and then went to sit with his wife in the first pew. Lily beamed up at her fiancé, then turned to hand Morgan her flowers.

"What were you and Aiden yacking about?" Lily whispered.

"I was just telling Aiden I'd kill him if he didn't make you happy," Morgan murmured back.

Lily laughed before giving Morgan a quick kiss. "Thought so. I love you, sweetie. Thank you for everything."

Father Michael cleared his throat, and the murmuring from the pews died away. Morgan tried to focus her attention on the beautiful wedding ceremony, but her mind kept drifting back to Ryan. For the past two weeks, she'd kept the depth of her feelings for him locked down. Even after they made love, snuggling together all night, first in the hotel room and then in the cottage Ryan had moved into near Paradise Point, Morgan had never once told him how she felt about him—that she loved him, and that more than anything she wanted to spend her life with him.

After all, what was the point? Unlike Lily and Aiden, Morgan and Ryan would never end up in this place, standing in front of Father Michael taking their vows and pledging to love each other forever. She was so happy the fairy tale was finally coming true for her best friend, but Morgan's happily ever after was proving as elusive as ever.

Ryan loosened his tie as he surfed the appetizer tables in the church hall. He hated suits. Hated ties. Hated dress shirts with stiff collars. He sometimes wore a sport coat when he was on duty, but more often than not he was in a T-shirt, jeans, and a ballistic vest. For his buddy's wedding though, he'd sucked it up and bought a real suit at one of the outlet malls in Freeport. He couldn't wait for the reception to be over so he could head home and take the damn thing off.

And get naked with Morgan, who he hoped would be down with that plan.

All during the ceremony, he hadn't been able to keep his eyes off her. She looked so totally hot in that slinky blue dress, as Bram had unnecessarily reminded him when they met up in the church foyer. Morgan, however, had only given him one brief glance from the altar. After the ceremony she'd gone off with the rest of the wedding party for photographs, including some on Lily's boat moored out at O'Hanlon's Boatyard.

Morgan had obviously been preoccupied with her maid-of-honor duties, but Ryan couldn't help getting the sense that she was avoiding him in a way he couldn't quite put his finger on. He got that she was feeling emotional about Lily and the wedding, which made sense. But was something else going on that he needed to know about?

Still, he figured they'd have plenty of time later to talk, though shallow bastard that he was, what he really wanted to do was take her straight to bed. They'd had sex every day at least once since the first time, and yet he was always hungry for more. He just couldn't get enough of Morgan. He didn't rattle easily, but that fact had started to seriously unsettle him.

As did the idea of walking away from her.

Choosing to ignore that for the moment, he sauntered over to the corner of the room where Micah was yukking it up with a few of the locals, all sitting around one of the tables and drinking beer straight from the bottle.

"Cool suit, man," Brett Clayton said. "Never seen you in one of those before."

"And hopefully never will again," he replied. "It's the first wedding I've been to in . . . well, forever."

He'd been to more than a few funerals so he had plenty of experience wearing a dress uniform and medals. But a civilian suit felt weird.

"Morgan might have something to say about that. You two are just about inseparable these days." Micah gave him an evil grin. "Just sayin'."

Ryan shot him a withering glare.

"I'm sure he means she might drag you to some other friend's wedding if you're still around," Josh Bryson put in quickly, laughing at Ryan's prickly reaction.

Brett's brows knitted in a frown. "Really? I though Micah was talking about Morgan and Ryan maybe getting—"

Ryan cut Brett off before he could finish another of his foot-in-mouth interventions. "Brendan, we're going to need you next week for that work on the doors and windows we talked about. Can you fit us in somehow?"

Brendan looked surprised. "That's sooner than I planned. You guys must really be busting your asses over there."

The town carpenter had it right. Ryan, Aiden, and Micah, along with some help from Josh, Brett, and Roy, had made incredible progress. The inn's roof and attic were completely repaired, and the damaged rooms upstairs had been drywalled and taped. They'd roughed in new windows, and a mainland electrician—a temporarily out-of-work construction guy Ryan had unearthed in Biddeford—had finished the second floor and was in the process of replacing the downstairs wiring. Fortunately, the more modern wiring in the annex hadn't needed replacement.

"Look, I know you're still swamped," Ryan said, "but we're dead set on reopening later this month. By the Blueberry Festival would be even better." Then he pulled out his trump card. "You know how much it would mean to Morgan and Sabrina after everything they've been through."

Brendan laughed. "Yeah, guilt-tripping actually works. Okay, I should be able to talk a couple of my clients into backing up their projects a few days. Everybody wants to see Golden Sunset get back on its feet."

"Fuckin' A, man," Brett chimed in.

"Bren, this guy does great construction work," Micah said, jerking a thumb at Ryan. "I've been telling him he could find plenty of repair work around the islands if he wanted to set up a little one-man business here. You've been swamped for years after all."

Ryan was still puzzled by that. "If you've got too much to handle, why don't you just hire somebody else to work with you?" he said to Brendan.

"I got into a trade because I never wanted to have a boss. And I sure as hell don't want to be one," Brendan said. "I'd be happy if there was somebody else local sharing the load. I hate to see folks have to call some guy in from the city, but I've only got two hands."

Josh craned around to look at the door to the hall. "Hey, they're back."

Ryan turned to see the wedding party starting to work their way through the crowd. Morgan had seemed to be heading for him when Lily grabbed her elbow and steered her at a ninety-degree angle toward Lily's grandfather, who was talking to fellow codgers Miss Annie, Roy Mayo, and Sean Flynn. Morgan managed to give Ryan a rueful smile as Lily swung her around.

Aiden, meanwhile, continued straight toward him. Ryan's friend looked completely at home in his black tuxedo, but then he'd probably worn them to baseball awards nights or dates with models and actresses.

"Well, here's a crew that's probably up to no good," Aiden said, grinning at the motley group sitting around the table.

"Kind of," Brett said. "Micah's on a campaign to get Ryan to move back here. We've been talking about how the town needs another guy to do handyman stuff."

When Aiden shot him a questioning look, Ryan lifted his gaze to the ceiling and shook his head.

"Guys, I need to grab Ryan for a minute," Aiden said. "We'll catch up later." He pulled on Ryan's arm, and they headed to a fairly quiet corner behind the platform where the band would soon play.

"What the hell, dude?" Ryan asked. Why would Aiden drag him off in the middle of his wedding reception?

"I wanted to run an idea past you." He rested a friendly hand on Ryan's shoulder. "When I heard those guys were on your case about sticking around, I figured now was as good a time as any."

Ryan gave a sardonic laugh. "Morgan talks to Lily, Lily talks to Holly, Holly bends Micah's ear, and presto, Micah's talking about how much repair business there is on the island." Thing was, he wasn't entirely sure how he felt about that.

Aiden frowned. "You think Morgan's behind it?"

"Well, she told me she could hardly imagine me leaving."

"That doesn't mean she's behind a conspiracy or campaign, asshat. And I'm not going to get into what Morgan and my wife talk about—as if Lily would tell me everything anyway. But it's pretty clear to me that Morgan's resigned to the fact that you'll be leaving soon. If you want to blame anybody for trying to get you to stay, blame Lily and me."

Morgan was resigned to his leaving? Ryan wasn't sure he could take that statement to the bank. Yeah, she was tough and resilient and she'd get over him, but that didn't mean she'd yet come to grips with him going. Not from what he'd seen.

Hell, *he* hadn't come to grips with it. When he held Morgan in his arms in the darkest hours of the night, he could barely imagine being away from her for months at a time. But when the sun came up in the morning, reality always came with it. Life had brought the two of them together for a while, and life would separate them again as they followed their own paths, just like it always had.

"It's not about blame," Ryan said. "My life's just not here, man."

Aiden frowned. "So you've said. But where is it, then? You're obviously not that happy doing your thing with Double Shield."

That wasn't the point, as far as Ryan was concerned. But he held his fire, not wanting to argue.

From the look on Aiden's face, he knew what Ryan would have said anyway.

"Look, I get it," Aiden said. "After I left at eighteen, not for one moment did I ever think I'd want to come back to Seashell Bay to live. Hell, I didn't even want to visit. But now, I'm happy with it. And not just because Lily's here either. This is a good place to put down roots. It's... peaceful. Good for the soul, and not in some New Age crap kind of way. It's real."

Ryan nodded. He understood that now—a lot more than he did before this summer.

"Back in high school, you and I couldn't see that," Aiden went on. "We were hell-bent on making another kind of life for ourselves on the mainland. But that's not the only choice, and I think maybe you realize that now."

Aiden was saying that guys like them just needed some time—maybe a lot of time—away from this little corner of the world. Maybe work whatever it was out of their systems. In Aiden's case it had been true, but was it true for Ryan too? Was it—whatever "it" was—out of his system?

He was far from sure. He had to admit that his feelings for the island were shifting from day to day. The only thing he was certain about was that saying good-bye to Morgan was going to be a hell of a lot harder than he'd ever thought it would be.

Screw it. The whole conversation made Ryan uncomfortable. It was great that his friends cared about him and wanted him to stick around, but he didn't need the pressure, even if it was unintentional. "Yo, this is your wedding day," he said. "You should be thinking about your beautiful bride and your honeymoon, not about me."

Aiden shook his head. "Yeah, but you might be talking to Double Shield before Lily and I get back. That's why I wanted to talk to you about something before we leave."

"And I figure you'll get around to that soon," Ryan said sarcastically, realizing Aiden wasn't going to let him off the hook.

His friend ignored the friendly jab. "Look, Lily and I have been throwing around an idea. We're a long way from opening the resort, but we're going to need to start hiring some key staff soon. Like security staff, for one thing."

Security staff. Ryan figured he was getting the picture but didn't say anything.

"I didn't have a clue what a security operation at a resort of our size should look like," Aiden continued, "so I talked to my friend Colton Booth. He runs a resort up the coast and is helping us get ours off the ground. Colton told me we'd be looking at a chief, plus about three other staff to cover all the shifts."

"And you thought of a certain ex-soldier you know?" Ryan asked drily.

"Exactly." Aiden said, obviously dead serious.

"A security guard, dude? Seriously?"

Aiden snorted. "I'm talking about chief of security, obviously."

Wow. Ryan hadn't seen that one coming. Was Aiden nuts?

Hotel security had never crossed Ryan's radar screen. Corporate security, yeah. He'd even been offered a financially attractive gig by one of the CEOs he'd protected, but he'd have had to spend half the year in Kuala Lumpur. But resort security? All he could think about was a guy in a dark suit knocking on the door of rowdy guests to tell them to shut the hell up so people could sleep. Or dealing with somebody losing her purse and thinking someone stole it.

He'd die from boredom in a week. "We're talking about Seashell Bay, Aiden. All those security people sounds kind of excessive to me. You might need to keep Daisy Whipple from pilfering some of your potted plants, but I'm not sure what else could go wrong."

Aiden didn't laugh. "I'm serious, man. This resort aims to attract well-off clients. People like that expect top-notch security. The best technology, and especially the best people."

"Okay, but what do I know about hotel security?" Ryan parried. "Not much."

"Bull," Aiden shot back. "Those corporate types you've been bodyguarding must have demanded the latest in technology and tactics."

Ryan couldn't deny that. "Pretty much."

"Right. And there isn't anything you don't know about keeping people safe."

This time Ryan did sigh. "Yep."

"Then just think about what I've said, okay? We can talk about it again after Lily and I get back from Quebec City. We'll only be gone a week."

Ryan gave a little nod. "Look, I appreciate this. And I will think about it. But I'm not taking anything away from the island when I say that I still can't see sticking around here for long."

It was true that they'd both been determined to leave Seashell Bay, but Aiden had wanted to escape his family even more than playing pro baseball. Ryan loved his family, but he'd needed to see the world and life beyond the island. He hadn't been escaping anything—he'd been running toward something.

Aiden stuck out his hand, and Ryan shook it. "While you're thinking about it, remember this. Morgan's not the only one who wants you to stay—not by a long shot. People here have always liked you, and everybody admires your service to the country. But after they've seen everything you've been doing for Morgan and Sabrina this summer... well, let's just say that your hero status is rising to new heights." He clapped Ryan on the shoulder.

"Oh, please, what utter bullshit," Ryan said.

"Just telling the truth, man. So think about it."

Ryan exhaled a relieved sigh when Aiden headed off toward Lily's group. But the fact remained that Aiden had gotten him thinking about things—things that had been lurking below the surface for some days and would no longer be ignored.

But he had no intention of dealing with them right now.

All he wanted now was a beer and Morgan, and definitely not in that order.

"That suit of yours totally did me in," Morgan said as she lay plastered against Ryan's side. "You looked so freaking hot I thought I might have to pull you into a dark corner of the hall and have my evil way with you." She reached up and lazily ran her tongue along the hard plane between Ryan's navel and sternum, savoring the faintly salty taste of his hot skin. "But this was totally worth the wait."

Boy, was it ever. She and Ryan had cut out as soon as Aiden and Lily left the dance. The newlyweds were spending their wedding night in a Portland hotel before hitting the road in the morning for a five- or six-hour drive to Quebec City. Morgan had practically dragged Ryan back to his little cottage, and they only managed to make it as far as the sofa before he was inside her. After their first, almost frantic bout of lovemaking, they'd gotten themselves as far as his bed.

"You had me wondering for a while there." Ryan smoothed a big hand down her naked back. "You ignored me at the wedding and for half the reception."

Her heart jolted a bit that he'd noticed, but she forced a little laugh. "Poor baby. You have to admit I was a little busy with my maid-of-honor duties."

"Onerous as they were," he said sarcastically.

"It's not a real good idea to sass me when I've got your junk in my hand," she said, reaching down to cup him.

He tilted his head forward to smirk at her. "Do weddings always make you this horny?"

"First time," she said softly, sliding her hand up to his waist and snuggling even closer.

Ryan ran his fingertip along her jawline and tipped her chin up. "I have to admit I'm glad about that." His dark gaze was warm and tender.

"Really?" she asked doubtfully.

"Yep. Guess I can't help being a Neanderthal, at least when it comes to you."

"Well, then, if you knew my entire sexual history, you'd be completely thrilled." Though she said it in a joking voice, the words contained so much truth. She hadn't exactly been a nun, but she'd been averse all her life to sex just for the sake of sex.

"You can enlighten me if you want."

"Only if I wanted you to pass out from boredom. Besides, I have much more interesting things in mind once we've had our little rest."

"Rest and recuperation. I like it." Ryan raised himself up on an elbow and nuzzled her lips before flopping back down on the mattress. "We can always talk later."

Talk later. About what, how she'd fallen madly in love with him? And even if she did tell him, could it possibly influence him to stay in Seashell Bay, with her?

She had no idea. But one thing Morgan did know was that if she put her heart out there and got nothing back from him in return, she'd probably want to crawl into a closet and hide. Aside from what it would do to her emotionally, it could also put their work to save Golden Sunset in jeopardy. She'd become so dependent on him to help her pull through the latest crisis that she was terrified that a falling out would damage their working relationship.

Ryan wasn't looking for forever, and she knew that too. *So don't say it, then. Play it safe, like you always do.*

"Holly's going home the day after tomorrow," she said, taking the easy way out.

Ryan rolled onto his side to face her, frowning slightly. "I thought she was going to stay longer."

"Me too. But she's getting around fine with her crutches now, and she's desperate to get back to work."

"Don't blame her for that," he said, sounding wry.

Ouch. Was he also starting to miss his work—his real work?

She forged on. "Anyway, I'm going to go with her to Boston and stay over a day or two. Help her with shopping and getting her place organized."

"You're a hell of a good friend, babe." Ryan kissed her again, this time on the tip of her nose. "Since I need to go to Raleigh, I might as well go at the same time. That way we won't miss much time together."

He tipped her jaw up again and started kissing her neck. Her surprise warred with her instinct to give in to his ability to reduce her to a puddle of pleasure.

"You're going to see Double Shield?"

"Yeah. It's time I talked to my controller," he said, sounding distracted.

Despite the bone-melting sensation of his hot breath against her skin, something like a shiver went up her spine. "What are you going to say to them?" she ventured.

He paused for several long seconds. "I'm still working on that."

Chapter 22

$\mathcal{R}$yan's boss and mentor gave him one of his usual bone-crushing handshakes. Oliver "Cap" Capstone was a two-hundred-pound, grizzled rock of a man with a prosthetic leg—courtesy of an IED that had demolished his armored vehicle and left two of his Double Shield team dead. That had been the last field assignment for the legendary Cap Capstone, and Double Shield had given him a well-deserved desk job in Raleigh as a reward. From an unassuming office building overlooking a wooded ravine in the burbs, Cap now managed more than a hundred operators—mostly men but some women—who worked and traveled in the most dangerous parts of the world.

"Thanks for making time for me," Ryan said, taking one of the uncomfortable metal chairs in front of Cap's tidy mahogany desk.

His boss waved him off. "Hey, you hauled ass all the way from that chickenshit island in Maine. How the hell are you anyway? Good to see you haven't let yourself go soft. Yet."

"I've been logging a lot of miles in my kayak, paddling around and thinking about stuff."

Cap leaned back in his executive chair, giving Ryan an assessing stare. "Thinking about stuff. I'm not sure I like the sound of that."

"You taught me that there's nothing more important on a mission," Ryan said sardonically.

"You're not on a mission in fucking Maine, Butler. What's going on? You want even more time off?"

Ryan shook his head. "I didn't come all the way to Raleigh to ask for that."

When Cap thumped the desk with his fist, it shook his brass nameplate hard enough that Ryan had to snatch it before it slid to the floor. "So you're quitting. I can see it in your damn eyes."

Ryan didn't flinch in the face of his boss's belligerent growl, since it was mostly for show. "I appreciate everything Double Shield has done for me, Cap. And I'm grateful for all the support you've given me personally."

He paused, collecting himself. His boss continued to level his death stare right at him.

Man up, dude. Get it out there.

"Here's the thing, Cap, plain and simple," Ryan said. "The job just doesn't seem right for me anymore. I figured if I took some time off and went home, things might start to become clearer. And I guess they are. I still don't know what I want to do after this job, but I know it isn't to…" Ryan checked himself, not wanting to say anything that could be taken as devaluing Double Shield's work. It was good work, necessary work, and he had no regrets about his time with the company. "I know it isn't to keep bouncing all over the world."

Cap grimaced but nodded in understanding. "It's not an easy life. But you're damn good at it, Ryan. One of the best I've ever had. And your client evaluations have been top of the list. You can pretty much write your own ticket on assignments."

It was the first time Capstone had ever called him Ryan. And he was shocked by the compliments too. He knew he had Cap's respect for the work he'd done in the field but had no idea that his boss considered him one of his best operators.

"I really appreciate that. And you've been a great mentor, Cap."

Capstone studied him for several long seconds, then sighed. "I don't suppose I'll be able to talk you out of it, you pigheaded son of a bitch," he said with no rancor. "But you gotta know you're going to be bored out of your mind doing anything else. Guys like you and me are born for this, Ryan." His gaze skirted around the room. "I don't mean *this*, obviously. This desk job is pure bullshit, though it pays the bills. I meant we were born for the life. For what you do. For what I used to do."

The old whispers of doubt feathered through Ryan. He could hear the frustration in Cap's voice at being stuck behind a desk, the boredom that came with that kind of life. It worried him too.

Still, what he'd been doing wasn't right anymore. "I'd just like to stay in one place for a while. See how that works out."

Capstone snorted. "On that chickenshit island of yours?"

Ryan shrugged. "Somewhere in the States. No deserts. No jungles." He gave a little laugh. "For some reason, Seashell Bay seems like a good place to settle down for a while."

"Settling down with a wife and kids and a house with a good old, white picket fence? Jesus, that sounds like a recipe for disaster, at least for guys like us." Cap didn't mask his disdain.

Maybe not if you're with the right woman.

"Well, I'd like to have kids someday, and kids deserve to have a father around."

"Lots of our guys are married with kids," Cap countered. "Military wives know how to cope with jobs like ours. You know that."

Many could but a lot couldn't. And military girlfriends often ended up sending their boyfriends shitty Dear John letters, like the kind Ryan had gotten from Callie while he was overseas.

Still, despite that bitter personal betrayal, he couldn't really blame a woman who didn't want to spend most of her life coping with everything on her own while her husband was deployed, not to mention having to take nearly all the responsibility for raising the kids. "I'd never ask that of a woman."

When Cap didn't respond, Ryan spread his hands wide. "Look, I could be making a big mistake. You obviously think I am. But right now I feel like I have to change things up."

His boss brightened a bit. "Change things up, huh? Well, maybe we could do something about that. What if we could smoke out some assignments that'd keep you stateside a lot more?"

Ryan swallowed a curse. He hadn't planned on getting into a bargaining session with his controller. He'd just come to quit. Still, he might as well raise the one thing—the only thing—that could make him reconsider.

"I appreciate that, Cap, but actually the only thing that could tempt me to stick around would be one of the combat training jobs at the national center. But that's a non-starter since you've made it crystal clear that those only go to operators with years of service and a broad range of assignments under their belts."

Capstone didn't say anything for several seconds, as if he was really thinking that through. But then he gave a tiny shake of the head and put his palms flat on the desk to push himself to his feet. "Okay, Ryan. But if you have second thoughts, you know you're more than welcome to come back. Guys like you don't grow on those loblolly pines out there."

Well, that's it. You pulled the plug.

Ryan stood and extended his hand. The meeting had been as tough as he'd expected. And the fact that uncertainty still tugged at him suggested he wasn't nearly as convinced about his decision as he'd made out to his controller. "That's great to know, Cap. Thanks."

Because who knew how he'd feel in a month or a year? While his decision felt mostly right in the moment, walking out now wasn't going to be easy. It already felt like he was closing the door on the only kind of life he'd ever known. And he had to admit that the prospect, although exhilarating, was also intimidating.

Cap pumped his hand. "I'm guessing she must be one hell of a woman, Butler. Now get your ass out of my office."

Morgan filled the kettle and turned on Holly's high-end gas range to boil water for tea. "I can't believe how pleased the surgeon was with your progress. It's awesome news."

Holly smiled at her from the sofa in the open-concept living room of her Boston condo. The Marlborough Street brownstone was old, but the unit had been completely renovated before she moved in. Morgan was happy that her friend could afford a gorgeous apartment on a tree-lined street in central Boston, because she certainly deserved it.

But she was a tiny bit envious too. Morgan had once felt herself well on the way to financial independence, but that was nothing but a memory retreating in her mental rearview mirror.

"I attribute the progress to good sea air and a whole lot of TLC from the best people in the world," Holly said. "Starting with you, sweetie."

Morgan filled an infuser with loose-leaf green tea and readied the pot. "You'd do the same for me. And Lily would take care of both of us."

"Of course, but you were taking care of me in the middle of your own personal crises."

Morgan pulled a couple of mugs out of a cupboard. "It hasn't exactly been an easy summer for either of us, has it?"

"At least you've been getting laid. By one of the hottest guys on the planet, I might add."

Laid and how. "Maybe your big-shot New York investment manager will pay a visit soon and remedy your abstinence problem." Morgan grinned. "Might be interesting to come up with some new positions to avoid trashing your cast."

"Fat chance. Jackson couldn't even be bothered to come to Maine the whole time I was there. And to be honest, I'm just as glad he didn't. He's a lot of fun, but he can be a bit of a brat."

The kettle started to whistle. Morgan grabbed and filled the teapot. "Well, it doesn't help your relationship that he's in New York and you're here. Long-distance romance is pretty tough."

How many times had Morgan pondered that very problem when it came to Ryan? Would he ever want to keep the relationship going if they were separated for months at a time? Could it have any future, or would they gradually drift apart with another woman taking Morgan's place in Ryan's bed and heart? She had no doubt that, wherever he ended up, women would be lining up to date him.

It was probably all idle speculation anyway, because Ryan had never spoken in terms of their relationship extending past his departure this summer. And she sure wasn't holding her breath.

Holly shrugged. "You know that Jackson and I are more about having fun than anything deeper, so it's not really an issue for us. But I think if people truly love each other, they can make a long-distance relationship work. For a while anyway."

"For a while," Morgan said with a rueful smile.

"Speaking of long distance, you really don't have any idea why Ryan headed down to North Carolina today?"

Morgan shook her head. "He was so tight-lipped about it that I didn't want to press him. My guess is that he's going to try to talk the company into giving him a new kind of assignment. He did say that he's had enough of running around from one country to the next."

"Maybe he's going to tell them he's quitting and staying in Seashell Bay." Holly tilted her head. "He might, especially if he thought you weren't going back to Pickle River."

Morgan had been as tight-lipped about her plans as Ryan. Then again, it had only been in the last forty-eight hours that she'd gravitated toward a decision, and even now it remained uncertain in the face of the B&B's future. "On that note, I think I know now what I have to do."

Holly reached for the mug Morgan brought in and cradled it in her hands. "Honey, if your expression is any indication, you're not exactly certain."

"No." Morgan forced a smile. "Well, actually I do know one thing. I know I need to stay in Seashell Bay and help Sabrina with the B&B. And obviously not just for a few months like I'd originally hoped. The only question remaining is whether or not the place will survive at the end of the day. Even with renovations and a new focus, the jury's still out."

"That doesn't mean that you'll give up teaching for good, does it? You're thinking of a temporary situation, right?" Holly shook her head. "Teaching's all you ever wanted to do since you were a little girl."

Morgan's chest went tight. It was true—she'd always wanted to be a teacher. She'd loved school, and as she'd gotten older, she'd also realized how much she liked children, being around them and helping them to learn and grow. The idea of permanently giving up her teaching career seemed unthinkable.

"It still is. But Ryan and the guys have given us a second chance with Golden Sunset, and I have to go for it, especially for Sabrina's sake. I have to give it everything I've got. So yes, I've decided to take the plunge and cut my ties with Pickle River."

Holly's eyebrows shot up. "Um, I sure didn't see that one coming."

"But I'm still planning on teaching," Morgan said quickly. "Just not full-time and not in Pickle River. Portland is often on the lookout for experienced substitute teachers, and I'm hoping to be able to work a few days a week there while I help run the B&B. At least until things shake out."

Holly smiled her approval. "That sounds like a really good plan, actually."

Morgan breathed a sigh of relief knowing that at least one person whose judgment she trusted didn't think she'd gone psycho. Giving up her long-standing post in Pickle River might be the hardest decision she'd ever make, but she saw no other realistic option at this point.

"Have you told Sabrina and Lily yet?" Holly said. "They'll be delirious to have you moving back home."

"Not yet. I just made the decision over the last day or so. I kind of wanted to test it out on you first."

She realized now she'd been clinging to a fraying thread of hope that somehow she'd find a magic answer that would let her go back to her job and still do right by her sister and father. But continuing to put off her decision wouldn't be fair to anyone, least of all her principal and school board. They and the kids deserved to have a stable, permanent teacher, not one who kept extending her leave of absence for as long as they'd allow her.

"I wonder what Ryan will think when you tell him," Holly said, thoughtfully tapping her chin. "He should be happy that you're going to see the B&B through, especially after all the work he's put into it."

Morgan wasn't sure. "Maybe, but he also told me I shouldn't be living my life for other people. He'll probably think I'm crazy to walk away from a secure job that

I love." She shrugged. "But, hey, does it really matter what Ryan thinks? He'll be gone soon enough, and who knows when we'll see him again in Seashell Bay."

Holly didn't look like she was buying any of that but fortunately let it pass. "When is he due back from North Carolina?"

"Tonight, I think. He was a little vague on that. You know how he is."

"Well, I'm dying to hear what happened," Holly said with a sly grin. "Maybe he even quit. Now wouldn't that be something?"

Chapter 23

$\mathscr{T}$he sea breezes blew strong across Eagle Island's rocky shore, setting up a fierce chop. Still, Ryan had kayaked from Seashell Bay with little problem, loving the challenge of the hard paddle over. Now, as he stood on the lawn of the isolated home that once belonged to Admiral Peary, he gazed across the gray Atlantic and absorbed the solitude of the deserted state park.

He hadn't stopped thinking about Double Shield and the ramifications of his decision since leaving Capstone's office yesterday. Not even at the Pot, where he'd sat at the bar last night trying to somehow maintain a light conversation with Laura over a meal of burger and fries. This morning he'd hoped to focus on some detail work at the inn but couldn't really do much until Brendan showed up. Frustrated and missing Morgan like crazy, Ryan had put away his tools, suited up, and aimed his kayak in the direction of Eagle Island.

The stark serenity of the place seemed to reach into his soul with a calming touch. The little island was basically a rock with some trees, an old house, and a dock where tour boats and private craft moored and discharged visitors. The last tour boats of the day had already departed, and it felt like he had the entire island to himself.

And it felt good. Like his whole Casco Bay summer had felt good. The attic fire had kicked the hell out of them for a while, but they'd fought through the destruction and found daylight on the other side. Other than that admittedly huge problem, he'd been blessed with a fair number of quiet hours in his kayak, and with the satisfaction of working every day with his hands as he repaired the inn.

Most of all, there was Morgan, and she'd made all the difference. The thought of going back to Double Shield and shepherding rich guys through the world's shitholes had started to feel like something he didn't want to do anymore. Not after his time on the island, helping friends and family, building something up and seeing it take shape under his hands.

He'd forgotten how good that kind of work could feel.

That didn't mean he wasn't still dogged by second thoughts about his decision. The peace he felt at the moment did funny things to him. It made him want to stay and build a life here, maybe with Morgan if she was willing—though who knew whether she'd end up in Seashell Bay or Pickle River.

That question and his uncertain future in terms of work on the island—hell, *life* on the island—continued to nag at him. Who knew how long this sense of peace would last? What would happen in the winter, when much of the population abandoned the place to the cold, stormy weather? Seashell Bay seemed like paradise now, but Ryan wasn't naïve enough to forget that life there could be pretty damn tough and isolating.

Then there was Morgan and her career. What if she did decide to go back upstate to Pickle River? Ryan had found out firsthand what could happen when a man and a woman lived apart for a long time, and none of it was good. He'd gotten damn serious about Callie Strohmayer, convinced she might be the one. They'd had their issues and their fights, but Callie had always said she'd support him if he decided to stay in the service.

What a sick joke that had turned out to be.

Although Ryan couldn't forgive Callie for the lies, he could understand how hard it had been for her to deal with the separation that came with long deployments. They sucked, took a huge toll on relationships, and were to be avoided whenever possible.

He glanced up at the clouds scudding across the sky. It was getting late and past time to head back to the island. If he could, he wanted to get back to Seashell Bay before Morgan got home. If she found him gone, she'd be looking for him and probably worrying too. She worried about everyone and everything but herself.

As he pushed off from the shore, he thought about her comments of a few weeks ago—when they were talking about their futures or lack thereof. Morgan had said that all they had was the present, and the moments they were together. That sounded about right. For now, he would focus on her and on the inn and let the rest sort itself out.

He had no idea where either of them would end up. He had no answers to any of the questions about his life, beyond the fact that he'd left Double Shield behind. The best he could do was just live for today and for his time with Morgan.

Tomorrow would come soon enough.

*   *   *

Morgan hurried across the gangway straight into Ryan's embrace. Thrilled to see him waiting for her, she wrapped her arms around his waist and lifted her face up for a kiss. He obliged with an enthusiasm that attracted the attention of more than a few tourists and grinning locals waiting to board the ferry.

"I guess you missed me," she said breathlessly, after he finally let her up for air.

"Hell, yeah. And I intend to show you exactly how much in a few minutes." Ryan let her go and grabbed the handle of her small suitcase. "Ready to go?"

Morgan nodded. "Sabrina said she'd pick me up, so I wasn't expecting you." *But I'm so glad you came.*

"I kind of insisted," he said. "Besides, she's been pretty busy painting the upstairs bathrooms."

Morgan grabbed his arm. "She's been what?"

"Yeah, you told her to let me and the guys handle the painting, but she said she wanted to prove to you that she could do a good job. So she's taking on a couple of the bathrooms. She said she hopes they'll be so good that you'll let her do more."

Morgan and Sabrina had engaged in a brief tussle of wills earlier in the week when Sabrina made noises about wanting to help paint the renovated upstairs rooms. Morgan had put her off, remembering a few previous occasions when her father had let Sabrina pick up a paintbrush. The results hadn't been pretty.

"That little sneak. She waited until I was gone," Morgan said, not knowing whether to laugh or groan.

"She's trying really hard," Ryan said, his left arm securely encircling her waist as they strolled down the pier to the parking lot. "Doing new stuff. I think it's great."

She leaned into him. "Let's see if you still say that after you have to repaint those rooms."

He kissed the top of her head. "It'll be good for her spirits, Ms. Control Freak."

"Control freak? Watch your mouth, buster, or you won't get within a mile of my bed tonight."

Ryan shot her an amused glance. "Are you sure about that?"

"No," Morgan admitted. "Not after I've been thinking all about you and what you can do to my body. It's been a long three days, I can tell you."

Ryan slowed and dropped a lingering kiss on her lips. "I've been thinking exactly the same thing."

"Sweet. So, uh, in that case maybe we could make a quick pit stop at your place before we head over to the B&B?"

His wolfish grin had her going soft and damp in an instant. How utterly mortifying, especially since Mrs. Bryson, Josh's mom, was giving them a cheeky smile and wave as she walked by them.

"That could definitely be arranged," he said in a low voice that made her belly tumble.

Ryan stowed her suitcase in the bed of the pickup and opened the door for her. A moment later, he had them on their way.

"Holly sends her best," Morgan said. "She's doing great—the surgeon's really pleased with her progress."

"That's good. You were sweet to help her out like that."

Morgan shook her head. "Not really. We always take care of each other." She decided to push the envelope a bit. "Like you've been taking care of me."

"I'd say that's been a mutual thing," Ryan said.

Morgan glanced at him. He looked totally mellow and laid-back, like he didn't have anything on his mind other than getting her in the sack. She was dying to know what happened in Raleigh but dreaded having to ask him outright.

Unfortunately, it looked like he wasn't going to be in any hurry to talk about it. Then again, what else was new? Ryan never wanted to talk about himself.

Suck it up, buttercup.

"So, what about you?" she asked brightly. "How was your trip?"

Ugh. Lame.

Ryan's eyes remained locked on the road ahead, even though there wasn't another vehicle in sight and he could probably drive the old island road in his sleep. "I met with my controller, and it was a little tougher than I'd thought it would be," he finally said.

When he didn't elaborate, Morgan gritted her teeth. It looked like she was going to have to drag the information out of him. "Why? Is it about some assignment they want you to take?"

"We didn't talk about assignments. Not really." The corners of his mouth eased into a smile.

Honest to God, she was going to kill him.

She yanked on her seat belt so she could twist around to face him. "But I thought that was why you went. To get a new assignment."

Ryan shook his head but still didn't catch her eye. "Nope. I went to tell him I was going to quit."

Morgan sucked in a huge gasp. Her reaction made him finally look at her.

"Morgan, the reason I didn't say anything before was because I wasn't a hundred percent sure I'd be able to go through with it. When my controller told me I was one of the best he'd ever had . . . well, it meant a lot coming from a man I really respect."

"But you did quit, right?" Her words sounded like a squeak.

Ryan nodded.

"That's . . . that's incredible," Morgan stammered.

"That's one word for it," he said wryly.

Go ahead—ask him straight out. Don't be a coward.

She gripped the edge of the cracked leather seat. "Do you have an alternative plan? Once you're finished up here, I mean."

Ryan turned onto the narrow gravel road that led to his cottage. A cloud of dust immediately enveloped the truck. "My alternative plan is to not have a plan. Not right away anyway. I'm going to take it one day at a time for a while. Like you told me, all we really have is the present."

Morgan felt like someone had just tasered her; she was so stunned. She'd been living in the present too, trying to make the most of her sweet days and nights with Ryan and pushing back the awful fear that she'd be a mess when he left.

Now she felt like she'd just received a stay of execution. "So very true," she managed.

"There's still a lot of work to do at Golden Sunset, like figuring out how to get the kayak operation off the ground and market it. But after that, who knows?" He paused. "Aiden thinks I should go to work for him at the resort."

Morgan grabbed the dashboard when they hit a rut. "What?" How could Lily have kept that from her?

"He hit me with it at the wedding reception. Sounded pretty serious about it too."

She just stared at his profile. Man, he still looked totally cool about everything, while she no doubt looked gobsmacked.

"What kind of job?" she asked.

"Chief of security." He gave a little huff. "I told him I didn't have a clue about hotel security."

"Does that mean you're not interested?"

She hoped her voice sounded neutral and nonjudgmental, but she was barely able to keep from blurting out that it sounded like an amazing opportunity, one that would change everything for him. For them. But she didn't have the right to do that, so she kept her big trap shut.

He pulled up in front of the two-story cedar cottage that had turned out to be a far cry from the dump Morgan had expected he'd have to settle for. The place had suddenly become available when a family cancelled their three-week reservation, and the owner had been so thrilled to get a last-minute replacement that he'd given Ryan a sweet deal on a week-to-week basis. Ryan had opted for this place over the one his mom's friend had offered because it was closer to Golden Sunset, not to mention a lot nicer.

Ryan leaned across the console and gave her a lingering kiss. Then he settled back into his seat. "They haven't even broken ground on the resort, so there's plenty of time for decisions on that and everything else." He slid his hand up the outside of her thigh. "Right now I've got something a lot more interesting on my mind."

When he nuzzled her neck, Morgan sucked in her breath as his stubble rasped over her skin, the rough feel making her even more crazy. Questions whirled in her brain, and she was desperate for answers, but her body definitely had other priorities. That was the only downside of sex between them—sometimes she thought they both used it as a substitute for talking about issues that really mattered.

Like the future.

"If you don't stop doing that, we're not going to even make it into the house," she said, squirming. "And doing it over a stick shift would present some challenges."

Ryan slid his hand up farther, going under her short skirt to finger the lace edge of her panties. "Oh, I don't know. We're always overcoming challenges together, aren't we?"

She gave him a playful little shove. "Forget it, big guy. I'm too old to have car sex, especially in broad daylight. And I might end up with that stick shift somewhere very unpleasant. But it's nice to know you missed me."

His gaze went from warm to hot in a nanosecond, practically scorching her. "A bit. Like about every minute or so I was thinking I couldn't wait to get inside you."

Wow. She'd have to peel herself off the leather seat at this rate.

But at the back of her mind she also hoped he missed more than just the sex. More than her under him, or riding him, or making love to him in any of the other dozen positions they'd managed to try so far. Because she'd missed him in body, heart, and soul, and the thought of saying good-bye simply seemed impossible.

Chapter 24

$\mathcal{P}$arched from his morning run, Ryan stripped off his sweat-soaked T-shirt and reached into the fridge for the pitcher of orange juice. He downed a full glass and then headed upstairs for a shower. There was no time for breakfast since he had to meet Brendan at the B&B to schedule the rest of the carpentry detail work.

Morgan's truck was already gone when he got back from the run. She'd spent the night—maybe their hottest yet—and he'd been looking forward to another round with her in the shower. They'd been crazy for each other till the wee hours of the morning, and he suspected that part of her enthusiasm resulted from relief that he'd quit his job and wouldn't necessarily be leaving town anytime soon. Still, he gave her props for not bugging him for additional info. He didn't have answers for himself, much less for Morgan.

Morgan and Sabrina were catching an early boat into Portland today to shop for the B&B, which was why she'd headed out. They'd make a day of it and even take a short trip down the coast to a company that manufactured custom weather vanes. Morgan had told him they deserved a girlie day together on the mainland after everything they'd been through, and Ryan totally agreed. Both women had paid their dues all summer long, physically and emotionally. If anyone deserved a treat, those two did.

He stripped off his shorts and dropped them and the T-shirt on the bedroom floor. The bed, with its flowery quilt and little fortress of neatly arranged pillows, was perfectly made. He couldn't help a quiet laugh. Morgan was obsessively tidy, unlike him. Ryan was the kind of guy who pretty much left his clothes wherever they landed. His mom used to kid him about not being housebroken, and he guessed that was pretty much true.

Or maybe he just hadn't been given the chance to get domesticated by a woman like Morgan.

His cell phone rang. Maybe Brendan was late and Ryan wouldn't have to rush over to Golden Sunset.

But it wasn't Brendan. It was Double Shield's Raleigh number. "Cap?"

"Yeah, it's me. I'd apologize for calling so early, Butler, but I figure you could use a wake-up call once in a while to get your lazy, retired ass out of bed."

"I just logged four miles, and in a few minutes I'll be heading to work. And by the way, my ass doesn't get to park itself in a cushy executive chair all day like some people I know."

Capstone chuckled. "Low blow, Butler. Low blow."

Well, enough with the pleasantries. "I haven't changed my mind, Cap, if that's what you're calling about."

"Never thought you would. But if you shut up and listen a minute, you might want to hear about a conversation I had with HQ late yesterday."

"Okay, I'm listening," he said cautiously.

"HQ thinks you're too valuable an asset to give up on. Don't ask me why," Capstone said with a snort. "I'm just a grunt so I didn't question the West Coast high and mighty."

"That would be a first," Ryan scoffed.

His controller chuckled. "Shut up and listen, Butler. When the ops director asked if there was anything we could do to change your mind, I told him there was only one thing that might tempt you, and it wasn't more money. It was a combat-training role."

His heart started pounding like he was under fire on a rooftop in Ramadi. Had Cap somehow managed to talk HQ into it? A position at the company's national training center near San Antonio, Texas, was exactly what he'd wanted.

"So after I told them that, the brass went off to examine their navels," Capstone said. "Last night, the director called and said they're willing to transfer you to the NTC, but only if you sign back on for a minimum three-year stretch. The guy slated for the job got T-boned in San Diego a couple of days ago and won't be working for a real long time, if ever. They had another operator in mind for the job, but when I told them about your situation, they came up with this offer."

Jesus. Ryan sank down on the bed, barely able to process. He'd never expected this and had completely written off a transfer—it was a promotion, actually—to the training center. Did Double Shield really want him to stay that badly? It was fucking amazing to learn that they apparently did.

"Holy shit, Cap, I don't know what to say. It's such a bolt out of the blue, especially after everything we'd talked about."

Capstone snorted again. "Tell me about it. I figured it was worth a shot to try the idea out on HQ. I knew they were high on you. Hell, they ought to be after all my performance evaluations. There was a whole lot of luck involved, but I have to say the bastards surprised me too."

"Yeah." His brain worked double time to process the implications of the offer. When he glanced down at the crisply made bed, he had a sudden and vivid image of how beautiful and peaceful Morgan had looked sleeping there this morning. Finally relaxed, finally happy. His throat tightened.

Shit.

"Besides the three-year commitment, there's one other catch," Capstone said.

Ryan's grip on the phone tightened. "There always is."

"It's not a big one. It's just that they need you there Monday. I know you wanted to be off all summer, but they won't budge on that, pal. They've got an instructor training class ready to go, so you need to be there by Sunday at the latest."

"No flexibility at all?" Ryan knew there wouldn't be, but the words just came out. He needed more time to think.

"Zero. You don't show, they'll promote the other guy."

Ryan's stomach was twisted like a tangled trapline. After everything he'd said to Morgan, how could he take off that soon? Talk about bailing out—on the inn, on Sabrina, and especially on Morgan.

"You'd better say yes," Capstone said, "or I'm going to look like a first class dickhead to HQ since I went to bat for you."

The job was exactly what Ryan wanted. He didn't have

to think about that part because it had been on his mind for months. Transferring to a training role was the only way to stay in the game but not live the kind of nomadic life that no longer made sense to him.

But he had to think hard about Morgan and what he was going to say to her.

"I appreciate everything you've done, Cap," he said. "But I'll need a little time to think."

"Jesus Christ, Butler, isn't this exactly what you wanted?" Capstone thundered. "Guys kill for these opportunities."

"Just give me a day, okay?" Ryan countered. "One freaking day. I made commitments to people here, and I have to get out of them."

Capstone cursed under his breath. "Okay, you've got twenty-four hours, not a damn minute more. I can lie and say that I couldn't get through to you today or some other bullshit thing, but tomorrow is the best I can do. Otherwise, it'll look like you're not serious, and they'll probably pull the offer. You know how they are at HQ. They never screw around. We're all just cogs in the machine."

Ryan figured if he couldn't make up his mind in twenty-four hours, he didn't really want the job, did he? "That'll do, Cap. And thanks a lot."

"You're not very fucking welcome," Cap growled. "Just make sure you call me first thing tomorrow."

"Count on it."

Ryan clicked off and stared blankly at the wall for what seemed like an eternity before he could even start to sort out his spinning thoughts. The moment his controller had dangled the training job, he'd almost screamed "yes" into the phone, thanking his lucky stars for an opportunity he'd wanted so badly. But for some reason, he hadn't been able to pull the trigger. Something had held him back, and that something was clearly the woman who had been with him in this bed last night—the woman he'd have to say good-bye to, maybe forever, if he headed to Texas.

One thing he knew for sure—that good-bye was going to be a lot rougher than he'd have ever believed possible.

He had twenty-four hours to make a decision, but deep down he knew he'd already made it.

Morgan sipped green tea from a tiny porcelain cup as she studied her sister across the little café table. Sabrina was devouring her Thai ginger noodles while Morgan was barely picking at her stir-fry vegetables and rice. One bite in, she'd discovered she had little appetite, probably because she'd learned that she could never be sure how her sister was going to react to any change in life circumstances. Her nerves were just a bit too jittery to make food appealing.

Energized after another awesome night in Ryan's arms, she'd picked up Sabrina at Golden Sunset and caught the eight forty boat into Portland. Less than an hour later, they were browsing the showroom at Down East Weather Vanes and talking to the owner about a custom-made vane—one featuring a lobster boat. She'd left a photo of *Miss Annie* for use as a model and couldn't wait to see Lily's face the first time she looked up at the B&B's roof and recognized the little replica of her boat.

Morgan wanted the new vane to be a visible symbol of Golden Sunset's new beginning and a tribute to her best friend.

Back in Portland, as they were strolling up the hill to the vegetarian bistro Sabrina picked for lunch, Morgan had decided to deliver her news there. She was pretty sure Sabrina would be happy, but if it turned out not to be the case, at least she figured her sister would be less likely to make a scene at a restaurant.

"At the rate we're going, I think our Labor Day reopening promotion is going to bring us a full house," Morgan said to lead off the discussion. "Inquiries are already coming in even though the online ads just started."

She'd received three e-mails so far, two asking for more details to supplement the sketchy information she'd provided about kayak tours in the ads.

"Great," Sabrina said. "But what about Ryan? Any more news?"

"About him leaving?" Morgan said, though she knew exactly what her sister was asking.

Sabrina gave her a wry smile.

Morgan wasn't sure how to convey what Ryan had told her because she wasn't sure what it meant. She didn't want to get her sister's hopes up only to have them smashed again when he decided to take off. "Well, for one thing, he just told his company that he's not coming back."

"Yay!" Sabrina said, punching her fist into the air. Then her elated look quickly morphed into a frown. "But I guess that doesn't mean he's staying here, does it?"

Morgan tried hard to keep both her expression and her voice neutral. "He only said that he's going to take it one day at a time."

Sabrina looked disgusted. "Then you'll just need to work harder on him," she said, putting down her chopsticks. "It's so obvious we need Ryan. I'm not sure we can do it without him, Morgan."

Though Morgan didn't think her sister meant that as a

criticism of her, it bugged her to think that Sabrina didn't believe they could carry on their father's legacy by themselves. Because she'd finally started to believe they truly could.

And wasn't that a nice bit of irony? She was the one who'd wanted to sell the place and take Sabrina back with her to Pickle River, and now Morgan felt totally invested in making a go of it. She couldn't help wondering how much of that she could chalk up to Ryan's presence.

"I sure hope we can," she answered. "In fact, I'm starting to get more confident that the B&B can make it now. And don't forget that Ryan said he won't leave until he gets the kayak operation up and running."

Sabrina shot her a skeptical look. "You're absolutely sure he won't?"

"That's what he told me. What do you want me to do, get him to sign it in blood?" she said with a smile.

"Yeah, that would be good," Sabrina said with a little smile of her own. Then she started fiddling with her chopsticks.

Morgan recognized the signs. "What is it, honey?"

Sabrina looked a little guilty and a lot nervous. "If things do turn out okay at Golden Sunset, are you going to head back to Pickle River like you originally planned?"

"Actually, no, I'm not. That was the other thing I wanted to tell you today. I've decided to quit my job, sell my house, and move back here."

Sabrina's eyes went wide. "You have? Oh my God, Morgan, that's awesome. I...I don't know what to say." Her blue eyes started to go a little teary.

"Just say you're happy."

"Hell, yes, I'm happy! And if Ryan stays, I know we

can make the new Golden Sunset a success. What a team we'll make!"

If only. "Let's not get too far ahead of ourselves, okay? We don't know yet about Ryan and, as for me, I'm only going to be part-time at the B&B." She hesitated a moment, clearing her throat. "So we need to talk about that."

Sabrina's gaze narrowed. "Part-time? What exactly does that mean?"

"It means I'm still going to teach. I'm just planning on doing it here in Portland instead of Pickle River, and part-time instead of full-time. I'm going to try to get work as a substitute teacher in the city."

"Oh." Sabrina looked deflated.

Here comes the tricky part. "I'm sure we can make it work, especially since I won't teach during the summer. But it'll mean that you'll have to take on a little more responsibility."

Sabrina stared at her and then pushed her plate away. "It's fine to say that, but you know there are things I just can't do. I wish I could, but..."

Morgan shook her head. "I'm not talking about taking responsibility for keeping the books and paying bills and promotion or any of that. I mean you can do stuff like ordering supplies and arranging for deliveries. And you'll have to spend more time taking care of the guests when I'm gone for the day." She smiled to take the edge off. "No more hiding out in the kitchen."

Sabrina's gaze darted sideways. "I don't know..."

Morgan took her hand. "Honey, you're definitely ready. I've watched you come out of your shell a little more each day, and now I can tell that you're starting to enjoy spending time with the guests. And I'm sure you're ready for me to gradually pass on some of the administrative work too. Really, it's the only way we can make it work, because I need to keep teaching. Sabrina, as much as I love the inn and the island, I can't imagine never having a classroom full of kids again. It would rip my heart out."

Her sister slowly nodded. "Since Dad died, every time you talked about your kids and your school it scared the shit out of me because I know how much it means to you. It made me think you'd never stay in Seashell Bay, no matter what happened. I felt like my heart was being ripped out too."

"But now?"

"Well, I'm okay, I guess. And I understand how much you love it. It's like how I love the inn." Sabrina blew out a breath and smiled. "Hey, even if you are only part-time at Golden Sunset, you'll still be living with me and working with me. I really, really hope Ryan sticks around, but even if he doesn't, I'm just so freaking happy that you're staying."

Morgan pulled her chair right next to her sister's. "You'd better give me a big hug right now, 'cause I really need one."

Sabrina hugged her as if her life depended on it. "I love you so much," she whispered in Morgan's ear. "Thank you for not giving up on me."

Chapter 25

$\mathcal{M}$organ had secretly hoped that Ryan might be waiting for them as the ferry nudged against the Seashell Bay dock. It made no sense since he'd know her truck was parked at the landing. But that hadn't stopped her from hoping that he'd be there, eager to be with her and help them with their stuff.

How girlie can you get, Morgan?

She chided herself for being a dope, even as she scanned the length of the pier for any sign of him. Maybe it was because the day had gone so well that she'd indulged in a little wishful thinking. Everything finally felt like it was coming together after a long time of feeling like it was all coming apart.

"It was awesome to spend the whole day with you in the city," Sabrina said as they lugged their purchases to the parking lot. "We won't have many chances to get away together once we reopen."

"Oh, the glamorous, twenty-four-seven life of B&B owners, right? At least ones that can't afford hired help."

"It's pretty sweet, actually," Sabrina said. "We don't

have to take orders from some dumb boss. And as a bonus, I get to spend lots of time with my sister."

That comment alone made Morgan feel like all the struggle and angst she'd endured along the way had been worthwhile. "I feel exactly the same way," she said.

"I've been thinking a lot lately about your idea to rename the place," Sabrina said. "And I guess I've changed my mind about that."

Morgan stared at her sister. "Really?"

Sabrina gave a quick nod. "How about calling it The Merrifield Inn? I think Dad would like that. It would be a nice way of honoring his memory, don't you think?"

"I absolutely love it," Morgan said, her heart overflowing. "It's a fabulous idea."

Morgan gave Sabrina a long, heartfelt hug and then they loaded the stuff into the truck and drove the short distance to the B&B. Morgan's heart did a silly flip when she spotted Ryan's dumpy, old golf cart in the driveway, simply because it was his.

She had it so bad.

Sabrina pointed down the slope to the beach. "Ryan's been out in his kayak again."

Shading her eyes, Morgan turned her gaze and saw Ryan slowly climbing the path. He wore only navy swim trunks and sunglasses. Against the ocean backdrop, with the sun behind him, he was like a freaking bronzed sun god rising up out of the azure sea. Just looking at him made every muscle in her body go weak.

"I'll take this stuff inside," Sabrina said. "I'm sure you two will want to…uh, talk." Her sister grabbed the various bags containing their shopping haul and disappeared into the annex.

As Morgan started down the path to meet Ryan, tendrils of anxiety whispered through her. Even from a distance, she could tell something was wrong. Though he was smiling, it wasn't the sunny smile she'd gotten used to, nor even the wry one when he was about to tease her or make fun of himself. No, this smile was tentative, maybe even worried.

She sucked it up and gave him a big smile as he came up to her.

"Sabrina and I had a wonderful day," she said after his hello kiss. "The weather vane place is going to custom make us an awesome lobster boat, and I'm getting it painted in Lily's colors. They said it'd be ready on Friday, so I was hoping maybe you could put it up over the weekend?" Realizing she was babbling, she stopped and took a deep breath. "How was your day?"

"Okay." Ryan let her go and eased away. "Can we go for a walk on the beach and talk?"

Oh, shit.

Now he was looking grim. And in her experience, when somebody said they wanted to talk, it meant nothing good was in store. Morgan instinctively looked down at her feet. Her low heels weren't really suitable for strolling on the pebble-laden beach, but she wasn't about to waste time running into the house for sandals or sneakers. Not with him looking like he had a parcel of bad news to deliver.

"What's going on, Ryan?" she said impatiently.

"Wait a minute and I'll tell you everything."

Everything. Ugh.

Ryan reached down and grasped her hand, leading her quickly down to the beach. Still holding on to her, he didn't say anything for a few moments as they started to pick their way across the seaweed and driftwood-laden mixture of sand and small pebbles. Though it had been hot again today, the breeze off the ocean made it feel cool. Maybe that was why Morgan had a sudden chill.

"I got a call early this morning. Right after my run," he said.

"From Double Shield?" she guessed. Had to be.

Ryan nodded. "From Cap. My controller."

It blasted through her in an instant, like a hurricane. *My God, he's going to tell me he's going back.* There was barely a shred of doubt in her mind. "He was trying to talk you into coming back, wasn't he?"

"He told me the brass at HQ didn't want to lose me," Ryan said, staring off in the direction of a lobster boat that was hauling traps a couple of hundred yards offshore. Then he turned his gaze back to her, shoving his sunglasses up on his head. His expression was somber but determined. "They're offering me a combat training position in Texas. A three-year contract for now, but it could be a long-term thing."

Morgan didn't need to ask if he was going to take the job. She could read it in his eyes. Everything she'd been afraid of was happening right now.

Nausea swamped her. How had she let herself think even for a moment that Ryan might stay in Seashell Bay? That he might actually give up the military life he loved and become an innkeeper, a handyman, a security chief, or who-knew-what on this little outpost? She'd been hopelessly naïve.

She dredged up every ounce of control and self-respect she had in her. After all, Ryan had never promised her that he'd be staying. He'd always been honest about that—honest that he loved what he did, just as she loved teaching. Really, how could she criticize him for following his dream?

"I understand. I really do," she said.

"I haven't agreed to take the job yet, but I don't see how I can turn it down," he said. "It's what I wanted. It's what I'm good at too, and I figure I could do it for a long time, right here in the States. Openings in those training positions are rare, Morgan. Really rare. I'm lucky they're even considering me, much less offering me the job."

She turned away, toward the ocean. She couldn't bear for him to see how gutted she was, how she struggled with an irrational sense of betrayal. "You don't need to convince me, Ryan. I said I understood. And I can tell you've made up your mind, so you don't need to try and justify it."

Shaking off his hand, she wandered blindly across the beach to a big jumble of rocks, one nearly as tall as her. She kicked off her shoes and climbed onto the flattest one, staring out to sea. A moment later, Ryan climbed up behind her and rested his hands on her shoulders. Though her instinct was to twist out of his gentle grip, she forced herself not to react so childishly.

"Okay, but we can still talk about it," he said.

"Please don't worry about it," she blurted out. "We always said we'd take it one day at a time. Things change, and we have to adapt. Like I had to after my dad died."

"True," he said softly. "Maybe the worst part is that I have to be there by Monday. They gave me an ultimatum to be there or forget about the job."

"Monday?" *How can this be happening? We made*

*love just this morning, and everything was fine. How can
it all be falling apart again?*

"I'm sorry, babe. It's tearing my guts out to think about
leaving before we get the kayak operation in business, or
the inn is finished. I could probably help some from a distance, but I know that would still leave you in the lurch.
That part really sucks."

And what about leaving her? Didn't that suck too?

Morgan had no hope right now of wrapping her brain
around what it would take to get the kayak operation running or what his leaving would mean to reopening and
rebranding the inn. All she could think about was what
his leaving meant to *her*.

"That's not your responsibility," she ground out.
"Sabrina and I will manage. We always do."

He put a little pressure on her shoulders to try to turn
her around to face him, but she resisted, planting her feet
even more firmly on the slick surface. She wasn't ready to
look at him. If she did, she might dissolve into a puddle of
tears, or maybe she'd even explode in anger. The jury was
still out on which. For the moment, she simply fought to
maintain control.

"Of course you will," he said, sliding his hands down her
stiff arms and letting her go. It was an echo of the absence
that was soon to come. "But as soon as I can manage a
chunk of time off, I'll fly back here for a few days and—"

A silent detonation went off inside her head. She
whirled around so quickly that she almost lost her footing.
When Ryan jerked out a hand to steady her, she knocked
it away.

"No!" she snapped. "When you go, I want you to stay
away for a long time, like you've always done. And please

don't think we could just pick up where we left off when you came back home for a visit, because that can't happen. I can't be your island booty call."

I can never let this happen again. Never.

It would kill her if she let him back into her life, knowing he would never stay.

His gaze went wide with shock. "Jesus, Morgan, it was never that, and you know it. I care for you, a hell of a lot."

She closed her eyes, forcing herself to throttle it back. She took several deep, slow breaths to calm her racing heart. When she opened her eyes again, he was watching her with a look that seemed both wary and anguished.

"I'm sorry, that was uncalled for," she said. "I know you do. But we both know what the reality is here, Ryan. So it's better for me if you just stay away for a while, okay? Give me a chance to find my balance again."

To get over having my heart shredded.

He took a step back down off the rock, holding up his hands. "Okay, I get it." He shook his head, and his jaw went tight with frustration. "Jesus, this sucks."

She sighed. His decision likely wasn't much easier on him than it was on her. Ryan was a good guy, and she was sure he felt like he was abandoning her, and Sabrina too.

"I'm sorry, Ryan. I'm just a little ... I guess it's just all too sudden for me to take in. You'll need to give me some time to sort things out. It's ... it's a big change from this morning, you know?"

His tender smile broke her heart all over again. "Believe me, babe, I know." He glanced out at the lobster boat and pulled his sunglasses back down before looking at her again. "It doesn't have to be over, Morgan."

His voice was soft and infinitely kind, but she heard no conviction in it. Morgan knew full well how he felt about long-distance relationships, since he'd mentioned it often enough. This was his guilt talking.

"Really?" she said. "With you in Texas and me in Maine? It's not exactly like you could pop back here for weekends. Let's not try to kid ourselves that we could make that sort of thing work for very long."

"Morgan—"

"I don't need your pity, Ryan," she said. "And you don't owe me anything."

That shut him up. He stared at her, probably trying to figure out whether she meant what she said.

"Maybe you're right," he finally said in a voice that sounded like it had been dragged over gravel. "But at least we've got a few more days together, and I've got a bit more time to work on finding someone to take over the kayaking project."

Morgan didn't think she could take it. Being with him day and night until he left, letting him in again but knowing he would then be walking away from her forever. It was an awful prospect.

"No," she said in low voice.

Ryan shot her a puzzled look. "Did you say no?"

"I think it's best that you just get on the boat and go. Or if you do stick around the island until Sunday, don't come around here. I mean it, Ryan. It's the only way I can deal with this." Like ripping off the biggest, stickiest Band-Aid in the universe, one the size of an entire planet. She could only do it once.

Nothing brought a relationship into sharper focus than ending it, and every bone in Morgan's body told her she'd been crazy to get in so deep with a guy who she knew would probably leave. It was her fault, and it was time she started digging out of the wretched hole she'd made for herself.

"Honey, at least let me walk you back to the house," he said. Now she could hear the anguish in his voice.

She shook her head. "No. I want you to go."

Ryan turned away and took a few steps down the beach. Slowly, she stepped down from the rock.

When he turned and started back toward her, she jumped. He shoved his glasses back up again, his gaze zeroing in on her with breath-stealing intensity.

"If that's what you really want, that's what I'll do," he said. "But be sure, Morgan. Be really sure."

No, it's the last thing I want! But it was what she needed. "It's for the best. Sabrina is going to be very upset, and I think it would be better if you two didn't see each other again before you go."

Sabrina would not only be angry with Ryan, she'd likely give Morgan hell for letting him get away. It was not going to be a happy discussion.

Ryan shook his head. "No, I want to say good-bye to her and explain why."

"Not until I break the news. And it'll be up to Sabrina, but I'll let you know."

"Shit," he shook his head, as if he couldn't believe it. "Well, I guess that's it then."

"I guess so," Morgan managed.

When he took a step forward and enfolded her in his arms, she didn't resist. But she turned her head away so he couldn't kiss her. So he couldn't see the tears flooding her eyes.

"Please go, Ryan," she said in a choked voice. "I'll call and let you know about Sabrina."

He held her tightly for a moment longer, stroking her hair before planting a kiss on the top of her head. "You're an amazing woman, Morgan," he whispered. "You'll always be in my heart."

She didn't look up when he let her go and retreated down the beach. She managed to resist for almost a minute. After that, she didn't take her eyes off him until he disappeared up the slope.

"I'll love you forever, Ryan Butler," she whispered out loud. "Damn you."

Chapter 26

$\mathcal{L}$ily tightened her grip on Morgan's arm as they inched down the ferry dock through the mob waiting to board.

"You sure you're okay to do this?" Lily asked. "It's hell saying good-bye here, even at the best of times."

Their glacial pace made Morgan feel like she was in a funeral procession. That somber analogy seemed almost appropriate, since Ryan's impending departure was just about killing her. She'd been telling herself for the last four days that she'd be fine, but it was so not true. Not only was she a wreck, she truly felt like there was unfinished business between them.

Morgan practically had to clamber over a huge pile of suitcases left in the middle of the dock by a noisy family of tourists. "I can't let him go without telling him how I really feel. I was a total coward not to tell him that day on the beach, when I had the chance."

"You're no coward at all, crazy woman. And I still might murder Ryan. Aiden and I have been fighting about it ever since you told me. Men always stick together on crap like this," she said with disgust.

"Thanks, sweetie," Morgan said, "but Ryan has to do what'll make him happy. I don't blame him for that."

Lily shot her a skeptical glance but didn't say anything more. Just ahead, Ryan and Aiden were in the middle of a pack of islanders waiting to catch one of the early boats into the city. The crowded scene wasn't exactly the setting for a quiet, tearful good-bye, and that suited Morgan just fine. She'd already cried enough to last her a very long time.

Since their fight on the beach, she'd been wrestling with the fact that she'd never told Ryan straight out that she loved him. Not that it would matter—not in any way that counted. Her life was in Seashell Bay, with Sabrina, while Ryan's life was clearly and probably permanently in Texas. Then there was the little fact that he'd made it abundantly clear that he'd never wanted a long-term relationship, much less declared any feelings of love for her. That was a fairly daunting impediment.

Still, if Morgan let him get on that boat without taking the chance to declare her true feelings, she knew it would dog her for the rest of her life. For her own sake, she had to put it out there. How Ryan responded was mostly beside the point.

Mostly.

"Aiden finally promised me that he'd take another shot at Ryan on the boat," Lily whispered as the approaching ferry edged sideways to butt up against the dock. "To try to convince him to stay."

Morgan grimaced. "Talk doesn't change people's minds, Lily. They have to want it deep in their hearts or their guts or wherever those emotions come from. Ryan's heart is telling him to go."

"No, his stupid head is telling him to go. The dope

could have the best woman on Earth *and* a great job with Aiden, and instead he's going off to teach mercenaries and bodyguards how to fight better? That's the definition of stupid if you ask me."

Morgan thought so too, although she couldn't bring herself to admit it.

The guys looked surprised when Morgan and Lily squeezed through the crowd to reach them.

"I didn't expect to see either of you this morning," Aiden said to Lily. "Shouldn't you be hauling traps right about now, babe?" He bent and gave her a kiss.

"The lobsters aren't going anywhere," Lily said. "We couldn't let Ryan slip away without a send-off, could we, Morgan?"

Morgan forced herself to smile at Ryan.

"You look amazing," Ryan said, taking off his sunglasses. His dark gaze locked on her with surprising intensity.

He obviously approved of her pink sundress—the one she stopped wearing last year after she gained five pounds. But she'd shed those five and a few more since her father's death. Oh, well, she'd always liked this dress, so she guessed that was a plus.

"I see Jack Gallant over there," Lily said. "Aiden, let's go say hello for a second." She pulled on her husband's elbow to get him moving.

"See you on board," Aiden said to Ryan over his shoulder.

Ryan nodded absently to his friend, keeping his eyes on Morgan. "I really didn't think I'd see you again."

She sucked in a breath for courage. "I had to come. I had to tell you something important before you go."

When a couple of teenagers bumped into her, Ryan took her by the arms and moved her to the side, shielding her with his body. She gave him a grateful smile, her heart breaking a little bit more at the way he so instinctively protected her.

"I should have told you the other day that I loved you," she said quietly. "Before that, really. I've never said those words to any man before, Ryan. But I do love you, with all my heart, and I needed you to know that."

If not so stricken, she would have laughed at the stunned look on his face, kind of like she'd just punched him in the gut.

He took her cheeks in his big hands as he leaned down to give her a brief but heartfelt kiss. "I'm glad you told me. And I'm really going to miss you, Morgan. I'm sorry for leaving like this. I'm sorry for..." He didn't finish his sentence, shaking his head instead.

Sorry for me falling in love with you?

Morgan guessed that might be what he was trying to say. But it wasn't his fault. It couldn't be, because she'd loved Ryan Butler for a very long time. She just hadn't been able to see it clearly before this summer, much less say it to him. "You don't have to be sorry about anything, Ryan. I have no regrets."

"Jesus, Morgan," he said. "I—"

She poked him in the chest. "Well, maybe I do have one regret. It's that you weren't able to mount my new weather vane before you left." She narrowed her eyes at him. "You did promise that you'd do it, you know."

His mouth dropped open. "Uh, well, you said it would be ready today, and I told you I could stay until Sunday. You were the one—"

She poked him again. "Idiot. I'm trying to lighten things up so I don't start blubbering all over you."

"Oh, okay." He gave her a hesitant smile before glancing at the crowd streaming onto the boat. "Aiden is driving me from the ferry to the airport before he goes to work."

"That's nice of him," Morgan said inanely. *Ugh.*

Now he was looking almost as nervous as she felt. "I'd better get on board before they pull the gangway," he said, hoisting his duffel.

This was it. The moment she'd been dreading all summer. In a few minutes he'd be out of sight and out of her life.

She went up on her tiptoes and pressed a kiss to his cheek. "Be safe, Ryan, and be happy."

But Ryan didn't move, not even when Aiden gave his arm a quick tug. He waved his friend away. Aiden got the message and hurried on board.

"I was just thinking that this is the first time in my life that I'm sad to leave Seashell Bay," Ryan said in a gruff voice. "You be happy too, Morgan Merrifield. Know that I'll never forget you."

He turned and strode across the gangway without looking back.

Lily appeared by her side and slipped an arm around her shoulders. "Are you okay, sweetie?"

Morgan shook her head. She wasn't okay. She couldn't watch the boat cast off. Didn't want to know if Ryan was at the rail waving or not. It felt like her heart had been ripped out and would travel away with him.

"I know it's practically the crack of dawn, but how does coffee with a shot of Irish whisky sound?" Lily said. "It might be just what the doctor ordered."

Morgan sniffled as she squeezed her pal's waist. "Two shots sounds even better."

Ryan didn't need to hear any more reasons from his oldest friend about why he should stay. He knew them all and hadn't been able to think about much else since Capstone's call. In fact, he'd been driving himself crazy with doubt since the moment he'd told Morgan he had to leave, and saying good-bye to her on the dock had almost done him in. It had taken all his willpower not to let her see how torn up he was, making their parting even more heart wrenching than it needed to be.

"Look," Aiden said, taking the exit to the airport. "If you take the position with me, I'll get the lawyer to put a clause in the contract giving you an out after six months. If it doesn't work—either with Morgan or with the job— you can always go back to Double Shield."

Ryan shook his head. "Like I said, I really appreciate everything you're trying to do. But if I don't take this opportunity now, I won't get another chance for years. And maybe never."

Aiden threw him an irate glance. "That combat training job really means that much to you?"

Yes. No.

"We're talking about the rest of my life here. The rest of my career, anyway."

"Sure, but jobs come and go. I used to think my life would be as good as over when I couldn't play pro ball anymore. I get that this opportunity is rare, but does it really mean more than Morgan? That's the question you should ask yourself one last time before you board that plane. Because after that it could be too late." He pulled up in front of the departure area drop-off and put the car in park.

Ryan figured what Aiden said was true enough. Once he and Morgan were two thousand miles apart and absorbed by work, life would move on for both of them. There would be no recapturing that lightning in a bottle.

Yeah, and the more fool you to pass up the chance.

Grimly ignoring that inner voice, he got out of the car. He grabbed his duffel from the backseat and leaned in the passenger side window to say good-bye. "Thanks for the lift, man. Thanks for everything."

Aiden shook his head, looking disgusted. "At least try not to be such a stranger, asshole. A lot of people here are going to miss you, believe it or not. Including me."

"I'll work on that." Ryan tapped the roof of the SUV and headed for the terminal.

Fifteen minutes later, he'd checked in, passed through security, and grabbed a copy of the Portland paper from one of the shops. As he was paying, he noticed a display of colorful sun catchers in a corner of the shop window. Birds, lighthouses, fish, and various other designs dangled from suction cups. But only one truly caught his eye—a green-and-white lobster boat, its bow riding high over choppy blue waves. The little glass sun catcher reminded him of weather vanes and Morgan's sweet but heartbreaking attempt to lighten things up on the dock as he was departing. It was just like her to try to make him feel better, and he'd gratefully taken it, shaking off the emotional intensity of the moment.

But now that moment when they'd said good-bye was replaying in his mind in living, horrible Technicolor, and it hit him hard. Installing her new lobster boat weather vane wasn't a big deal—Brendan or Micah could do it for her in an hour—but it seemed to symbolize what was beginning to feel like a total abandonment of Morgan and of what they'd meant to each other. When it came down to a choice, he'd picked Double Shield and packed his bags, leaving so much unfinished at Golden Sunset.

Including telling Morgan exactly how he felt about her. She'd had the guts to tell him, but he'd taken the coward's way out.

He absently wandered over to get a cup of coffee before heading back to his departure gate. His flight wasn't scheduled to leave for another hour, so he had plenty of time. But as soon as he started poring over the sports section, he realized he was reading the same paragraphs over and over again. His mind wouldn't focus, not even on the baseball coverage. Not on anything. He couldn't think of a damn thing other than that sad little half kiss Morgan had brushed over his cheek before he left and how he'd rushed off the island like his damn ass was on fire.

And he'd done it after she'd looked him straight in the eye and told him that she loved him.

Jesus.

He put the cup down and began pacing the departure lounge. He told himself he was just stuck in the moment, that he'd leave it behind once he put some distance between himself and Seashell Bay. That once he got to San Antonio and got working, he'd put everything that happened this summer with Morgan into perspective.

But as he stared blindly at the planes coming and going out on the tarmac, he knew he was kidding himself. He was actually dreading the arrival of his flight at the gate. What should have felt right to him—the start of a new life—felt all wrong.

He'd only been away from Seashell Bay and Morgan for an hour and a half, and already the thought of not seeing her and that dumb little island again for months or even years sucked. And it would likely be years, because she'd told him to stay away, to give her the chance to get over him. But would he ever get over her? Would he ever feel like he truly belonged anywhere other than Seashell Bay?

With Morgan.

Against every expectation, he felt completely right when he was with her. Like he could finally trust and be open again, instead of the closed-down jerk he figured he'd become after everything had blown up with Callie. He'd deliberately shut everyone out, including his parents and his friends, focusing on his work above everything else. His friends all joked and called him the mystery man. He still remembered how Morgan had called him Mr. Enigma on the ferry, the day he arrived in June.

But the truth? Fear had kept him in a rut, afraid of doing something different. And afraid of letting someone get under his skin, like Morgan had. Brave, funny, and beautiful, she'd taken the risk and let him in, even knowing how much he could hurt her.

He'd had her in his arms, in his life, and he'd let her go.

But it'll be worth it, right? After all, you finally got the life you wanted.

Movement out on the tarmac caught his eye—the plane that would take him away was pulling up to the gate.

Chapter 27

Morgan's hand was a little jittery as she held her coffee mug out for a refill. Lily had made her three cups already this morning and this one, like the last, didn't include a shot of Irish whisky. The generous amount Lily had poured in the first cup had calmed her down to the point that she'd suddenly had no desire to do anything other than hang around with her pal all day. After that, the two of them had taken a long stroll to Sea Glass Beach and kicked along the pebbled shore arm in arm, strictly avoiding any mention of Ryan Butler and talking only about all the good stuff happening at the B&B and with Sabrina.

You will be okay.

Sooner, Morgan hoped, than later.

Back at Lily's cottage, Morgan put her bare feet up on the coffee table. "I'm sorry you had to take the whole day off from fishing. I know I'm being a total wimp."

"Oh, stop it." Lily flopped down on the sofa. "Erica agreed that we both could use a day off, and what better way for me to spend it than kicking back with my main girl. Besides, do you really think I'd let you go through that kind of gruesome good-bye scene all alone?"

"No," Morgan admitted, "Ms. Mother Hen Lobster Boat Captain."

"Ha! You should talk. You've been mothering me forever."

Morgan had to smile. "What are friends for other than to be brutally overprotective?" She glanced at her watch for probably the twentieth time since they left the ferry dock.

Lily didn't miss the time check. "Can't let it go, can you?"

"Guilty as charged. Right now he's in Philadelphia waiting for his connection to San Antonio." She exhaled a little sigh. "How insane is it to be thinking about where the man happens to be at any given moment, like that makes a difference?"

Lily gave her a wry smile. "I'd be doing the same thing if it was Aiden."

"Maybe it's some kind of natural response," Morgan said. "An unconscious way of adapting to the change. Like I'm actually feeling him move farther and farther away."

"It's perfectly understandable. Some form of self-flagellation, but perfectly understandable."

Morgan sighed and hauled herself to her feet. "Well, I'd better pack up my whips and chains and get moving. Sabrina will probably kick my butt for slacking off all morning. There's a fricking boatload of work waiting for me if we're going to be ready for the Labor Day weekend."

Lily rose too. "I want you both to come for dinner tonight. In fact, I insist. I don't want you two sitting home reinforcing each other's gloom."

"Sabrina's actually okay, thank God. She'll miss Ryan,

but she's kind of happy for once that she gets to be the strong one." She gave her friend a hug. "Thanks, darling. You're the best."

"You know I'm always there for you, honey."

Morgan just smiled since her throat had gone tight again. She ducked out the door, gave Lily a wave, and headed for her truck. After she got in, she picked up her cell phone from the console and checked for messages. There was one text.

From Ryan.

"Ryan?" He could hear her voice go up on the second syllable.

"Yeah, it's me, babe. How are you?"

"Uh...okay."

In the background, the ferry gave a short blast on its horn to signal its departure from the terminal. Morgan would of course be intimately familiar with that sound.

"Ryan, where the hell are you?" Now her voice had gone sharp.

"I'm at the terminal, and the boat's pulling out right now. Look, I know this is going to sound totally weird, but could you pick me up at the dock? I'll need a lift, so I'd really appreciate it."

When Morgan didn't answer right away, a shiver of apprehension raced through him. Was she so pissed off at him that she didn't even want to see him? Ryan had hoped to surprise her—in a good way—but maybe he'd miscalculated. "If you're tied up, I can always call my mom," he added quickly.

"But why aren't you on the plane?" Man, now her voice was shaking.

"I'll tell you everything when I see you, okay?"

He didn't want to torture her with suspense, but he really did want to spring his surprise on her. Well, another surprise, since not taking his flight had obviously knocked her for a loop. Hell, he could barely believe he'd done it himself. He'd made the toughest decision of his life because his gut and his heart had told him he'd be the idiot of the century if he got on that plane.

"Okay, sure. I'll see you at the dock." Morgan was sounding a little more confident now. "But you've got some splainin' to do, mister, that's for darn sure. And it won't be pretty if I'm not satisfied with your answer."

Her parting shot had him grinning. Any lingering doubts that he'd made the right decision slipped away on the cool harbor breeze.

Morgan had never been as freaked out in her life. She almost wished she smoked, just so she'd have something to do with her trembling hands. But how could she not be out-of-her-mind nervous? The next few minutes held the potential to change her life forever.

The ferry was closing in on Seashell Bay. Morgan couldn't seem to get enough breath into her lungs as she sucked gulps of air through her dry-as-dust mouth. Crap, she should have grabbed a bottle of water. If Ryan actually wanted to kiss her, she would be like smooching a piece of toast.

Please, God, let me have another chance with him.

As soon as she hung up with Ryan, she'd raced back into Lily's cottage and told her astonished friend the news. She'd barely been able to spit it out amidst her wild, breathless excitement and shuddering, naked fear. Every cell in her body screamed out the belief that Ryan was on his way back to her. Still, she was scared spitless. Too many things had gone wrong in the past year for her brain to actually believe something was about to go right.

As the ferry approached, its big bow swinging out to line up with the dock, Ryan suddenly appeared on deck, his duffel slung over his shoulder.

He brought his duffel. Did that mean he was planning on staying? A night? A week? Forever?

Morgan would happily take forever and never look back.

Ryan leaned against the starboard rail and let his gaze scan the crowd. She just barely stopped herself from jumping up and down and somehow managed to give him a wave and a half smile. He smiled and waved too, but his ball cap and sunglasses obscured his expression.

The boat nudged gently against the dock. *Wait. Just wait for him to make his move. Leave it in Ryan's hands.*

That's what Lily had told her. But that sage advice was easier to say than to obey. Morgan had to grab the railing and plant her feet to keep from rushing into his arms as soon as he crossed over the gangway.

Then she realized she'd have had a hard time throwing herself into his arms anyway since he had his heavy duffel over his left shoulder and a flat box tucked under his right arm. A huge flat box.

What the heck?

Ryan picked his way through the milling crowd while Morgan remained rooted on the west-side rail of the dock. It seemed to take forever for him to reach her, and she stared at him the entire way, trying to read his face. He dropped the duffel and set the box down, propping it against his thigh.

"Well, are you going to kiss me," he asked as he took off his cap and lifted his sunglasses, "or are you going to insist on explanations first?"

His crooked grin completely did her in. *To hell with playing it cool.* She flung herself into his arms, closing her eyes as their lips met.

Apparently, that was all Ryan needed. One brawny arm looped around her waist and the other clasped her back as he crushed her to his chest. When his tongue forced her lips to open—not that she resisted—the white-hot intensity of his kiss turned her knees to water. Her mind blanked, and she gave herself up completely to the strength of his embrace, her arms falling limply at her sides.

"Oh my God," she said, gasping after he finally broke away. She had no more coherent words.

Ryan sucked in a huge breath as he eased her back down on her heels. "Well, I call that a hell of a welcome back."

You ain't seen nothin' yet, dude.

Morgan wanted to jump up into his arms again, but she mentally cautioned herself to hold back until he told her what the hell was going on.

She glanced down at the box. "Is that monster box the surprise you were talking about?" She had a weird feeling that she should know what was inside it.

"Yep. How about we load this stuff in your truck and I'll show you?" He slung the duffel back up over his shoulder and picked up the box. Though Ryan was a total hard body, he bent his knees and slowly lifted the awkward and clearly heavy parcel.

Halfway down the dock, she suddenly got it. She poked the box that was now wedged securely under Ryan's arm. "Ah, that wouldn't be my new weather vane by any chance, would it?"

Ryan laughed. "Good guess, Merrifield."

Okay, this was getting weird. "Obviously, I should have known that."

"They did a beautiful job," Ryan said. "You're going to totally love it." Despite all the weight he was carrying, he picked up his pace, making Morgan hurry to keep up with his long strides.

A few moments later, Ryan laid the box in the back of her pickup and broke the tape that sealed the top of the package. Her heart firmly lodged in her throat, Morgan stared as he slid out a couple of bars of polystyrene and then the weather vane, wrapped in blue plastic. He quickly stripped off the wrapping to reveal the perfect depiction of Lily's lobster boat that Morgan had hoped for.

"Oh, Ryan, it's . . . it's awesome," Morgan breathed.

"I'll have it on top of the inn's highest gable within an hour," Ryan said, obviously pleased. "Sure is going to beat that dumb old rooster."

The nerves that had tightened Morgan's insides now twisted them into an agonizing cramp. She sucked in a couple of gasping breaths as she closed her eyes. Had Ryan only come back so he could make good on his promise to put up the weather vane? Given the superhot way he'd kissed her, that seemed crazy, but she wouldn't put it past him. She knew how much he hated walking away from an obligation.

You've got to be more than an obligation to him, right?

"Honey, what's the matter?" Ryan said, grasping her shoulder. "Are you okay?"

She opened her eyes. "I'm fine. Just a little stomach thing, I guess."

His dark brows knitted into a frown.

"Must be all that Irish whisky I drank after you got on the boat this morning," she said. His eyebrows shot up at that, but she rushed ahead. "Since you brought your bag, I was just wondering if you were planning on staying... uh, well, longer than it'll take to put up the weather vane."

Ryan's smile returned. "Well, that depends."

She narrowed her gaze. "On what, pray tell?"

He slid his hands onto her hips and pulled her close. "On whether you'll forgive me for being such a moron to think I could ever leave you."

Her heart skipped a beat. Well, several. In fact, it felt like it actually paused, and that time stopped too. Then it started up again, beating solid and strong. It was a pivotal moment, and a perfect one. A moment she'd remember for the rest of her life.

Morgan wrapped her arms around his neck and hugged him as hard as she could. "The only thing that matters is that you came back to me," she whispered.

"I'm not going anywhere, babe. As long as you're here in Seashell Bay, that's exactly where I'm going to be too." His mouth was muffled against her hair, but she heard the catch in his voice.

He pulled back just enough to tip her chin up, and then he claimed her mouth in a kiss that was first tender and then as hot as any kiss in the history of the world had ever been.

When they came up for air, Ryan held her at arm's length, his gaze intent and serious. "You want to know what happened? Why I didn't get on the plane?"

She gave him a breathless nod.

"It's kind of crazy, really. I saw a lobster boat sun catcher in the airport, and suddenly all I could think about was that I'd promised to put that damn weather vane up for you. And how much I *wanted* to put it up, to make good on that promise—on all the promises I made to you and then some." He grinned. "So I took a cab to the vane company and convinced the owner to let me take it."

"The bill must have been something of an epiphany too," she said. "I know exactly how much this darn thing cost."

He laughed. "Yeah, but it's totally worth it."

Morgan hugged him again, resting her head on his muscled chest. "I'm not dreaming, am I? You're really not going to Texas? You're really going to give up that job?"

And would he come to regret that in time?

He cradled her in the shelter of his body. "I can always find another job, Morgan. I can't find another you." He kissed the tip of her nose. "I love you."

"I love you too, Ryan," Morgan whispered. "I've loved you forever."

The fact that he was willing to give up so much for her lit her up like fireworks on the Fourth of July. She'd do whatever it took to make him never second-guess his choice. "You said you'd have the weather vane up in an hour?"

His mouth kicked up in a questioning smile. "More or less. It's a pretty simple job."

"Why don't we make that two hours? As much as I'm dying to see this cutie on the roof, I have a much better idea for how to spend your first hour back home."

Home. That Ryan was home sounded so incredibly right.

"I like your idea," he said, smoothing his hand down the back of her T-shirt until it rested on her butt. "But let's make it three hours." His hand started to slide under the waistband of her shorts.

"Yo, Butler," called a voice from across the parking lot. They both turned to see Bram Flynn loading some boxes into his truck. "Get a room, you pervert," Bram yelled with a huge smirk on his face.

He wasn't the only spectator either. Several locals who'd come in on the ferry and were heading to their cars regarded Morgan and Ryan with amused interest.

She let her head thump against his chest. "That is *so* embarrassing. I was ready to let you grope me in front of half the town."

He laughed. "Then I'd better get you straight home before you do something you might regret."

"Never," she said, smiling up at him.

As Morgan rushed around to the driver's side of her truck, the Casco Bay ferry tooted its horn to signal its imminent departure. It seemed to be giving her a salute, saying it had done its job in bringing Ryan back to her.

Back home to Seashell Bay, where they belonged.

Epilogue

Mid-October

$\mathcal{M}$organ was glad that Ryan was taking it slow as he steered the golf cart down the freshly graveled road. A hundred feet in front of them, a pickup truck spewed a thick cloud of dust that threatened to engulf them if they didn't keep it to a crawl.

"Hard to believe this used to be a grassy little goat track to Bram's cottage on the bluffs," Morgan said, waving at the dusty air. "Now it's a construction road. And then there's the other new road on the west end of the Flynn land too." She gave a little sigh. "It reminds me of that Joni Mitchell song about paving paradise to put up a parking lot."

Ryan flashed her a smile. "I prefer to think of it as progress. The resort is going to be good for the island."

"Ha! You have to say that because you're on the payroll, Mr. Chief of Security," she said, ribbing him. It was only a part-time job for now but would gradually become full-time as construction went into high gear over the next couple of months.

He laughed. "You got me."

Actually, Morgan thought the ecoresort would probably be good for all of them. She'd pretty much discarded her worries that the fancy complex would drain business away from the B&B. Aiden was obviously sincere in his desire to create a positive working relationship between the two. The resort would focus on ecology and conservation tourism, while The Merrifield Inn would specialize in providing a homey atmosphere along with its focus on paddling sports. B&B guests could get in on the resort's ecotours at discounted prices, while resort patrons could use the B&B's kayaking facilities and programs.

She snuggled closer to Ryan. Being plastered against her smoking-hot lover always carried its own rewards, but today it had the added bonus of warding off the chill of a blustery October afternoon. The weather was distinctly not cooperating with Aiden's plan for a festive ground-breaking ceremony for the resort, with overcast skies and a bone-chilling ocean wind gusting across the bluffs.

The gates of the six-foot-high construction fence were wide open today as Ryan drove through, swinging the cart around some heavy equipment to park beside a big white tent, its canvas sides partially down to protect against the elements. As soon as Morgan got out, the biting wind leached away the warmth from sticking close to Ryan. Her ivory linen dress and lacy black shawl just weren't cutting it.

Ryan immediately wrapped his arm around her shoulders, pulling her close as they made their way into the tent where forty or fifty people were milling about in advance of the speeches and cocktail reception. He was an incredibly protective man, and especially so with her. She'd been on her own for so long that she sometimes couldn't believe that she now had someone to lean on when she needed to. It was a blessing for which she would always be grateful.

And soon they would have their own place, instead of bunking between her room at the inn and his rental at Paradise Point. They'd decided to build a separate suite for themselves in the annex. That way Morgan could still be close to her sister but have the privacy she and Ryan needed. If all went well, they'd move in before Christmas.

Ryan, naturally, had insisted on footing the bill for the addition, firmly stating that he and Morgan were now partners in everything.

And sometime next year, they'd also be husband and wife. She stole a quick glance at her diamond ring, as she did about a hundred times a day since Ryan slipped it on her finger a few evenings ago over dinner at Diamond Cove. Her engagement and all the other changes still felt a little unreal, but in the best possible way. In a matter of months, she and her sister had gone from grief to believing once more that life could be and was, in fact, really good.

While a few people had taken seats on white plastic chairs, most stood around in groups at the front of the tent or around the entrance. Inside, Aiden was holding court in a circle near a low dais. Lily rested her hand in the crook of his arm while a proud-looking Sean Flynn, dressed up for the occasion, flanked him on the other side. Bram, also in jacket and tie, was in animated conversation with Sabrina, Micah, and Jessie Jameson.

"Well, look at you, Mr. Big Shot," Ryan said as he stuck out his hand toward Aiden. "All fancy in your coat and tie." He glanced down at his leather jacket and dark chinos. "I guess I'm underdressed for this crowd."

Morgan rolled her eyes. "Ryan hates ties with a passion that never sleeps. I couldn't get him to wear a sports jacket either."

"Hey, it's cold out today," he protested. "I bet you wish you were wearing more clothes too." Then he leaned over to whisper in her ear. "Although I like you best wearing nothing at all."

"Behave yourself," she hissed, trying not to laugh.

"I hate the damn things too," Aiden said, sticking a finger in between his neck and the tight shirt collar. "But my wife said I had to do it for the publicity photos."

Lily yanked on his arm. "You want to look like a slob in the Portland paper? After I had to whine and beg them to send a photographer out here for the groundbreaking?"

"Yes, dear. Whatever you say, dear," Aiden said, his voice warm with laughter.

"Hey, Ryan," Micah said as he joined them. "I was surprised to see the construction gate wide open with no guard in sight. Since you guys are so big on security, I thought you might at least have a couple of men out there stopping traffic and checking invitations." He gave Ryan a taunting grin. "Gotta watch out for all those killer deer roaming around this place."

"We thought about it, but I figured the presence of the town deputy would strike the fear of God into the local criminal elements," Ryan said sarcastically.

"You mean like Bram?" Aiden said.

"Fuck off, bro," his brother cheerfully replied.

Everyone laughed.

"Yeah, well," Micah said, his gaze turning serious,

"with all the noise you and Aiden are making about security around this place, some might almost think you don't trust the sheriff's office to deal with any problems that might crop up."

Lily frowned. "Oh, Micah. That's not true. Of course they trust you."

Aiden patted her arm. "He's just sandpapering my ass, babe."

Micah grinned. "Had you for a minute there, Lily, didn't I?"

She stuck her tongue out at him.

"Seriously though," Micah said, looking at Ryan, "I'm happy you took the job. I look forward to working with you. It's great to have you back on the island."

"Thanks, dude," Ryan said. "That means a lot coming from you."

Morgan had to blink back a few silly tears. She was just so darn proud and happy, especially when Sabrina slipped a hand through Ryan's arm and started discussing plans she had for setting up box lunches for the kayaking crowd. It had been a particular joy to see Ryan and her sister growing so close and to see how well Sabrina was doing. Morgan had worried that so many changes in her life would throw Sabrina for a loop, but so far so good.

When Lily got in on the conversation with Sabrina, Ryan moved back to stand next to Morgan, slipping an arm around her waist.

"You okay, babe?" he asked. "Not too cold?"

She smiled up at him. "Not when you're around, Soldier Boy."

He smiled back. "Hey, it's part of the job, along with keeping you happy."

She rested her hands on his chest. "And you're doing a fine job. You have no idea how happy I am, Ryan Butler."

He leaned down and kissed her. "I feel exactly the same. You've made me happier than I ever thought possible, Morgan Merrifield. And I'll be even happier when all these damn speeches are over and I can get you back home and have my evil way with you."

She laughed. "Just remember that good things come to he who waits."

Or *she*, in Morgan's case, and it had been more than worth the wait.

Aiden Flynn returns to Seashell Bay
to sell his family's coastal land
to a developer. But beautiful
Lily Doyle will do whatever it
takes to convince him to save
their island home—and
the love that still burns
between them...

Please see the next page
for an excerpt from

Meet Me at the Beach.

$\mathcal{A}$iden stared down into emerald eyes just as bewitching as he remembered—eyes that now also held a depth and maturity that sucked him right in. As much as he might have liked to deny it, he felt the pull toward Lily as strongly as he ever had, and he'd be willing to bet his parcel of land she felt the same.

But frigging darts...really? If Lily had no intention—sadly—of leaping his bones, he would have expected her to get down to business right away, pumping him for info about his position on the development project.

He glanced away from her challenging, amused stare to take in the avid gazes of the crowd, waiting with bated breath for his answer. And his destruction, he suspected, given the nasty smiles of anticipation that lit the faces of at least half the people in the bar. It was Thunderdome, Seashell Bay style, with Aiden tagged as the loser.

Just swell. Nothing like a little ritual humiliation to cap off his fabulous homecoming.

Lily Doyle had always had a touch with darts, just like Aiden had the God-given ability to hit baseballs. Most people thought it was simply a matter of natural coordination, but there was more to it than that. Lots of people had great coordination. Damn few, though, could hit a ninety-five-mile-per-hour fastball or throw a dart with perfect precision.

Lily had coordination in spades and a sweet, sweet form.

Aiden clapped a hand to his chest, trying to look like a wounded puppy. "Such a coldhearted way to welcome a native son back to the island. Since you're the top dog in these parts, I reckon you have some ulterior motive for wanting to whip my ass in front of the entire damn town."

Her gaze cut off to the side for a few seconds, surprising him. Lily was never one to dodge a question or a direct challenge. But then she looked back, dazzling him with a glorious smile that fried the logic part of his brain.

"Oh, I don't know," she replied with a throaty purr that made Aiden want to lift her over his shoulder and haul her out to his truck. "I guess I'm pretty good, but you're a *professional athlete*, after all. You're not afraid of a little old game of darts, are you, Aiden Flynn?"

"You tell him, Lil," Boone Cleary said, leaving his bar stool long enough to weave over and see what the fuss was all about. "Nobody walks away from a challenge on Darts Night. Not on this island, anyway." He belched as if to emphasize his weighty intervention, which prompted a whack to the back of his head from Miss Annie and a lecture on minding one's manners in public.

Bram whispered into Aiden's ear, "He's right, bro. Look, just keep saying stuff that'll get her rattled. You can start by reminding her of that time when you and me tailed her down to Bunny Tail Trail and saw—"

"Shut up," Aiden said through gritted teeth.

Lily had crossed to the dartboard but now came back to Aiden, still giving him that sexy smile that said, *What are you afraid of, big boy?* His brain might have been addled by waves of hot lust, but he couldn't shake the feeling she was somehow trying to manipulate him.

"Well?" She held her palm out, daring him to take the three darts that lay there.

Instinctively, he reached out, his hand swallowing hers and the red-tailed darts. Her skin felt hot and almost as smooth as he remembered from that long-ago night, when her hands had been all over him. That surprised him, given the work she did. Of course she wore gloves on the boat, but she set and hauled traps all day long. Both his dad and Bram had always suffered from unending cuts, scrapes, and chewed-up hands from snapping lobster claws.

He froze for a few seconds, her small hand trapped in his, and his mind became swamped with images of the battle-hardened warriors who fought the cold sea and the unforgiving elements to eke out their living. He could only imagine what Lily had gone through all these years he'd been away. While he'd been playing and partying in the glamor of big-city pro baseball, the slender, fine-boned woman before him had toiled long and hard on her lobster boat, facing down the dangers—and the dangers were real and ever-present—of a brutally unforgiving family trade.

When Lily tilted her head, her half-smile curving with an unspoken question, he released her.

"You go first," he said, sliding his hand across the swell of her hip to gently turn her toward the throw line.

"You are such a gentleman, sir," Lily said over her shoulder, flashing him a mocking yet heated smile that went straight to his dick. "Okay, we play the usual rules here—501, straight start, double finish."

In that sultry voice, even the scoring rules sounded like an invitation to bed boogie. "Fine. Say, who's that girl keeping score?"

He nodded toward a tall, young woman at the side of the board who was staring intently at him as she gripped a black marker. She had cropped, dark hair and wore a black T-shirt and leggings so tight she couldn't possibly have been wearing a scrap of fabric underneath them. Though he didn't recognize her, she sure seemed to know him.

Lily swung around and shot him a look somewhere between puzzlement and annoyance. "That's Jessie Jameson."

Aiden couldn't hold back a disbelieving laugh. He remembered Jessie as a scrawny, preteen tomboy who hung around the boatyard. It was yet another lesson that not everything on Seashell Bay Island had stayed the same.

As Lily turned into the throw line, positioning her flip-flops at a slight angle, Aiden's eyes automatically locked onto the way her beautifully rounded ass filled out the little denim skirt. *Nice*, his libido muttered, imagining how easy it would be to slide his hands underneath that well-worn fabric and—

"Good one, Lily!" a blond woman said from a table near the board. "You give him holy hell!"

He jerked his attention away from Lily's very fine ass to the board. Her first dart had landed in the double twenty ring, no doubt exactly where she'd aimed it. She didn't turn around and gloat, though, instead giving her arm a little shake as she set up for her next throw.

Aiden glanced at the woman who'd shouted out the encouragement. "I know that blonde's a friend of Lily's, but I can't dredge up her name," he said to Bram at his side. It was starting to piss him off that he couldn't remember the names of people he'd known all his life.

"That's Morgan Merrifield," Bram said. "She's a teacher up the coast now, but she comes back every summer to help her dad at the B&B. Hell, she and Lily are so freaking close they might as well be married."

Aiden's mind went blank. "You don't mean that they're..."

Before he even finished his sentence, Bram looked at him like he was a freak. "What the fuck, bro? Did you get hit in the head with a baseball and not tell me? Lily isn't gay, and neither is Morgan."

"Nothing wrong about it if they were," Aiden said defensively. He didn't give a shit one way or another about anyone's sexuality, except for Lily's. That seemed to matter a lot to him at the moment, way more than it should.

Mumbling something that sounded like *fucking bonehead* under his breath, Bram turned to watch Lily while Aiden glanced discretely at Morgan. Now he remembered her. She, like Lily, had been a couple of years behind him in school. The girls had been close back then too. He probably hadn't recognized Morgan right off because she was thinner than she'd been in high school and because she'd worn wire-rimmed glasses back then.

Aiden returned his focus to Lily and watched as her dart just missed the double ring. A couple of seconds later, she sent her last one on a perfect arc into the double twenty ring again. Scoring one hundred on her first set was pretty sweet.

"Woo-hoo!" Morgan yelled. "Let's see you top that start, Mr. Big Shot."

Aiden ignored the taunt, just as he'd learned to ignore far worse from opposing teams' fans as he patrolled the outfield. Morgan was trying to rattle him, just as Bram had wanted him to do with Lily. But Lily's easy mastery of the game made it plain he was in over his head.

Story of his life, when it came to Lily Doyle.

"Let's go, Aiden! You can do it!"

He glanced to the bar where Laura was pumping her fist. He grinned at her, thankful that he had at least two supporters in the bar tonight.

Aiden held his first dart lightly in the pencil grip he favored. *Don't think, man. Visualize the tip of the dart hitting the target and just let it go.* He repeated that mantra twice and let the dart fly, a part of his mind jeering that he was taking a darts game so seriously. But it was Lily and it was Seashell Bay, so it mattered.

The dart headed straight for the top of the twenty but clanked against the double ring and dropped to the floor. *Bounce-out.*

Amid hoots from the crowd, Lily made a little shrug that held a lot more mockery than sympathy. Undaunted, Aiden launched his second dart. This time it angled perfectly between the wires for a double twenty.

Lily's eyes narrowed as she gave him a golf clap in response—all motion and almost no sound. Her cheering squad suddenly went quiet. Apparently the game mattered to them too.

Aiden took a deep breath and held it as he threw his last dart, this time aiming for the more difficult triple ring. How better to set sweet Lily Doyle back on her heels than to score a triple twenty the first time he was up?

And... *thunk*.

He did it. To the sounds of breath being sucked in from all sides, Aiden casually strolled over to the board, plucked out the two darts, and then bent to pick up the bounce-out. When he straightened, he gave Lily a deep, exaggerated bow. Damned if he didn't feel as good as if he'd just thrown out a runner at the plate.

"Jackass," Morgan Merrifield muttered from behind him.

Lily simply tilted her head, looking more intrigued than worried. "Decent," she finally said, then eased up to the throw line for her second turn.

Aiden moved in close, practically whispering in her ear. "Not to blow your concentration or anything, but why the hell was Miss Annie so freaked out just now? It's not like the stuff with the developer and the car ferry vote is a big secret."

Okay, maybe he *was* trying to blow her concentration, but as he inhaled her scent, the years melted away. He swore her hair smelled exactly the same as it had that last night in his car, when his lips were trailing kisses over her long, perfect neck and his hands were exploring the gentle swells of her breasts and ass. Her gleaming auburn hair was as sweetly fragrant as the roses that bloomed all over the island.

He couldn't hold back a smile. Yes, Lily had changed, had grown up. But she'd also remained essentially the same, and he found that incredibly appealing.

Clearly unfazed by his comment—or by the fact that he'd crowded her sweet bod—Lily launched her dart and then turned to face him. "I'm sorry about that. Gràny's memory isn't what it used to be, and she sometimes thinks people are keeping her in the dark. You remember how much she hates not being in the know about absolutely everything that's happening on the island."

"Got it. But she sure still looks and sounds sharp to me." Annie Letellier might be in her eighties, but she looked like the same fireball he remembered from when he was a kid. He hated to think it might be otherwise.

Lily shook her head, her hair gently brushing over her bare shoulders. "She's definitely still our Miss Annie, but you'll notice some differences in her, for sure." For a nanosecond she looked sad, but then she lifted an eyebrow. "If you stick around long enough, that is."

She was probing for clues again, but he wasn't ready yet to give up that kind of info. "I don't know how long I'll be here. Depends on a lot of things," he said.

But after seeing you, babe, I may not be out of here quite as quick as I'd thought.

Lily let out a derisive little snort and turned to throw again, scoring a twenty.

"This match could be close," she said over a shoulder that Aiden wanted to caress.

"Don't count on it," he replied absently, letting his gaze drift down to her shapely ass.

She turned to him and blinked, as if startled that he stood so close. A faint blush washed over her cheekbones, but then she put her hands on her hips. "Then maybe we should make a little wager before we get too far in. What do you think, city boy? You up for the challenge?"

The gentle taunt in her voice tweaked his competitive instincts. "Name it," he said.

Lily tapped an index finger on her chin, as if pondering a weighty question. "Let's say if I win, my tab tonight is on you. If you win—like that's going to happen—I pick up yours."

"Even if I stay and close the place down?"

"Even if. In fact, be my guest. On Darts Night, I usually don't go home too early."

Which means you do every other night? He liked that idea. Lily tucked up in her bed safe and alone—preferably in a skimpy nightie that only he would ever see.

"You're on, then," he said.

Lily thought she'd done a fairly respectable job preventing Darts Night from deteriorating into full-blown war. Not that Bram would ever lay a hand on a woman, much less one almost three times his age, but Granny had lots of supporters in the Pot. Any one of them would have been more than willing to throw a punch on her behalf.

Aiden had done his bit to keep the situation under control too. He'd reacted calmly and decisively, keeping his stupid brother locked down and treating Granny with a sweet, old-fashioned respect.

And she had to admit that his understated confidence turned her on a little too.

Okay, he was pretty much melting her panties.

Once a high school hunk, Aiden had now matured into an incredibly sexy man with a laid-back assurance and masculinity that vacuumed up the attention of every woman in the bar but Granny. Every cell in Lily's overheated body was telling her that he felt the pull between them too, and that he was more than willing to act on it. Should she use that attraction to get closer to him and probe for info? She hated the idea of using such sleazy tactics, no matter how just the cause, and the idea of getting involved with Aiden was even more anxiety provoking. She felt pretty certain that would be a one-way boat ride to a whole lot of heartache.

But Gramps had made her mission crystal clear—find out where *the boy* stood on Seashell Bay's future. Would he honor his mother's inheritance, or would he side with his jerkwad of a father? From the few clues Aiden had dropped, she sensed that he had yet to make up his mind. Aiden wasn't the kind of guy to let his father—or anyone else—force him to make a decision before he was ready.

So there was time to push back, especially if he hung around for a while. And if he did, Aiden just might be a temporary fix for the other problem that was keeping her awake at nights.

If she could get him to agree to it, and that was a very big if.

She flashed him a bright smile when he hit the double ring to score another twenty-six points with the third dart of his turn. "Very nice."

Lily didn't need to fake her compliment—he was damn good. Now it would come down to the first person to hit the double needed in order to check out.

He casually rested his hand on the base of her spine as she took up her position. His hand, big enough to nearly span her lower back, sent heat through to her skin. The sensation forced her to lock her knees to hold her stance.

"Feeling the pressure yet?" His deep voice made her

want to press her thighs together. "You must really hate the thought of losing in front of the home crowd."

"Lose? In your dreams." She mentally winced at the squeaky note to her voice.

He was teasing, but his words contained an element of truth. Lily hated losing, and there were a few people watching who would find pleasure in rubbing it in. Folks in Seashell Bay took their darts seriously, and she'd been whipping their asses for years. Still, she'd developed a game plan, and she had to stick to it.

Think big picture and get over yourself, girl.

"Put him away, Lily," Morgan shouted, her face lit up with loyal enthusiasm.

"She's gonna bust," Bram retorted.

Lily shut everything out and threw three straight darts just outside the double nine, scoring zero for her turn. Perspiration prickled along her spine where Aiden's hand had rested only moments ago. It took skill to throw a game and not look suspicious.

"Ah, so close," Aiden said with a mock sigh as he moved up to the line.

"Let's see you do better, pal," Lily shot back, secretly hoping he'd put his first dart straight into the double seven to check out.

Deputy Micah moved in close, just off to her right beside Morgan's table. He scowled at the board like he wanted to pull out his gun and blast it. Given Micah's long-standing antipathy to the Flynns, she knew he was going to be pissed when Aiden won the match. Lily and Micah were old friends, and he wouldn't take kindly to Aiden beating her.

Despite the noise and catcalls, Aiden's hand was steady as he tossed his dart to score the double he needed. Just like that, the match was over, and Lily was on the hook for his beer tab.

Small price to pay.

"Yes!" Bram leaped out of his chair, knocking it to the floor. Once he finished pummeling his brother on the back, he swung around to sneer at Morgan and Micah. "How about that, huh? A Flynn wins!"

Aiden hauled him back. "It could have gone either way, bro. Lily just missed by an eyelash. She's a great player." Then he flashed her a seductive smile, turning her brain to fish bait. "Want to go again, Lily? Get your revenge on the city slicker?"

Morgan jumped up from her chair and whispered urgently in Micah's ear. Clearly, she'd figured out that Lily had tossed the game and wanted to keep Micah from acting like a bull-headed deputy.

"What? Now you want to stick me with Bram's beer too?" Lily said, struggling to find a light note.

Aiden shook his head. "No, and you don't need to buy mine either. I just like spending time with you. I always did." His voice was deep and sincere, a quiet undertone cutting through the raucous bar.

Lily was afraid she might melt on the spot, just when she most needed to focus.

"If you really want to give me a chance to get even, I just got another idea," she replied, trying not to sound breathless. She told herself the tight feeling in her chest was only about the crazy plan she was about to drop on him. "Are you up for a *real* challenge?"

He gave her a lazy grin that curled its way right down between her thighs.

Lord, the man could smile.

"Lily, have you ever known me to back down from any kind of challenge?" he asked.

She'd been counting on that, but not on the predatory heat in his gorgeous, dark eyes. He looked as if he was hoping she would suggest a wild night of strip poker as her next challenge. Now *that* would be a disaster. Getting a look at Aiden Flynn's naked body would be as dangerous as going out on the *Miss Annie* in a winter gale.

Bram was practically standing on his tiptoes behind his brother as he strained to eavesdrop. Micah started to move forward and Morgan scrambled after him, ready to run a little interference.

"You always loved watching the lobster boat races, right, Aiden?" Lily asked.

Every summer, up and down the Maine coast, various harbors hosted the races. Aiden's father had often raced his boat, though never once had the bastard allowed either of his boys to go with him. He'd been determined, she suspected, to keep any glory to himself.

"Sure," Aiden said, suddenly wary. "Who doesn't?"

Lily gave him an easy smile. "Well, the Seashell Bay races are this weekend, and I'll be racing my boat."

When Aiden's jaw tightened, she knew he'd caught her drift. "So?" he said.

"So, even though it hasn't raced in a while, I figure your dad's boat might still be one of the fastest out there. Right, Bram?"

Bram looked as stunned as a deer caught in headlights. "Uh, you know Dad can't race anymore, and neither can I."

"No, but this big, strong *professional athlete* surely can," Lily said, pouring on the sugar. "Do you think you could beat me, Aiden? Could you outrace a girl?"

Aiden let his thoughtful gaze roam over her. As always, he wouldn't rush to answer. "Let's just say for a moment that I agree to this little idea of yours," he finally said. "What kind of bet are we talking about? What would I win when I whip your butt?"

Oh, I think you'd like to spank my butt, wouldn't you?

Lily forced that too-enticing image from her mind. "Well, I was thinking the loser could grant the winner a wish. Say, something that involved a *personal service*." She tried for as much sexual innuendo as she could without going completely hot with embarrassment, hoping he would take the bait.

"Come on, Flynn. You're going to take that bet, right?" Micah needled, taking an aggressive, wide-legged stance. "Or has the Boy Wonder just come home to sign away his heritage and hustle back to the big city again?"

Crap. Lily had to repress the urge to smack Micah upside the head. If the well-intentioned loyalist of the Doyle clan managed to mess up her plans, she'd kill him. "Micah, come on. You know that's not the way we do things in Seashell Bay," she said in a firm voice. "Aiden will always be one of us."

Her friend grimaced but remained silent as he glared at Aiden.

Aiden's balled fists slowly opened, and he turned his gaze from Micah to Lily. He let the silence between them drag on for too long but then nodded. "I appreciate that, Lily. And if you want me to take a shot at the races, fine. As long as *Irish Lady* is up to it." He glanced back at his brother. "Can we get the old girl in shape by the weekend?"

If there was one thing the Flynns had in quantity it was

pride, so it was no surprise when Bram started to look enthusiastic. "It'll take some work, but damn right we can, bro. And it'll be great to kick some Doyle ass again, even one as sweet as Lil's."

Though Aiden was still looking wary and skeptical, Lily had been right in thinking he couldn't refuse the challenge. Especially from a girl, and worse yet, a Doyle.

But Mr. Aiden Flynn had no idea what he was getting himself into. After all, she'd won her class in the Seashell Bay boat races for the past two years.

And he'd be in for an even bigger surprise when she finally laid out the penalty for losing.

Fall in Love with Forever Romance

POWER PLAY
by Tiffany Snow

High-powered businessman Parker Andersen wears expensive suits like a second skin and drives a BMW. Detective Dean Ryker's uniform is leather jackets and jeans... and his ride of choice is a Harley. Sage Reese finds herself caught between two men: the one she's always wanted—and the one who makes *her* feel wanted like never before...

RIDE STEADY
by Kristen Ashley

Once upon a time, Carissa Teodoro believed in happy endings. But now she's a struggling single mom and stranded by a flat tire, until a vaguely familiar knight rides to her rescue on a ton of horsepower...Fans of Lori Foster will love the newest novel in Kristen Ashley's *New York Times* bestselling Chaos series!

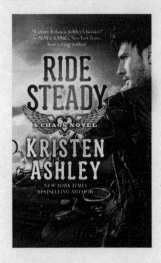

Fall in Love with Forever Romance

SUMMER AT THE SHORE
by V. K. Sykes

Morgan Merrifield sacrificed her teaching career to try to save her family's bed-and-breakfast and care for her younger sister. So she can't let herself get distracted by rugged ex–Special Forces soldier Ryan Butler. But her longtime crush soon flares into real desire—and with one irresistible kiss, she's swept away.

LAST CHANCE HERO
by Hope Ramsay

Sabina knows a lot about playing it safe. But having Ross Gardiner in town brings back the memory of one carefree summer night when she threw caution to the wind—and almost destroyed her family. Now that they are both older and wiser, will the spark still be there, even though they've both been burned?

Fall in Love with Forever Romance

A PROMISE OF FOREVER
by Marilyn Pappano

In the *New York Times* bestselling tradition of Robyn Carr comes the next book in Marilyn Pappano's Tallgrass series. When Sergeant First Class Avi Grant finally returns from Afghanistan, she rushes to comfort the widow of her commanding officer—and ends up in the arms of her handsome son, Ben Noble.